Owls, Doughnuts, and Democracy

By Jason A. N. Taylor

Owls, Doughnuts, and Democracy
By Jason A. N. Taylor
Copyright © 2024 Jason A. N. Taylor
Published by Jason A.N.Taylor via Amazon
ISBN 979-8333346148
First Paperback Edition

Edited by Dennis E. Bolen
Cover art by Angie Stacey

All rights reserved. No part of this book may be reproduced or used in any manner without the prior written permission of the copyright owner, except for the use of brief quotations in a book review.
To request permissions, contact the publisher at BigJayTaylor2@gmail.com

Disclaimer: Owls, Doughnuts, and Democracy is a work of fiction. The author fabricated the actions, dialogue, and situations involving people, places, and things that exist in the real world as part of this work of parody and satire. Suppose anything in this book seems too close to 'reality.' In that case, it is 'reality' that is wrong… Or the copy in your possession has fallen through a wormhole into a parallel universe where Direct Democracy is a real Canadian political party.

Foreword

Owls, Doughnuts, and Democracy (ODD) takes place on the territory of theLəkʷəŋən (Songhees and Esquimalt) Peoples. The author is grateful to live, work, and, most of all, play on Ləkʷəŋən territory. The author asks readers to share in this respect and acknowledgement of Ləkʷəŋən Peoples by learning about their culture.

"The possibility that empathy resides in parts of the brain so ancient that we share them with rats should give pause to anyone comparing politicians with those poor, underestimated creatures."
Frans de Waal

ODD is dedicated to all the people who listen to my crazy ideas. All have helped me write this book. I am extremely grateful for the brainstorming, discussion, feedback, support, and friendship that has led to ODD. In a very real way, ODD was written democratically with your input and inspiration. Thank you!

Special thanks to Amanda, Angie, Chris, Christa, Mom, Dad, Mel, Dana, David, John, Karysa, Megan, Rick, Samantha, Sheldon, Soressa, Dennis, Sue, and Parv. Ms. Bees was one of my many great teachers who specialized in learning disabilities. YAY! Thank you!

I hope ODD models the values of diversity, equality, and equity I try to follow. It is said doughnuts and democracy have nothing in the middle; ODD hopes to fill in the hole. I hope ODD shows that equity does not equate to sympathy but empathy for difference. I think politics must be based on people's needs, not isms dictate.

Thank you! YAY!

🦉 Owls, Doughnuts, and Democracy, by Jason A. N. Taylor 🦉

1.

The walk from Bea's crappy apartment to the James Bay Home for Seniors took her past the British Columbia Legislative Assembly. Passing by the building caused great resentment in her. She had wanted to be in the halls of government since an elementary school class tour of the Legislature.

Sixteen years ago, Bea had slipped out of the tour into a washroom to change into a mime costume. She then snuck onto the House floor in protest of being unable to vote as a twelve-year-old. Of course, no one listens to a mime or a twelve-year-old. Her protest achieved nothing. She got detention, which was worth it. The comedic artfulness of a mime protest warmed her heart.

She'd learned from her silent demonstration that she needed to be loud. By age fifteen, with a budding social media world growing around her, sex seemed to be the best way to get attention. She had been blessed by the booby fairy, and they definitely got attention. In an effort to get them onboard with proportional representation, she sent topless pictures to key members of the provincial Legislative Assembly. A government security person contacted her parents to let them know she could be charged with distributing child pornography. The incident was one of many to cause a rift between Bea and her parents.

By age sixteen, the audience, message, and method came together; her audience was easy: teenage guys. The message was to vote for Bea. The method was the attraction of tits. She understood political promises. Once elected class president, promises were forgotten. Few really cared that she did not follow through, and those who did got a private viewing.

These were not the reasons she was resentful of the Legislature. She was disqualified from being in the halls of government because of something that should not matter in the 2020s. The open, equal, inclusive society she was promised was a dream exchanged for traditional shame and debt. Worst, the shame was caused by something she was proud of.

She thought of changing her route because of the resentment, but walking by the harbour and past the Legislature was beautiful any time of the year, especially on a frosty winter's morning. James Bay on a Saturday morning was always quieter than one would expect for an area next to downtown Victoria. There was always the chance of seeing one of the local birds like the Bald Eagles, Cooper's Hawk pair, or her favourite, Josie, the Barred Owl and her family.

A few more minutes of walking took Bea to the Home. The automatic door opened, and she sniffed for the old person's smell. She never smelled it; she did not think it existed.

"Hi Bea," Karen, the manager, spoke from the reception desk. "You've got a customer. Ms. Anderson has turned her internet off and won't listen to me."

Bea strode past Karen on the way to the lounge, providing IT's universal solution. "Tell her to turn it on and off again."

"LOL! That's too advanced for her." Karen quipped.

By the games and hobby rooms, Bea thought: 'entertained till the inevitable.' She felt her life was aimless, passing the time just like the people here.

When Bea was voluntold by her lawyer to volunteer, she chose to help older people with computers. She reasoned that older people do not like computers, so she would not have to interact with them much. She wanted to do other things with her time but continued because she had nothing better to do; she got free stuff, and they needed her. She identified with the pervasive feeling that life was passing them all by. The future only had banal choices, "Will it be the mashed potatoes or white rice?" Oh, the suspense. However, seven years of volunteering resulted in her bi-weekly visitations with her son, Sam.

On good days, Bea still thought she could get the residents to explore the virtual world. She could show them that there are games for any age. She hoped that the veterans would like one last chance to shoot a Nazi, even a pretend one. But she knew a win was showing someone how to play Candy Crush or how to play music on their cell phone. Most days were filled with Ms. Anderson. "Good morning, Ms. Anderson. I hear you are having problems with your tablet again?"

"It's not working. My daughter sent me an email, but I have not received it. It has been hacked. I know it. And when I tap on the internet, I get a dinosaur cartoon… that's a virus, isn't it?" Ms. Anderson shoved the tablet in Bea's face. "Look!"

"It is not a virus. It looks like you are not on the Wi-Fi. Here," Bea took the tablet and held it so they could both see. "See, there's no Wi-Fi icon. Just swipe down and tap on the icon."

The tablet connected to the Wi-Fi. A cacophony of email dings sounded from the tablet. Ms. Anderson shrieked, "Ooo, it's been hacked! My personal information!"

"Ms. Anderson, the noise is the notification of new emails. It is nothing to worry about. See, there's a notification from your daughter. The other emails are spam, so don't open them."

"I don't eat near my tablet. How could I get Spam on it?"

Bea stifled a laugh, "Don't worry about the other emails. Just open the emails from your children. If you don't know who an email is from, see me."

"You are such a help, dear," Ms. Anderson took the tablet. "Oh, look how big she's grown."

With no other urgent questions, Bea found a recliner near the window and reclined. She scrolled through the *Province* newspaper's subscriber site on one of the Home's tablets to get her political fix. She had successfully made the case to Home's board that online subscriptions were cheaper and had more content. They had cancelled all their subscriptions to paper newspapers. Really, it was so she could have free subscriptions. She was doing the oldsters a favour by making them walk to get a paper.

Bea got other benefits from volunteering. Free coffee and snacks. Liberated toilet paper and other supplies. The odd purloined dinner that would not be missed. Even small Christmas gifts.

The music caught Bea's attention. *Won't Get Fooled Again* was playing much quieter than The Who should ever be played. Every time she volunteered, she admired the general commitment to good rock and roll. The oldsters listened to the music their parents chastised them for listening to in their youth. "Meet the new boss. Same as the old boss."

Owls, Doughnuts, and Democracy, by Jason A. N. Taylor

Down the hall came a bellowing, "Do you have a *Province*?" There was silence for a second. "No paper! You are going to make me walk to the store. It is icy and cold. I'll break a hip." Again, silence, "I don't want to use a tablet to read the paper. Next, you'll tell me to use a keyboard to wipe my ass!" Unintelligible grumbling moved closer to the lounge.

This conflict had been brewing for weeks. Until now, fortune had smiled on Bea, and the curmudgeon found a paper before getting to her. She did not feel lucky today as it was the coldest day of the year, and the sidewalks were icy, so it was possible no one might have bought a paper. The grumbling had turned to a mumbling just outside of the door. She told herself, "Turn this into a win." She pulled the lever on the recliner and got up, tablet in hand. She asked the hunched, doddering old man, "Did you say you were looking for the *Province*?"

"I am looking for a paper. The kind that keeps our pulp mills going and the economy strong, not some plastic toy."

Bea knew the old man: "The Honorable member Harold Gordon, former MP (member of Parliament) from Courtenay Mid-Island, it is an honour to meet you."

Harold's demeanour changed. "Miss, you have the better of me…" He stood to his full 6 feet 2 inches. "Do I know you?"

"When I was a kid, I saw you campaigning. That was eighteen… possibly nineteen years ago. If I were old enough, I would have voted for you. You were honest and reasonable. I had a schoolgirl crush on you. But now, I'm sad to say, I'm more on the left."

"Honey, I've served up more bullshit than an organic farmer. Don't give me that schoolgirl crap! Hell, I am left of my party these days because I'm not a fascist." Bea stood mouth agape. Harold continued. "Calling them fascist is too harsh; they are too ignorant to know they are fascists. I guess that one woman from Ontario is good, but mostly because she's a woman."

Bea closed her mouth, "Still honest. Still reasonable." She was not at all convinced she would turn this into a win.

Harold laughed and extended a hand, "Harold is fine."

"Bea."

"Really? Bea or Beatrice? Nobody's named Bea anymore."

"This from an octogenarian." Bea shook her head. "And it's Beatrix."

"Yes, I am old... almost a nonagenarian, and you are good-looking. Does that help me get a paper?"

"The Home's Board of Directors voted that they will be providing online subscriptions for a variety of newspapers including the *New York Times, National Post, Globe and Mail, The Jerusalem Post, the Vancouver Sun, the Province, Times-Colonist, Ottawa Gazette, the Daily Telegraph, Ottawa Herald, Chicago Sun-Times* and a bunch more."

"That's a relief. I can get all of Conrad Black's opinions. Just give me a *Province*."

Bea tapped the tablet to get to the *Province's* menu page and handed it to Harold.

"Dearie, you handed me a plastic coaster."

"It has all the stories you want. Tap on the title." Bea saw that Harold could not see the print, "Is that too small?"

"No, I'm too old. I need my glasses." Harold patted his shirt for them.

Bea used two fingers to zoom in. "You can make the words bigger like that. You can also use it as a coaster - it is water resistant."

"Wow, I can read that without my glasses! Show me what this electric coaster can do. Remember, the last time I used a computer... I never really did. I always had a secretary."

"Ok... I'll start from the beginning." Bea turned it into a win, but after a few minutes, Harold seemed to be overloaded. "Some articles look like a news story but are really ads." Bea pointed to the spot on the screen. "Don't tap into them. If you do tap on one, look for the close button or X to get out of the ad."

"A news story that is an ad?"

"Advertorial or Native advertising is the name for it."

Harold looked confused.

"Here, I'll show you." It took no time for Bea to swipe to an advertorial. "Here's one: 'What's in your heating vents could be causing ill health.' And down at the bottom, it gives you the best vent cleaning company. It's bullshit. Stick to the actual newspapers; they at least say it's an advertorial."

"I'll give this device a chance for the next week..." Harold smiled. "If you get me a couple of Empire Donuts when you're here next."

"You have a deal if you tell me who's going to win the election this fall."

"It won't be my old party. Those jackasses can't see further than the oil patch. Their message doesn't resonate past Winnipeg. They have no chance without strong support in Ontario and some in Quebec."

"What about Junior's (Justin Trudeau) scandal?" Bea was giddy. "That's got to turn off a bunch of Liberal voters."

"In my day, that crap would not have come out. We would have kept it inside Cabinet. The bigger picture is that J.T. was saving jobs in Quebec for a Quebec company. Add this to a weak Bloc Québécois and an NDP that will not get another Quebec seat... bing, bang, bong, Liberal majority."

"That scandal would not have come out with the Progressive Conservatives?"

"We all got into the game for the same reason: to advocate for our constituents and get them a better deal. I know it's hard to believe, but even this PC got into it for the people. I was smart enough to know socialism would not work. Then twenty years go by, the power seems real, and you fly an Airbus full of money into a Swiss bank."

"You know they named a town in Saskatchewan after Mulroney?" Harold looked confused.

Bea dropped the punch line: "Moosejaw."

Harold nearly spit out his dentures and did not stop laughing for twenty seconds.

"You must have stories..." Bea narrowed her eyes. "Any Swiss bank accounts?"

"I was never smart enough for that kind of intrigue. But I have stories... if you have an afternoon."

"Just an hour today. Next week, we'll have Empire Donuts too." Harold happily told war stories of his glory days. Bea was happy to listen.

The muffled sound of the Imperial March from Star Wars interrupted them. Bea patted herself down for her phone. "SHIT! Marcus is calling. What time is it?" She found the phone. "Hi Marcus, sorry I lost track of time. I'll be there in five minutes."

"Get here as soon as you can. Amy and I have a lunch reservation."

"Five minutes." Bea hung up the phone and grabbed her bag. "Harold, I'm late for visitation with my son. I must run. Doughnuts and discussion next week."

She needed to get from James Bay to the kids' playground in Beacon Hill Park, a ten-minute walk, in five minutes. As she ran, a cyclist was on the sidewalk. "Get the fuck off the sidewalk!" The cyclist moved onto the road, glaring at Bea as she passed. "Asshole!" Beacon Hill Park had its fair share of asshole tourists. She let the tourists know what she thought of them as she ran past. At the cricket clubhouse, she stopped to catch her breath before seeing Amy.

Coming around the corner, Bea saw her wonderful little boy Sam whizzing down the children's zip line. She called, "My man, Sam!"

"Momma B!" Sam jumped off the zip line, feet moving too slow to keep up with his upper body. He hit the soft ground hard but stood up smiling, dusting himself off. "Did you see me jump?"

"Good job, Sam." Bea gave him a hug.

A waif with heavy makeup and designer gym sweats with JUICY on the ass ran over. "Bea, don't encourage him like that! He'll break something like when you let him break his arm."

Bea stopped herself before saying what she thought. "Hello, Amy." Bea thought her ass was too flat to be called juicy. "Sam's tough, right Kiddo."

"But Momma A, the cast was cool. Everyone at school signed it. Next time, I want a black cast."

Bea answered before Amy, "But Kiddo, how will kids write on it if it is black? And hopefully, you will never need another one."

Amy looked at Bea, "If you play safe and don't do foolish things, like when you broke your arm, you won't need a cast."

Bea wanted to slap her more than normal. "You are looking well today, Amy. Do you put your makeup on before or after you go to the gym?"

"I didn't go to the gym."

A man called from twenty metres away, "Hey, Sweet Cheeks, let's get going." Bea instinctually turned to what had been her pet name. She did not know how Marcus could use that nickname for Ms. No Ass.

"Play safe, Sam." Amy gave the boy a hug and kiss. "Don't let Momma B get you in too much trouble."

Bea resisted the urge to kick Amy in the crotch.

"Momma B, watch me on the zipline!" Bea watched Marcus and Amy get into the brand-new Range Rover, wanting that life. Momma B, indeed. "I'm gonna jump off at the end."

Bea swallowed her regret and turned to her love. "Should I get my camera out, Kiddo?"

"Yeah."

"Best jump ever!" Sam did his thing, as Bea videoed. "I think I'm done jumping. Can we go look for the owls?"

"Of course, we can. But don't get your hopes up."

"I know where they are…"

"We haven't seen them since fall."

"They're by the stinky compost." Sam held his nose. "That's where the rats are."

Bea wrinkled her nose. "Lead on."

Sam led them down paths and next to homeless people camps. "I hope the owls have owlets. Remember last summer when Elmonzo dropped a pellet and looked at it like a poop, that was funny." After an hour, they had seen no owls. "Momma B, I'm not sure we're going to find them. I'm getting cold."

Bea noticed an old lady with big glasses and an old guy balding with a long-lensed camera, "Let's try this one last spot."

Approaching, Sam recognized the old lady. "Owl Lady!" He ran ahead. "Where are the owls?"

The Owl Lady smiled. "The female barred owl, Josie, is just in the tree over here... this way." The two walked off the paved trail into the leafless bush under a cedar tree.

Bea found a downy feather. It felt so fluffy that she had to stroke it along the back of her hand.

"Isn't this the best?" The old man with the camera spread his arms wide to encompass the grandness of the park. "Downtown Victoria...an owl over there and the beach over there. Amazing."

"Rich..." Bea giggled a little. "That Sublime sweatshirt cracks me up."

"Tie-dye suits my personality."

"Get any good shots?"

"No... too many branches." Rich changed the subject, "Is Junior going to pull off a second win this year?"

"Politics..?" Bea snickered. "While owl-watching?"

"Always politics while doing anything. Is there anything more important?"

"I suppose not. Funny, I was just talking with Harold Gordon, Honorable member from Up Island. He thinks the Quebec vote will keep him in."

"Gordon..." Rich scowled. "What a PC shill. Sold the forest industry to the U.S. with Free Trade."

After a few minutes, a WHO COOKS FOR YOU! WHO COOKS FOR YOU ALL! Owl call interrupted their political talk. Josie was waking up for the evening.

Bea's day was perfect.

2.

Friday night, Bea was multi-tasking, mining the dark web for leads she could use at work and, as her avatar Kira B, engaging in salacious repartee with Bubo.

Bubo: Can you believe they dug up two pictures of Justin in brownface?

Kira B: Who cares! It is obvious he's not a racist.

Bubo: Thanks, white girl. For telling a brown guy when to be outraged.

Kira B: If Sophie wants to roleplay BBC scenarios, why should we be in the bedroom too?

Bubo: Oh, so that's what our fling was.

Kira B: No. Our fling was ABC—a, for average or adequate.

Bubo: How come my neighbour pounded on the floor because of the moaning and screaming?

Kira B: Ever watched When Harry Met Sally?

Bubo: No.

Kira B: Here is the link.

The banter was cut short by the Imperial March—Marcus and Amy's ringtone. Anxiety kept Bea from answering immediately. Marcus had no reason to contact her. She'd had her visit last week. The time was odd, too, after eight on a Friday night. "Bea, I need your help," Marcus said.

"Is Sam ok? Did he get hurt? Is he sick?"

"Nothing like that. Snow has cancelled our flight out of Ottawa. The nanny can't stay with him overnight, so can you take him?"

"Tonight? Yeah. What time?"

"As soon as you can."

"I'll get there quicker if I can get a cab."

"I'll give you cab fare. Keep the receipts."

Bea hung up her phone.

Bubo: You were faking! I am hurt. I was not faking.

Kira B: Sorry, Bubo, I must go—family emergency.

Bubo: Hope everything is ok.

Kira B: Nothing serious.

Bubo: Good luck.

Ecstatic to be seeing Sam, Bea rushed out of the apartment. She stopped at the local Fairway market to get popcorn and goodies for the movie night. It was after nine o'clock by the time she picked up a sleepy Sam.

The cab got them back to Bea's apartment just in time to see her drunken neighbour's ex-girlfriend crying at the front door. This was normal for Villa Paulina. In fact, this ex-girlfriend was here last weekend with eyes dripping mascara and a bottle of rye.

Tonight, Bea did not want to deal with the drunk woman. "Hey Sam, wake up."

"I wanna sleep, Momma B."

"We're going around back. I thought I saw an owl."

Sam was instantly awake, "An owl!"

"Sssshhh, we have to be quiet."

Bea got her receipt, then sneakily got Sam out of the far side of the cab. They crept around the building by the park side. "Oh, I think the owl flew away."

"Rats... that's what it was looking for. Do you think it was Josie?"

"I don't know. We are kind of far from where we see her." Bea unlocked the back door, and they made their way to her apartment. The hallway smelled of pot smoke. She put the movie goodies on a hall table. "Kiddo, I am going to the washroom. Find something to watch."

Bea only heard the thump of some neighbour's music when she came out of the washroom. She was expecting Sam would be watching TV. But he was asleep in her bed. She fell asleep watching TV.

"Momma B, wake up!" Sam pulled the living room blinds open, letting the sun in.

Bea stretched and sat up, "I'm awake... what time is it?"

"Almost nine... on Saturday morning, Momma A lets me watch cartoons for an hour. Can we watch them?"

"We're doing something special this morning. First, it's Empire Donuts for Mr. Gordon at the seniors' home, then we're going to look for owls and get ice cream."

Owls, Doughnuts, and Democracy, by Jason A. N. Taylor

"Momma A won't let me have ice cream in the winter."

"Get moving, Kiddo, the best doughnuts sell out first. And take a banana; it is a long walk."

The doughnuts in the Empire Donut display case had a cartoon quality to their glaze, with colours straight out of the Simpsons. Sam stood drooling in front of the display of doughnuts. Bea asked, "What doughnuts do you think Mr. Gordon would like?"

"Hmmm... definitely a pink one and a green one. I want a blue one or a pink one. Can we get one of each? There are too many to decide."

"Ok. We can share ours so we can have more choices." Bea paid, and Sam carried the box of doughnuts. They walked through the quiet downtown. Bea watched Sam flying the box down the street like a plane in turbulence. "Sam, try to keep the box flat and don't jiggle it. The icing might get stuck to the box."

An annoyingly high-pitched, 'DING, DING," caught Bea's attention, and she realized she was on the pedestrian crosswalk of a bike lane. Some weekend warrior on a road bike did not want to stop. She instinctively yelled, "CROSSWALK ASSHOLE! YOU NEARLY RAN OVER MY KID!" She followed up with the finger. She realized she was swearing in front of Sam. "Sam, don't yell like that. I should not have yelled like that."

Sam giggled, "I know Momma B. Daddy is always telling Momma A that you have a foul mouth. But Daddy is worse."

Bea responded flatly, "What a nice guy." Sam spent the rest of the walk talking about the bike he had gotten two Christmases ago. Bea humoured him but was hurt she was not able to buy it for him. Hopefully, this year, she would get him a mountain bike for his birthday.

Sam ran into the Home first. Karen greeted him, "Sam, are you here to help with the computers? Ms. Anderson needs help."

"She has probably turned the wifi off again. I'll help her." Sam stomped down the hall.

"Hi, Karen. Sorry about Sam. I got him on short notice."

"No problem. Everyone here loves Sam."

Owls, Doughnuts, and Democracy, by Jason A. N. Taylor

When Bea got to the lounge, Sam had already helped Ms. Anderson. Harold sat working on his tablet. Sam approached. "Are you Mr. Gordon?"

Harold stopped looking at his tablet. "You have the better of me, young man. Indeed, I am Mr. Gordon."

"This is my son, Sam." Bea stepped near. "Do you mind if he joins us? We have doughnuts."

"I'll sit with anyone offering Empire Donuts. Does anyone want something to drink?"

Sam answered first, "Coffee, please!"

Harold asked, "Aren't you too young for coffee?"

"That's what Momma A says, but I'm with Momma B today, and she says I'm old enough. I'm almost nine."

Harold turned to Bea, confused, "If your Mom is ok with it."

"Decaf... or just a small cup." Bea felt judged but tried to shrug it off. "One for me, too."

"Come with me, Sam, we'll get the coffee."

The three of them sat around a table eating doughnuts. Once the coffee and doughnuts were gone, Sam wandered over to an old lady working on a puzzle. "Can I help?"

"If your mother is fine with it, yes."

Sam smiled impishly, "I have two moms, Momma A and Momma B."

"Well, I never."

Laughing, Bea said, "He can help with the puzzle."

Harold was confused. "Are you a..."

"Lesbian? That's none of your business, old man," Bea admonished Harold with a chuckle. "I wish it were that simple, and it is none of your business. Sam just knows that if he says he has two moms to oldsters, he'll get a rise. Momma A is my ex's wife, Amy."

"She is Momma A, and you are Momma B. That has to hurt."

"It did for the first few years. I'm used to it."

Harold changed the subject, "You were right; the tablet is better than a paper. I used it all last week. However, I have some questions."

"An old man likes technology! OMG!"

"That is one of my questions. What is this OMG?"

"OH MY GOD! Hahaha..." Bea's cackle caused all to look at her. "That's what it stands for."

"It is an acronym. I thought the government had license over all the stupid acronyms. I was wrong. Let me show you the next thing." Harold tapped and scrolled on his tablet, then turned it toward Bea. "Who or what are these notes at the end of the article?"

Bea looked at the tablet. "Those are comments from readers."

"Can anyone comment?"

"Yes. You have to create a profile first, though."

Harold sat up straight, "How democratic. In my day you had to write a letter to the editor that had a sparrow's chance in a hurricane of getting published, even in a small town's rag. This is powerful stuff. If we had this in my day..."

"Powerful stuff? Have you read the comments?" Bea said with incredulity. "They are from idiots, trolls, sock puppets, and bots."

"Some of the comments are idiotic, but some people are idiots. Like this one, he didn't get a bag for his marbles." Harold put on a dumb voice to read the idiot's comment, "'*Globe and Mail,* why did you censor me? It is my First Amendment Right to say what I want!' Is this what Canadian education has come to?"

Bea responded, "That might be a sock puppet and an idiot."

"What is a sock puppet?"

"A sock puppet is a person who uses a pseudonym to post comments to promote something else. I think this person is a Russian sock puppet because their name is the type of name you come up with if you search common Canadian names. 'Gordon Crosby' is obviously Gordon Lightfoot or Downy combined with Sydney Crosby. The avatar is a moose playing hockey, yet the idiot does not know we don't have a First Amendment." Bea clicked on the commenter's handle to see other posts, "Bingo... look at that post, some BS about Putin being hotter than J.T. (Justin Trudeau). And the next is about Canada wasting money on its NATO commitment in Eastern Europe."

"Why would a Russian care?"

"Sock puppeteers who work for countries get paid per post to influence people in other countries. The Russian Government and many others pay people to post." Bea loved lecturing old white men on new politics. "This guy probably has other bots that post the same on other papers when a similar story comes out. I'm going to copy some of the posts about NATO, then go to another Canadian paper with a similar story. I'll find his comment by using 'find' and pasting the snippet to search for it... I called it... this guy has the same post here." Bea did a little happy dance in her seat and then resumed the lecture. "Bots or 'robots' post the same content for similar stories on different papers to bombard the comments with their message. Then some naïve person like you sees the same sentiment in many places and thinks maybe I should think like those people because they think Justin is a weak, pretty boy too."

Harold shook his head. "I cannot fathom that Russia cares enough to pay people to do this."

"Every country wants to look good; we give foreign aid to look good. Sock puppets hardly get paid anything in Western terms. Paying them is way less than foreign aid and probably more effective."

"For heaven's sake, why are Russians allowed to 'post' on a Canadian paper?"

"Canadian papers could limit who posts to Canadian IP addresses or something like that, but they want people to read. People love a lively comments section; it brings more stupid readers. Media today is all about the attention you can get." Bea paused, scrolling through the comments. "Come on, where is the troll?"

"Troll, what do you mean?"

"A troll trolls the comment section, posting to get people to bite. Kind of like trolling for salmon."

"Do you fish?"

"No. My Dad does, but he does not catch anything. He is more of an asshole than a troll. Trolls post the opposite view of an article to get a rise out of people, like this gem on an article about the opioid crisis, 'Have a rave for all the addicts and give em' free fentanyl. Problem solved.' You can see the results: a string of 'think of the children' replies, followed by the troll's ad hominem attacks on the snowflake tree-hugging lefty. And a flame war ensues. A flame war is when people sling insults at each other online."

"Sounds like fun. Seriously, how do I post comments?"

"Really..?" Bea looked at Harold. "Be prepared. The people don't pull any punches."

"Missy, I was in Parliament for nearly 30 years and in Cabinet for a few. I can sling mud like a pig in a trough. Sign me up. I'll be able to tell the writers what I think. And they need to know."

"Ok. You'll have to make up a handle, a name. A picture for your avatar is good, too."

In a booming voice, Harold answered: "Honorable member Harold Gordon."

"Most sane people use a pseudonym." In reply, Harold took hold of the lapels of his house coat and looked dignified off into the distance. Bea tapped on the tablet. "Honorable member Harold Gordon it is. At least the name hasn't been used. To sign up, you need an email address, What is it?"

"THM, no space, HaroldGordon@hotmail.com"

"Hotmail!" Bea snorted. "You really love the title. You'll have to sign up for the other papers if you want to comment on them."

"I have another question. Can you go to the front page? There was a question or something. I did not want to tap it because Ms. Anderson said it would infect the tablet."

Bea quickly navigated to the front page, where a poll was asking the question, "What do you think of the re-negotiation of NAFTA? Bea asked, "Is this what you were talking about?"

"Yes. I worked on the original North American Free Trade Agreement."

"It is a poll. You can select the answer you want. Which do you want to choose?"

Harold read the answer a couple of times, "Go with, 'There is no need for change.'"

"Looks like you are in the minority."

"Who answers these polls?" Harold scratched his head. "Could it be a specific group?"

"Readers, of course. It would be easy to limit who could answer, but why would *The Sun* want to do that?"

"Could it be limited to voters from a riding?"

"I'm sure it could."

"Has it been done before?"

"Has what been done before? You are confusing me, Harold."

"If you could make a poll like this and restrict it to only people who lived in a riding, we could have direct democracy! The MP could run on a platform of voting for whatever the poll's outcome is. Imagine that. Like the Greeks intended."

Bea was gobsmacked. "I don't know if it's been done. I don't think so. At least not in Canada. I would have heard of it. Is it legal?"

"It is probably legal. It probably has not been done because no politician wants to give people the power." Harold smiled. "I want to be the person to do it. I got in the game to tell Ottawa what my people wanted. I am going to make a comeback with the Direct Democracy Party!"

"Are you serious?"

"Serious as the plague, dearie. We will need to find out if it is legal. I can contact Derek Nelson; he's a good lawyer… Hah, sorry, I misspoke. There's no such thing as a 'good' lawyer. He is knowledgeable of the law. I think I have enough money. The campaign will really be for highlighting the idea… maybe to empower others to do it in the future; I have enough for that. Do we know if it has been done before? It doesn't matter. If I've not heard of it, it can't have been done… or done right." To Bea, Harold asked, "Can you do the computer stuff?"

"You're serious?"

"Do I look like a Stampede Clown?"

"You are serious." Bea felt giddy. "I know how, but there is more to it than knowing how. Doing it securely and privately while at the same time being transparent is beyond what I know how to do. But I do know a guy who does."

"Great, contact your friend. The election is next fall."

Owls, Doughnuts, and Democracy, by Jason A. N. Taylor

"Ajay is not exactly my friend... but he'll be excited to talk with me. He is excited anytime he sees me." Bea felt a prying stare from Harold. "I don't want to talk about it."

"There's a lot you don't want to talk about. And I don't want to hear it. Use his excitement about seeing you to get him to help us. Direct Democracy is a game changer. It's about time people got their say," Harold's voice boomed. He looked more like 60 than 88.

"Do you think you can win?"

"No, but we cannot be sure until we try." Harold maintained his loud tone. "I wasn't sure I could win the first time I ran. Even the party did not think I would win. But I was stubborn enough to try."

Bright-eyed Bea said, "If it can be done it would change things. I always wanted to..."

"MOMMA B! MOMMA B!" Sam came racing into the lounge. "One of the old ladies has cookies. She said I have to ask you if I can have one. Can I have a cookie?"

"Sure Kiddo." Bea beamed as Sam ran off.

Harold asked, "You always wanted to... what?"

"Oh, nothing."

"Another thing you don't want to talk about..." Harold shook his head. "Well, finish teaching me how to post comments. I think it might be a good way to start getting some hype for Direct Democracy. Trolling gets people's attention, eh?"

Harold and Bea spent more than her hour scheming. They plotted until Marcus called. Marcus wanted to get Sam earlier than normal. Bea left to ensure Sam got the promised ice cream and owls.

Bea was preoccupied with giddy thoughts of being part of an absurdly conceived political campaign. It stirred something inside of her she had not felt in a long time. Passion and youth, she had no such feelings since all those things she did not want to talk about happened.

Sam found one of the owls by the Harrison Yacht Pond. Sam was sure it was Josie as it was big, but Bea could not tell. Josie was close to the ground and lit well by the low winter sun. They took turns taking pictures with Bea's cell phone.

Finding Josie in such a nice spot gave Bea the strength to message Ajay.

Kira B: Hi Bubo, I hope you are doing well. I have a wild idea you might want in on. Can we meet to discuss it this week? Early evenings are best for me.

Bubo: Meeting in real life OMG!!! I must be dreaming. When and where?

Kira B: Bard and Banker 5:30 pm Wednesday.

Bubo: It's a date.

3.

"Please, don't call my girlfriend," The male's voice on the line was cracking. "She does not need to know about this."

Bea would have to run to meet Ajay on time, but she was hopeful she would get a great commission from the call. "David, that is in your power. You can work out a payment plan with me, or I can contact your girlfriend. What will it be?" David started to sob. Bea let him cry for ten seconds. "David, be a man; pay up. I don't want to call your girlfriend. She should not have to take care of you... you're a man, aren't you?"

"Fine. Three hundred a month."

In five minutes, Bea was out of the call centre, running to meet Ajay. Rain was pelting as she ran across Government Street. A bicycle bell dinged at her. She responded, "Fuck you, asshole!" She ran into the bar, dripping wet but on time.

A quick scan of the tables and booths did not reveal Ajay. Bea took a seat at the bar and ordered a Manhattan to warm her up. He had not arrived by the end of the drink. She fished through her purse for her phone. It was 5:45 pm.

Bea began to have doubts. It had been almost eight years since she'd seen Ajay in person. Online, Ajay was a barrel of monkeys, always a laugh. But in real life, he was a reminder of things she did not want to talk about. It did not help that he was living the life he wanted as a data mining guru of Tech-toria. She was not sure if she should message him asking why he was late or forget about him and this absurd lark by getting drunk.

"Princess Leia, you're wet," came from behind her. From the reflection in the mirror behind the bar, she saw a body builders' chest in a muscle shirt.

Bea spun around and kicked for the guy's crotch. "Back off, buddy or I'll connect next time." The toe of her foot just barely touched the creep's junk.

The guy buckled at the knees and groaned, "Sorry, Bea. I couldn't help it. You look exactly like you did in university."

"Oh my God! Ajay?! I'm so sorry."

The bartender interrupted, "Is everything ok?"

"Sorry, it was an accident," Bea assured the bartender.

"It was a joke gone wrong." Ajay tried to smile but only grimaced. "Why does a tap hurt so much?"

The bartender smirked. "A drink will help. What'll you have?"

"Two of what she is having," Ajay said.

"Have a seat." Bea looked Ajay up and down like a man would a woman. "You look really great."

Still pained, Ajay answered, "I'll stand for now. And you look really well, too."

"Don't ever call me that again. This is not online." Bea fixated on Ajay's chest. "What changed? You were... how can I say this... uhm, chunky. Lots of people like the bear or dad look. But wow! I mean, look at you now."

"You changed me, you and your sex-positive outlook. Our little amore made me care about myself. Before our fling, I'd... never... well, you know."

"I figured you were all talk."

"You gave me the confidence to love myself. I'm kind of hoping we..."

"I'm happy you grew..." Bea blushed. "But no."

There was an awkward silence. Ajay filled it by shifting from side to side and looking pained at the bartender. Bea tried to tell if Ajay's pain was from her kicking him in the balls or breaking his heart.

The bartender set the drinks down. Bea broke the silence. "I'm sorry if you thought this was a date. Especially, with our history and that Kira B and Bubo flirt online. I can see how you could be confused. After everything with Marcus, I'm going solo. Although, your new look has me reassessing my decision."

Ajay pulled out his phone and tapped the screen, "You got me wrong. I'm in a relationship." He turned the phone to Bea. A picture of a buff man on the beach was on the screen.

Bea gasped. "You're shitting me!"

Ajay chuckled, "Just fucking with you." Bea punched him in the shoulder. He said, "Why did you want to meet in person?"

"I wanted to have a serious conversation about business. Not the type Bubo and Kira B have." Bea slugged back half her drink.

"Business it is," Ajay said.

"Remember in university how we would talk about changing politics? That politicians did not listen to the voters."

"You were running for the student society, and I volunteered to help. I did that because I had a crush on you."

"That was obvious, Ajay," Bea rolled her eyes. "I might have found a way to change politics to give the people more say. An oldster I help with computers came up with it. The old guy, Honorable Member Harold Gordon, a Progressive Conservative MP in the 80s and 90s, thought of it when I was teaching him how to post comments on newspaper articles. He is a natural troll, too. "

"Who are the Progressive Conservatives?"

"Basically today's Conservative Party."

"Okay. So what is the idea?"

"That an online poll of the constituency could be used to vote for bills before parliament."

"Oh?"

"Do you know if it's been done before?"

"Sounds interesting, though it might be impractical." Ajay took out his phone. "Let me search Wikipedia."

"No one has done it because no politician wants people to have power," Bea spoke flippantly.

"Here we go, Electronic Direct Democracy…" Ajay poked at his phone. "Blah, blah, in Sweden, a party called, I'm not going to pronounce this right, Direktdemokraterna or DD believes in directly influencing their representatives through online voting. Guess how much of the vote DD got in the last election?"

"I don't know. 2%"

"You are off by 25 times. DD could not even get their friends and family out to vote. They got 0.08% of the vote. And Sweden is much more progressive than Canada. No party will go for it."

"No?"

"The government wants the illusion of democracy… do you want the people of Walmart voting on the right to die?" Ajay chuckled. "A fun idea, but why do you think it would fly?"

Bea took a pull from her drink, "The people involved. Harold was excited about it, and I am, too. I'd bet the Swedish DD party is full of commies and anarchists. Harold is an old-school conservative who values individuality, fair play and equal say but is not a hippy. He has all his old contacts and name recognition."

"Let me look him up." Ajay stabbed further at this phone."

Bea ignored Ajay's screen fixation. "Harold wants to make it happen. He says he has the money to do it. He even said he was contacting a lawyer. Derek Nelson is his name, the one infamous for the DeLoria Scandal. Harold wants me to look for someone who could make an app. Someone like you."

Ajay spoke to his phone. "Search Wikipedia for Deloria Scandal. Hmmm... Derek Nelson is real, too. In the late 90s, he found a way to make a deal with an Indigenous People to approve a tar sand project that was a vital marsh on the North American Central Flyway. Years later, questions about kickbacks, gifts and trips to a Vancouver Gentlemen's Club with NBA Players came to light. Nothing unlawful was proven." Aay looked up, smirking. "But I wouldn't leave him in a room with my sister."

"Harold is on the level."

"This lawyer guy sounds like the kind of person you need for this. The whole thing sounds like a laugh... but honestly, I got enough real projects on the go—the kind that make money."

"I know what you mean..." Bea slumped in her seat and gazed at her drink. "This is the type of escapade we might have gotten up to in university, but... I'm working all the time and not getting ahead."

"Sorry to hear things have been tough for you."

"Oh, I'll be all right. But it was so invigorating seeing Harold at almost ninety glow like a child when he talked about his idea of Direct Democracy." Bea knocked back the rest of her drink.

From down the bar, the bartender noticed. "Do you want another?"

"No."

"Have another one," Ajay interjected. "I don't want to finish this alone."

"I would like to, but I can't afford it. Sam's birthday's coming up. I need to get something as good as Amy." Bea spat out the last bit.

"I got it," Ajay called to the bartender. "Another round."

"Thanks... you are a good friend. If only I was smarter back then and knew when to let things go. I could have been like you, doing something amazing and fun. At least, I could be the communications person for an advocacy group. I fought the law, but the law won... ok, not actually the law, but I fought social norms, but he won." Bea leaned with elbows on the bar, head in her hands. "If I were smart, I would have at least had half of Marcus's fucking house and Range Rover."

"You did some amazing things. Remember the Voting Party?"

"How can I forget?" Bea hit her head on the bar lightly. "I met Marcus there."

"You did more to get young voters to the polls than anyone I know. It was genius: get in free to the best party of the year with an **I Voted** sticker or pay twenty bucks if you didn't vote. Crazy! You even got a shout-out from Rick Mercer."

Bea plunked her head on the bar again. "I sent Rick a racy love letter when I was 16. I even made a YouTube video of me reading it. I was too stupid to know he is gay."

"You changed things. Voting Parties are held at every Canadian university for all levels of government; it is a rite of passage."

Surprised, Bea looked at Ajay, "Really? It did some good?"

"Students I mentor rave about it. I get so much cred when I say I helped you throw the first Voting Party. I can honestly say I feel all the student union shenanigans you participated in did good."

"That's a big thing coming from you. Direct Democracy is a good thing. If it works. The worst that might happen is we win. Come on, make an old man and me happy. I need you."

"I can see if it is feasible," Ajay spoke while melting at Bea's smile. "I might get one of my mentees – is that a word – to look into it."

"I could hug you!" Bea got up and hugged Ajay.

Reminiscing over another drink, Bea began to feel tipsy and had to ask: "Is it ok if I feel your chest?"

"I thought this was not a date?"

"Oh God. I am sorry, Ajay. Don't get me wrong, I'm really happy to see you. Thank you for looking into Direct Democracy and for the drinks. I have to go." Bea got up from the bar stool and held her arms wide. "A hug before I go."

"I won't hold it against you." Ajay hugged Bea.

"Sorry… thanks and see you." Bea hoped it was not raining out because she was certain if it was, she would get a ride from Ajay. She wanted nothing like that from men.

4.

The internet reached by Google was a far more commercial and uninteresting place than Bea had remembered, particularly on a Friday night. It seemed hard to find something novel that was not sensationalized commerce. She did not have the money to buy anything. But if she went through the looking glass beyond Google's turf, she'd likely find Bubo online. She desperately wanted to chat about Direct Democracy or anything else that might come up. She knew chatting with him would not be productive.

Maybe YouTube had some new cute owl videos. The only new owl videos were of a Russian woman with a pet owl that seemed to hate the woman. Bea watched it but was unsatisfied because the owl never pecked the owner's eyes out.

She went to the darkest depths of the internet: the comment sections on news stories. It was entertainment that always left her feeling shameful. She tried to hide her embarrassment by telling herself it was to see if the Honorable member Harold Gordon had posted anything.

Bea found posts by Harold. His posts touched a chord, and there were likes and dislikes and replies from sympathizers, idiots, and trolls. In total, there were twelve posts, eleven more than she had expected. She felt good; the posts made it feel as if there was progress forward.

"On your left!"

The box of Empire Donuts nearly left Bea's hand as she pretended to lob it at the cyclist. The cyclist swerved. She followed up with, "Fuck you! Asshole!" and kept walking. She was in a good mood and excited to talk with Harold.

He was waiting in the lounge with Jerry when she came in. "I got us doughnuts," she held up the box.

"I hope you got one for Jerry." Harold's voice was gruff. "He just got back from a fantastic cruise. But I'm sure you will hear all about it because he can't get his camera to talk to his phone. He could use his phone to call someone who cares, but he would have to stop showing me hundreds of badly lit, out-of-focus pictures of the same statue. Next time, get a book from the gift shop, I tell him! Then the pictures will be good, and you won't have to waste my time."

Bea stepped back and addressed Jerry. "Let me give him a doughnut to help his blood sugar, and then we can download your pictures."

"You can't have doughnuts without coffee," Harold grumbled. "I'll get us some."

Bea took her time helping Jerry. This further aggravated Harold. This amused her. She hid her joy with giggles directed at Jerry's shitty photos.

"Thanks, Bea. I would never have figured that out myself."

"A word of advice, Jerry." Harold taunted. "Don't show those pictures to your kid; he may not want to see you again."

Jerry did not respond, walking away.

Bea moved to Harold's table. "What was that about?"

Harold did not answer. "Did you see your man about Direct Democracy?"

"Yes. Ajay is going to help."

"What does that mean?"

"Ajay said he would see if it is feasible."

"Feasible, is that your word or Ajay's?"

"Ajay's... and he is going to get one of his students to look into it."

"I don't like people who use the word feasible, it is bureaucratic for not going anywhere. And putting a lackey on it is not good. When is this guy getting back to you?"

"It was hard enough getting him to investigate it. I was not in the position to give him a deadline."

"Next time show a little more leg," Harold snarked.

Bea stared Harold in the eye. "That is over the line."

"You said he had a thing for you. This is serious stuff."

"If it is serious, Harold, take it seriously and don't degrade the people helping you. Apologize."

"Fine. I am sorry, it may happen again but hopefully not often... I am old and it was 'okay' in my day."

"Thank you. Why are you so grumpy?"

"It's my daughter's birthday this week." Harold sighed. "I haven't spoken with her since the divorce back when I was in government. June and my son Ron will not forgive me for breaking up with Anne…"

"I'm sorry. That's hard. I can relate. But you don't have to tell me about it."

"The kids won't listen so you can. Besides, you might learn something about the jerk you're working with." Harold took a sip of coffee. "Our marriage was over long before the divorce. Anne and I fought all the time but not in front of people. We both had affairs. The only time we would talk after the kids went to university was on social occasions. Even before that, we would find ways to not see each other. I stayed in Ottawa or the cottage. She lived in the house. I did a lot of fishing back then, it was great. When the kids came home for the holidays, we'd grin and bear it."

"Why drag it out..?" Bea interrupted.

"Politics. At the end we had the Reform Party nipping at our heels. We… Anne and I knew it would be bad to divorce. She liked the lifestyle and I wanted to stay in the game. We made a deal not to divorce until I left politics. She agreed and abided. We grew even further apart." Harold stopped and rubbed his face.

"That doesn't sound so bad. Adults make arrangements."

"That's not the part the kids are upset with. Anne, God rest her soul, did not tell me she was in the final stages of breast cancer. She didn't tell anyone until right before the end. Right before the divorce Derek, my lawyer, and a mutual friend, called to tell me she died."

"Oh my God! That's terrible."

"The kids had both gravitated to Anne after the divorce. I had not spoken with either in about a month. I was giving them some time. I found out from Derek, whose wife was close to Anne, that Anne was going to tell me too. Anne didn't get the chance. She only told the kids a couple weeks before. I tried to talk with them but they were inconsolable. They cannot believe I did not know. They think I left Anne knowing she had cancer."

"That is horrible. But time heals all…" Bea did not believe her words even while speaking them. "Your kids will come around."

"It has been over twenty years."

"I don't know what to say. I can relate but..."

"...you don't want to talk about it."

"I was saying, I can relate with your kids." Be a struggled to not sound angry. "I have a similar parental situation and there is nothing that will change it."

Harold opened his mouth but said nothing.

Bea changed the subject: "Nice work on the posts you put up last week. It ruffled a few feathers. We'll need that to get the message out."

"I would have posted more, but tapping it out letter by letter takes forever. Why are the keys so small and the keyboard so illogical?"

"You can't type?"

"I had a secretary; she could type as fast as I could talk."

"Your tablet can do that," Bea moved from sitting across from Harold to sitting next to him. "Let me show you. Go to the main menu. Hit the notepad icon. See the microphone-looking thing. Then speak." She tapped the microphone when she stopped talking.

"What should I say?" The computer typed what Harold said. "That's amazing!" The computer typed that as well. "Stop it! How do you stop it, Bea?"

Bea tapped the tablet. "If you hit the microphone button again, it'll stop. It takes some getting used to."

"Perfect, this will help get the message out. I've read social media is the best way to get voters these days. How do we do that?"

"Have you heard of Instagram or Facebook?"

Harold looked puzzled.

"Facebook is where old people go to be racist and remember when the country was great... are you sure you never heard of it?" Bea paused for a response. Harold shook his head. "Instagram is for slightly younger people that are all trying to show that their life is better than everyone else's."

"I've heard of Facebook... at least I've read about that alien-looking billionaire who owns it. Seemed like a scam to me. Never used it."

"We need to be on Facebook and other social media to get followers. The more followers we have, the better. Controversy, shock and argument gets views. That gets followers." With a strong feeling of Deja vu, Bea continued teaching the ins and outs of social media: memes, privacy, groups, etcetera. They practiced using Messenger. She friended him. They looked for other 'friends' that could help get the message out.

Harold listened intently as Bea taught him to search for videos on YouTube on how to fix any computer problem. Harold became enthusiastic, keen to sign up for a YouTube Channel, but Bea coached him to get used to Facebook first.

Soon Bea's time at the Home was almost done. "Harold, I've got to go get Sam. If you have questions, ask YouTube… if that doesn't work message me. I'm going to send you a link to Commentiquette, it is the kind of humour you'll like and will show you how to comment on the internet."

"What?"

"Internet Comment Etiquette…"

"There's such a thing?"

"No…" Bea laughed. "But his channel on YouTube will show you the different crap you can do to get followers. Also a good example of the type of trolling to not get caught by. We want to stir things up but not scare people off. And I think you'll find it funny."

"Thanks. I learned lots. But I think we missed something; what is Direct Democracy's message?"

"We don't need a message right now; we need followers. Once they are following us, we don't need a message."

"I don't get it." Harold furrowed his brow. "How can we get elected if we don't have a message?"

"We don't have a message. Direct Democracy is the voice of the people, as diverse as they are."

"I get what you're saying, Bea, but that sounds like Hippy-Commie bullshit."

"Focus on the followers." Bea looked at her cell phone. "I have to go. Good job."

"People need to be heard again. Even in Canada, there is too much money spent on politics. Maybe we can shake it up. I feel like we got started today."

"Me too." Bea silently admitted to herself that the session had truly been fun.

She met Sam at the park as usual. There was no admission charge at the Museum, so they spent the afternoon there. Seeing the wildlife photos got Sam hankering to see his owls.

Their search was unsuccessful even as the sun was going down. "Momma B, I think it's time to stop looking. Josie wants some privacy."

Before Bea answered, she saw Rich up under one of the cedar trees. "Sam, I think you should check one more tree. That one, over there."

"Ok, one more."

Rich saw Sam walking up to the tree and pointed to the branch Josie was on. Sam stood watching Josie preen. Rich walked over to Bea.

"What's new, Rich?"

"Everything is good except for Mayor Moonbeam tearing up half of Dallas Road for more bike lanes and taking away parking spots. Where am I going to park my car in the summer? The park will be packed. If I knew she was going to do this, I wouldn't have voted for her."

"Funny, Harold Gordon has a solution for the problem of your elected representative voting for something you don't want. At least at the federal level."

"What's that old gas bag's idea?"

"Allow the constituents of the riding to vote on every bill via a secure online poll. The MP only votes for a bill that gets 50 percent of the constituency's votes. Direct Democracy."

Watching Josie, Rich said, "How would you get everyone to vote? Only thirty-year-olds living in their parent's basements will have time to vote."

"Right now, the only people who get a voice are cranks who can hound the MP, donors and corporations. With Direct Democracy, you would at least have the chance to vote for what you want."

"As much as I hate Harold Gordon and his defunct party, I like the idea. I like the idea because I like politics. But most people don't care about politics. They want convenience. Once they vote, if they vote, they're done. They sit back and watch the show. It is fun dissing what your politician just did. It is like that Dead Kennedy's album, Give Me Convenience or Give Me Death."

Bea was hurt by Rich's criticism, mainly because she knew it was true. Who wanted to vote on everything? Brightening, she said, "The program we are making for Direct Democracy will have an option to set your vote on a bill by category and party. When your Direct Democracy representative gets in, you can set your votes to what you want. You are a Green on the environment, toggle the Green section for environmental bills. But if you want a strong military, click the Conservative selection for defense. And you can leave the setting that way for the rest of the term."

Hmmm, that could work." Rich rubbed his chin. "It would be nice to get the politician away from politics. Canada is better with donation limits, but let's face it: all MPs work for the donors. The last defence Minister just got a job with Lockheed Martin."

"That wouldn't happen with a Direct Democracy candidate."

"You say you're creating an app?"

"Harold is checking to see if it's possible. I have a friend looking at the platform. I would say it is a long shot, but we're going to try."

"Keep me in the loop."

"No problem. What's your email? I'll send you Harold's new Facebook profile." Bea smirked. "If we don't get Direct Democracy this thing off the ground, you can at least harass him online."

Josie exploded out from under a cedar tree, flying low over Bea and Rich.

"Momma B!" Sam yelled. "Did you see that?"

"I felt it, Sam. That was amazing!"

"Wow, that's the closest I've ever been to an owl." Sam gazed wistfully off in the direction Josie had flown. "Momma A said there is a place in Ottawa where you can hold an owl."

Bea fought back the hurt from what Sam had said. Why was Amy telling Sam about owls in Ottawa? Owls were Sam and Bea's thing.

Rich turned to Sam. "There's a place in Duncan where you can hold an owl. The Raptors has all kinds of birds of prey."

"Duncan, that's not far, right?" Sam appealed to Bea. "Momma B, can we go?"

"It's not far." Bea knew deep down it was impossible. "We'll see…"

5.

Upon hearing, "Please give me a chance," from the desperate man on the phone, Bea tuned him out. She had heard it every workday.

In fact, she herself had a similar story of debt and hardship that was not of her own making. But she'd figured out how to take control, paying the debt down. Each payment was its own scab pulled off the wound that was her relationship with Marcus. All the lawyer did was waste her money. Then she had to pay and pay and pay. She had only paid the debt down last summer. That left her in student debt. Meanwhile, Marcus got Sam a wife, a house, and a Range Rover.

"That's why you need to give me a break," the man continued. "I'm begging you… Please."

"I can understand where you are coming from. The best thing to do…" Bea paused as she heard the Imperial March playing softly from her purse. She stared at her bag, unsure what to do.

"What can I do? Help me out."

"The best thing to do is set up a payment plan with me." Bea hurriedly gave him a number he could not refuse just to get him off the phone. Her haste would bring her average down and put her bonus in jeopardy. But a call from Marcus at work was concerning.

Bea checked his message, "Hi Bea, Amy and I have a chance to go to Ottawa on short notice. We want to take Sam along… it is on your weekend. Maybe you can have him the following weekend? Give me a callback."

The message did not end. Amy's muffled voice said, "Don't cave to her; she got an extra weekend a few weeks ago."

Marcus replied, "I just want to be fair; she might not…" the rest was too faint to hear.

Bea was just able to make out Amy say, "If this goes well."

Marcus said, "Shit! The phone didn't hang up." Repeating the message did not give Bea any more clarity.

An instant message from her team lead, Mike, popped up on Bea's computer: "When you have a minute, come by my office."

Bea wanted the team lead position. She resented Mike for getting it. The first time she applied, she was told she had all the ability but was not aggressive enough. She became more aggressive. The second time she applied, she was told she had all the ability, but she was too aggressive to lead. This was exactly the type of hidden discrimination she learned about in women's studies. Studies showed male interviewers skewed in favour of other men. This was Y (like the chromosome), and Mike got the position instead of her. She was an aggressive bitch, and who wants a boss like that? The third time the position was posted, she did not apply.

Mike was not the problem. He was a pretty good guy with a wife and kid. It was the system. Bea wished it would be fair. Her ability against his on a level playing field. Democracy stood for the equality she wanted. Each person with an equal chance of success based on ability as much as possible. She did not live in that world. Once, she thought she could level the playing field. It only set her back. She was slowly spiralling down the drain of inequality.

Changing jobs was too risky; she could not afford a month with no job. She could not get the time off to go to an interview. She could not go back to school; she already had more debt than she could handle. She was too proud to find a man to save her. Her hope was to hustle her ass off collecting debt, paying her debt off in a few years, then finding something better. Something with a pension, a thing she was not sure existed anymore.

Long, slow breaths helped Bea squelch her negative thoughts about the world and her position in it. She knew a meeting with Mike at the end of the day was probably not a good thing. She walked into Mike's office. "What's up?"

Mike pointed at the ceiling, "Above your head… usually."

"That never gets old, Mike," Bea smiled at Mike's running gag that stopped being funny a long time ago.

"Close the door and have a seat." Mike pointed to a chair. "I got a complaint from one of your accounts."

"Of course you did. Nobody likes a debt collector."

Mike sat back, manspreading in his chair. "Yes, Bea, it's part of the profession. I have no problem humouring people, but you must follow the rules. I had a guy named Andrew Chow chew my ear off because you called his work."

Bea was happy she wore pants today so she could mirror Mike's expanded sitting position. "Did he tell you he works from home?"

"Ah... no... no, he didn't." Mike seemed unnerved by Bea's posture and assertive query. He sat up, "Look, I'm letting you know as a courtesy. I hung up on the mouthy asshole. Bea, I was a collector, too; I know you guys push the boundaries... Just don't break the rules."

"Mike, if you're worried about us breaking the rules, go back to the commissions we had three years ago. We get better numbers now, yet we get less commission."

"Ah, I don't control that."

"But you can ask for it, especially for a team that's killing the numbers."

"Noted. I'll bring that up with Terry."

"Don't worry about Andrew Chow; he's drunk most of the time. Liked calling me a dirty slut and telling me how sexy I sound. All while working from home." Bea put air quotes around her last three words.

"That's good... Just wanted to give you a heads-up. Have a good evening."

"You, too." Bea got up to leave. "But do remember to ask Terry about the commission."

Knowing Mike's reply did not matter, Bea stomped out of his office. She barely stopped to turn her computer off and grab her bag. In her agitated state, she hoped to see a cyclist on the way home, especially one on a racing bike.

Walking home, Bea was reluctant to call Marcus. Something was not right.

In fact, the whole Marcus obsession was not right. She had misjudged him, or she had only seen her side of the relationship. In university he had acted like a woke person. He was going to be an environmental lawyer, fighting for the wilderness and helping indigenous peoples get what was theirs. She was going to be a community leader and one day get into politics.

She dreamed they would be equal forces for good, certain that he was all in for the dream, too. He would be fine if she was the primary income earner. When they had kids, they would truly split the parenting - lawyers can work from home. When she thought of all this, she could not believe how naïve she was.

When Bea got pregnant, Marcus changed. He became his father. He wanted the Nuclear Family and a white picket fence. She did not find this out until he forbade her from going back to university. She had to take care of Sam. He would say to her, "When Sam is in preschool, you can take some courses." Worse, the parents on both sides did not support her – particularly the women. The consensus of the parental units was that a mother away from home was bad for the child. She could not live with this. She could not live with a man who would not let her be a person.

Bea often argued with herself about whether Marcus deceived her or if she was blinded by love to who he really was. Lately, the self-deception argument has won more often. It did not matter. She made the decision to cause the shitfight the separation and custody battle turned into. She could have changed into a woman acceptable to him and the families if only she stopped being so uppity.

The underlying problem was that uppity was still a common word some Canadians used to describe women in the 2010s. She wanted to follow her dream. But she lost her kid and her dreams.

The light turned red at the T junction pedestrian intersection. Bea was starting to cross when she saw the cyclist about to run the red light. This happened all the time. She hated it. It was exactly the specialness cyclists believed they were entitled to. Everyone should follow the same rules, she thought. She took out her cell phone and immediately had it recording. She stood videoing as the cyclist approached, slowing only slightly. As the cyclist got to the stop line, where cars had stopped, she yelled, "RED LIGHT! RED LIGHT! RED LIGHT!"

"What the fuck!" The cyclist was still going too fast to stop and had to swerve.

Bea smiled as she stepped onto the sidewalk. Stopped at the intersection, a second cyclist shook his head. She thanked him for stopping as she walked past. She could not wait to post the video.

The incident brightened Bea's mood enough to call Marcus, dialling as she walked. She was grateful she did not have to question that Marcus wanted the best for Sam. Even Amy was all in for Sam. At the same time, Bea resented Marcus and Amy for being so good. Bea worried Marcus saw her as bad for Sam, and she felt that was not totally untrue. Bea tried not to dwell on this.

"Hi Bea, how are you doing?"

"Fine. Why does Sam need to go to Ottawa?"

"Amy's family is there. There's snow, and he likes snow."

"He needs to go because of snow?" Bea had more to say but did not say it.

"I know he does not 'need' to go… but this would be fun for him. It is an opportunity."

"He'll be out of school, too?"

"Yes. It'll be five days," Marcus paused for Bea's response. He did not like the silence. "He can miss the time. It's only grade three."

"Is Amy's family well?"

"What?"

"Weren't you stuck in Ottawa when I took Sam for the night?"

"Yes, they are fine."

"I'm happy to hear they are well. Why are you going there so often?"

"Work is lobbying for changes to the environmental assessment process." There was an uncomfortable pause. "Look, I don't want to fight about this. It would be nice for him to go on a trip. Amy can take him to all the sights. He could get to play hockey on the Rideau Canal. Tell me you want to deny him that?"

Bea took a deep breath. "Let's let Sam decide."

"Give me a second," Marcus called for Sam.

Bea braced for Sam's certain decision to go to Ottawa. She could understand why he would want to go. Still, it would hurt.

"Momma B wants to ask you a question."

"Momma B!" Sam's effusive voice over the phone buoyed her mood. "Have you seen any owls lately?"

"No Kiddo. Not since we last saw Josie. But hey, do you want to go to Ottawa instead of having our weekend?"

"I want to do both!"

"You have to choose, Kiddo."

"How about this... you come?"
"That's not possible."
"Could I go and then see you right after?"
"You mean you come with me the next weekend?"
"Yes. And see owls!"
"I am fine with that. Ask your dad if he is fine with that."
"Dad?"
Marcus came onto the phone. "That sounds good."
"I get Sam the week after."
"Yes."
"Have a good trip." Bea was hanging the phone up as Marcus said bye.

At home, Bea went straight to her computer to upload the bike video. Within minutes, it was getting likes and comments.

She opened her browser to the dark web and clicked into a forum called Doxed. It was a place where members could buy and sell personal information. It was how she found out who a debtor's girlfriend was when a debtor's Facebook profile was private. Any type of private information could be found here, like credit card numbers, sin numbers, and passwords. But she only skimmed the surface by spending the odd faction of a Bitcoin for the details of one of her clients.

Today, Bea was not looking for information. She was here for some anonymous vengeance. She understood why debtors hated her. She forces them to clean up their financial mess. Something that, in the long run, was freeing. Indeed, the hard choice she gave them to pay off the debt quickly and help her get a bonus was an opportunity. It levelled the playing field for the debtor, so they were on an equal footing again, able to live a good life when the debt was paid. She posted drunken Andrew Chow's information on the Spam Hell thread. He would be getting calls, texts and emails from every shady scammer on the internet for days and nights.

A flash on the menu bar caught her eye. She pulled up the message.

Bubo: Yo! Killa! I got some news on the DD.
Kira B: Let me guess, the idea sucks?

Bubo: Quite the contrary. I've chatted with a few people, all of whom are ready to vote DD. The app is easy, I'm sure you could make it. The security is hard, it needs someone with skill and who knows the law… like me… and…
Kira B: And?
Bubo: I'm in. If the honourable member can pay me.
Kira B: Do you know how to cash a check? I will send the honourable member an email to his Hotmail account.
Bubo: LOL! Let the honourable member know.
Bubo: Killer, I only got time Tuesdays and Thursdays after 6 and 8 pm.
Bubo: I got this crazy thing going with a girl from the gym. The other nights of the week, we do this intense session that ends with an intense passion. ☺
Kira B: Is your name Epstein?
Bubo: No.
Kira B: Then you mean woman from the gym.
Bubo: Oooh… touchy today.
Kira B: I don't think this woman would want to hear you calling her girl. If she does you should lose her. My dinner's burning. Smell you later.

Bea closed the browser, not wanting to hear about Ajay's new woman.

6.

Bea did not reach the monthly bonus goal. She wanted to berate a cyclist, but that was unlikely on this crappy ass night. She wanted to feel sorry for herself while eating salty Skor bark from Rocky Mountain Chocolate while watching a movie. But she had to follow through with an old white man's dream of changing the world one last time. She thought, 'He doesn't need my help; old white men's dreams are inevitable.'

Rain beat down on Bea's umbrella as she jogged down Blanshard Street to the Home. She double-checked each street on the dark night.

A silhouette on the chain link fence surrounding a school caught her attention. A car drove past, illuminating the barred owl perched three metres away.

The owl did not move. Bright-eyed, Bea stood watching the owl. She took out her phone to get a picture. The owl looked right at her.

"Is that you, Josie? The left arch over your eye is wider than the right. I think it is you," Bea said softly. "The light's bad. Can I use the flash?" Bea took a picture. The flash did not seem to bother Josie.

Josie flew down to the edge of the field next to a garbage can. The owl was a metre from Bea. Josie grabbed something with her beak and then flew back onto the fence.

Bea stood there for minutes, transfixed. Josie kept hunting, seeing things Bea could not, as rain beat down and cars drove by.

"Thank you, Josie," Bea said. Josie took no notice. Bea put her umbrella on the ground so she could cup her mouth with her hands as if she were warming them with her breath. "Who cooks for you? Who cooks for you all!"

Josie stared at Bea and toward a flashing white light behind her. After a few seconds, Josie flew over Bea's head, messing Bea's hair. Bea started laughing and started walking to the Home.

A flashing bike light grew closer. Bea thought, could the night be better? Then she yelled, "Turn off your fucking blinking light! It scared the owl!"

The cyclist sped away.

Owls, Doughnuts, and Democracy, by Jason A. N. Taylor

Bea's reflection smiled back at her as she opened the door to the Home. The clock over the reception desk indicated that she was 15 minutes late. She stopped at the reception desk. "Rita, look WHO I saw on the way here." Bea shoved her phone between Rita's knitting and her face.

"Oh, what's that Bea?"

"That's the local barred owl, Josie. She was hunting by South Park Elementary... in downtown Victoria."

"That's amazing. I never..." Rita was interrupted by what sounded like a loud 'bullshit' and some inaudible words. Then what sounded like 'keep it down,' from a woman's voice. "Deary, you're here with that brow... young fellow to see Harold?"

"Yes."

"They are in the lounge with one of Harold's friends. I don't think Harold likes your friend."

"Harold does not like anyone. Wish me luck."

"You'll need more than luck." Rita went back to her knitting.

Harold walked out of the lounge, shoulders back and chest out, as Bea started down the hall. Harold did not see Bea and turned down the hall away from her. He grabbed for the hallway rail, hunched over, his gait changing to an old man's shuffle.

Bea considered if she should call after him but thought better of it.

Ajay would be easier to calm than the honourable member. She turned into the lounge. Ajay was sitting on the edge of his seat, turned away from the door, chest puffed out and elbow planted on the armrest, ranting to the older man. "How can you not see a need for a guaranteed income? Even billionaires know automation and robotics are decimating manual jobs. It has already happened!"

The older gentleman said, "There are always jobs for those willing to work. If you give people free money, there is no incentive to work. The Soviet Union proved that." He turned to Bea, "You must be Bea."

"Yes. And you are..?"

"Derek Nelson," Derek stood to shake Bea's hand as he did, he said, "Harold's description was right. He said to look for a beautiful woman."

Normally, a remark like Derek's would have been met by Bea's acid tongue, but his demeanour was deferential and seemed honest. Combined with the buttery voice and pleasant words, she had no comment. She thought, was he a lawyer? She blushed a little, then remembered the scandal with a gentleman's club and said, "There is a first time for everything... including Harold being right." She then turned to Ajay, staring at his chest without meaning to, and said, "I could hear you down the hall! What's going on?"

Derek answered politely, "A passionate discussion of current events."

Ajay was not polite, "Bea, in the fifteen minutes I've been here, Harold has found every way to belittle me. He said my clothes were gay... and any trained MONKEY could do my job because he can use Facebook... and called me a liar for saying how much I get for an hour of consulting... then he called me a Communist. I'm getting the vibe he does not like people like me. No offence Derek, you've been gentlemanly, if wrong."

"No offence taken," Derek responded. "A guaranteed income is socialism and wrong."

Bea said, "Calm down, Ajay."

"I'm about to walk," Ajay got up.

A woman sitting with another group spoke up, "Young man, the honourable member is... How can I put this politely..."

"Harold's waggling his dick at you," another woman in the group interrupted. "Trying to show you he still has one. Let it slide, he can't keep it up long."

Ajay did not know what to say but sat down.

Bea laughed, shaking her head.

Derek winked at the inappropriate lady. "Astute observation."

"Oh Irene, you did not need to be so vulgar."

"Wendy, get with the times." Irene addressed Bea, "Are you part of this conspiracy too?"

"Ah, conspiracy?" Bea used that opening to practice her Direct Democracy elevator speech. "I guess we are trying to change politics. What do you think?"

Wendy answered first, "It is not polite to talk about politics."

Irene thought for a second, "You're saying I could vote against the pipeline but vote for the rest of the Liberal platform?"

"Sure, you would have to set your profile up that way."

"Profile!? I don't want to be part of any 'electronic' dating scheme!" Confused, everyone looked at Irene.

Bea sat down. "Voting profile." She turned to the two women.

Bea felt a kick from Derek. He was winking and tilting his head to the door as if saying, 'Leave with me.'

"I don't know why I thought that." Irene giggled. "I like the idea; tell me if you get anywhere with it." She got back to playing cards with Wendy.

"You were thinking of that hairstyle of a Prime Minister." Harold boomed. "We don't need help from a Liberal."

Not looking up from her cards, Irene said, "Wiggle that little member somewhere else. At least the Grits still exist."

Bea turned her glare to Harold. "What is this BS, Harold? Who are you fighting? We're all on the same team. Even Irene. Our party is about everyone having an equally valid opinion. One person, one vote. We need Liberals, NDPers, Conservatives, and even communists, socialists, anarchists, and libertarians. But you're slinging shit at the people trying to make this happen. Ajay can make this happen and he nearly left. We are on the same team!"

Harold leaned forward, hands on the arm rests, starting to get up. Derek put a hand on Harold's. Harold sat back. "Forgive Harold, he did not mean to offend you, Ajay. As we go forward, our campaign finances become extremely important. Harold was upset because if Ajay makes the amount he says he does, we cannot hire him. It would use all our funds. We are not in the United States, there are strict donation limits."

Bea said, "Could Ajay volunteer?"

"I'm not doing this pro bono; it is too much work."

"Contributions of services by a self-employed professional must be counted as a donation of time at the same cost as charged normally," Harold grumbled. "At Ajay's rate for computer jiggery-pokery, the campaign would be able to get about a half hour of his time before hitting the spending limits. Eh, can you make this thing in 30 minutes?" Ajay laughed and shook his head.

"I did not think so. Sorry, I was tactless earlier; you can see why. It seems we are wasting your time."

Bea sat up. "Is that it!?"

"Unfortunately, it is only as the campaign gains steam that there might be enough funds to pay for the program," Derek said. "Ajay, realistically, how much would the app cost?"

"Between thirty and fifty thousand dollars."

"In the Victoria Capital riding, a candidate can spend about a hundred and twenty thousand. Making Direct Democracy a party would increase that. However, getting contributions to hit that number would be miraculous for a new party." Derek rubbed his eyes. "Our total contributions might not hit thirty thousand."

Bea slumped back into her chair. "That's, it."

"That can't be it." Ajay closed his eyes in thought. "The 'girl' I'm seeing is really into Direct Democracy."

"That's the real reason you're here?" Bea shook her head. "And for God's sake, call her a 'woman' or come up with a name like everybody else. Dick!"

Harold seemed not to have heard the bickering. "I think we can go forward without the thingamajig, but it will be harder."

Derek said, "I think it is a long shot if we can't show people what we're talking about."

The group sat quietly for an awkward amount of time.

Irene piped, "Make a video of how it will work."

"It is not that simple," Harold rebuked her.

Ajay rubbed his chin, "Maybe it is that simple. Derek, can a volunteer provide time free of charge if he is not self-employed doing the same work?"

"Yes."

Ajay mused out loud, "It might work. The hard part is the security. But you don't need the security until after the election. The easy part is the voting app; Bea can make that."

"I like your confidence in my skills, Ajay, but I've not coded anything in a while."

"You have the skills. And I can hook you up with one of my mentees if you get stuck."

Harold smiled. "Forward movement. Thanks for your help, Ajay. You are free to leave."

"We love the idea," Ajay said. "Is there anything else I can do to make Direct Democracy a thing?"

Bea rolled her eyes at Ajay.

Harold said, "Unless you have accounting skills, no."

"Harold, I think Ajay can help," Derek said. "Have you heard of a Third Party?"

"Derek that's a great idea," Bea enthused.

"Isn't that a rule in hockey?" Ajay looked around, confused.

"Ajay…" Bea sighed. "You're thinking of the third man in rule fighting in hockey. A Third Party is Canadian for Super PAC. It's a group of people that supports a political agenda but is not a political party and they don't run a candidate. Like those dicks at Canada Proud that troll social media to get Justin out of power. You would be so good at that Ajay!"

"Marvelous summary of a Third Party, Bea." Derek grinned lecherously in Ajay and Bea's direction. "In Harold's and my day there was no such thing. Times have changed, one cannot run a campaign without online support. Third Parties can highlight the importance of an issue. They are a real force multiplier even if they are limited by caps on contributions and spending."

Bea squinted at Derek. She was unhappy he was checking her out.

Derek continued: "Direct Democracy needs at least one Third Party, possibly more. Bea is right to say we need all political stripes; a Third Party can cater to the political group we want to sway whether they are left or right. We must appeal to diversity as Bea so wisely points out."

Derek's praise warmed Bea. She felt validated and a little turned on. "Yes Derek, a Third Party arguing 'I know how to vote on policy better than any politician' would certainly catch on. It would be a classic Libertarian view. Ajay, I'm sure your tech bros would eat this up."

"Yeah, Bea, they'll eat it up. I've only told a half dozen or so, and all but one love it..., and that guy is a bit on the spectrum, anything outside of the norm, and he gets leery about it. My woman is so into it she did not want me to tell anyone in case they stole the idea."

"Your woman!" Bea could not help herself. "How long have you known her, Ajay? Two weeks!? Really? What is her name anyway? And if the idea is to get Direct Democracy, why would anyone keep the idea secret?" Bea thought she might have gone over a line. The fact everyone was looking at her told her she had.

No one was sure if she was upset at Ajay's words or just jealous.

Sheepishly, Ajay replied, "Cat thought that online idiots could steal the message before we could brand it as Direct Democracy."

"That's a good point," Harold jumped in. "We need to own the brand. How are we going to do that?"

"Sorry, I was harsh, Ajay. I want to make sure you are doing this because you want to. Not because you're trying to impress Cat. Remember how we met?"

"Yes, I do. It is not like that." Ajay addressed everyone, "How are we going to keep this on brand?"

Bea replied, "Harold has a pretty good if new, online presence commenting on newspapers, Facebook, and trolling Dex Duffy."

Ajay interrupted, "Who?"

Harold growled, "That fucking Newfy dingleberry who once hosted Cross Country Check Up. Now he's a mouthpiece for Conrad Black."

Ajay still looked confused. Bea continued, "But Harold still needs an actual website with our platform or lack of one. I can build something simple this weekend with Harold. Once it's up, Ajay can start posting questions that lead back to it."

"Great starting point, Bea," Derek said. "A suggestion for the website: consider making its focus Direct Democracy and not Harold."

Harold glared at Derek.

"We need to keep in mind that Harold is divisive," Derek continued. "Many, if not most, of our supporters could sour on the party if they see Harold's politics first."

Harold groaned, "Derek's right. This is about implementing Direct Democracy, not people. How do we make that point?"

No one said anything for another awkward amount of time.

"Gin!" shouted Irene. To the group she said, "It's obvious, show the people their parties don't vote for what they want."

"Thanks Irene," Bea responded. "That's a good place to start."

Harold added, "If the Liberals had avoided that behaviour, WE would not own a pipeline that will never be completed."

Irene shot back, "And the free trade agreement was good for all those western Conservatives working in sawmills?"

"Irene that's not the same..." Harold fumed. "That was an unintended consequence. I fought to keep the mills here when it happened, but the American companies bought them."

Bea said, "All parties vote for regionally bad ideas or short-sighted projects. The point of Direct Democracy is to let the people make those decisions... not the party. Let's move on by finding those wedge issues so we can highlight them. The big one is the pipeline." Bea turned to Irene, "Do you want to be part of this, Irene?"

Irene answered, "As long as the honourable member is not going to dominate."

Bea said, "I'm sure Harold will believe he's in control. But he believes a lot of things that aren't true." Derek laughed out loud at Bea's remark. Bea continued, "I'll be here on Saturday making the website if you want to help. For the rest of us, I'll send around an email with all the wedge examples of parties not being true to their constituents. Any example will do, but do your best to find ideas relevant to our riding. Let's check in two weeks from now. Any other actions we should take?"

"I'll get Ajay some information on Third Parties," Derek answered. "Next meeting, we should look at who's taking on what role for the campaign. If the election happens on the latest date, October 21st, we have seven months before the campaign begins."

"Thanks, Derek," Ajay replied. "I will start sowing seeds of discord..." He smiled manically and made a tent of his fingers. "Excellent..."

Bea said, "Great, we have a plan."

"Thanks Bea..." Harold stood up. "I can take it from here. Everyone, do what Bea said."

Bea and Irene were talking amongst themselves, as were Derek and Ajay. Harold stood there, lost for a minute or two, then started for his room.

Bea caught up with Harold in the hall, shuffling toward the elevator holding the handrail. "Honorable member, hold on for a minute."

Harold let go of the rail, straightening up while turning to Bea, "Did you get the Liberal on board?"

"Irene is on our side. I'm so happy we are doing this. It feels right and I can't believe it. Can I give you a hug?"

"Sure." They hugged. "I feel 60 again. And it's good to have something to rail against. Ajay is a communist, nice guy otherwise."

"The guy who won't volunteer his time is a communist, right." Bea smirked. "Socialist, maybe, but that doesn't matter. I gotta see if I can get a lift from him. I'll see you Saturday with some doughnuts."

Bea noticed Derek and Ajay talking at the front door. When standing, Derek looked much younger. Derek was in the same good shape as Ajay. Derek was dressed in a stylish suit that went well with her fantasy of his scandal at a gentlemen's club. She censored the rest of her thoughts; they were working together, and Derek had to be in his 60s.

Ajay waved to Bea as he left. She tried to tell him to wait but he continued. She started toward the door as quickly as she could.

Derek intercepted Bea with a touch on her elbow, "It was lovely meeting you. I would like to talk with you for a moment."

"Sorry, Derek, I need to catch up with Ajay. I don't want to walk home. It is pissing out."

"I would be glad to give you a ride. Listening to you joust with Harold was a joy. You have certainly invigorated him. It seems you have a fine talent for organizing. Ajay's a fine young man too; however, he's not as refined or tactful as you."

"A ride would be great. It is awful out." Bea stepped close enough to the automatic door that it opened.

Derek stepped in front of Bea, umbrella in hand. "No reason for both of us to get wet. I will bring the car around."

The chivalry irritated Bea, but she told herself to go with it. No one had ever brought a car around for her. In less than a minute, a black Mercedes pulled up. She thought it was an S Class. She resisted the urge to go around the back of the car to check the model. Derek released her door from inside the car. She got in, enjoying the leather smell, "Nice car. Thanks for getting me wet... excuse me... from keeping me from getting wet."

"It is a fine automobile," Derek responded, tapping something on the touch screen.

"Is it an S Class?"

Derek nodded in response. "Where am I taking you?"

"I'm near Quadra Village. Hopefully, that's not out of your way."

"It is. I am on Dallas Road."

Bea wanted a place on Dallas Road. "House or condo?"

"A house. The view is great. Especially on stormy days like today. I have Harold to thank for it. He pushed me to buy it. Now it is worth a mint. But the view's worth more."

"I can imagine," Bea put together Derek's looks during the meeting, bringing the car around and talking of his house. He wanted her. Derek exuded a certain power she was attracted to, but she knew from experience lust only complicated politics. In any case, Bea viewed all interactions with lawyers as transactional, including complements.

"The front window is so big, I've got a bar and full-sized couch in front of it. The primary bedroom on the top floor also has a window as wide as the house. It is high enough no one can see in. Again, it was Harold that sold me on the huge windows. I am eternally grateful to have him in my life."

"Ooooh, my ass is hot!" Bea tried to recover, "The seat is really warm… too warm."

"I'll turn the seat warmer down." Derek fiddled with the touch screen, "Would you like to try the hot stone massage in the seat? It vibrates."

"No! This is not happening, Derek. I find you attractive, but this is business. Stop coming on to me. I am not putting Direct Democracy in jeopardy with this."

"Bea, I am deeply sorry if you thought I was making a pass at you."

"Don't deny it! What was all that winking at me, gesturing at me, kicking my leg and ogling at me during the meeting?"

"I wanted to get your attention so you could see Harold. I wanted you to see that he can barely walk. I love the man. I owe everything to him. I will help him with whatever he wants to do. But I do not want to see him hurt. I am not sure he has another campaign in him."

"What about the leering at my chest?"

"If you must know, I was looking at Ajay's chest."

"You're gay..? Not that that matters."

"Yes. It is why I like Direct Democracy. When I was a Conservative, our lives were private. We were fiscally conservative, not socially conservative. I like to think we were discreet. Now, you cannot be a conservative without being socially conservative. Direct Democracy lets people hold seemingly contradictory ideas – at least in today's divided political landscape – at the same time, such as wanting less regulations and taxes while being gay."

"But the scandal at the strip club!"

"Yes. I found it ironic. The stories in the papers were much more interesting than what actually occurred." Derek paused. "As I said before, I owe everything I have to Harold. I will help him with anything he wants. I cannot stop him from doing what he wants to do; however, I do not think he is able to run again. That said, he was more energized and vigorous than I have seen him in years. He is even using the internet!"

"Right! The Honorable Member has a lot of piss and vinegar in him," Bea laughed out loud.

"How did you come to volunteer at the Home?"

"If you want to know the truth..." Bea did not like this question from a lawyer. "I needed to look good to keep custody of my kid. My lawyer said volunteering would be a way to do that."

"Why would you need to look like a good mother?"

"None of your business."

"How long have you volunteered?"

"Seven or eight years."

"And you only started talking with Harold a few weeks ago?"

"Yes."

"Why?"

"Good fucking question. I'm not an altruistic divorced soccer mom. I keep going there because I get free coffee, I don't have to do much, and the rest of the time I steal whatever I can. Just little things no one would notice, like movie streaming and online newspaper subscriptions, food, and toilet paper. I also get the odd gift from senile people who think I'm their child. It is close to where I meet my kid every two weeks for the lame-ass custody arrangement my expensive lawyer got me. I did my best to keep my head down and download movies. But I pissed off Harold by getting the management to go fully digital. I had to persuade him to use the tablet or lose all those free subscriptions. Amazingly, the old man understood the internet. Before you started questioning me, I thought Direct Democracy was a fun shenanigan that gave a little light to an old man and me. God knows I could use some light. If you haven't noticed, I'm so poor that volunteering at an old folk's home is a nice way to get free shwag."

"Hmmm..." Derek intoned. "All very interesting."

"Interesting it may be, but if this interrogation doesn't stop, I'm out."

"Forgive me if you feel cross-examined. Let me confess my historical background with Harold."

"Please do."

Owls, Doughnuts, and Democracy, by Jason A. N. Taylor

"When it comes to politics, Harold does not participate in shenanigans. In 1993, the writing was on the wall; we knew the Progressive Conservatives were going to lose badly. The free trade deal did not go well. Canada and British Columbia had been in a long recession. Mills were closing. Harold had become a pariah in the logging towns that elected him. They even burnt him in effigy. A millwright in Port Alberni said on the radio that if Harold could come down there and stand up like a man for his part in it he might vote for Harold again. Harold immediately got in his truck, drove there, knocked on the guy's door, and got a shit kicking. Then the guy took pity on Harold. They went to the pub for beers. I got a call from Harold's wife to go pick him up the next day because his eye had swollen shut."

"I call bullshit," Bea snorted. "I follow politics pretty closely. If I knew about a BC Premier's wife, Lillian's, tragically 80's fashion sense—the woman who had a headband for all occasions—I'm sure I would have heard about Harold getting beaten up for votes."

"The story did not make the official news, but the myth travelled. The PCs went from a majority to only three MPs after that election; Harold was one of the three. So, you see, Harold is serious. He will pursue Direct Democracy until it has beaten him. Now that I am retired, I will help Harold as much as I can. What I am asking in a roundabout way is how committed are you? What do you want from this?"

Bea wiggled in the comfortable seat, fantasizing. She wanted to be part of something. She wanted to make a difference. She wanted to help everyone to be heard. She wanted to be important. She wanted to live in a nice place, have a pension, give Sam nice things and travel. She wanted a manservant. She wanted a second chance at her youthful dream. She wanted to be in parliament. She said, "Right on Hillside. Then left on the next street. It is that shitty apartment at the end of the block. Just behind the cop car is good." She knew that was a dream. She had wrecked any chance of being a public person.

"Bea, what do you want from Direct Democracy?"

"Derek, I want to be part of something. My life sucks. I live in an apartment easily identified by the ever-present cop car. I work as a collection agent. I barely have the money to buy my kid a bike for his birthday. My biggest hobbies are yelling at cyclists, looking for owls with my boy, volunteering at an old folk's home, and being a troll online. I want to use my three years of a bachelor's degree in political science for something. I will do what I can for Direct Democracy but if it does not pay it will be hard to do a lot."

"My my..."

"Right on Hillside. Then, left on the next street. It's that shitty apartment at the end of the block. Just behind the cop car is good."

"Everyone will get paid. As we start getting donations, we will be able to pay some of the people in the campaign. It will not be much at first. Of course, if the candidate wins, he..." Derek paused and turned toward Bea. "Or she, gets a salary of $176,000 a year for five years with money for an office, travel vouchers, and other expenses, for a job any warm body could do." Derek smiled mischievously. "You did say your butt was hot, which would make you qualified for the job."

Part of Bea's mind was already laughing in a first-class Air Canada lounge, ordering Camembert cheese with honourable member Wilson-Raybould and discussing the renovation of her primary residence. But that dream was quashed by her past; she struggled against herself not to even dream of such an impossibility. "Really, Derek... forget me and politics. I'm out. I can't risk being in the media's crosshairs for Sam's sake."

"It was a bad joke, Bea. I am sorry."

Bea searched for the door handle. "Having a Rockstar lawyer tell me I've got the talents to make Direct Democracy a winner while sitting in a Mercedes is hard for me to believe. Normally, when a woman living in the Villa, Paulina, has an older man talking up her talents in a hot car, it ends with a cash exchange and a stop at the pharmacy for plan B. So, you can see why I'm feeling overwhelmed and worried about getting fucked."

"I can see why you would be concerned," Derek laughed. "I can assure you; you won't get fucked. I only have eyes for Ajay. And Irene was pretty certain the honourable member cannot keep it up."

"Ew! I'm going to gag..!" Bea was laughing, too. "I kind of think of Harold as grandfatherly." She thought, 'Harold and Derek may be serious people, but Direct Democracy is still a dream. A joke that does not even have the credibility of the Rhinoceros Party.' Bea said, "It's been fun getting to know Harold and hearing some of his stories. Talking with you has been nice, too. I do want to hear all your salacious stories. Hopefully, Direct Democracy will have more chance of taking off than the Natural Law Party's yogic flying platform."

"I remember the press conference with the Yogi using his crossed legs to bounce around on a mattress and claiming he was flying! I nearly died laughing." Derek turned serious, "Harold wants Direct Democracy to happen; therefore, it will. We will have a candidate in the next election. I would rather that candidate not be Harold, but I cannot stop him. I think you are a great choice as the candidate."

"I can't be the candidate. I cannot leave my job for a flight of fancy. I've got things I do not want the public to know."

"Nobody cares that you swear at cyclists. Though I think you could be more creative because 'fuck you, asshole' is so common."

"What?"

"I'm one of the cyclists you swear at. In a jersey, helmet, on a road bike, I look different."

"Oh, you're one of THOSE cyclists! You deserved it."

"Sadly, yes."

"I'm doing my civic duty. I have a YouTube channel dedicated to shaming cyclists. I hope to get famous for hating bikers. That's not why I don't want to be the candidate. I'm not going to tell you the reason. Besides, Harold has been more invigorated every meeting we have. He said he was feeling sixty last time."

"All I ask is that you reconsider. You are perfect for it. I agree. Harold has been more active since starting this. So far this has been good for him. He has been depressed and less active over the last few years; I was growing concerned."

"Thanks for the lift. Will you be at the meeting next week?"

"Yes."

"I'll bring some doughnuts," Bea opened the door and put a foot out into the rain.

"Keep the receipt; it is an expense," Derek winked. "Did you know Lillian Vander Zalm wore a headband to see the queen?"

"Really?"

"Yes. It was quite the coup."

Bea giggled, "Tell me more on the weekend. I'm getting wet. Thanks again."

"Great meeting you, Bea."

The Mercedes pulled away. Bea watched it leave. The cop in his car stared at her as if a crime had occurred. She glared at the cop, taunting him to do something. He returned to his computer screen.

Even with a cop in front of the apartment, Bea looked around for any trouble. She saw a gray shape fly into a tree behind the Villa Paulina. She ran down that way, stopping where the playing field got too wet. It was too far to take a picture, but she could see a barred owl on an oak branch. She thought, 'Two owls and political intrigue, what a night.' It was not reasonable to assume the owls she saw were the same bird, but she believed it was Josie. Rationally, she knew Direct Democracy was a party in the same way the Marxist-Leninist Party of Canada is one, but she fantasized that she was in parliament regardless.

Bea did not let her past interfere with dreams on this night.

Owls, Doughnuts, and Democracy, by Jason A. N. Taylor

7.

Dawn Saturday morning looked Spring-like, with one of the cherry trees sporting blossoms. Bea knew that tree bloomed a month before the others, but it did not mean it would be warm out. All Friday night, she had worked on Direct Democracy's web presence. There was no more work she could do before leaving for the Home. But she had too much restless energy. She put on an outfit for running she had not worn since Sam was a baby. Thankfully, the tights and sports bra stretched. She checked herself out in the mirror before leaving. She was the curviest she had been since being pregnant.

Bea was happy with her first run in years. 5k was a good distance. She only walked up a couple of the steeper hills. She got to listen to some birds and yell at a biker. She stopped to feel the velvety pussywillow and magnolia buds; she had to touch fluffy things. At the traffic light before her apartment, she caught a guy walking his dog, checking out her ass as she jogged on the spot. She smiled and winked, hoping the man would notice as she trotted off. She felt great. She picked up the pace for the last block home.

As Bea closed on the Paulina, she noticed the front door had been wedged open. On the driveway next to the building was the idiot in a scooter that wedged it open. Michael Night from 302. Knight Rider rolled his way to the corner store, not caring that the open door would invite in every crackhead and thief in the neighbourhood. She yelled, "Close the fucking door!" Either Knight Rider did not hear her, or he was ignoring her calls. To get his attention, she shouted, "I hope you get murdered by a burglar!" She knew he heard this as his mirror glinted sun at her. She followed up with a middle finger and then closed the door on her way in.

After a quick shower, she ate a peanut butter banana, grabbed her laptop, and left for Home, running down the stairs. Bursting out the fire exit to the lobby, she noticed a new sign in black Sharpie and bad handwriting.

Bea, the tenant in 206, threatened a disabled person and locked the front door on him. Legal action will be taken against

the building if 206 is not evicted. The Paulina discriminates against disabled people.

As usual, there was no name on the paper, and it was placed out of the sight line of the door camera. Bea knew exactly how to respond to this. She dashed back upstairs for a Sharpie of the same colour and drew three penises on the note, and initialled it MK 302. Grinning and giggling, she walked past a cop car, pulling into the spot reserved for it.

Doughnut box in hand and still smiling about the penis drawing, Bea strode into the Home, waving to receptionist Karen without stopping. Multiple conversations could be heard coming from the lounge. She stopped at the entrance, amazed at the activity. Four of the recliners were occupied by residents awkwardly manipulating tablets. Harold was moving about looking over the shoulders of oldsters, directing them on comments to like and responses to make.

"Are you a Communist?" Harold bellowed over Jerry's shoulder. "Because I'm pretty sure Lenin said that."

Jerry rebutted: "Yes, Lennon did say that. John Lennon."

"Our audience will get turned off by that pinko crap," Harold spat.

"Men, we want controversy," Irene chirped. "The internet is all about emotions. Politics of the messenger doesn't matter if Direct Democracy's message gets heard."

"Oh God, the Liberal is right. Thanks for focusing us." Harold changed the topic, "Anyone need more coffee?"

"I'm not sure I have enough doughnuts for all of us," Bea called. "But we can cut them in half."

"No worries, deary. I can't have any," Wendy said. "Diabetes."

Harold held out his tablet. "Doughnuts can wait, Bea. I have a bunch of questions. I watched Internet Comment Etiquette. It was funny but a little advanced for me."

Bea hid a laugh with the doughnut box.

"Tell me, what is this branch-looking thing?" Harold continued. "When I tap it, email, F thing, Bird thing, and other weird things pop up?"

"That's the share icon," Bea explained. "The email lets you share the story using email. The F is for Facebook. Bird is Twitter. They're social media apps."

Irene interjected, "Exactly what I told you, you old fart!"

"Get stuffed, Irene!"

"Honourable Member, listen to the others in the group," Bea admonished. "You're acting eight, not eighty-eight."

"Lucky I'm able to act at all," Harold grumbled.

Bea asked, "Is Derek coming?"

"It is Saturday and sunny. He'll be late and wearing god-awful cycling tights that make him look like a florescent advertising peacock."

"Ok." Bea stifled a laugh. "Let's have coffee and doughnuts, then I can answer all your questions." They put aside their tablets.

When the doughnuts had been distributed, Bea cast her tablet's screen onto the Lounge Room TV. The audience was astonished to see their comments on the TV. She started with a pep talk, giving the group kudos for the accounts they had made and comments on posts. She taught them how to follow each other on the different comment sections.

"I noticed Harold's post gets a bunch of likes almost immediately after he posts," Jerry asked. "But mine do not. Why?"

"Because I say more important things than you," Harold puffed. "People listen to me."

Bea jumped in quickly: "Those quick likes are not because Harold is more popular. Ajay has bot accounts that automatically like everything Harold posts. I will be sending him your usernames too and your comments will get more likes."

Bea tapped her tablet to get to the first iteration of the Direct Democracy home page. It showed what Direct Democracy is about and the party's goal. It had an overview of the Voting App. A donation button would be added when finance management was sorted out. She assured them the website was free for the first month, that the website was a starting point. The oldsters were too dazzled by technology to see how basic the site was.

🦉 Owls, Doughnuts, and Democracy, by Jason A. N. Taylor 🦉

There was a tapping of steps down the hall. Derek's entrance had Harold saying: "The fluorescent advertising peacock arrives."

"Sorry I'm late," Derek responded. The morning was too nice, so I had to ride a little longer. Bea, please continue…" He sat down and took off his cycling shoes.

Bea continued, showing where a future tab would have links to a Discord. The group looked confused as to what a Discord was. She tried to explain what Discord was but saw even her most enthusiastic members were not getting it. She left it at, 'it's for communicating with the group.'

Bea's lecturing on the behind-the-scenes data-gathering capability of the website lost her audience. Nevertheless, knowing how important the information was, she forged ahead with instructions about how data was used to make a profile of the person's web presence. Their social media usernames. Targeting those who came to the website with Direct Democracy 'propaganda'.

Harold stepped out to get more coffee.

Bea struggled on, describing how controversial topics would be mined from the person who landed on the website's social media. She described how Direct Democracy's foot soldiers would friend or follow the interested person on social media to inject Direct Democracy's' propaganda' into their feed. When she finished talking, it was clear the audience needed a break.

"Why don't we freshen our coffee or tea?" Bea said. The four oldsters groaned and shuffled their way to the cafeteria.

Derek stayed seated. "Bea, great strategy. Get troops moving, give them something to do. 'Theirs not to reason why. Theirs but to do and die.'"

"That's not right. It is 'not mine to reason why, it is mine to do and die.' That's the quote."

"The folks," Derek waived to the group getting coffee. "Don't need to know it's a strategy. They need action. Show them how to use Facebook."

"Really? Facebook..? I don't even have an account."

"Great! You will be able to show them how. Old people love Facebook."

Bea fiddled with her phone, not wanting to show that she was pissed. She could not understand why the group might not be interested in the most interesting part, the strategy. She noticed a missed call on her phone.

She turned to Derek. "I must check this message."

Derek raised a hand to say go ahead.

A few seconds into the message, Bea spat, "Fucking Knight Rider." She ended the call. Punching back the number, she said to Derek, "Listen to my side of this conversation in case I need a witness." She put the call on speaker.

"Hello, Constable Wu speaking; how can I help?"

"Constable Wu, you called me. Beatrix Jansen."

"Yes. Ms. Jansen, we got a call from Mr. Knight."

"Of course you did," Bea let out a big sigh.

"Mr. Knight said you threatened to kill him."

"I did no such thing. I said, 'Close the fucking door! I hope you get murdered by a burglar.' Write that down in your little notebook."

"I understand why you feel upset. Please calm down. We need to determine the seriousness of Mr. Knight's concerns."

"Serious, HA! The only issue here is Michael Knight leaving the door open so a defenceless woman like me can get raped and murdered by a sexual predator. Do you know where the last killing happened in Victoria, Constable Wu? Two blocks from my apartment. A single woman raped and strangled by an intruder."

"Ms. Jensen, please look at this from Mr. Knight's perspective. He's mobility challenged, unable to easily open the door."

"Mobility challenged! He had no problem running over my six-year-old's foot with his scooter. Please read the notes from your CIPC database before jumping to conclusions."

"Look, Mr. Knight is willing to let this matter go if you apologize."

"I did nothing wrong. Knight Rider is a disease in our building. The tenants and owner of the building, including me, have been victimized by him for years. You are one of his tools for bullying us. I have done nothing wrong, yet I have the police calling me on a Saturday morning, telling me to apologize for sticking up for my security. Constable Wu, imagine if I was a nice lady and you called.

I would be terrified if the police had called me. I would do everything to smooth over this misunderstanding. I would be terrified of seeing Knight Rider in the future because the last time he called the cops. I would be intimidated into apologizing."

"We must follow up on all calls," the Constable stammered. "If you are feeling threatened by Mr. Knight or anyone else, you have every right to call the police. If you can safely video the interaction, do so, but always…"

"I am not going to waste your time. Knight Rider is a bully you are helping. I am a victim of his bullying. Unfortunately, bullying is not a crime. I am not apologizing. Write that in your little book. If you want to come and arrest me, I will be at the James Bay Senior Home for the next hour, volunteering with people who suffer from dementia. Please do not come until my shift is almost over; they need my help."

Bea stared at Derek, expecting a response. Derek sat passively with a car salesperson's grin. From behind them, Harold broke the silence, "Knight Rider sounds like a dick."

Derek almost started to laugh but stifled it by saying, "His name is Michael Knight, like David Hasselhoff?"

Bea nodded.

Derek continued, "His scooter is Kit?"

"Yes." Bea and Derek broke out laughing.

"What's so funny?" Harold did not get the reference.

"He has the same name as David Hasselhoff's character from the bad 80s TV show Knight Rider," Bea replied. "It features a car that talks, Kit." She turned to Derek. "Did I say anything I shouldn't have?"

"I am not a criminal lawyer. It is best to limit what you say to the facts, and if you suspect you are a suspect to call your lawyer. You did not say anything incriminating. Antagonistic, yes. Funny, yes. But you don't have to worry."

"Another reason I shouldn't be the candidate."

"I am the candidate for Direct Democracy," Harold declared. "I've got name recognition, experience, money, and a face that makes J.T. look like week-old, chopped liver. There is no leadership question here."

"Harold..." Derek sighed. "We are going to have a leadership race for Direct Democracy. That will make us a party, not an independent. We will be able to raise more money. Sorry, I did not tell you this sooner."

"You don't have to worry, Harold," Bea reassured. "Direct Democracy can't have a leader that yells at cops and 'harasses' disabled people. And that's the tip of the iceberg."

"Bea, the way you handled that call demonstrated great potential for leadership." Derek paused for effect. "A leader needs to be able to respond to authority unflappably while not crossing boundaries, like you did. What do you think Harold?"

"I'm glad Bea has baggage."

Bea took the camouflaged compliment. "We had better get back to teaching our team about Facebook."

Facebook had been a bridge too far for Bea's online snobbery. She disliked social media. The closest she got was trolling Reddit. Even then, when Reddit asked her if she liked the app, she answered the people are shit. She stuck to old-school online forums. In her volunteer role, when the oldsters would ask about Facebook, Instagram, or WhatsApp, her assistance would be half-assed at best. At worst, she would scare them off social media with horror stories of stolen data and Big Brother watching. But now she had a Facebook account.

Word had gotten around that Bea was going to teach Facebook. Three more residents found their way to the lounge with tablets in hand, including Ms. Anderson. Bea's task looked daunting. Irene and Jerry said they used Facebook often, so Bea recruited them to assist with questions. Bea had Ms. Anderson sit next to her. Bea cast her screen to the TV and walked the group through the process of signing up to Facebook.

Bea tried to tell the oldsters to use an alias or at least not totally real information for their Facebook profiles. But that seemed to be something they could not fathom. Soon, they were all sending friend requests to old schoolmates, business partners, and family, except for Bea. Bea intentionally did not look at the friend requests on her new profile. She only sent friend requests out to those in the group and Ajay.

"Here are all my children's pictures!" Ms. Anderson exclaimed. Similar murmurs came from others.

Bea went over to Harold to see if he needed help. Really, she wanted to look at who came up in his suggested friends. Of the four suggested people visible on the banner, two were Conservative Members of Parliament and one was a reporter. The list buoyed her spirits and made the possibility of Direct Democracy more real.

Harold noticed Bea. "Can you give me some advice?"

"Yes. Friend the MPs and reporter. We need them to know about Direct Democracy."

"I am going to... but she is my daughter," Harold pointed to the woman in the middle. "Is there some protocol or rule for family that disowned you?"

"There is no convention. You can hit the remove button and not see them. I know how you feel. I specifically used a fake name, so I did not get my family suggested. But it is only a matter of time before Zuckerberg's algorithm figures out those connections."

Harold tapped the add friend button for the two MPs and reporter. Then he scrolled through his list filled with the who's who in Canadian politics. Harold sent friend requests to all of them, even those he referred to as dumber than a bag of hammers, as smart as bait, and with only sawdust in the sawmill. He smiled with glee when he saw Rex Duffy's profile, requesting his friendship too. Bea thought that was unlikely. Harold reminded her that Mr. Duffy was as egotistical as President Bucket of Orange Jello in the States, so it was a sure thing Mr. Duffy would friend Harold.

After about twenty minutes, the group settled down and Bea got them to join the official Direct Democracy Facebook group. Attention faded as lunch neared. Before they broke up Bea reminded them to post at least once daily promoting Direct Democracy on an online newspaper article, a relevant Facebook post and invite anyone to Direct Democracy on Facebook. She showed the group how to link the website.

As Bea was leaving Derek clip clopped in his riding shoes to catch up. "You could be a tap dancer," Bea smirked.

"I dreamed of being Fred Astaire, but my dad cut my lessons short. He thought they were turning me gay."

"Hah. Little did he know."

"Little indeed. But never mind that. Nice work in there. This was a real start."

The automatic door opened as they approached. "I'm not sure a website, Facebook group, and an internet army of nine, including seven oldsters and you and me, is the start of a revolution."

"All movements start with one, but like a snowball rolling downhill, they grow. Great job today. I mean it." Derek patted her on the shoulder and then went toward where his bike was locked.

"Thanks..." Bea called after him. "But Facebook was your idea."

She stood outside in the pre-spring sun's warmth, thinking this was the best day she had had in years. And it was only noon. She was not sure she wanted to go home, so she strolled to Beacon Hill Park to see if she could find some owls.

Daffodils were about a week from blooming, but the trees still had no leaves on them. Josie was not at any of her usual roosts. The day was nice enough that owls were not needed to make it better, but Bea still searched. Near a Blue Sspruce, Rich was pointing his long-lensed camera into the tree. Bea knew this to be an owl sign.

"Hey, Rich, who's up there?"

"It's Grumpy Cat Great Horned. She's thick in branches."

"Yup, branches with a hint of owl. I love those yellow eyes. She glares so well."

"Have you read the NDP's new platform for this year's election?" Rich spoke while eyeing the foliage through the lens.

"Nice segue. Change the subject much?"

"What else is there to talk about?"

"Good point. Do tell. What about the NDP platform?"

"Jagmeet's taking a page from the Grit's and Tory's playbook. He's kowtowed to Quebec, putting the pipeline east in the platform. All because the Bloc shit the bed last election and gave the NDP a bunch of seats they did not earn. The NDP won't get the seats again this year, mark my words. The Greens will pick up votes, resulting in less NDP seats."

"Most likely, if even half of what you say comes true."

"Sad but true."

"You know there is a way to solve this?"

"If it includes Harold Gordon, I'm not sure I can be part of it."

"Direct Democracy is not about personality, it's about getting to vote for and against the bills you want. Harold is great to argue with. We got a website and a Facebook group for it. Harold is going to run in the fall election."

Rich broke away from the camera and pulled his phone out. "Direct Democracy group." He tapped on the screen. "I've joined. Do I get an armband or something?"

"No."

"You're sure it's not a cult?"

"It is not a cult. We don't have a logo yet. We just need members to post on social media as much as they can and direct interested people to the group."

"Okay...maybe."

"And you're welcome to join our meetings at the James Bay Seniors Home on Saturday mornings."

"If it doesn't interfere with owling."

"I get you."

Bea was nonetheless bright-eyed and smiling at Rich's pushing Direct Democracy to ten members. That was a start.

8.

The debt-collecting leads were not as good as they once were. To make the most of them Bea was mining the dark web. This Thursday night she was focused on finding information that would get her bonus. Every bonus she did not get was another month she had to work the shitty debt collection job.

The previous bonus, this bonus, and the next pay period's bonus were earmarked for Sam's birthday gift, a super cool mountain bike. Bea was a few hundred dollars short because she did not get her last paycheck's bonus. The thought of using a credit card for the gift crossed her mind but it got hit by the Mac truck of regret she had for her current debt. She would not entertain those thoughts. With a little luck, her bonus calculation will be correct for her upcoming paycheck. Her bonus would bring her within a hundred bucks of buying the bike. She was certain she could scrounge the rest of the money even if it meant binning for bottles. It was 20 minutes until her company deposited her pay on Friday at 00:03.

A direct message from Bubo appeared: Kira B! I got something you have to see.

Kira B: What? I'm kinda on a mission.

Bubo: A mission to spread the good word about Direct Democracy?

Kira B: No. Work. Getting info to softly extort money from debtors.

Bubo: I'd thought you would be working on DD. There has been a lot of discussion about it. Qualify that; some vs. none is lots.

Kira B: That's the Army of Oldsters. 14 of them post a few posts a day. I been teaching them about "the social media." It is fun.

Bubo: Cat has been working on some heavy artillery for your army. I'm so proud of it I want to show you the unpublished version. Cat wants to give it one last edit, but I had to share. It will blow your mind: www.linkitylink.com

Kira B: Thanks.

Bea was disappointed with the chat. It had none of the witty, sexual innuendo that messaging with Ajay once had.

Bea clicked the link.

Owls, Doughnuts, and Democracy, by Jason A. N. Taylor

The video started with computer-generated animation of a hunter-gatherer group in a green forest scene. Drumming was in the background as a male narrator with an indigenous-sounding voice spoke. "Long, long ago, for a very, very long time, all people lived in tribes. Within these groups of a few hundred people, it was easy to have your voice heard." The animation shows a person talking to a leader. "The boss did not always listen." The chief laughed at the person's idea. "That was the exception; the chief had to listen most of the time, or they might not be followed. Each person had an important role in the community and listening to them was vital for the community's success. It was a democratic system before there was a need to invent the word 'democracy.' But communities grow. Being heard became harder." The animation of the clan grew into a town, then a city.

The camera focused on an ancient Greek amphitheater with mythic music playing, blue sea and sky in the background. A caption read "Athens, the Theatre of Dionysus." A strong female voice with a slight English accent said, "Imagine six thousand or more of your fellow citizens gathered to vote on laws." The theatre was filled with people raising their hands to vote. "Each with the same say as the man next to him. The Greek word for this system was demkratia. Demos for people and Kratos for power. Democracy. All democracies today have roots that go back to Ancient Greece in 500 BC. Athenian Democracy was direct democracy, citizens voted directly on the issues at hand in the Ecclesia, the assembly. There were no politicians or parties, only people with one vote each. Everyone with the same power."

The view focused on a person standing on the theater's stage. "It was very different from today's representative democracy. Today, lawmakers are elected on promises to uphold their party's platform and values. And how good is a politician's promise?"

"In ancient Athens, an orator who did not hold decision-making power would argue the merit of a law to the assembly. The people of the assembly would vote on the law. Direct Democracy thrived for nearly a century in a sea of monarchies, tyrannies, and oligarchies. Those who wanted to consolidate power for the elite eventually won.

Uneducated people could not be trusted with making laws and democracy was too slow to fight wars. These were the elite's arguments; they did not care about arguments, only stealing power. Athenian democracy fell to tyrants." The orator morphed into an owl that flew away as the mythic music faded.

Imperial music started playing. Two hills with towns on top and wolves fighting over food with a blood-red sunset, Rome, filled the screen. An aristocratic narrator spoke—Bea recognized the voice as Ajay's— "Democracy was best left to idealist young people. Maybe a city-state could hold it together under that system. An empire cannot. Rome required the power of monarchy, tyrannies, and oligarchies to keep its empire underfoot. A set of political systems that can be boiled down to oligarchy, a small group of people—elites—having power over a state. The elites that had power changed, sometimes they were clergy, generals, kings, or merchants—but never the people." Images of a maniacal group of stereotyped priests, warlords, royalty, and traders danced in flames as the video rolled. "Some call this the Dark Ages. It was good for us."

"It could not last forever. An information revolution occurred; the printing press was created. Bibles could now be printed in the languages of their parishioners. People began reading the Bible themselves. Interpreting the Bible themselves. When they did, they saw their rulers as people too. Revolutions became possible. From Martin Luther's reformation to France's Revolution and the American Revolution, people were becoming important again. At least European people." The blood-red background transitioned to orange as animated Bibles were pressed, a person nailed treatises to a church door, heads rolled from a guillotine, and Washington crossed the Delaware.

"As had been traditional for the elites, the rebellions were put down with the usual vigour. Armies marched, heretics were burnt, and scapegoats purged, but the ideas behind this new rebellion steeled the people's resolve." Scenes of armies hacking their way into each other dissolved into a woman burning at a stake and Jews being forced from a burning village. But a helix spun with animation of resilient people overcoming persecution.

"The elite learned that democratic institutions limited revolution. More accurately, representative democracy was the carrot. As few carrots were given out as possible. Voting was always limited to groups allied with the elite's goals—white men. The representatives were of the elite. A representative always had the power to vote against what their constituency wanted if it did not align with the party's or elite's goals. Power was kept to the powerful." The animation showed a group of white men being separated from the population with a carrot, the other group pushed into obscurity by police. The white men voted for another white man. That man joined the group of stereotyped clerics, generals, sovereigns, and tycoons—the elites—on the left of the screen. The men on the right yelled 'no war,' while the elites voted for war.

The slightly British-accented female voice took over narration as the orange animation lightened. "Cracking the door on democracy let in other benefits to society. People who vote needed to be educated so they did not vote the wrong way. Education, even if the purpose is indoctrination, raises people. Idealists held those in power to follow the intent of constitutions and charters. Slowly increasing the electorates from white men to other races and even women. And from time-to-time, good representatives were able to make the world better." Scenes of people learning, arguing about laws, and making declarations rolled while the narrator spoke.

"But all was not well. A second information revolution occurred. Internet and social media came to life. On the surface, these are intrinsically democratic, and anyone can say what they want on Twitter or Facebook. Underneath, the elite were able to use the data to divide natural allies. This led to parties whose representatives were elected on the promise to vote for the right side—the most popular—of a wedge issue like immigration. On all other legislation, the legislator looks to their donors for guidance. The voter only sees the action taken by the party member to stop immigration." An animation of a divisive meme on immigration zooms in on the post's 'like' counter, counting ever higher. An electronic matrix appears at the microscopic level of the 'like' counter, making links between user accounts. The linked profiles morph into a protest with two sides arguing for and against immigration. Then a candidate celebrated in front of No Immigration signs. The members of government, hidden from the protesters, with elites whispering in his ear, signed many bills for other things. "From the day after the politician is elected to when the next election cycle starts, he does not have to listen to constituents. During that time, donors host many dinners for law makers. And party considerations take precedence over local constituent's views. Who has more influence with the politicians in that time? The people? No, it is the donors and the party. Does this sound like democracy or oligarchy? Remember, an oligarchy is a small group of people who control a country." In the video, a limousine passed a group of protesters. A person looking a lot like an orange Jabba the Hut or an American President exits the limo.

The hue of the video lightened to yellow. The Parthenon consolidated in the middle of the picture with a statue of Athena, eyes bright and gleaming as described by her epithet. Bea thought the face of bright-eyed Athena looked familiar. Athena spoke with a slight British accent, "The internet can bring back Athenian Democracy, Direct Democracy. It is no longer unwieldy to have millions of people vote securely, nearly instantaneously, on any topic. The world already uses Direct Democracy to pick the best European Song and ship names." A cut of a Eurovision Song played, then Boaty McBoatFace's happy silhouette flashed on the screen. "In any representative democracy a representative, Member of Parliament, or Senator could create a secure online polling system all their constituency would use to vote on some or all legislation. In Direct Democracy, the elected officials cast their vote for whatever the will of the people is. The side that gets fifty percent or more of the vote." The video shows people voting on their cell phones. A Member of Parliament receives the results and votes in Parliament thusly. "Why has this not happened? Is it because you cannot understand the issues? There are no qualifications a politician must meet to be a politician."

🦉 Owls, Doughnuts, and Democracy, by Jason A. N. Taylor 🦉

The silhouette of the orange blob or President of the United States appeared on screen with thought bubbles of a man, woman, person, camera, and TV bursting above his head, referencing the President's amazing ability to ace a dementia screening test. "How are they smarter or more qualified to vote on an issue than you? The reason Direct Democracy has not happened yet is power. Our representatives do not want to give up their power. Or, more correctly, they do not want to give up your power. A vote is a citizen's chance to have a voice. Giving that voice to a politician who has other's interests in mind before yours does not sound like democracy. Use your power to make Direct Democracy happen. It is your way to be heard." The camera panned across bright-eyed Athena with an owl landing on her shoulder and towards the Ecclesia, the assembly, where people raised their hands to vote. The narrator finished by directing viewers to Direct Democracy's website and other groups pushing for democratic institutions.

Skipping back, Bea took a second look gleaming eyed Athena. She was shocked to confirm her face and bright eyes were Athena's.

Bea was in disbelief at the quality of the video. The message was clear. It avoided left and right ideology as much as possible. The elites were evil for all. The references to a better, older time in classical Greece and prehistory drew out people's desire to be connected to the ancients. The orange gelatinous mass was a little too political, but those people would be too stupid to notice. And the owl! She was tingling with giddiness. Most of all she was jealous. She wanted to be making media like this, with a partner supporting her. Instead, she was mining for dirt on her clients while waiting to see if her bonus came in at 00:03.

At ten after midnight, Bea signed into her bank. There was her paycheque, too small as usual, and the bonus was not there. She double-checked with her last payday and bonus to see if they came in at the same time. They did. She recalculated her numbers twice. Each time, the numbers said she should have hit the threshold. She hit her desk with frustration. How would she get Sam his bike?

It was time for the contingency plan. Bea took off her gaming headset and could hear the dull thump of bass from upstairs. Her shady neighbours were awake. Better to do this now rather than tomorrow. 'What clothes would be best for this?' she thought. She knew it did not matter to Tim, the skeezy guy upstairs, who could get you anything you want off the back of a truck. Watching strippers was the closest to laid that he got. The sensual clothes were for her. She settled on PJs with enough buttons open that a breast could slip out, slippers, and a messed up bedhead. The mirror said she was still sexy.

The smell of pot got thicker the closer to Tim's apartment. Knocking on the door did not work; Bea had to bang on it. The music turned down. She moved back to ensure she could be seen through the peephole. A latch, deadbolt, and bar could be heard opening from behind the door. The smell of burnt pot slapped Bea in the face when the door opened. Tim took up most of the doorway. Sheepishly he said, "Sorry. We got an intense gaming session on. We'll turn the music down." He went to close the door.

Bea was offended that Tim was not going to chat her up or leer at her ass if she walked away. She put a hand out to stop him from closing the door, "It is not about the noise. Can I come in? I have a favour to ask."

Tim's face brightened, "Come in."

The apartment was lit with a string of Christmas lights and the TV. A second guy sat on one end of a badly stained and cigarette-burned couch. "Tiny Tim," the guy called loudly. "Where are your manners? Introduce me to the lady. Offer her a beer and roll one." The skinny guy's manic grin and the small mirror on the table in front of him said cocaine. "I'm Carter. What brings a fine-looking woman like you here so late at night?"

"It's Bea. A beer would be great." Bea looked for a seat, there was a crappy armchair next to the sofa, but she chose to sit in the middle of the chesterfield between them. Tim brought a beer then started rolling a joint. "Thanks. I want to get this bike for my son." She showed a picture of the bike on her phone to them. "But I didn't get my bonus and can't buy it from the store. Is there any chance you can get me one?"

She made sure to hold the phone so Tim could see her side boob and possibly some nipple through the buttonholes.

Carter was ogling her like a man who habitually searched for MILF's on PornHub. It was clear her presence was all the titillation he needed. By peripheral vision, she saw him adjusting himself.

"That's an expensive kid's bike," Carter said. "I've seen one around the hood."

"Don't take it from a kid!" Bea glared at Carter. "If you can't take it from a store, I don't want it. Stealing from a kid is fucking heartless."

"Insurance will get them a new one," Carter argued.

"No." Bea stood up to leave.

"Carter'll get you one," Tim said. "Straight from the store. A hundred bucks."

"I've seen them outside the bike shop on Bay Street," Carter said.

Bea threw an arm around Tim for a half hug and wiggled her butt as she sat back down. "My kid's birthday is two Saturdays from now."

The joint broke the ice. She had not been stoned since university and had forgotten how much she liked it. They played Fortnight. She found the game absurd. She laughed at the two men and shrieked when it was her turn, having great fun trying to distract them from the game. Naturally, the distraction became more flirtatious. Raunchy thoughts filled her head.

Bea was glad when Tim went to get more beer. It was great timing because she had wicked cotton mouth. Carter broke out a tiny bag with powder in it and cut up lines on the mirror. Bea accepted the mirror and snorted a line, another thing she had not done since university.

The dopamine rush came quickly. Bea was feeling great and horny. She was considering what the best position for a threesome on the couch would be and if Tim was as big as he was big. Then she remembered she was as fertile as the Virgin Mary. She suspected that Tim was not confident enough to have condoms on hand, likely only using those that the hooker would supply. On the other hand, Carter would be the type of guy who would never use a condom. She did not have any at her place, but she hated them too. She did not want to miss work to stop at the sexual health clinic. She would have to take care of this herself.

"Hey Carter, can I get another bump?" Bea asked.

"Sure beautiful." Carter cut three more lines. "Tiny, get us some shots too."

Tim brought out three shot glasses and a bottle of Jägermeister. They took their medicine. Bea chased it with the last of her beer. They all did another line. When no one was watching, Bea took a bud from the table, the PJs with pockets were a good choice. Shortly after, Bea took her phone out, concerned at what she saw. "Shit, my kid is awake. I gotta go and see what's wrong. Tim, can I take a beer for the road?"

"Sure."

"Thanks. Remember the bike for three weeks Friday." Bea left, grabbing a beer from the fridge. She turned back and smiled to see the guys staring at her ass.

Back at her apartment, Bea cycled feverishly between activities. She scratched her itch. She shilled for Direct Democracy. She found more places to share her boss's private information to irritate the fuck out of him. She searched for leads. She rewatched the Direct Democracy video. She was not sure how many times she mentally wandered through these activities. After the beer, she opened an old bottle of wine. She was surprised at the number of YouTube videos there were on how to smoke pot without a pipe or rolling papers. At some point, she was drunk, stoned, and tired enough to sleep.

A giant coffee with a combination of Tylenol and Advil was not enough to diminish Bea's malaise and headache. Worse, none of the leads she had researched the night before had panned out. The hangover had taken all her persuasiveness. At lunch, she decided she needed something stronger than coffee. Maybe a Monster Energy drink would get her out of the funk. A drink that tasted like aspartame and urine must be curative. But it made her less able to concentrate and more irritable. She went from doing a half-ass job to fucking the dog.

Bea was too intently watching her screen to see Mike come to her workstation. "What is this, Bea?"

"Checking the weather..." Bea closed the window at the sound of Mike's voice. "...to see if I will need an umbrella today."

"Don't give me that. You look like something the cat dragged in and you've done a quarter of the calls that you normally would. What's wrong?"

Bea resisted the impulse to tell Mike to fuck off. "My bonus was not with my cheque. I got the numbers to get a bonus. Where is it?"

"Did you read the newsletter from two weeks ago? The calculation has been changed. If a recovery gets a complaint from the debtor, it does not count toward the bonus calculation."

"Fuck! You didn't think this change was worthy of a team meeting?"

Mike gestured. "Let's take this to my office."

"Oh no, the principal's office." Bea followed Mike to his office. As they got there the faint ring of a cell phone could be heard. "What is that noise?"

Mike rushed to his desk. "My cell phone has been ringing off the hook with spam calls. I need it on for a call from my wife." He took the phone out of his desk and hung up on the call.

Bea hid a snicker.

"Where is this attitude coming from? It is not like you to come in dishevelled."

"I count on the bonus!" Bea attacked. "This change cost my son the birthday gift he wanted. Great communication, boss."

"Reading corporate communications is part of your job."

"It's a fucking newsletter with the reception's joke of the week, staff pet pictures and HR's favourite recipes. It is definitely not a serious communiqué."

"I know how hard it is to let down a child. I've let mine down before. But your language and behaviour today are unacceptable. Take the rest of the day off. We will talk about this Monday."

Bea was shocked. Meekly, she said, "Are you firing me?"

Mike responded, "No. We will talk about the consequences on Monday."

"Look, I'm sorry I was rude. I was up all night, upset that Sam won't get his bike." Bea did her best to look like she was going to cry.

"You'll get him something he'll love. I'm sure of it. Go home." Mike's phone rang again.

Bea got up to leave. The energy drink made her anxious. She had to continually tell herself she was not going to get fired, and there was no way Mike could find out it was her behind the spam calls. 'A run is what I need,' she thought.

A block from Bea's apartment she could see Knight Rider loitering in front of the building, holding a sign. He was protesting again. Every time she came home early, and the weather was 'okay,' he was outside with a pathetic sign. Walking past him would cause a scene. The right thing to do was use the back door but it hurt her greatly to sneak around in broad daylight because of an entitled idiot playing the victim. If anyone was the victim, she was.

Bea turned at the top of the street to go down the alley and into the back of the building. Quickly she changed into her running gear and was out of the back door running, fast, using bike lanes and the road to dodge pedestrians. She got to yell at cyclists twice. At what she thought was five kilometres she turned back. The closer she got to home the faster she tried to run.

Almost at a sprint, Bea approached her apartment. Again, she saw Knight Rider and was certain he saw her. Her pride would not let her enter once more by the back door, so slowing to a walk Bea took out her phone, starting the video. She was not going to do anything to incite Knight Rider, but she was going to quietly walk past. This was her home too. He tried to hide the sign, but she was able to read it: Beatrix Jensen, the Paulina, discriminates against disabled people.

"Didn't the police tell you to stay away from me?" Knight Rider growled.

"No." Bea stopped and raised the phone. "The cops said continue my business as normal, document my interactions with anyone threatening me and continue ensuring the security of my building." She pointed to the front entrance. "Why is the door open?"

"Don't video me. You don't have my permission."

"We are in public. There is no expectation of privacy." Bea videoed the sign. "What does that say?"

"Nothing."

"Everyone else can see it, but I can't. You are discriminating against me. You coward."

Knight Rider threw the sign to the ground and charged Kit, the scooter, toward Bea, Canadian flags flapping from the acceleration. She easily danced aside, giving the finger and continued to bob like a boxer, jabbing her middle finger out. Kit lurched forward again. Bea sprang out of the way and over to the sign to get a close-up shot of the message on it. "My name is on it, you asshole! How did I discriminate against you?"

"You close the front door that I wedge open," Knight Rider shouted, looking as if he was trying to decide to dismount Kit. "You're a foul-mouthed hussy with a disrespectful brat!"

"I discriminated against you by closing a door to ensure the security of the building. A single mother is not allowed to make her home secure from rapists and murderers?" She picked up the sign and started skipping around Knight Rider with it. "Victoria's last rape and murder happened down the street."

"Thief! Thief! Give me my sign back! Thief!"

"Here is your sign." Bea stopped two metres behind Kit. "Come and get it."

Kit lurched in reverse.

Bea sidestepped at the last second. "Trying to run me over again like when you hit my kid?" She tossed the sign on the lawn. "Go get it." She walked backward videoing and fingering Knight Rider all the way to the wedged open front door. "And close the fucking door!"

Inside her apartment, Bea was elated from the run and the confrontation with Knight Rider. The dopamine rush spiked with adrenaline was better than last night's lines. She got comfortable in front of the computer, updating the website with directions on how Direct Democracy converts could spread the message. Most of what she was adding was the directions she had given to the oldsters on how to promote Direct Democracy on Facebook.

Owls, Doughnuts, and Democracy, by Jason A. N. Taylor

There were some other modifications to the website Bea wanted to make, too. She messaged Bubo to get the permanent link to the video. The tab on the website titled "Voting App" was changed to "the Ecclesia" with "Voting App" in parentheses. Although Ecclesia was hard to read, it was the best name for the App. She knew the others would probably say it was too esoteric and suggest the Assembly. Until then, the App would be Ecclesia.

A message from Bubo pinged on Bea's computer: Here is the link for the video: www.linkitylink.com. Cat, has it premiering tomorrow. She's got it being reviewed on BC Budds on BC, Canada's Other Pastime, R.R. McNorton, and some others over the next few weeks. Puts me to shame, the only name I got to promote with more than 10K subscribers is *Libertarians on Guard for Thee*. It will be big.

Killa B: WOW!!!

Bubo: Direct Democracy will be a thing in a couple of weeks. Get your army to comment like mad.

Killa B: The video is awesome. Can you send me Cat's email? I want to thank her.

Bubo: Babou71@gmail.com and she's on here as Babou71.

Killa B: Thanks. She is a talented woman.

Bubo: She has a nice ass too.

Killa B: Do not reduce people to how they look.

Bubo: I'm not. Cat is talented and has a great ass.

With the potential for hundreds of thousands of people seeing the video, Bea let Ajay's comment go. Even getting BC Budds on BC to review the video would be a coup, causing a cascade of other suckfish YouTubers to review it, too. Direct Democracy was feeling less like a lark. She had to make sure the message on the website was clear so people would be captured by the idea.

A couple of hours later Bea got a ping from Bubo: www.reddit.com/r/VictoriaBC/Karenharassesoldmanonascooter

Clicking on the link took Bea to a shaky video from a phone in portrait with distracting blurred bars to either side. But as bad as the video was, there she was dancing around Knight Rider, giving him the finger with one hand and phone in the other. The video was from a balcony across the street. The person taking it could be heard laughing. It started halfway through the incident and was not flattering. There was no chance she would be seen as anything but a self-righteous Karen. It was already at five hundred upvotes and rising. She was certain that if it got to a bigger sub, it would easily hit the 10K mark. The number of comments was rising as she watched. Scrolling down the comments had her snickering at the vitriol. But when she searched the comments by controversial, she found her supporters. It seems at least ten others had run-ins with Knight Rider. Most had seen his protests, some had been in altercations, a few had been sued by this leach. She decided she could not care less about Reddit infamy.

Kira B: It will be the most upvotes I will ever get, and I won't get the Karma. LOL

Bubo: It will always be far behind your Star Wars videos.

Kira B: Karen's are hot on media. It might take the top spot.

Bubo: Seriously, you need your side of the story up. Post your video. You can't run for DD with this out there and no rebuttal.

Kira B: I'm not going to be the candidate. Harold will be.

Bubo: That old fart is too divisive. You are much better than him.

Kira B: LOL! He's been an MP, and DD is a-political.

Bubo: You watch; he'll bring all his old politics to the table. This was made for you.

The thought of an MP's salary was tempting, but that was a fantasy. Harold was tested. He was the best candidate. Bea did not want to be a public person. If Direct Democracy took off, she would be part of it and get a job from it. That was enough. She did not respond to Ajay or upload her video.

The rest of Bea's Friday night was spent perfecting the website and working on Ecclesia.

Saturday morning was a step closer to spring with the sun out. There were more birds singing, more cherry blossoms blossoming, and daffodils blooming. Bea was getting to the Home earlier than usual; she had no box of doughnuts to slow her down. By the Legislature, she was surprised to see Harold, Irene, and Wendy walking. She easily caught up with them.

"Greetings, Bea," Harold called. "Our morning constitutional got us hungry. But you d on't have any doughnuts."

"My paycheck was not what I thought it would be, Harold. I couldn't get doughnuts."

"We can stop at Discovery Coffee," Wendy said. "They have Yonni's doughnuts. It will get us a few hundred more steps of walking."

"God help us!" Irene exclaimed. "The Honorable Member will have another five minutes to pontificate. Please join us, Bea. We need you to save us from Harold's ego."

The three women laughed. Harold grumbled.

"I haven't seen you out walking before," Bea remarked. "Is it the nice weather?"

"We must get in shape for the race," Harold declared. "This is training."

"I've started running, too," Bea added.

"Good show," Harold huffed. "My goal is to get to five thousand steps in the next three weeks. I hit four thousand yesterday and was only a little achy today."

The oldsters walk to get doughnuts and to the Home was irritatingly slow. It made Bea late for the volunteer time. When they got to the lounge room the recliners had been arranged classroom style. Five people were waiting for them. Rich, the owl photographer, and Ms. Anderson were the only ones she recognized. She turned to Harold, "Wow. I'm a little unprepared."

"They want to learn," Harold patted her on the back. "Teach them about Facebook and Direct Democracy."

Bea stood at the front of the class. "Sorry, we're a little late. Please take a minute to freshen your coffee. I have to set up." She turned to Rich, "Great to see you here. Do you have a computer?" Rich showed her his smartphone. "You can grab a coffee down the hall. Wendy or Irene can show you." She pointed the two women out for Rich.

The impromptu lesson Bea settled on started with teaching them the basics about Direct Democracy, then showing how to use Facebook. The group's size meant she could put those who knew how with those who did not. She insisted they solve their own problems within the group before coming to her. Amazingly, they did. Rich was adept with Facebook, liked passing his knowledge on and flirting with the old ladies. He was a great help.

Derek clickity-clacked his way into the room halfway through the workshop in his peacock-like riding attire and sat next to Harold.

During the workshop, Bea entertained herself by looking up Cat's online presence. Bea started by figuring out Cat's username, Babou71, which she did by searching Cat's social media. Babou was the neglected Ocelot from Archer or Salvador Dali's pet cat. Archer memes were a staple of Cat's Instagram so likely Cheryl's Babou was where the name came from. Babou generally caused havoc by destroying and spraying everything in his path. Bea could relate to Babou. The 71 was not obvious to Bea. There was no way Cat was born in 1971. Cat did not seem to be enough of a hockey fan to add Evgeni Malkin's number to her handle. Nor was Cat overtly religious so it was unlikely she would use its biblical meaning. Other than being a lucky number for Cat, the most likely reason to add 71 was to use it like 69. Bea liked 71 better than 69, and in Archer, women are always getting fucked bent over a desk.

Of course, a gamer tag could mean very little. Bea's handle, Kira, was from the anime "Death Note." In it, Kira is the name of the owner of a notebook that grants him the power to kill people by writing their name in the book. Kira seeks justice with the notebook by killing criminals. Bea chose it because Marcus and the world pissed her the fuck off and she wanted justice. In her younger years, she believed she was dispensing justice online. Really, she was a troll. But the name did not mean a thing.

Cat had a big online footprint.

Instagram had Cat living her best life, from handstands at the gym to vegan dinners and yoga balanced atop driftwood on the shoreline of Clover Point. In between the lifestyle posts were a sprinkling of social justice and feminist memes. Bea was glad to see Cat's feminist posts, so many women today saw feminism as a good way to ruin a date.

Linked-in was full of Cat's accomplishments. She had a degree in communications and certificates in social marketing and social media management. She worked for the city government in communications but had a sideline company working on media campaigns with not-for-profits. Bea was impressed.

Twitter was full of Cat's witty trolls. She had thousands of followers. Bea knew that if she was on Twitter, she would have more followers, but she's allergic to Twitter.

Cat's YouTube channel was monetized with some videos with 10 thousand views. She had a few thousand subscribers. The content was yoga and fitness training in nature, with a small number of rants on social topics. Bea thought Cat was showing her Lululemon yoga pants off too much, but Ajay was right about her ass.

Cat was killing TikTok too. Most of Cat's TikToks were shorts of yoga and fitness training videos. Bea played a TikTok that looked like a rant, "Antinatalism is the only way we will save the earth. A Canadian uses ten times more resources than a person in the developing world. Every child you have will continue to use at an unsustainable rate. Stop having children. We do not need any more." Bea was surprised but knew Cat was right.

Reddit was full of Cat's posts on Antinatalism and the dystopia we live in.

Antinatalism resonated with Bea. She wondered where she would be if not trapped by a man wanting a child and him knowing what was best for both of them. Cat's social media was like a mirror to where she would be if she did not have a kid. She was certain she would be in politics or advocating for what was right to those in power, but Sam. She loved Sam, but she did not want a child.

Bea tapped her coffee mug with her keys to get the attention of the group. "I would like to show you how to use Twitter. Then we can watch the Direct Democracy video that is premiering at noon." She did her best to explain Twitter to them. But no one understood because none of them were idiots. She then cast the Direct Democracy video for them.

The crowd was quieter than Bea had expected or hoped during the video. After the video, nobody said anything. She hoped this was because they were polite, not speaking up before being spoken to. Loudly, she asked, "What do you think?"

"I don't like it," Harold answered instantly. "It's childish. Cartoons are juvenile. It says we are not serious."

The group gasped at Harold's comment. A man new to the group was about to agree with Harold but Irene silenced him, "Ok Boomer! The animation was great, the video message was perfect. Your view that, 'Cartoons are juvenile' stopped being true in the 80s." Everyone dog-piled on Harold, letting him know he was wrong. Harold took it stoically, but Bea could see he was seething.

"Ok!" Bea stood up. "Harold heard your view. He has a point and I personally love the video. Direct Democracy will win because we embrace diversity and allow different views. I think this video is a perfect start. But we need a message that appeals to people who find this one 'childish.'" She did her best not to roll her eyes when she said 'childish,' but she was pretty certain she did.

Rich put his hand up squirming but not wanting to interrupt. Bea gestured for him to speak, "Hmm, I aww, I think Bea has a great point. If Direct Democracy's advantage is having your say on a bill before parliament, whatever your politics are, then we should have messages tailored to the different political points of view."

Wendy followed up, "Specific messages to people with different views. I like that."

Bea noticed the clock. She had to leave soon to meet Sam. "Rich and Wendy, think about how we can expand on this idea. Let's all take a few minutes to share the video. I'll be showing what to do on the TV if you want to follow along. However, I must leave in 10 minutes."

When Bea finished demonstrating how to share videos on Facebook, Twitter, Email, and comment sections, Derek came up to the front. He addressed the group, sounding official but looking like he just biked a hundred kilometres. "I am Derek Nelson. To make Direct Democracy into a legitimate party with a candidate running in the next election, we will have to elect people to key positions. The spots we need to fill are Campaign Manager, Financial Agent, and Auditor. I put forward that those signed up to our website by the date of our internal election are eligible to vote. Can I have a show of hands on this?" Only Ms. Anderson did not raise her hand, she was looking confusedly at her tablet. "That's settled. I also put forward that the vote occurs two weeks from today. Can I see a show of hands?" Everyone raised their hand.

Irene jumped in, "Who gets to run again..?"

Harold had daggers in his eyes.

"Thank you, Irene. I knew I forgot something. Anyone who is a member of Direct Democracy can run in our election. Do know that there will be an open vetting process for those who run. This will include an interview in front of the membership to ensure the candidate does not have any baggage that could cause the party problems. The elections will require the candidate to get more than fifty percent of the vote. If the vote is split between three or more candidates, we'll do a runoff between the two front runners."

Bea did not stick around, running to meet Sam. But a text from Amy said they would be twenty minutes late. To kill time, Bea checked out the video on YouTube. It had nearly a thousand views and had only been live for forty minutes. There were fifty-ish likes. The comments were mostly positive and seeking more information. She was stunned and jealous of Cat, wanting to be part of it and go home to keep the support building.

"Bea!" She looked up to see the no-assed Amy striding up with Sam in his team's hockey jersey. "Sorry, the game went into overtime."

"Did your team win?" Bea asked Sam.

"Yes. We get ice cream after a game, but I had to come here."

"We can get ice cream from the drive-through."

"I want Cold Stone Creamery ice cream with my team," Sam then ran off to the zip line.

"He's in a bit of a mood," Amy stepped close. "He really wants to be with his team. I can drive you over there." Bea did not answer. It was odd for Amy to offer anything. Instead, Bea tried to get Sam's attention. But calls of Sam, kiddo, ice cream, and owls did not get Sam's interest. Amy said, "If we leave now, I'm sure we'll catch some of the team there." Bea called Sam one more time, but he did not respond. Bea accepted Amy's offer. Amy called to Sam; he came running over.

The car ride was almost unbearable. Sam pointed out to Bea the places Momma A would take him, like his best friend Oliver's house, their favourite restaurant, the dentist who thought he was tough because he did not cry when a tooth was pulled, and the pottery store where Dad had made an owl plate. Bea felt like she did not know who Sam was. Bea was like Sam's new friend, getting driven around by his mother for the first time and hardly said a word.

Luckily, the drive was only ten minutes. At Tim Horton's, some of the kids were out in the parking lot getting ready to leave. Sam asked if he could go see them. Amy and Bea knew there was no stopping him, but both told him to be careful and watch for cars. Bea thanked Amy for the ride, then followed Sam.

Bea walked over to where the children's parents were chatting, next to their trucks near the boys. She tried to socialize with the four parents of the kids. But she did not know what to say.

"Hi there!" One of the parents noticed Bea. "I'm Jenn; this is Brad."

"I'm Bea. Sam's mom."

Jenn frowned. "Sam's mom is Amy."

"Amy is Sam's stepmother," Bea tried to not sound defensive to this overly protective Karen. "I'm his biological mom. He wanted to see his teammates, so here we are." She smiled painfully.

"Funny, Amy never said anything."

Bea wanted to throw a punch but said: "Funny, I don't tell my friends much about my ex, Marcus."

The resulting cold silence was interrupted by pings from Brad and Karen's phones. Brad read his and said, "That was Amy. Bea's taking Sam today."

Jenn added, "You can't be too careful these days. Last week there was an amber alert for some poor child taken by the ex-husband."

The mom in Bea craved an apology but knew that was not going to happen. "You can never be too careful."

For the next ten minutes, Bea was the fifth wheel in a conversation that revolved around houses, schools, and trips to Mexico that she could not relate to. The conversation turned to parenting and she was also unable to contribute.

The two families left with Sam's friends. Bea and Sam went into Tim Horton's. None of his team was inside. After a small meltdown, she was able to get him to sit down and eat his $14.87 ice cream. She did not get an ice cream. He had half a dozen spoonfuls of ice cream and then stood up. "I don't like this," he said, picking up the treat and throwing it in the garbage.

Bea was gobsmacked. "Why did you do that!? I would have eaten it!"

Sam shrugged his shoulders. "I didn't like it. I want the strawberry one. Get it for me, Momma B!"

"You are not getting anymore. We are leaving." Bea took Sam by the hand, leaving the doughnut shop. Outside, she crouched down in front of Sam at his eye level. "Sam, I love you. And I will not put up with you wasting food like that. If you don't want it, you ask, 'Momma B do you want some?' Do you understand?"

Sam was holding back tears. "Yes. Can we get some strawberry?"

"No."

"Momma A would get it for me." Sam started tearing up.

Bea hugged him to hide her tears. She wondered if she was his mom. Intrusive thoughts told her she never wanted a kid, she wanted to be like Cat. The thoughts left after a minute. She put on a smile, "Kiddo your birthday's coming up. Do you want to go to the mall and look at toys? Then to a movie? Finally, we can go to the park to look for the cranky cat great horned owl near the Gorge Water Way?"

Sam snuffled, "Let's do that Momma B."

The mall was a trying ordeal for Bea as well. Sam wanted everything and she could buy him nothing. She did get him a book on owls that would have her eating KD till the next paycheck. He got her to send pictures of the gifts he wanted to Momma A. He was certain he would get all of them. At the toy store she handled every owl stuffy, unable to resist the fluffiness.

Owls, Doughnuts, and Democracy, by Jason A. N. Taylor

They went to a matinee movie that lengthened Bea's debt payment plan by two weeks. During the movie she was fixated on the questions of if she was a mother to Sam and if she wanted to be one. Hanging out with him was fun but was that because she got bite-sized chunks of his life? Did she fight for custody out of custom and spite? She was glad when the movie was over.

Carrying the half full bag of popcorn that would be a good dinner for Bea next week, they walked into the park. As the tall Douglas fir forest closed over top of them, Sam said, "Momma B, did you know Momma A's family has a cottage in the woods with an owl box?" Bea shook her head no, then listened. "It is a seven-hour plane ride to Ottawa, then two hours in a car. I have not been there. They have a family of owls every year. It is on their property so there will be no crowd of people. You can watch them all day. We're going for the summer. Until Dad gets the house ready."

"You're going to Ottawa for the whole summer? And what do you mean, 'Dad gets the house ready?'"

"We are going to Ottawa while Dad gets our house fixed."

"Oh, your house in Victoria is getting renovated when you are in Ottawa."

"Yup."

Bea would have to talk with Marcus.

They found some whitewashed trees, some feathers and a pellet, but no owls. Ten minutes after sundown, with the forest darkening quickly, they heard the duet Hoot-hoo of the great horned. But by this time the forest was too dark and spooky for Sam. They left for home.

9.

Direct Democracy had broken its inertia. It was moving forward without Bea or Harold's involvement. Cat's video was being discussed by YouTube pundits. The Army of Oldsters was commenting everywhere on everything, all leading back to Direct Democracy. The vast majority of IP addresses hitting the website were from outside of the group. Derek was posting the roles to be filled and formalities that must be followed for a legitimate political party. Bea found it funny that none of the Election Canada YouTube Channel videos describing how to run a campaign that Derek linked had more views than their two-week-old video. It was exciting.

Ajay, Cat, Derek, Irene, Rich, and Wendy had all petitioned Bea with emails to run. She replied to all of them coyly but did not back away from her position to stay on the sideline. She was flattered, and it felt nice, but for Sam's sake, she could not run. Eventually, she yielded after calls from Derek and Ajay—with Cat in the background—begging her to take the chance. She realized that in the absence of anybody else, she had to run. But she reassured herself that she did not have to win. During the vetting process, she would be honest. No group in their right mind would want a loose cannon like her as a leader.

The Friday night before the leadership election meeting Bea gleefully answered an email from Harold asking how many people had signed up as Direct Democracy members. He needed to know how many doughnuts to buy. The website showed that 14 people had signed up. She sent Harold the information, feeling good that she did not have to buy doughnuts for the leadership election tomorrow.

That night, Bea slept well, dreaming of sitting in Parliament with Josie, the barred owl on her shoulder, arguing in front of the Speaker of the House. "Mr. Speaker, none of what the MP from Butt Fuck Nowhere (BFN) is saying is untrue or illegal. It is a beautiful, natural, artistic act that he would not have a problem with if he engaged in it more often." The assembled legislators roared. The MP from BFN responded with a patronizing, unintelligible sound like the teacher from a Peanuts cartoon. The Speaker said something equally incomprehensible. Bea banged the desk. Josie leapt into the air, winging straight for the MP from BFN while Bea yelled, "If the MP from Butt Fuck Nowhere cannot close his eyes when he sees something offensive, I will do it for him." Josie's talons plunged into the shoulders of the MP from BFN, then the owl pecked his eyes out. Josie and Bea left Parliament to see Sam skating on the Rideau Canal.

A Saturday morning run had become a routine for Bea. She let fantasies of an MP's lifestyle with an expense account, jetting around Canada, and fancy dinners in the halls of power put a kick in her step. She ran a little longer and faster, but it made her a little late getting to the Home for the election. She'd hustled through downtown to the legislature where she got stuck behind her usual gaggle of shuffling greybeards. The four old men took up the extra wide sidewalk. She wanted to push past but going between the rascal and elder with a walker risked knocking one of them over. She chided them, calling, "Pick a lane."

"Single file boys. Let the lady pass," the voice was unmistakably Harold's.

"Good morning, Harold. Where's Irene and Wendy?"

"The Liberals." Harold's entourage grumbled at his words.

"Aren't we all part of Direct Democracy?" Bea asked.

"Some more than others," Harold stopped with his crew and turned to address Bea. "Young men, this is Bea my right-hand man…"

"Woman," Bea corrected.

"Yes… woman, in Direct Democracy. She does all the technological jiggery-pokery. Bea, meet our three newest members, the lads." The old men smiled like it was funny that Harold called them young. "John, speedy Cameron our getaway driver, and young Morty using the walker." Harold gestured to each as he said their names. "They got me up to six thousand steps. But I think Cam is cheating."

Bea walked with the old fogies to the Home.

The lounge room was nearly full of people finding seats or hovering around a table of multi-coloured Empire Donuts. "I took doughnut duty in hand," Harold remarked. "Irene was flustered trying to get the orders organized. I thought it would be easier to place one big order. Besides, she was going to get those inferior doughnuts from Yonni's. She can't organize her way out of a paper bag."

"Afraid of the competition, eh?" Bea did not let Harold reply, "I have to set up the Zoom meeting."

Derek approached Bea as she worked on the computers and cameras. He had ditched the cycling gear for a suit. "Good morning. Fine day to pick a leader. It amazes me the amount of work Harold put into this formality. Did you notice the new members signed up today?"

"Yes. And the far from subtle jabs at Irene. Oh, can't forget the Empire Donuts, so much better than Yonni's," Bea laughed.

"Irene doesn't worry Harold."

"Who else is running? Tell me it's Ms. Anderson. That would be hilarious."

"It's not Ms. Anderson." Derek eyed across the room where Harold was being uncharacteristically sociable. "He's shaken every person's hand twice. You have him concerned."

"That's news to me."

"He sees what Ajay, Cat, and I see in you. You are formidable, relatable, and personable. This is a win-win situation for you. If you win the election, you are set for life. If you do not win, you win anyway because of the experience. I guarantee Direct Democracy will go far enough to make anyone who was part of it valuable to other parties."

"Won't I get a similar experience with less risk from being the Right-Hand Woman of Harold?"

"Not as much as being the candidate."

"Won't I limit where I can work after if I'm identifiable as the face of Direct Democracy?"

"Maybe... but," Derek appeared to be struggling to complete his argument.

"Derek, I've made my decision...," Bea winked. "I'm going to run."

"Thank goodness."

Derek called the meeting to order promptly at 10 am.

Owls, Doughnuts, and Democracy, by Jason A. N. Taylor

Bea had the online members visible on the monitor and a camera focused on the podium. Bea, Derek, and Wendy sat at a table at the front of the room next to the podium. Wendy had volunteered to be the note-taker. Derek efficiently outlined the rules and agenda for the meeting from memory. The members understood Robert's Rules from strata meetings and community groups. Derek kicked the voting off by nominating himself as chairperson. Everyone agreed, but Bea had to coach Harold's lads on how to enter their online votes.

"Direct Democracy's first order of business is to elect a leader. This will be a three-part process. First, nominees coming forward. Second, vetting of the nominees. This will be an interview in front of the membership. Third, a vote on the nominees. The winning candidate must get more than 50% of the vote. If this does not happen after the first vote a runoff between the two leading contenders will occur." Derek paused. "Questions?" The room remained silent. "Can I have a member put forward a motion to nominate candidates?" The floor quickly seconded the motion. "Can I have candidates raise their hands?"

Harold's was the first to go up. Then Irene's. Bea let Derek make a second call for candidates during which the room grumbled for her to throw her hat in the ring. Bea raised her hand slowly. About half the room sighed with relief.

"Great, three candidates. Harold, since you have more experience than the others, can you go first?"

"Certainly."

"We will flip a coin for who goes second," Derek pulled out a toonie. "Irene, call it in the air." He tossed the coin high enough for Irene to compose herself enough to make a decision.

"Heads."

Derek caught the toonie, "Tails. Bea, do you want to go second or last?"

"Last."

Derek stepped aside from the dais and spoke formally: "Harold, please come to the podium."

Harold stiffly got up and shuffled to the front of the room.

"Before we start," Derek continued, "the ground rules. The vetting is to ensure there is nothing that could disqualify the nominee from running. We are not here to judge the actions of the candidate or moralize or drag them through the mud. The nominee is encouraged to freely bring forward anything of concern. Everything heard here stays here. None of the discussions are for public ears. If you believe the nominee has disqualified themselves, do not vote for them."

Harold stood behind the podium. His expression was somewhat mocking. "Where to start? When I was in my twenties I had too much spit and vinegar. I may have gotten in a fight or two and ended up in the drunk tank. I was a logger. Obviously, that's not good behaviour, but I can hardly remember sixty years ago. The Progressive Conservatives did not care about a few dust-ups when they allowed me to run. Did I tell you that I won every election I ran in from 1979 to 2000? In '93, when the PCs were routed, I was one of only three to hold their seat. I retired when the Reform Party merged with the PCs to make that lump of horse shit that calls itself the Conservative Party." Harold snorted. "I've wiped better things off my boots than the Conservatives - populist wingnuts." He stepped back, ready to go back to his seat.

Derek stopped him with a question: "Can you tell us about the Deloria deal?"

"There is no reason to get into that. Besides, you know everything."

"I do, Harold. But this is for the membership."

"There's no real need, Derek…"

"I can tell them if you would like?"

"Oh very well, if you insist. I can give them the gist. Early in the development of the tar sands, Deloria Oil wanted to secure mineral rights to prime land. I had a connection to the Indian band whose land the oil is on. In the nineteen seventies I logged with their hereditary chief. He wanted the band to thrive, naturally. The right deal with Deloria Oil could make that happen. Derek and I worked as intermediaries to make sure the deal went through. We had to incur some expenses to get the Elected Chief and Band Council on board.

Some saw this as kickbacks, but it was the way the Indians did business in those days. Long story short, there was a lot of smoke but no fire. No charges were laid, but of course, the press was bad."

Derek pushed, "How bad was the press?"

"Lucky for me the story didn't break until after the two thousand election. If I didn't retire ahead of the PC merger with the Canadian Alliance/Reform Party, I probably wouldn't have won. I got it from all sides; the environmentalists were pissed because of the lost habitat; the industrialists were angry because the band got too good a deal. And the law-and-order vote thought I was a crook." Harold sniffed. "But I stand by my actions. The Indians now have the money to give their kids a head start."

"Harold," Rich half put his hand up. "What happened with the Clayoquot protests in the 90s?"

"Speak up. I can't hear you."

Rich repeated the question.

"I did the right thing," Harold replied, indignantly. "I stuck up for my constituents. It's not my problem the protester did not understand gravity. He recovered."

"Harold," Derek prodded, sighing. "Please tell us the entire story."

Harold wiped his hand down his face. "In the middle of the Meres Island kerfuffle, some of the boys from the local mill and I went to give the public the other side of the story. Their livelihoods and way of life were at stake. One protester strung himself up in a tree amongst a tangle of deadfall. The silly kid did not anchor himself well enough so before I could inspect the line holding him up, it failed. He hit the ground, luckily only dislocating his shoulder, and bonking his head. The boys and I evacuated him out to the hospital because the dingbats didn't have a vehicle to get him out. One hippy environmentalist tried to accuse me of sabotaging the line. It was a lot of hot air over nothing. No one in the riding supported the protests."

"How could you say that?" Rich was fuming. "There's video of you mucking with the line. You only helped the kid because you were guilty."

"The RCMP investigated. They found I did nothing wrong. The video is just me telling the kid the problem."

"Rich, this is exactly what we need to know," Derek took control. "However, let's not try to re-litigate the event. Our discussion here needs to be like a conflict-of-interest inquiry. Whether or not the conflict of interest happened is less important than the perception of one. As you point out, this instance definitely does not look good."

Harold piped up, "It ends when the police say I was in the right."

Bea raised her hand, "I think we know what we get with Harold. Most of his life is in the public record." She looked to the assembly. "And in the past. But his language is one of those gifts that is definitely not in the past. 'Indians' is not an acceptable term for indigenous people today. His use of 'gay' is disparaging; he calls women 'gals', and he uses aphorisms and colloquialisms that are problematic."

Harold nearly jolted from his seat. "Frank, my Indian best friend, told me to call them Indians! How could that be 'problematic'?"

"Oh my god!" Bea shook her head. "You just used the racist aphorism, 'I'm not racist. I have a black friend,' to defend yourself. What more is there to say?"

On the TV, Ajay was rolling his eyes, and Cat was acting as if her head had just exploded. Derek, Irene, and Rich nodded to what Bea said, but the rest of the audience was confused.

"Politically Correct poppycock," Harold declared. "Nobody that votes cares if I'm PC. In fact, it is endearing to Joe Six Pack. It's how he talks."

Bea noticed Cat yelling at the camera. "Cat, you are on mute."

Cat regained her composure, "I think this is a serious issue. Direct Democracy must be inviting to all groups. Diversity is the only way it'll get a winning following. It must be the biggest tent. Micro-aggression turns people away. By saying something Politically Incorrect, but appealing to Joe Six Pack, you are offending everyone else. It is a dog whistle to closet racists."

Harold boomed, "I am not a racist!"

Bea replied, "We know you're not, but your language can be."

Cat nodded in agreement.

"I think the point's been made," Derek reasoned. "Let's move forward. Are there any other questions from the members?" Thirty awkward seconds passed. Finally, Derek turned to Harold. "I have one last enquiry. There are rumours of infidelity. Is there truth to this?"

Harold wiped his hand down his face. "Yes. And no. It is true before my marriage officially ended; I was involved with a gal from my office." That got the stink eye from the women in the room. "It was the early eighties and consensual. Anne, my ex-wife, and I weren't living together. I'm pretty sure she was in a relationship too. I don't think it can bite me. Anne passed away almost 20 years ago, and my kids avoid anything to do with me."

"Thank you, Harold." Derek was conciliatory. "This kind of thing isn't easy."

Harold lumbered back to his seat.

"Irene, please come to the podium. Since you're not as well-known as Harold, can you give us a brief bio?"

Irene held the lectern in front of her like a shield. "I was born in 1947 in Comox. My dad was in the Royal Canadian Air Force. We were the only mixed-race family I knew of. My dad was continually having to tell colleagues that mom was Chinese and not Japanese. Once finished high school I moved to Vancouver and got involved in the hippy movement. I participated in many anti-war protests and proud that I was part of the Abortion Caravan that traveled from Vancouver to Ottawa to fight for abortion rights in nineteen seventy. It took eighteen more years to change the law, but we kept at it. I met my partner in nineteen seventy-four and my activism slowed down. Somehow, I ended up as an accountant..."

A polite chuckle issued from the crowd.

"Did you know that counter to what most people would think..." Irene spoke with a sly smile, "...accountants as a group are very empathetic? In two thousand I became politically active again. Mostly to pass the time. I volunteered for the Liberals federally and the NDP provincially. In two thousand fifteen my partner died of cancer. In two thousand seventeen I moved here. I don't have family to help me."

"Thank you, Irene," Derek said. "Are there any questions?" Bea's hand shot up, as did Cat's virtual hand. Harold raised his more slowly. "Bea, Cat, I don't know which of you was first. Please, sort it out yourselves, then Harold can go."

Bea and Cat gestured for the other to go first politely for so long Harold laughed, "End this Canadian standoff! Speak up, Bea."

Bea spoke, "Abortion Convoy? I've never heard of it. What happened?"

"In nineteen seventy, abortions were mostly illegal in Canada," Irene answered. "The law had to change. In the previous fifteen years, over a hundred and fifty thousand back-alley abortions were carried out, with many women dying or being left infertile from the procedure. The Vancouver Women's Caucus decided to drive from Vancouver to Ottawa to be heard, like the On-to-Ottawa Trek during the Depression. We travelled in a VW van with a coffin on the roof representing women who died trying to get healthcare. When we got to Ottawa, we marched into a meeting at Parliament, demanding to be heard. None of the Trudeau leadership would meet with us. We declared war on the Government of Canada. Then we marched to twenty-four Sussex, occupying the lawn. This didn't work, so we escalated." Irene stood straighter and her expression firmed with pride. "We sneaked into the House of Commons and chained ourselves to seats in the gallery. It was the first time in the one hundred and three-year history the House of Commons was shut down."

"I don't know why I never heard of this," Cat remarked.

"You forgot to tell us that you were arrested!" Harold exclaimed.

"Yes, I was! I am very proud of it. We had to act."

Bea applauded. Cat joined her amid most of the other women's nodded approval.

"Getting arrested is instant disqualification in my opinion," Harold said, his cadre of three murmuring agreement. "We can't be led by a criminal."

"Says the man who admits to getting in fights," Irene was livid. "Last time I looked, assault is truly criminal."

"A small-town scrap is no different than a hockey fight. The police agreed with me. I was never charged."

"Harold!" Derek took control. "We have heard your concerns. It is time to move forward."

"What was your partner's name?" Harold pressed.

"Helen."

Harold scanned the room for shock and support. Only his trio of henchmen nodded in support. Most avoided his gaze. The others rolled their eyes or shook their heads in condemnation of his attack. Seeking support he said, "Her partner was a woman…"

"That's enough, Harold. Thank you, Irene, you can sit down. I apologize for Harold; he can get stuck in the past."

Arms crossed, Harold muttered, "If my infidelity mattered so does her sexuality." His lackies grumbled.

"Harold, we are moving on. Bea, can you come up?"

Bea walked up to the lectern casually, placing one hand on the stand and the other on her back pocket and phone. "If I described myself I would say I am a bad person because of circumstance. Not criminal or violent, but bad." She let the crowd be stunned in silence for a minute. "In University I partied. Drinking, smoking pot, doing cocaine if it was free. As recently as a week ago, I invited myself into my neighbour's house for a few tokes, some drinks, and a couple of lines. At twenty I met my ex. I got pregnant shortly after. We married three months before Sam was born. Eighteen months after that I filed for divorce. My ex wouldn't let me continue university. He wanted me home with Sam. I was not going to be a housewife. The divorce was messy. I wanted joint custody, but my ex fought for sole custody. He had the support of his family and my parents. My parents literally disowned me over it. My parents even took out a peace bond against me because of an incident we had. I believe they will use it against me if I am the candidate. I had to be told by my lawyer to volunteer here so that I would look better in court. I wasted a ton of money I did not have, only to get Sam once every two weeks. In the eyes of the court, I wasn't a good enough mom to raise my own child." Bea paused to let that sink in.

"With massive debt from school and the custody battle I had to find a job that would pay well enough to get me out of debt. I could not practice one of the traditional money-making professions women have, you know, being an escort or stripper, because I would lose custody of Sam." There was a gasp from the elderly women. Bea winked. "I found a job as a debt collector. It had good bonuses and allowed lots of overtime, but over the past little while, the job has gotten steadily worse. No raises. Less bonuses and overtime. But I don't have the stability to change careers. As you know, everyone hates debt collectors. And make no mistake, I'm not just a debt collector, I'm a shady one. I don't break people's legs, but I do blackmail debtors. I use the information I find on the dark web, like a family member's name and threaten I will tell them about the debt. It works really, really, well." Bea swore she heard a "Well, I never" from the group. "I don't think what I do is illegal, technically. But certainly, it is immoral. But you know, in a way I'm helping. Getting out-of-control borrowers out of debt quicker than they would on their own."

Bea could easily tell her speech was being received in the negative way she wanted. "And another thing about me…" She took out her phone, casting a YouTube video. Cyclists filled the screen. "I have a YouTube channel devoted to publicly shaming bad cyclists in Victoria." Derek's peacock cycling uniform filled the screen. "You know this guy." In the video, Bea yelled for him to stop at a crosswalk. He did not. "Not my best work, but I do like to name-drop."

The video continued with Bea walking across a bike lane crosswalk with her phone camera pointing at a road bike cyclist racing at her, not slowing. "This is the one I am most proud of." She pretended to drop something, crouching to pick it up. The cyclist slammed on brakes and veered into the other lane. The other lane had an on-coming cyclist going too fast. They slowed enough to soften the head-on collision. Both could not get their feet out of the pedal clips and so comically tipped over. Bea could be heard laughing as the cyclists fell, perfectly in frame.

"Don't get me wrong," She turned to the crowd. "I like cycling. More people should bike. But they gotta follow the rules. If you can't stop for a crosswalk, you are travelling too fast. This video has over ten thousand views. There are like two hundred videos on the channel." Half the audience awkwardly chuckled.

"But that's not my most viewed video on the internet," Bea smirked, doing her best to cover a lie. "This is..." The video showed Knight Rider in front of Bea's apartment building, protesting. The perspective was from the second floor of the Paulina. An unknown female voice narrated: "This guy has been going out every day for the last week protesting. I can't read his sign. He hides it whenever a resident walks past."

A woman and child carrying slabs of cardboard walk into the frame. "That looks like Bea and her son. What are they doing?" The two took up positions on either side of Knight Rider and held up their signs. The narrator continued: "I don't know if you can make out the signs. The kid's reads: '**Mental Health Care Needs More Funding**.' Bea's reads: '**Mental Health in Crisis**.' That's pretty funny. Oh my, the guy on the scooter's getting upset. He's yelling something."

Bea and Sam laugh as Knight Rider yells at them. They start dancing like sign twirlers. Kit starts rolling inches forward then back as Knight Rider tries to move away. "Oh my God!" The narration continued. "The scooter hit the kid and he fell over." Bea races to Sam while yelling profanities at Knight Rider loud enough to be heard on the video. She then starts kicking Kit. Knight Rider tries to hit Bea with Kit. "Oh no! A fight. Call the police, Hasan!" In the background, a male can be heard giving the details to the 911 operator. Bea can be seen about to push Knight Rider. The narrator yells, "The police are coming! This is all on video!" Bea and Knight Rider move away from each other. The video ended.

The room was quiet enough to hear the beat of an owl's wings. Bea broke the silence. "There are a few other videos of me and Knight Rider. One a few weeks ago on the Reddit sub-r/VictoriaBC got a thousand upvotes. I have not been on Reddit in a while, it could have gone truly viral on r/cringe or one of the bigger subs. It could be on TikTok, Twitter or Instagram, I don't go on those platforms."

Bea took a long pause, looking to the ceiling as if trying to remember something. There was no sound in the room. "That's the stuff I remember. I'm sure there is much much more. The big message is that I may not be a criminal, but I am pretty immoral, not a good person, and come with heavy baggage." She scanned the silent room. "Any questions?" Silence. "Oh... one last thing. I love to fart on elevators. Particularly if there's a person, I can blame it on." Amid the continued stunned silence she left the lectern, happy with her mic drop. She wished she had recorded this.

Back of the room, "Good God woman, you are sick," floated across the stillness.

Derek stood at the lectern. "One thing we should all take away from Bea's disclosure is that she is honest." He paused to let that sink in. "She is honest and able to talk directly to her mistakes."

"Derek, these were not mistakes," Bea resented how Derek was spinning her story. "I do not regret them."

"Exactly what I was trying to highlight, honesty and responsibility." Derek moved the meeting forward. "Now that this is done, none of us will speak of the details. We will take a fifteen-minute break and come back to vote. Remember, if you are not here or online between twelve- ten and twelve-fifteen, you will forfeit your chance to vote."

At twelve-sixteen Derek called the meeting back to order. "The vote count is three for Irene. Bea and Harold are tied with seven each. The runoff vote will be twelve twenty-five to twelve-thirty."

At twelve thirty-one Derek again called the meeting to order. "The vote count for the runoff is eight votes for Bea and nine for Harold. Congratulations Harold, you are the first leader and candidate of Direct Democracy." A cheer led by Harold's cronies and followed by everyone, including Bea and Irene, came up from the room.

Bea congratulated Harold first.

In the crowd, Derek took Bea aside. "I knew what you were trying to do, and you lost by one vote. That says something."

Irene found Bea soon after, "Our party must be inclusive of all. Harold is a strong, charismatic man, but I'm not sure he can change direction. We'll need to pull the reins to keep that old war horse on the right track, Bea."

10.

The mountain bike of Sam's dreams was filling up the short hallway to the front door, so Bea had to put on her runners in the living room. She was ecstatic. The tags of the big box store from which Carter had liberated the bike were still on it. She added to the tags by tying a birthday bow to the handlebars with the card. She was almost as happy that she still had one hundred and fifty bucks left of her present savings fund. The extra money would go to a new helmet and other accessories. Sam would have a great birthday.

After her run, Bea donned an old but still stunning floral summer dress that suited Victoria's spring weather. She left the Paulina, walking to the Home, pushing the bike. About a third of the way there, in North Park, a kid started yelling at her and pointing, "My bike! My Bike! Mom, Dad, my bike!"

The kid was across the street, halfway down the block. Bea thought he was far enough back that she could just keep walking. Glancing down the block, she saw a momma bear appear. She sped up and considered riding the bike but she had not ridden a bike in over ten years, let alone a kid's bike. She was startled when a middle-aged hipster with stereotypical goatee, glasses, longish wavy hair and skinny jeans stepped from behind a telephone pole, poster in hand.

"Morning," the hipster said unconfrontationally. "Nice day. I can't help but notice the bike you have is like the one stolen from my son yesterday. I can see the tags… May I have a look at it so I can assure my son it's not his?"

"No! It's my kid's birthday present." Bea pulled the bike closer.

"It is probably a coincidence." The hipster displayed the poster. "But the bike does look like the same model."

Bea peered at the photo. "They look similar, but this is not that bike. I'm late for my kid's party."

Momma bear was lumbering near with the kid running ahead of her. She had her phone out, recording. "Murph!" She yelled. "Should I call the cops?"

"Hold off a second, honey… I think it's a misunderstanding." He spoke directly to Bea. "You have a child, so you understand. I'm sure the bike is not his. Let me have a closer look."

"Dude, don't touch me. I don't know who you are or why your fat wife and unruly kid are accosting me. Back the fuck off!"

The hipster held up his hands. "I'm sure this is not my kid's bike. But I want to give him some closure."

The boy arrived and grabbed onto the bike inspecting the price tag on the bike. "The price tag is for the Trail Rider Adult! This is the Trail Rider Junior! It is my bike!"

"Give my kid his bike!" Momma bear bellowed. "Or I'll call the cops!"

"It's my bike…" Instinct had Bea pull her phone out to record the situation. "I bought it off a guy on Craig's List!"

The hipster grabbed the handlebars. "Lady, call the police or let me see this bike."

"Murph, I'm going to call the cops!" Momma bear turned to her son, "Oliver, how do I make a phone call while videoing?"

The boy ignored his mother. "Give me my bike!"

"Fine!" Bea pushed the bike at the hipster.

The hipster turned it over. Under the bottom bracket was a number ground into the metal. "I put this number on my kid's bike. This is his bike. Where did you get it?"

"I got it from some guy on Craig's List." Bea took a step back. "I had no idea it was stolen, it had tags on it."

The momma bear growled, "I've got you on camera, thief! Call the police, Murph!"

Bea backed further away. "I'm a single mom with a shitty job trying to get a good gift for my kid. I had no idea the bike was stolen. The guy on Craig's List said it was a final sale so he couldn't return it. I thought I was getting a deal. I wanted to get my kid the bike he wanted. I'm sorry. Take it."

"You are a piece of shit!" Momma bear frothed. "Call the cops!"

The hipster handed the bike to his son and took out his phone. The kid started taking the tags and ribbon off and saw Sam's card. He flicked it past Bea.

Bea sprinted after the card.

"She's getting away!"

"Have a heart, Donna," Murph replied. "Her kid's not getting a birthday gift."

Card in hand, Bea struggled to keep from crying while her fast walk turned into a run. But she could not run from the feeling of failure. The adrenaline was wearing off as she neared the Home. She sat down to sort herself out, perched on the curb, bawling. How was she going to explain this to Sam? Crying was helping.

A man approached on the sidewalk and saw Bea crying. "Are you ok?" He asked. "Do you need help?"

"Fuck off! Leave me alone!"

The man held out his hands. "Whoa. I just want to know if I can help. Should I call the police?"

Standing up, Bea used her dress to dry her eyes, then brushed herself off. The man still stood looking at her. "Mind your own fucking business."

Bea resumed walking and tore the card to pieces to drop them into a garbage can. Finally, she arrived at the Home. Stomping through the front door she did not acknowledge the manager.

Harold was in the lounge. "Grab coffee and a doughnut, Bea. We got two new members today. Everyone is chomping at the bit to figure out Instascam."

Dryly Bea responded, "It is Instagram."

"That was a good one Bea. You didn't even smile. What's wrong?"

"I don't want to talk about it. Something has come up. I can't lead the meeting today. Give me some space," Bea strode to the corner farthest from the refreshments and leaned against the wall, looking into the corner. She pulled out her phone and dialed Marcus.

After a few rings Marcus picked up. "Hi Bea, what's up?" The sound of children playing was in the background.

"The bike I got for Sam was stolen. I don't have a gift for him." Bea's voice cracked.

"What happened? Did your apartment get broken into? Are you ok?"

"I don't want to talk about it. I might be late…" Bea took a deep breath. "I need to get something else for Sam."

"Of course."

"He'll be so upset about the bike." She started weeping. "I can't even get a birthday gift for my son."

"Why don't I give you a minute…" Marcus was genuinely concerned. "I'll call you back."

"Okay." Bea hung up the phone. She cried for only a moment, then forced herself to Google gifts for Sam. An arm around her shoulders and she turned to see Irene standing close. Harold stood behind Irene, keeping others away.

"Let it all go, Bea…" Irene hugged her. "Crying is good. And when you get it all out, we might have a gift for Sam." After thirty seconds she let go.

"Thanks, Irene. I needed that. I'm feeling better."

"That's good, dear."

"But I have to go find a present for Sam."

"Sam loves owls?"

"He does."

"I have a good friend…" Irene smiled. "Really more like family. They run the Raptors in Duncan. I'm sure I can arrange a special tour if you can get us up there."

"Derek can drive you," Harold chirped. "He loves showing off his Benz to the ladies."

Bea chuckled at that, wondering if Harold knew Derek was gay. "Sam would love that. When could we go?"

Irene answered, "I have to check with Sandy, but possibly tomorrow."

"Speak of the devil," Harold said as Derek clacked his riding shoes into the room. "Derek, we need to help Bea. Her kid needs a gift. Irene knows someone at the Raptors. Can you give them a ride in your Benz tomorrow?"

"Well, hello everyone…" Derek smiled. "Sure thing. I love driving the Malahat. Any reason will do."

"I'll check with Sandy," Irene said. "I'm excited, this will be fun,"

Bea was overwhelmed at how easy this new gift was coming together. She thanked them. As she told them she needed to confirm about taking Sam, the Imperial March sang out from her phone. "Hi Marcus. I think I have a gift sorted out for Sam. One of my friends can take us to the Raptor's for a private tour. I'm hoping I can have Sam tomorrow to go there?"

"That's a relief," Marcus sighed. "Opa Peter got the bike for Sam."

"What the fuck Marcus..! My parents are going to be there! The judge placed an order on me to not see them. I don't want to see them!"

"Calm down, Bea. A peace bond only lasts a year. It's been almost eight years. I've talked with your parents. They won't speak with you."

"You didn't talk to me!" Bea shouted at the phone. "How do you think I'd feel arriving at the birthday and there they are?"

"This is a big birthday for Sam. We want him to be happy. It's getting too hard to have separate parties with your parents coming to one and you to the other. We knew if we told you, you would not come, so we didn't tell you. You won't have to interact with them. We told them not to talk with you. Let's be adults. Make it a great time for Sam. Ok?"

Bea was not sure why nine was an important birthday for Sam. She put that aside. "Ok...I'll be there. But I want to take Sam to the Raptors tomorrow."

"I'll have to check with Amy. Give me a minute." Bea heard muffled tidbits of conversation like Ottawa, parents at the birthday, a long time, stolen bike, who's driving, time for getting the house ready. Marcus returned to the phone. "Amy wants to know how you're getting to Duncan."

"Derek Nelson is driving, Google him. He's a lawyer."

"Where have I heard that name before?" Marcus paused. "Anyway, you can have Sam tomorrow, but we will need Derek's info."

"Great..." Bea wanted to tell Marcus to fuck off, but he was only being a good father. "I'll see you when the party starts." She hung up the phone, slumping against the wall. "Fuck." She was not sure if she had the restraint to act civilly or ignore her parents.

The meeting commenced. Most of the group seemed to grasp the concept of Instagram and then practiced their new skills with those who did not. That this group of oldsters continued to follow Bea's lead bolstered her spirit.

Harold banged a gavel when it was clear Bea had demonstrated what she had hoped to. In Bea's eyes, it was more pomp than necessary.

"From now on there will be an official business portion as part of these meetings," Harold announced. "The purpose will be to organize our activities. The agenda will include membership stats, finances, and activities." The more Harold talked, the more the officialness made Bea believe Direct Democracy was something. The members seemed to think so too.

Bea provided a discussion of internet metrics during the new business item. None of the members understood, but they nodded and said, "Right," as if they were experts. Bea continued remembering how far Harold had come from asking what an online poll was.

Afterward, Irene and Derek confirmed with Bea to ensure the plan for the Raptors was solid. Bea's heart was warmed; she had not had anyone spontaneously help her since childhood when on the odd occasion, a teacher would. Bea's parents certainly never had.

Walking up Circle Road to the lawn by the Rose Garden and across from the Beacon Hill Petting Zoo Bea noticed at least three families with flashy SUVs driven by soccer moms. Birthday balloons and kids clustered inside the vehicles. She felt certain these people were here for Sam's birthday and an overheard child confirmed it. The hipster parents carried a well-wrapped gift and a bottle of wine. The party took up an area bordered by the Rose Garden, a Douglas fir grove, cherry trees, and rock outcrops. Picnic tables were covered with food and gifts. A large tent covered two of the tables. The only precipitation the tent stopped was a light pink snow from the last of the cherry blossom petals. More than ten kids were gathered about Sam or chasing each other around. The parents were grouped at the picnic table with wine on it. Some parents sipped from plastic wine cups; the minority had coffee. Amy and Marcus were at the center of things.

Bea felt out of place, of course, because she had neither a large gift, bottle of wine, or man to hang off. She warily scanned the group for her parents. They were not yet there. Hopefully, she could get a glass or two of wine in her before they showed up.

Sam saw Bea coming and ran to her, arms wide. "Momma B!"

Bea caught him with a hug, remembering why she was here. "Happy birthday Sam! I am so sorry I couldn't get the bike you wanted. But I think I have something better."

"I don't care. Dad told me the bike you got me was stolen. Opa Peter is getting it for me."

"Yes, Kiddo, it was stolen. What I got you has to do with owls but that's all I'm telling you."

"Can we see owls after the party?"

"Maybe... maybe we will hear Josie. She probably knows it is your birthday," Bea looked at the already overflowing garbage can. "She'll be happy to eat all the rats attracted by the leftovers."

"Josie will get a gift too," Sam giggled. "I'm going to go play with my friends."

Amy and Marcus welcomed Bea with a call. She returned it, then made it to the wine table, hoping not to talk with anyone. That was too much to ask. A parent, too close by to ignore, engaged her with small talk. A too-chubby-for-Lululemon blonde woman in leggings introduced herself. "Your dress is so summery. I'm Tanya."

"Hello, Tanya."

Tanya pointed to a child who did not see her. "Mine is Olivia. Which one is yours?"

Bea poured while answering. "Sam is mine."

"Your boy's named Sam too?"

"I gave birth to Sam."

"Oh..." A moment of confusion crossed Tanya's face, then recognition. Without further words she turned and walked toward the kids, shouting, "Olivia!"

Bea was happy with the response her answer caused.

Marcus approached Bea from her blind side. "Look how happy Sam is."

"He sure is."

The two parents watched their son play.

"Direct Democracy is a great troll," Marcus remarked suddenly. "How did you get Harold Gordon and Derek Nelson in on the prank?"

Bea was shocked he did not want to talk about Sam. "It is not a prank. Harold came up with the idea when I was showing him how to use a tablet. He said it is what he got into politics for; giving his constituents a voice."

"You're telling me you still volunteer at that old folk's home? And you met Harold Gordon there? And he has the idea for Direct Democracy? I don't believe it. It smells too much like a troll. How is Derek Nelson involved?"

"He is the party's electoral officer."

"That's exactly what he said when I called him," Marcus confessed. "Who's doing the computer stuff, like that video? It's slick."

"The video was made by our third-party, Alliance for Direct Democracy."

"ADD… you are kidding me? Is it a joke!"

"Yes, I made up the name Alliance for Direct Democracy. But the third party is real. I honestly don't know the name of it. Ajay from University is a big tech guy in Victoria. His girlfriend, Cat, and him are making content promoting the concept of direct democracy."

"Ajay," Marcus smirked. "That fat brown guy with the small dick you had pity sex with."

"You thought something small down there was an asset when you wanted a threesome with him." Bea turned to leave.

"Wait, sorry. That was uncalled for…This is all a little absurd."

"You've got that right."

"But good, though. Good like you were in university."

Marcus's last words hurt Bea much more than the Ajay comment. She steeled her expression. "I agree. But this 'absurdity' is taking on a life of its own. We have a membership of twenty-four people so far. Mostly oldsters. All of them actively promoting DD on social media."

"Old people on the internet... If I was telling that story, its genre would be fantasy..."

"Call it what you will."

"...And you still insist it's legit?"

"Of course."

"Who's making the voting app?"

"I am."

"Knowing a little HTML is a far cry from writing an app," Marcus laughed.

"I know a lot more than you think. Ajay has confidence in me."

"Whoa...small-dick-man has confidence in you!"

"I don't know why I'm bothering to explain all this. I already know you don't believe in me."

"Hey, Sweet Cheeks," Marcus blushed and corrected himself for calling Bea her old pet name and Amy's current one. "Sorry... I meant Bea." His expression turned serious. "Look, it's great you've found something to get you out of your rut but be realistic. DD is an assault on what politics is about, power. If Harold Gordon or any other political person wins as a DD candidate, do you think they'll surrender their personal power to make decisions? No, they will not. Plus, do we as a country want uneducated morons able to vote on every bill that goes through Parliament? I don't think so. Stop being so idealist."

"I guess realistic was what you were striving for when you sold out and took a job lobbying for oil and gas. What happened to fighting for a better world? You want Sam to play hockey on an outdoor rink, don't you?"

"Yeah."

"Stop shilling for climate criminals."

"I'm part of the Association for Natural Gas. Nothing to do with oil."

"Not exactly, but close enough."

"NG is a greener product. It's a bridge that'll be needed to solve the intermittency of renewable energy. Environmental assessment processes will need to be changed." Marcus sounded scripted. "It's a step in the right direction."

"Oh please. Don't give me talking points. You sold out."

"Sure, okay. Maybe my job doesn't perfectly align with my beliefs back in university. But I had to grow up and provide for my family. You should too." Marcus became more serious, "Bea, this troll you are participating in better not pull in Sam. If it does, that will be the end."

"Are you threatening me?" Bea's question hung in the air. "Direct Democracy is not a troll. My involvement is in the background. Aside from Sam getting free doughnuts at the meetings there's no way he'd be involved."

"I didn't think so. Keep it that way."

The rising heat of their conversation had attracted Amy. "Are you two getting back together?"

"Has hell frozen over?" Bea replied.

"I'm glad to hear that." Amy batted her fake eyelashes. "Bea, I thought you'd like to know your parents have arrived. You know…in case you want to be on the opposite side of the party."

"Thanks, I am truly grateful for the heads up." Bea finished the wine she'd been sipping so she could fill it again and found her way to the other side. Everywhere she went she practiced the Direct Democracy elevator pitch, including to children.

The party progressed with games for an hour, then it was time for cake. Then presents. Sam was asked to pick which present he wanted to open first. "Momma A," Sam shouted. "I want to open Momma B's present first!"

Bea struggled to stay smiling with everyone hearing she was 'B' to Amy's 'A.' But Bea beamed for her son, bringing the card to him, "Here you go, Kiddo."

Opening with too much enthusiasm Sam ripped the card. He struggled to read the disjointed writing but jumped for joy when he did.

"What did you get?" Amy asked.

"A VIP afternoon at the Raptors! I get to hold the owls!"

None of the other gifts got the reaction the Raptors did. Bea was smug and grateful.

Ottawa Senator's or 67's merch made up a large portion of the other presents. Bea found this odd as Sam was a Canucks fan.

After two pieces of cake, a few glasses of wine, and touting Direct Democracy to everyone possible, Bea decided to leave and look for owls. She found Marcus to confirm the pickup details for tomorrow. "Three sets of parents here are now on Direct Democracy's mailing list. A fourth said they would look it up. So, you see, it is not a troll." She walked away, waving goodbye to Sam, telling him she would see him tomorrow.

Walking out Bea heard someone calling and turned. Her mother and father were following. She stopped, stunned.

"You did that on purpose!" Her father yelled. "Getting Sam the better present! You're always trying to make us look bad."

Bea inhaled deeply and exhaled slow; the only way she could stop from yelling back. The hair on the back of her neck stood up. Her arm was raising as if on its own to point at them. But two more breaths and literally biting her tongue, she allowed the moment to pass. For Sam, she would not engage her parents.

"You're making your poor mother and I look bad." Her father continued to scream. "Say something!"

Bea turned to leave.

"It's obvious we did the right thing." Her mother joined in. "Look at all the great people Marcus and Amy know. Did you see their cars? What are you driving? Right, you don't drive. What kind of life would Sam have had with you!?"

Memories of her parents' betrayal dominated Bea's thoughts. She told herself it was not worth walking that road again and fought to replace bitterness with pleasant thoughts of taking Sam to the Raptors. But the battle was being lost.

"WHO COOKS FOR YOU! WHO COOKS FOR YOU ALL!" The call came from the swamp and older growth trees near the Beacon Hill city nursery.

That focused her. She strode fast toward the owl calls and heard that they were receiving a response from a suiter. The real caterwauling began just as she found Josie and Mister. Spring was definitely in the air. She was thrilled to get a bad cell phone video of the two mating. Owlets were definitely in the offing. A couple minutes behind her Sam rolled up on his new bike in time to see the cuddling couple.

Exactly at a quarter before three Derek pulled up in his Benz. In the time it took for Bea to notice Irene in the front seat Derek had hopped out and opened the back door for her.

Inside the car; Bea asked, "What is with the suit?"

In a British accent, "I am your chauffeur."

"He's been pretending to be a driver from England," Irene added, smiling. "He is an odd man."

Derek stayed in character all the way to Sam's house, passing many houses that looked chauffeur-worthy. The Oak Bay house they pulled up to was modest compared to the mansions but definitely would be worth more than two million dollars. Derek opened Bea's door and then the other in anticipation of Sam.

Marcus emerged as soon as he saw Derek's car, eyeing it closely to see what class of Benz it was. He then ran down the front stairs to ogle the car like a kid seeing a Lamborghini for the first time. He assailed Derek with car questions, who dutifully answered as a chauffeur.

When Sam approached Derek politely told Marcus to bugger off, then assisted all passengers into the car. He had them all laughing when he secretly turned on Sam's seat massager. Bea and Sam appreciated Derek's very fast driving, so fast Sam only had to say, "Are we there yet" twice. Irene was not so comfortable with the rate of speed.

At the Raptor's Sam was immediately worried by the closed sign. Irene reassured him that it would open for them. As they walked through the dirt lot, Sam took a detour to a nearby enclosure. The barred owl 'Wellington' greeted them with a whining screech. It was like the begging steam kettle noise an immature owl makes, but deeper. Bea and Sam were happy to watch and listen. Irene continued to the entrance with Derek.

Bea and Sam were still watching Wellington when Irene and Derek came back with a woman Irene introduced as Sandy.

"You like Wellington?" Sandy asked.

Sam and Bea nodded yes. "She has not flown today. I'll get her." Raptor glove on, Sandy entered the enclosure and emerged with Wellington perched on an arm.

"Momma B," Sam spoke with awe. "This is the closest to an owl we have ever been!" This was the start to an overwhelming owl experience that included:

Flying Wellington, Ziggy, the barn owl and Sven, a great grey owl

Holding Wellington, Arcturus, a great horned owl, and Taiga, a western screech owl

Touring of all the owls at the Raptors

Derek took pictures, hanging back from the birds.

Flying the owls was what Bea and Sam loved most. Having the owls silently soar over their heads was awesome, wings gently brushing their hair. Derek jumped when 'Sven' brushed his head, but he was thrilled with the photo.

They learned that all the flying birds were bred in captivity. Sandy explained that the strange, deep call of Wellington was the contact or begging call of a barred owlet coming from a full-grown owl.

Sandy told them the birds could fly away if they wanted but stayed for the food and companionship, having bonded with their keepers. 'Ziggy' then gave them a demonstration of how the birds did not always listen. Like the rock star Ziggy was named after he flew away, not listening to Sandy or coming for the food. Instead, Ziggy took a few extra laps, trying to hunt some mice. Bea and Sam loved Ziggy's attitude.

Watching Sam hold the owls made Bea want to hold one too. But when Sandy offered, Bea declined. Bea knew that if she held an owl, she could not resist petting it. In Bea's mind the owls were too fluffy not to stroke. Petting the owls was not allowed.

Three quarters of the way through the owl experience Bea could not hold any more owl facts in her head. She let Irene and Sam have Sandy to themselves.

She and Derek hung back. "You're not a bird lover?" Bea asked. "Let me guess, birds' poop on your car so you don't like them?"

"Birds freak me out a bit," Derek dropped the English accent to answer seriously. "But I love kids at Sam's age. When my kids were his age, I would put on the chauffeur's act and take them to museums and other places."

"No wonder you're so good at it. We can't thank you enough for doing this. Sam will remember it forever. I'll remember it forever. I'm so grateful. I've never had the support Harold, Irene, and you have given me." Bea smiled tightly. "My world has suddenly become hopeful."

"No need to thank me, Bea. Your energy and ability are why Direct Democracy is happening. Seeing Harold and the oldies come together over technology is nearly miraculous. You did that. The idea for Direct Democracy may have been Harold's but you are the one who sees that at its centre is equality. You see how it can bring people of all political stripes together."

"You flatter me…"

"It is true, though. You are the heart and soul."

"Oh maybe.

"That is why I'm so confused. Why did you vote against yourself at the leadership meeting?"

"What? I voted for me," Bea lied.

"Don't make me do an audit. You voted for Harold. Why?"

"If my past is revealed it will take Sam away from me," Bea snapped. "I'm not taking that chance."

"Then why enter the race at all?"

"My reasons."

"Had you voted for yourself you could have forfeited the nomination when you won. It is strange."

Bea did not comment further. Instead, she joined Irene and Sam, asking Sandy owl questions.

But the questions Bea asked were not the ones she was truly pondering.

Why indeed did she run if it was only to lose by her own hand? She had wanted to be seen losing, so the question of her being the candidate would not come up again. But she loved speaking to the crowd.

It was obvious that if she had not shot herself in the foot, she would have easily won the race. If those people felt she was worth voting for, why didn't she? All answers ended by remembering the world collapsing around her as she fought to break the mould her ex-family had forced on her.

Had she gone with the flow, she would be Momma A to Sam, taking him to hockey and soccer, having a nice car. Her biggest worry being when to schedule manicures, not having to work. But she'd wanted to be a person with a life beyond family and not be seen only as Marcus's wife or Sam's mother.

A terrible thought entered Bea's mind: that she had fought for the privilege of failure. Everything she had done since the divorce was to maintain the status quo so she could see Sam. She had stood up for the freedom to be a person but had not used her freedom. In order to keep her one day with Sam every two weeks she feared acting as she desired.

Was there any chance that even with her debt paid and the realistic prospect of a more lucrative job, she would get more custody of Sam? Did she want more custody of Sam? Society's pressure to be a mother was so great that she could not think about this question objectively. Could going back to school get her to where she wanted to be? Again, she did not answer the question as she knew a positive outcome was too far in the future to even dream of.

As Bea watched a smiling and laughing Sam hold one last owl, Taiga, she sensed that the fight for Sam was just a pyrrhic victory. She had lost everything she wanted to gain from divorcing Marcus. This was the best her life was going to be. She started to cry.

Derek noticed Bea's tears through the view finder of his camera. He gestured to Irene, who reached into her handbag for a tissue. Bea gratefully took it, dabbing her eyes and wiping her nose. "Thank you. Tears of joy," Bea lied. "This has been a great day."

"Momma B," Sam called. "I'd hug you but I'm holding an owl."

Irene gave Bea a hug in Sam's absence.

Bea's new friends brought her a smile and confidence that things would be better. Direct Democracy had already made her life better.

The owl experience at the Raptor's wrapped up with the visit with Taiga. Everyone thanked Sandy for the private tour. Bea did her best with Derek and Irene to let her pitch in on the fee, both said there was no cost. They said the joy it brought to Sam was more than enough for them, but Bea knew they were not telling the truth.

To entertain Sam on the way back home, Derek showed him how to view the pictures on his camera. Sam was extremely excited by this because his dad never let him touch his camera.

Bea viewed over Sam's shoulder at the owl images, thinking she was like them; tethered by the past. She could only fly so far without fear of all she had done. Her past was like the jesses around Ziggy's legs, reminding him he had a cage to be in with food, minimal companionship, and little freedom.

'Why did it have to be this way?' Bea asked herself. Maybe the nine years was far enough from her past to fade away. Maybe the world had changed enough for her past to not be seen as disqualifying her to be a good mother. People with children would always see her past as wrong for a "good mother." She was sure the world would see what she did as forgivable if she would beg for forgiveness and be repentant. But why would she ask for forgiveness and repent for something she knew was not wrong. Her past was something she was proud of. Just as she could not walk past a plush toy without petting it or risk holding an owl because she would stroke it; she would certainly fight to show that her past was not wrong. Boldly fighting for something the vast majority of society sees as repugnant for a mother to do would only reinforce how deviant and wrong her beliefs are to the majority. Fighting to show that her past was not shameful would take away Sam. And it would be her fault because she was an uppity woman that would fight.

Bea thought that if her past was the past of a man, the story would be different. It would focus on the true wrong done; was it illegal, did it hurt others, was it a youthful mistake. A woman would not be given that reasonableness, the story would focus on the perception of immorality. On the spectrum of morality, she would be compared to the model of motherhood. The bar for a man would be closer to what was illegal rather than what was immoral for a mother. She would be pilloried for the superficial. A man would only be ridiculed after deep consideration. To her, this was best illustrated by the way Anthony Weiner was able to salvage his political career while sexting for six more years. Weiner was only taken down by a criminal act six years after the scandal broke. But Congresswoman Katie Hill was destroyed in months by revenge porn. She thought, Katie Hill did have sex with subordinates but that was not the cause of her downfall. It was the pictures. In her mind, both events should have been non-events until there was criminality or at least treated the same, but the world does not work that way.

Bea turned away from the pictures.

The rest of the ride home the adults discussed politics.

They arrived in Victoria near sunset. Bea had to wake Sam, then half carry him to the house.

Derek drove down Dallas Road to watch the sunset. Near Cook Street, Bea said, "Can we stop here for a few minutes? I want to show you, our owls."

Bea led them into an older growth section of the park. Many large Douglas fir and maple trees near the Story totem pole darkened the path as the sun sank. At the edge of Beacon Hill, a barred owl's call boomed out.

"What was that?" Derek asked. "A monkey?"

Bea quickened the pace. "It was Mister, our male barred owl."

Mister sat amongst pine trees with the last of the day's light shining on him. Derek positioned himself to get photos. A second barred owl responded from behind them.

With gleaming eyes, Bea giggled, "It sounds like someone's getting lucky tonight."

Irene was confused, "What do you mean?"

Bea said, "That was Josie telling Mister that she is in the mood."

Mister started calling again, ending the call with a squawking that almost sounded like a rooster. Mister exploded into the air toward Derek as he took pictures. A wing brushed his head.

Bea tracked Mister and got a fleeting glimpse of owl mating action. It was done almost as soon as it started; it did not look satisfying. Bea was happy she was not an owl.

"Best picture ever!" Derek exclaimed.

Irene and Bea both agreed that Derek's capture of an owl in aggressive flight could likely be in National Geographic. Driving them home, Derek would not stop talking of his photographic coup.

Bea was happy to have an owl memory that did not make her sad.

11.

Checking the Direct Democracy website email box had become a daily event. The number had steadily risen to a dozen a day. Most were from members asking for help, such as forgetting how to sign into a comment section. The rest were new people interested in Direct Democracy.

Today there was a different email. It was from Canada's Other Pass Time (COPT), one of the YouTube Channels on which Cat had promoted the third-party video. It was seeking an interview with Harold. Bea leapt from her chair and did a happy dance. The downstairs neighbour banged on the floor. She danced louder.

To test if Harold was up to the task, Bea checked if he was on Messenger. He was. She video-called him. It rang more than five times. As she was about to hang up, he responded, "What in tarnation is this bullshit? Probably a fucking ad. Where did they hide the close button?"

"Harold don't close the window. It's Bea!"

"Why is my picture in the corner?"

"It is a video call over the internet."

"Eh?"

"I'll explain later. I have big news."

"Did you call my phone number?" Harold was confused. "I don't have video calling."

"Messenger, the instant messaging app I chat with you on Facebook can host video calls. I saw you online, so I called you. Why don't you try calling me?"

"Holy doodle! Woman! I'm not Ms. Anderson. I answered. I can call. Just tell me the big news?"

"The YouTube Channel, *Canada's Other Pass Time*, wants an interview!"

"What is that?"

"They are the third most viewed Canadian political channel on YouTube."

"Never heard of them. Isn't YouTube only how-to videos and shots of guys getting hit in the balls? I like that *Commentiquette* guy but it's not serious media."

Bea sighed and proceeded to youngsplain. "COPT gets similar numbers as the CBC's YouTube videos, Harold. More young people watch YouTube Channels than the CBC for news because they don't have cable. Trust me."

"It's not Power and Politics but I suppose we have to start somewhere," Harold sighed. "Anyway, this will be good practice for when we get on TV."

"Good practice…right."

For the rest of the call Bea taught an impromptu lesson, with Harold following along as a less than enthusiastic student. He didn't think lighting mattered and thought headsets were dumb.

After the call and with slightly less enthusiasm Bea replied to COPT's email. It was not more than two hours before COPT answered, asking to slate the interview for a webcast the next day. They had already contacted Cat, who was going to be on the stream too.

Bea saw Harold on Messenger and called.

Two rings in, Harold answered, "I'm honoured to hear from you twice in one day. Did another aspiring TV journalist ask us for an interview on his pretend news show?"

"Harold don't give me that."

"Don't judge me too harshly. You will despise reporters in the same way a rummy who's pissed himself despises the bottle that's out of his reach."

"I'm not even going to try to understand that. *Canada's Other Past Time* wants an interview tomorrow. It'll be hard for me to get to the Home in time for the live stream…"

"Live stream?"

"It's a live broadcast, Harold. Pay attention." Bea got back on track, "I can get there to assist you if I take a cab. Or I can join the call from a private room at my work. What's your choice?"

"Can't Canada's whatever push the time back?"

"They're based back east. Our segment will be seven forty-five pm in Ontario. Four forty-five here."

"Toronto," Harold grumbled. "Center of the bloody universe. No need to be here. I can do this myself."

Owls, Doughnuts, and Democracy, by Jason A. N. Taylor

"I like your naive confidence, but Murphy's Law governs internet communication. We must have a backup if one of us cannot join because of technical difficulties."

"I see your point. Send me the information and we'll talk tomorrow."

"Harold, we need to practice more on using the technology. You definitely need a headset. There's too much background noise at the Home. You need a spot with good lighting. I also think you should have someone assist with the technical work. Irene is pretty good at that."

"I've done more interviews than you've seen sunny days, Sweetheart. I'll do great."

"I'm know you'll kill. But it is the tech I'm worried about."

"You're being a worry wart. I made this call, didn't I? Send me the details for connecting and I'll get one of the lads to help me. But it's suppertime. Right now, I have to get going before they're out of Yorkshire pudding. Have a great night. Break a leg." Harold hung up the call before Bea could respond.

Bea was sure that if Harold got help from one of his lads something would go wrong. She emailed Irene with the interview details and instructions to be online. Then she sent Harold the COPT invitation.

The clock in the corner of Bea's work computer was edging up to four thirty pm. The sad story on the other end of her phone was like a bad country song with a dog running away in Saskatchewan, it kept going and going. She had dropped the debt payment as low as possible. Half listening, at four thirty-two she checked her phone to see if Harold was online.

Harold was not online.

Desperate to get the debtor off the phone, she offered a too-low figure to the debtor, knowing she would get a talking-to from Mike. She logged off at four thirty-six.

Stepping close to the meeting room's closing glass door, Bea flattened her dress and took a second to admire her reflection. She sat down putting her headset on.

Mike opened the door.

"I have the room booked," Bea barked.

"You can't have a job interview in our office."

"It's a tele-doctor's appointment."

"How come you're all dressed up? You never wear dresses here."

"Not that it is your business," Bea shrilled. "But I may need easy access to the problem area." Not showing anything, Bea splayed her knees to make the point.

Mike reddened. "I'll put the occupied sign on the door." He checked that the blinds were closed and slinked out of the room.

Bea laughed at her ruse while tapping on her phone. She was put on hold by the producer. She used the time for a second time to ensure she looked good. She did.

"Bea, Cat…" the producer came on the line. "You're on in one minute. Harold hasn't joined the call. I will include him when he does. Cat will be first to field questions. Bea and Harold will follow."

The show came up. The two hosts, Melissa and Ryan, segued from the previous segment on the less than fifty-dollar barrel of oil's impact on Alberta's provincial politics to Direct Democracy. Melissa said, "I'd bet that many Albertans want a new option to be heard in Ottawa."

"Our next guests have a new way for Canadians to be heard. It's called Direct Democracy. We have Cat Lavoie from the advocacy group Canadians for Greater Democracy and Bea Jensen of this new federal party to tell us about it."

Cat and Bea smiled and waved as Ryan introduced them.

"We're also hoping to have ex-Progressive Conservative MP, Harold Gordon, the newly elected leader of Direct Democracy talk with us. We're experiencing technical difficulties with his line."

Bea cringed at the double-edged sword of Harold's history. Every interview would be prefaced by the words "former Progressive Conservative MP".

Melissa asked, "Cat, can you tell us how direct democracy works? It sounds really new to me."

"Direct democracy is an old idea first documented in ancient Athens, though that was not the first place direct democracy thrived. Most egalitarian societies use it in some way." Cat took them through a four-minute overview, including origins, how representative democracy is becoming less representative, how direct democracy is the ultimate in representation. "It's possible now. There will be a direct democracy option: Direct Democracy."

Bea listened, marvelling at Cat's poise and the clarity of her points.

"Thank you, Cat," Ryan transitioned. "That sounds intriguing. I salivate at the idea of being able to vote for every bill that comes past the House of Commons. But I'm a political geek with a YouTube channel dedicated to Canadian politics. Honestly, I see the average Canadian being overwhelmed by the choices. Bea, how does Direct Democracy overcome that?"

When Bea did not answer immediately, Melissa added, "It reminds me of trying to decide on toothpaste. There are too many choices."

"That's a good analogy, Melissa," Bea said brightly. "When I go shopping, I have a list of what I want. The list doesn't change much, and it gets me out of the store quickly. Similarly, people have a list of political desires that don't change often, like the staples on a grocery list. With our Direct Democracy App—in development—constituents will be able to select how they vote by different groupings of issues. Like healthcare. The App interviews me on my political leanings for a multitude of topics then allows me to decide if I always want to vote one way on a topic or if I want to be notified to vote on individual bills. For example, environmentally I identify with the Green's platform, but on defense I'm Conservative all the way. I had family in the forces. For these topics I can set the App up to always vote Green on the environmental issues and Conservative on defense. The average voter would be interviewed once for their voting profile and need not sign-on again until and unless they change their mind. A political geek like me could vote on all individual legislation. Someone with less political obsession could just action their voting preferences.

The App can be set up for any variation between those two extremes."

"Sound's simple, but what is simple to me is not simple to my father," Melissa laughed.

"That's so true," Bea joined her. "We have a plan for that. Our party started at senior's home. We have a great group of octogenarian user acceptance testers to ensure our App will work for everyone."

"Sorry, did I hear that right, Direct Democracy started at an old folk's home?" Ryan was astounded. "How could that be, it is based on technology?"

"You heard right. Let me tell you the story." Bea told the story.

"That is amazing," Melissa exclaimed. "Who would have thought an idea like this would resonate with so many different people?"

"There is a bigger question here," Ryan interjected. "Is the average person qualified to vote on every bill? Surely, we elect a politician because they have at least some qualifications."

Bea knew this question was coming and had hoped Harold would answer it. Her gut told her to attack: 'How dare you question the competence of the citizenry. But the vibe of the interview felt too light to smack the question down. She responded, "There is no level of education or competency requirement for an MP, and they vote on all legislation."

Melissa said, "I think the election process itself is how an MP proves his competency. The average person doesn't spend the time educating himself on the issues."

Bea felt an argument brewing that had no winner. She brought it back to the system, "If a voter doesn't feel confident to cast a ballot on an issue, the App allows them to vote along their preferred party's line."

"Melissa has a good point," Ryan dug deeper. "What if a political group on one side of the issue wanted to influence voters with outright lies. Wouldn't it be easier to change the mind of a naive person rather than a savvy politician? Especially now with social media so prevalent."

Owls, Doughnuts, and Democracy, by Jason A. N. Taylor

"Good question, Ryan..." Bea felt the ship sinking. This was an argument they should not engage in. "There's an entire industry for influencing politicians. To my mind that is the main reason trust in the political system is waning. If direct democracy was the way of Canadian politics the political influencer would have to change the mind of millions of people, not just one."

"I can see lobbyists changing focus from politicians to influencing the population." Melissa thought aloud. "I think that might be easier, like a PR campaign."

"That's why education is important..." Bea knew this wasn't strong enough and wasn't sure she believed it either. "I trust an ecosystem of information will develop to keep the electorate informed."

Ryan interrupted, "We now have ex-Conservative MP and Leader of Direct Democracy, Harold Gordon, online."

A unicorn appeared. "Hello... Hello... am I on..?" The unicorn spoke with Harold's voice. "Someone said I'd be put on the air. I see Bea, Cat, the hosts, and a unicorn in a small box. Holy doodle! Morty, is this thing working? I don't think the doohickey is working."

The four others were biting their tongues to keep from laughing.

Muffled and not in the picture, Morty answered, "I followed the instructions my son gave me exactly. It is working. The unicorn is always there."

Melissa started laughing. It was contagious. The others joined in.

"Fiddlesticks!" The unicorn bayed. "Did I get transferred to a comedy show by mistake?"

"Harold, the unicorn filter is hilarious, but you can turn it off now," Bea laugh-talked. "It should be on the right-side menu of the phone." She messaged Irene to help Harold.

"Unicorn! Filter! Speak English, woman! What do you mean?"

"You have an electronic unicorn mask over your face."

"The unicorn is ME! Morty, turn it off!"

Almost drowned out by laughter, Morty said, "This is how it looks when I call my son. Maybe you should call in again."

"Harold don't hang up! We can continue with the filter on," Bea coached.

"Oh that was a good laugh." Melissa wiped an eye teared up from laughter. "If you don't mind Harold, we can do our best to overlook the filter."

Ryan added, "That's a first. Thanks for the laugh."

"The unicorn filter Harold had on is an over-the-top example of how politicians prepare for interviews like this." Bea brought the show back on topic. "They judge the audience beforehand and create a mask of talking points to frame the message for the audience in front of them. This puts the best side of the issue forward. Harold did this accidentally, politicians do it purposefully. Right Harold?"

"Uhm... yes... I ah... the last time I was in office I would have different points for different towns, events, or TV channels." Harold spoke softly at first but became more strident. "It was to put the best spin on a topic. Swaying a few people to my side could be the difference between winning and losing. For example, for free trade I would hit the benefits for exporting timber to small towns. For the city's cross boarder shoppers, I would sell the savings on groceries." Harold paused as what looked like Irene moved through the frame behind him. "Bea, can you take over a second... Irene is here."

"Certainly Harold. A Direct Democracy MP does not need to mask the party's position by framing an issue positively..."

The unicorn filter vanished.

"Who's the coffin dodger?" Harold joked. "Bring back the unicorn to hide this old monster. It is me! Time has not been kind. Seriously... when I got into politics it was to bring my constituent's voices, Vancouver Island voices, to Ottawa. Once in Ottawa I found that most of my job was to make the Progressive Conservative message palatable to my constituency. I hated doing that, but I told myself I would hold to my guns on what really mattered. I hope I did. I know there are times I did not. If my younger self had had the option of Direct Democracy, he would have fought for it because it gives an opportunity for each man to be heard on the issues he values. A Christian's religion comes before his party. For me, democracy comes before my political views."

Bea loved what Harold said and continued fervently, "Having one's say and being heard is one of the most validating things in life. However, I hear from people every day that our leaders are not listening. This is what I think causes people to disengage from political discourse. Direct democracy gives a voice to all people. It allows people to have their diverse political views counted because the constituency can vote differently than the party bound traditional MP. If that view won the majority, the Direct Democracy MP will vote with the majority in the House of Commons. Direct Democracy is the party of diversity of thought."

"Wow, I love that passion," Ryan interjected. "I wish we had time to continue the revolution."

"You'll have to have us on again," Harold said.

"I'm sure our viewers will want an update on Direct Democracy. Thank you, Cat, Bea, and Harold. Have a good night! Hustle hit and never quit!" Melissa signed off with COPT's obligatory hockey saying.

Bea, Cat, and Harold waved as the call dropped off.

The meeting room door reflected Bea's smile back to her. The interview was great. Harold's technical difficulties made it even better. She bounced and squealed in her seat. A ringing phone stopped her. "Hello?"

"Bea. Harold. I'd like you to come debrief over dinner. I've got the kitchen to make us Yorkshire pudding."

Bea thought of her dinner options, KD and Ramen noodles. "Sure."

On the way out of the office, Mike called to Bea, "Is everything alright?"

Bea turned, "It went great. Better than expected." She smiled, waved and walked out of the office like a model in a woman's razor ad. Only when she was out of the building did she remember she had told Mike it was a doctor's appointment.

The dining room was almost empty at five twenty-eight pm. Bea easily found the table with Harold and Irene.

Irene spoke first, "Good God, I am glad to see you, Bea. I've been trying to tell this lummox I don't eat meat and I've had dinner.

But he insists that we will be getting Yorkshire pudding. I'm doing my best to tell myself the only way a chauvinist knows how to thank a person is with meat."

"Irene!" Harold was genuinely shocked. "You don't eat meat? You should have told me."

Irene rolled her eyes.

Bea said, "That was a great interview."

"Don't lie to me Bea. I was only following Morty's instructions. I'm not sure he knows what he's doing." Harold picked up his wine glass to toast, "But you two saved it. I should have listened to you. Next time we'll practice. Cheers to Bea and Irene!"

"The entire interview was great." Bea offered her glass to be clinked. "The unicorn will be remembered."

"Don't mention that damned thing!" Harold cried.

Irene rubbed it in, "The unicorn was the best part. I nearly choked with laughter."

"Harold... Irene and I are grateful for your thanks and glad you understand we can help, but this was a huge success. There's a good chance the unicorn will go viral. That'll get us lots of views. Our message was strong."

Harold furrowed his brow. "Hmm, maybe you're right. They say any media is good media. Thank you, Irene, and Bea."

Irene got one last jab in, "Thank you for all the laughs."

The three of them ate four dinners and viewed the interview. All agreed that it was great. Even better was the fact that the unicorn clip was going viral. Bea got a message to the elderly internet army to share everything everywhere, posting it on Reddit, Facebook, Instagram, TikTok and Twitter.

Before the group went their separate ways Harold asked Irene: "How many steps do you have?"

"Eight thousand."

"Hah! I might win tonight. I have six thousand. Unless you get another two thousand tonight," Harold gloated.

"I'll win." Irene winked. "I sleepwalk dreaming of my wife a lot."

Harold saw Bea's confusion. "Irene and I have a contest. How many steps we can get in a day. If I get half the steps she does, I win her dessert. When she wins, I hand over a drink ticket. I have yet to win. The real goal is fitness, and we're both winners on that front. I feel like a millennial."

"I don't," Irene said. "I'm in it to win it… loser."

Harold thanked Irene and Bea once more and all went their separate ways.

Bea found her way into Beacon Hill Park, rounding out her great day with four owls. The pair of great horned owls and the pair of barreds.

12.

The next morning when Bea opened the Direct Democracy inbox there were forty-seven new emails. For the first time the minority were from members in need of technical assistance. Around twenty were from people interested in joining. Eight were from political or humour YouTubers requesting appearances. A few more were influencers trying to get rights for the unicorn video.

Bea could not arrange appearances on the YouTube channels around her work schedule, so she emailed Ajay, Cat, Derek, Harold and Irene to practice the technical side of the interviews. By morning coffee, all had gotten back to her for a practice run that night. Ajay emailed that he could not attend but would set up meetings to practice on different platforms. The rest would be at the Home. Harold even saved her from choosing between KD and Ramen again, inviting her to dinner.

A fresh ocean wind whipped fallen cherry blossoms around James Bay. Though the cherry trees had few if any flowers, tulips bloomed in front of the Empress and the first camas flowered in Beacon Hill Park. It was well into spring, but Bea was glad to have brought her Cowichan jacket and worn fuzzy leggings under her spring dress. James Bay was always cool because of frigid the Salish Sea being so close.

There was fine food and company at dinner. By quarter to six the group got down to business. Ajay sent out meeting requests for Zoom, Skype, Teams, and Messenger. Cat and Bea demonstrated to Derek, Harold, and Irene how to use the meeting apps. Then Derek, Harold, and Irene would try it themselves.

It was a tough go at first. Harold was getting frustrated. Irene was not helping by laughing at Harold's frustration. Then it happened. Harold yelled, "Why don't they make these damn things like cars! Every car has a gas pedal, a brake pedal, a gear shift, and a steering wheel."

"They are like cars!" Bea screamed back. Then she grabbed the tablets from each of them, signed each tablet onto a different meeting app, and lined them up on the wall. She screeched while pointing at the appropriate icon, "Zoom, gas pedal. Skype, gas pedal. TEAMS gas pedal."

Cat began to laugh. Then Derek did.

"Eureka! I get it!" Harold exclaimed.

Derek, Harold, and Irene did one last run-through using the different apps with few mistakes that they easily corrected themselves. Harold declared the training a success.

They moved on to scheduling the next interviews. Priority was given to the YouTubers Cat had originally gotten to review the video. The next two interviews, Bea would stay quiet as a backup, with Harold speaking and Irene providing technical assistance. After those two shows, Harold, Irene, and Derek would be on their own. Harold was, as always, confident. Bea had faith in Derek and Irene.

Derek excused himself immediately after the meeting. Harold was quick to follow but not before asking Irene how many steps she had today.

Irene answered, "7000-ish."

"I've got you this time woman! I'm at 6295, and it is seven-thirty. There's no way you'll get 13000," Harold beamed as he stiffly shuffled away.

"I will still win."

When Harold was out of earshot, Bea asked, "Why are you so confident?"

"Have a drink with me in the lounge and I'll tell you."

"Bea," Cat interjected. "I have an opportunity for you and an idea for Direct Democracy. Can I join?"

"Certainly," Irene answered. Bea went to get drinks and the two ladies found a table.

Bea brought glasses of wine and sat down.

"Harold challenged me to a step contest," Irene explained to Cat. "I thought why not. Maybe the old lummox will get fit, and I can always use the drink credits. But I've been cheating." She leaned close to her two listeners and spoke in a low voice. "I found that using my Hitachi gets me lots of steps. Every night using my magic wand I fantasize about when my partner and I were young and beat Harold in the step challenge."

"Irene!" Bea said, then was overcome with laughter.

Cat looked confused. "Hitachi?"

Bea said through laughter, "A personal massager."

Wide-eyed, Cat replied, "Oh my."

"Don't be so shocked. I'm old, not dead."

"Cheers to getting more steps than Harold. Great, if he talks about the contest, I'm going to start laughing 100%." Bea changed the topic, "I'm glad you guys are getting on top of the tech."

"I always understood," Irene assured. "And Harold doesn't seem scared of apps anymore. He'll be fine. I have an idea I want to run by you two. Whether we like it or not, our supporters will fall into groups that basically follow the traditional party lines. Socialists will identify as NDP. Capitalists will identify with Conservatives. I think we need to embrace that by establishing our own conversation leaders for each political group. For example, I'm a Liberal these days, I would focus on sending out a Liberal message to those of like mind in Direct Democracy."

Cat jumped on board, "That's a great idea. We could use an app like WhatsApp to push out messages with political content that aligns with her politics, with the same underlying Direct Democracy message. By customizing our content to the party she identifies with, we do not risk losing a member with a message targeted at a person who leans a different direction politically."

"Sure… let's tell Harold," Bea said.

The conversation changed to who might be the best leader for each political group. Their consensus had Rick as the NDP leader. Irene for the Liberal spokesperson. One of the Harold's lads as the Peoples Party of Canada's sharpest tool. They all knew Harold would want to be the Conservative chief but thought the leader of Direct Democracy should not have a political agenda.

When that discussion petered out, Cat exclaimed, "Oh Bea, I almost forgot. Ajay heard from Dr. John Fridman from the University's poly-sci department. The professor finds Direct Democracy intriguing and wants to see if someone, you, wanted to speak to his class about it. Ajay wanted you to speak to the class on your own, without Harold. Ajay said that Dr. Fridman remembers you from your undergrad."

"That's really flattering. But I think Harold should be there. He's the face of the party."

"Bea, do you think a class of Gen Z's are going to listen to grandpa tell them how good the old days were and that they're lazy? They won't listen to him. Or the time will be taken by budding Conservatives wanting to hear war stories from an old Conservative warhorse and not learn about Direct Democracy."

"Good points. And I still think he should be involved."

Irene tut-tutted, "You can speak to that demographic better than Harold. Don't let the fearless leader overshadow what you have to offer. It is your invitation, not his. If you tell him, he will push himself in. It's all he knows."

"You can't let Ajay know I told you this," Cat said slyly. "Ajay mentors a computer science student in the class who's odd and wicked smart. He's apparently even worked on security and transparency for a First Nations voting app. If Harold was there this guy would likely be turned off by all the colonial old white man-ness floating around."

"Oh, stop being coy," Irene rolled her eyes. "You're trying to set Bea up with this mystery man."

"No, I'm not!"

"I'm not looking for a hook-up," Bea chided. "This is business to me."

"Exactly," Cat said. "Direct Democracy needs this man's help."

"Well, okay. If Ajay and you think doing the class without Harold is that important, I'll do it."

The conversation meandered.

Irene mentioned how happy Sandy had been to take Sam on his birthday tour.

"Irene, I almost forgot," Bea said, then fished around in her bag. "I got you this necklace for arranging Sam's owl evening."

"Ooo that's nice." Irene put on the necklace. "It suits my outfit. Where did you get it?"

"The James Bay Market," Bea answered. "From Bug and Buddha. Angie, the vendor is great. She had paintings, stained glass, upcycled China jewelry, like what I got you... Oh, she makes book covers too."

"I will check her out next week." Irene gave Bea as stern look. "You didn't have to get me this."

"It's nothing."

"You shouldn't have. Seeing Sam so happy was enough for me."

"Sam sounds like a great kid," Cat said. "I'm not really a kid person."

"I love Sam but I'm not sure I'm a kid person either."

"What do you mean? Ajay told me you fought hard to get custody."

"I did... but it's ah, complicated." For the first time since the breakup Bea felt she could share how she felt. "It was the summer before my third year of university. I was madly in love with Marcus, possibly obsessed. We had moved in together. I certainly thought we would marry sometime down the road. He fully believed at some point when we were settled, we would have kids. He believed there is a time when a woman's biological clock goes off and all she wants to do is push out babies. It seemed as if every woman in my life was saying when you find the right man or when you near thirty a switch will flip, and you'll want a kid."

Bea paused for wine, "I was good with not wanting a kid at twenty. Who knows who I would be at thirty. I did know that if I had children, it would be in an equal relationship, one where if I had the better job he'd do childcare. But mostly it was not something I thought of... Come to think of it, maybe I didn't think of it because I didn't want any." Bea gazed into the distance. "I usually only dream of what I want."

"Makes sense," Cat added. "I've never wanted children and I never think or dream of them. Unless some little bastard is throwing a tantrum at a store. What a nightmare."

"It became a moot point, though I've always been cautious with birth control. I had heard somewhere that antibiotics can mess with birth control. I had been on them for strep throat. A few weeks later, I was late. I bought a Dollar Store test, it was positive. I got a pharmacy test, it was positive."

"The Dollar Store sells pregnancy tests?"

"Uh-huh, an aisle full of them." Bea was disdainful. "But no condoms."

"That says something," Cat quipped.

Irene said, "How did you get pregnant?"

"The old-fashioned way! I thought it was the antibiotics, but Google said it was not them... then Good luck... then because the world was out to get me... but in the end, it was statistics. There's a one percent chance of getting pregnant on the pill. In a real-world setting, like with women not being perfect about taking it, it is more like ten percent."

Cat tapped at her phone. "Whoa, in typical use over a year, nine in one hundred women will get pregnant taking the combined pill."

"I hadn't thought of what I'd do if I got pregnant. I was so cautious I was sure it wouldn't happen. He was supportive of what I wanted but called the pregnancy a miracle. He argued that it was inevitable we'd have children. It was happening sooner than planned, that's all. I'd get Sam off to a good start and when Sam was old enough, I'd get back to university. His family would make sure I would not have to work. I remember crying, being confused, and not ready for this. He backed off, suggesting we take a couple of days to let it sink in and then discuss it seriously.

"I thought I was..." Bea stopped speaking, took a deep breath and continued. "I thought I was well educated enough to make an informed decision with no need to talk with counsellors. But now, when I'm struggling to talk in the abstract about that time of my life, I see how naive I was. This is almost contradictory, but I don't think I could have made a decision that was right for me without having an uninvested person to help sort my thoughts out."

Irene patted Bea's hand. "It is not contradictory at all."

"That was only half of it. I had all the objectivity of someone madly in love. I could not see any future that did not have Marcus and happily ever after in it. All the things that would later become the reasons we split up were there, but I didn't internalize them. Things like 'it is a miracle you are pregnant,' 'if you want to go back to school when Sam's older,' and 'you would not have to work.'"

"Bea, a miracle?" Irene gasped. "Do you think Marcus tampered with your birth control?"

"It crossed my mind. But when I say I was cautious about birth control, it was more like paranoid. I kept it on my person at all times. A few times a day I checked to see that I'd taken it. I made sure.

"Anyway..." Bea got back to the story, "We had only been going out for eight months. Three months of that time we weren't exclusively dating each other. To be honest, the relationship was monogamish or swinging until the pregnancy. We had only moved in together two months before. How could I believe I knew someone when I had only lived with them for a couple of months? But I was madly in love, maybe obsessed.

"It should have struck me as weird when Sabrina, Marcus's mother, called the day after I found out. She told me, she had Marcus earlier than she wanted. I'm sure that he had told her I was pregnant. I found out later he told her everything... but I'm pretty sure she called on her own. He hated when she interfered, and she loves manipulating."

"Codependent cow," Cat muttered,

"Because of work, I didn't see Marcus until late the next night. I took another test; it was positive again. I hadn't moved much beyond the shock of it. I was happy when he said he wasn't ready for a serious conversation; I was all for postponing it. He said he was going to take the day after tomorrow off so we could talk."

"In the meantime, I worked my two server jobs. I was too busy to give my situation the thought it needed. And I didn't have anyone I trusted to talk with."

"No family?" Irene asked.

"Only child. And I didn't trust my parents' opinions even on serious matters like what dish soap to buy. I certainly wasn't going to take their advice on children. My only close female friend continually told me Marcus was a catch. She parroted that it was fate. As a naively optimistic twenty-year-old, my mind was dominated by the possibility of a super couple splitting the childcare duties while fighting for social justice."

"That said, I was technically, if not emotionally ready for a serious conversation. I researched all options, including not having Sam." Bea tapped on her phone as she talked. "This is what happened." Bea turned the phone toward Cat and Irene.

The screen showed Bea standing on the edge of a picnic blanket covering the rocks of Finlayson Point. She was more beautiful than the view of Clover Point, Trial Island, and the glass calm ocean she was looking at. The green of the shore and lightly clothed beach goers indicated that it was warm. Marcus's arm could be seen adjusting the frame a little. Bea gazed at the ocean as Marcus positioned himself on a knee in front of the camera. "Bea, I love you. Will you marry me?"

"Huh?" She turned. She put a hand to her mouth.

"Will you marry me?" He said louder then opened a box with a large diamond ring in it.

"What?!" She started to cry.

"I love you, Bea. Will you marry me?"

"Say yes!" a guy on the beach yelled. Many more people joined in.

"Yes." Bea answered through tears, almost too softly to be heard on the video.

The people clapped. Marcus put the ring on her as she sobbed. He stood to kiss her. It took some time before the kiss could be considered romantic."

"There was no need for a discussion after that." Bea stopped the video and wiped a wet eye. "We spent the rest of the day ensuring I was pregnant."

"A knight in shining armour saved you?" Cat said sarcastically.

"It was Disney or Hallmark to begin with. Marcus proposed the week after Canada Day. His family wanted the wedding the last weekend of August. In the two weeks we had dinners with all his family and mine to meet everyone. We had to arrange for a place, catering, and all the rest. I quickly found out all I had to do was identify what Sabrina wanted and do that. It was chaos but at the same time I was being treated like a princess. The little girl in me was loving every minute."

Irene identified with Bea. "Before I met my partner, I would become a linebacker when the bouquet was thrown. This at a time when legally I could not get married to who I wanted to marry."

"I hate children," Cat chimed in. "But I love baby showers. Weirdness."

"The closer we got to the wedding the busier I was. No matter, I loved the attention. Our big day came. It was perfect. A freak thunderstorm drenched us during our pictures at the Oak Bay Golf Course. The best part was that it gave us cover for why we looked so disheveled and flushed for the pictures." Bea winked.

"At the reception, Marcus's parents told us we would no longer have to pay rent to live in their condo so we could save for a house. We got a honeymoon trip to Kaua'i the day after the wedding, too, at a five-star resort. Way nicer than anything I had ever experienced. My parents bitched that they had to pay for the open bar. I'm pretty sure the only reason they paid for that was because they didn't want to look cheap. They certainly got their money's worth."

"Oh God! I almost forgot. It was only almost perfect. When creatively hiding from the rain, we found a dead barred owl in the bush at the golf course. Poor young owl."

Cat and Irene both went silent.

"Midway through the honeymoon," Bea became more serious, "I got my first taste of reality. Marcus was online signing up for his classes in the fall semester. I was so busy I forgot to do mine. I was livid that he didn't say anything to me. His answer was patronizing, I was pregnant and should not go to university in my state. I flipped. I would just barely be six months along at the end of semester. I said, if I can still fuck at six months pregnant, I can damn well go to classes. Late signing up, I didn't get the classes I wanted. From then on, every time I had morning sickness or griped about being pregnant, I would get a barrage of calls for me to stop going to school and give up my part time job. It only made me want to continue. By winter semester I was worn out. It was easier not to fight. And once Sam was out, I reasoned, I'd be back in university."

"Was Marcus lying to you?" Cat asked.

"Marcus didn't lie, he was just vague. For example, he would say, 'when you don't have to take care of Sam.' I couldn't tell if this would be when a nanny took care of Sam or when he was out of high school. I assumed it would be when we settled into a sharing routine."

"When Sam was around four months old, with the fall semester nearing, I wanted to take at least one course. By this time Sabrina was taking Sam three or more times a week. Marcus could take care of Sam while studying. There was no reason I couldn't take a course. Instead, I ended up with a personal trainer for me to lose the nonexistent baby weight."

"Chauvinist pig!" Irene blurted.

"I'm exaggerating. The trainer was my fallback idea. Marcus went for it because the gym was close to the condo, and it would work around his mother's time with Sam more easily.

"I might not have been in the classes, but I had all the work I could handle. Marcus was struggling and I picked up the load to make the argument I could go back to school. Over the fall semester, I wrote half of his papers and edited the rest. There were few assignments of his I did not work on. I wanted to show him I could do it and it would help me when I got back to school. He was all too ready to play up how tired he was from Sam keeping him awake to get me to do his work."

"It became blatantly obvious what our families wanted from me Sam's first Christmas. My mom talked up how nice it would be to have two grand kids. She said I would have been better with a brother. I would be less spoiled." Bea snorted, "Because getting clothes at Value Village is spoiled. Sabrina had written a letter to Santa from Sam asking for a brother or sister. To follow that up Sabrina had Sam give us a romantic Valentine's Day to Tofino for storm watching and to make a brother or sister for him."

"Isn't that too soon to have another kid?" Cat asked, outraged.

"Technically no, but there are risks. Marcus's family had a tradition of close siblings."

Bea got back to the story. "During the fall semester, I would say I fell out of obsession with Marcus. I still loved him, but he could do wrong. By Christmas I was starting to see the ideological differences we had. Like I was not sure I wanted the kid we had, and he wants a second… It was then that I decided he and I needed to discuss the future in a concrete way. I believed we could work it out. Before Sam, he had seemed to be on board with both of us striving for high-powered careers and sharing responsibility. I wrote a list of what I wanted; to go to university, have a career, not sure about more children, that kind of stuff. I showed it to him after Christmas. He did not get it. He responded by asking if I had ever had it better materially. He did not use 'materially', but that was what he meant. I answered honestly, that yes, I did indeed have more 'materially' than I had ever had. He then asked if that was true, why did I need to go to university or get a job? I told him it was my dream, that I was unhappy just taking care of Sam. I wanted more. He couldn't get that I wanted more than to be happily bored, taking care of the kids in nice dresses. I did get through to him that I wanted us to get counselling. Or I mostly did. Seeing the distance between Marcus and I was greater than I thought, I did not push to get back to university.

"Marcus did arrange counselling for me. Going on my own did not set off any alarms because I assumed that each of us would start with an individual session or two before joint ones. But the sign on the counsellor's door saying she specialized in post-partum depression should have been a hint. When I did the depression screening, I was not depressed. When I told the counsellor the rest of the story, she suggested couples therapy. I told her that's what I suggested to my husband, but this is what I got.

"Doing therapy showed me how blind I was to reality. I was isolated. The only people in my life not family were this counsellor and my trainer. Though the therapist was professionally neutral, the fact Marcus's family was paying for the sessions made me less open. I went to three, during which I made plans to either get the freedoms I wanted or exit the relationship. It was a nine-month plan."

"The first three months would be used to salvage the relationship if possible. I still loved Marcus. In my mind he was innocent, it was a combination of fear and a solution provided by his family that changed his beliefs. I started with meetings between us where we were to discuss what we wanted from the relationship and a bunch of other bullshit I found in relationship books. The meetings got off to a bad start. In the first one we fought over why I was back on birth control when it was obvious, we wanted another child. That argument lasted until our next discussion. But I was hopeful because he understood that I did not want another child in the next year. He decided to support me on that."

Bea gazed out the window and said, "In this first argument there was this part of my mind that was yelling. It screamed, 'Marcus is framing the argument to make another child the only option. Don't get sucked in! You did not even want the child you have.' But the voice was lost in the dirty diaper of reality."

"Marcus was granite as the weeks passed. He would not move. I was getting more worn down than he was. Worse was that we could have this heated argument, then he could disengage, moving on without it affecting him. Like he could go from our fight, to loving husband making dinner or bringing daffodils home and we'd be lovers again without missing a beat. I would fall for it. It is what makes him so good at his job, he can consistently press his points and be your buddy. The progress was glacial. Nearing the three months mark, his position was that I could go to school when the kids were in school."

Cat clarified, "Kids?"

Bea nodded, "Yup. Kids. He had backed away from having a second one right away. But still brought it up as a way for me to get back to university sooner. At the time, I thought this was progress. I was considering extending the three months or lowering my expectations. Then I overheard one of Marcus's calls with his mother. She was browbeating him over the phone. She was telling him what he wanted. He wanted another kid soon. He wanted me to take care of the kids. All he had to do was to be firm, kind, and patient. If he did that, inevitably I would come around. I lost it. In a rage, I confronted him. Yelling that his mother was a conniving bitch. Accusing him of loving her more than me. Belittling him for being a momma's boy. He cried, admitting he loved his mother and listened to her too much. It was the only time I saw him truly weep. Then he made fondue. We made up. As the week went on, I was closer to trying to meet in the middle than ever before. Just before Marcus and my recurring discussion, my dad called me. He only called if someone died, except this time. He called because mother was broken-up over Marcus and my fight. I had no idea how they found out. He said there was no place for me at their home if I got divorced – not that there was in any other circumstance. I should stop being so uppity."

"Your father is an old school asshole," Irene confirmed.

"That sums dad up. The call was fresh in my mind when Marcus and I had our discussion. And we were back at square one. No change. A fucking immovable object. I was incensed. I took a walk to ponder my situation. I was so lost in my thoughts that I did not see an owl until it swooped at a squirrel on the maple tree next to me but missed. I can still hear the scratching of the owl's talons on the rough tree bark. The owl watching quieted my mind."

"What's with owls and you?" Cat asked.

"There are lots of owls around Victoria. I like owls so I notice them. Owls seem not to hate me. Or most owls don't." Bea got back to the story. "It was clear from my father's call that Marcus had support from both families. There was no middle way. I had two options: submit or leave. I decided to leave. The situation went against everything I believed. Regardless of wanting children or not, I wanted to live equitably with Marcus. I wanted to have my say and be heard. I wanted decisions to be made that considered both of our desires. I knew this meant compromise for both of us. And likely more for me as opportunities are better for men – male privilege. I was ok with that if the decision we made was made with reasonableness. For example, there was every chance that if I was able to take a course when Sam was four months it would have been too much. If that was the case, I was ready to stay at home. I did not get the chance. It was not Marcus's fault, not totally. It was mostly caused by beliefs and traditions that make the equality we have less equitable. Like a rich person getting a fairer trial than a poor one. Or in my case, the wife's traditional role dominating how the families and

Owls, Doughnuts, and Democracy, by Jason A. N. Taylor

Marcus saw me. It is that pressure to conform to the norm of the group, like women crossing our legs when sitting, even when wearing pants." Bea splayed her legs wide while wearing a dress. "But I did not want to become how they saw me. That made me want to fight. Because I was forced into this decision, I decided to fight for at least half custody of Sam. I would also be righteous by not fighting for spousal support beyond getting settled in a new place. I felt I had to prove I could do all the things Marcus did not want me to do."

Irene spoke, "It's the same fight I've been fighting since the sixties. Equality in the law is not equality in real life. Men making more money than women, literally makes men worth more than women. The equality provided by the Human Rights Code is less equitable for a woman because of social factors beyond the law."

"When I got home, I Googled getting divorced. In BC, the grounds for divorce were separation of a year, adultery, or physical or mental abuse. Marcus was not abusive. Neither of us was committing adultery, yet."

"From what I've heard," Cat interrupted, "Marcus was being mentally abusive. Not giving you equal say in the marriage or considering your desires is abusive to me. Crushing your dream while he lives his best life? That's fucking cruel." Irene supported what Cat said.

"It was the Judge's opinion that mattered, he didn't see it that way. But I'm getting ahead of myself. When I got home, I separated our lives as much as possible in a 950 square foot two-bedroom apartment. While Marcus was at university, I moved everything I had into the bedroom with Sam. Thankfully, I did not have much stuff. When he got home, he noticed all my shoes moved to inside the door of my new room. It looked sad. He asked what I was doing. I told him I wanted a divorce, and we were separated. He said, 'Sleeping in Sam's room will make you responsible for taking care of him when he wakes up.' I told him that I already did that. He went to his room. I think he already knew it was coming or was in shock."

"Who cares what he thought!" Cat exclaimed.

"The first couple weeks, I had great resolve. I only stepped into the other areas of the apartment when Marcus was there for the necessities, food, washroom, and to go out. I talked with Sabrina sometime in the second week. She had come to help with Sam. She started crying as I was getting ready for a run. She begged me to talk. I agreed. She could not understand what changed from the wedding when she and I got on well. I told her what I wanted. She said, 'Naive girl, we all have dreams like that… but we must grow up.' I told her, I did most of his work at university, it should be me going to law school. She countered by saying that I was getting to do the academic work I wanted. She then lectured me on the roles of men and women. Her philosophy boiled down to the wife supporting her man because men will get further than women, regardless of her ability, it's just the way the world works. He was to treat her like a princess, and in time there would be room for her to pursue her dream but after her husband and children. She guaranteed her boy would treat me like a princess and in time I would, like she did, find great joy in married life. She asked if he had treated me like a princess. I said yes but I wanted to be treated like a partner. I got back to my run. I had a similar call with my mother except it had more four-letter words and name calling."

Cat huffed, "I'm sure they vote Conservative and would be for 'making Canada great again' if the saying was not associated with the President Pussy Grabber."

"My parents are supporters of President Tiny Hands." That left Cat speechless. "Marcus's parents are mostly Green but socially conservative. The Green party has some strange religiousness to it."

Irene asked, "You were able to make a clean break from Marcus?"

"God no! We were pretty good at sleeping in separate beds, but it wasn't three months before we were fooling around again. My lawyer told me this would be a big problem for a contentious divorce because Marcus could argue we were acting like a married couple. This is when I was really glad Marcus got me a trainer. It made the reason for divorce much easier. If there is adultery, the year separation can be skipped. There was one big challenge, it would not be as easy as me saying I slept around. Our relationship was pretty open. If Marcus caught me fooling around, he would say it was an open relationship. His mother was a different story. If she caught me, it would be over. The hard part was getting the trainer and me caught by her. What I thought would be a one-time tryst to end the marriage became a saga. Getting the trainer interested was easy. All I had to do was ask him for a ride..." Bea paused. "Home. What was his name? I'll remember. The plan was to park in front of the condo and get caught by her in the back seat. I figured we had a ten-minute window to get caught. After a couple minutes, we were cleaning up and he was apologizing for being too excited. I told him I was flattered at how turned on he was, but next time more foreplay please. He was muscular and big but inexperienced. I was willing to give him some training. A half-dozen attempts met with the same problem. No matter the amount of practice he was quick. I should have noticed when he gave me classes for free, brought me flowers, and other gifts, that he didn't get the situation. It seemed obvious... but whatever.

"I pulled out all the stops the time we got caught. We were in the condo totally naked. I waited till Sabrina was walking up to the entrance with Sam's stroller to start the main event. He was thrusting away, with his back to the entrance way. I was lying on the dining room table. I saw her watch for what felt like a minute before she said, 'Marcus... that's not Marcus!'"

Cat gasped. The peanut gallery said a communal, "Well I never." Irene toasted Bea, smiling with approval.

"The trainer did not hear her. I said take a picture, it'll last longer. She screeched, 'What are you doing! Sam is in the room, have you no shame?! Get out!' When the trainer noticed, he ran to the living room. I threw the trainer his clothes. Then I stood between the trainer and her, ushering him to the door. She was pretending to feel faint, asking where she could sit that had not been defiled. Mostly naked, I took Sam's stroller into my room and put on a large hoody. She yelled through the wall, 'Now you're going to beg me not to tell Marcus? To think my husband wanted to give you and Marcus this condo. But I knew you were a tramp. Thank God he listened to me.' I said to her that I wanted out of the marriage and if Marcus had listened to me more than you, it would not have come to this. I think she was hoping I would beg for forgiveness, and then she could blackmail me into staying. I felt I had freed myself."

Irene praised Bea, "No wonder you got pregnant on birth control, you got a damn big pair of ovaries."

"The drama was not over. I had enough of listening to Sabrina grumbling at the Morie Povich show in the other room. I went for a walk with Sam. During the walk I got a call from the trainer... arrgg... I still can't remember his name. He professed his love to me. Told me, it was all his fault for thinking with his dick. He said Sam and I could live at his place. If I was worried my husband would harm me or Sam, he'd protect us. I said it was sweet of him to offer but I did not need a place to stay. Bluntly, I told him I was using him to get divorced and I would not be seeing him anymore as a trainer or trainee. Then I hung up because Sam and I had stumbled on to a pair of owlets in Beacon Hill Park. It was so long ago I don't think it was Josie or her family. Sam was pointing and smiling at the owlets screeching their steam kettle call. He always loved owls."

Bea returned to the story. "The trainer called me for a few weeks. He was more pathetic with each call. The poor guy had it bad. I truly believe he was worried about Sam and me. He was sounding more depressed with each call. I had to tell him to get counselling. He did. He emailed me a few months later that the counselling worked. He was grateful I helped him learn who he was. He also found out he had anxiety, and the medication fixed his quickness. He wanted to show me. I was tempted to find out, but my life was falling apart. God, I feel so bad I can't remember his name."

"Bea! You're a horrible woman," Cat said jokingly. "That's two men you've made better with casual sex. And you can't even remember one of their names."

Irene was confused by the comment. Bea was confused for a second too, until she realized Cat was referring to Ajay. Bea said, "It's a shame I never get the fruits of my labour. Even Marcus turned out better but there was more drama to come. My mother helped with Sam too. I knew there was going to be a scene when she came to get Sam a few days after I got caught. I prepared for it because when I was in my early teens, Mom and I would get in physical fights. Most of the time I was the first to get physical. My home life sucked. Selfishly, I wanted Mom to still provide some free daycare for Sam after the divorce. Free childcare was one of the few things Mom gave me. I had planned to get away from Mom when she arrived at the condo. I would push Sam out of my room into the living room run through the kitchen back to my room, the opposite way from the direction Mom would come."

Bea let out a long sigh. "It did not work out that way. Marcus met Mom at the door. I pushed the stroller out, saw Marcus in the kitchen, thinking Mom would be behind him. I went down the other hall where I literally bumped into Mom. She said, 'What's that awful smell?' I had nowhere to go. I was trying not to slap her. But she made it worse, she said, 'Ew, it smells like whore.' She pulled out a bottle of cheap perfume spraying me in the face. She said, 'This'll cover the smell of your stinky twat.' She knew perfume gives me migraines. She continued spraying me with it like it was a water gun. Enough that it blinded me. I lost it. I started swinging at her. Not slaps but punches. Marcus got between us. Most of my punches got him. When I heard I was hitting him I stopped. By then the damage was done. I beelined it to the washroom to get the perfume out of my eyes. My mom was crying that her eye was swelling shut. She called the police. The apartment smelled awful. Sam was balling. When I could see, I went to open the windows. Marcus was leaning over the kitchen sink, nose bleeding badly. I told him I was sorry and helped him pinch off his nose. He understood. I threw a bag of frozen peas to my mom. She related this to the 911 operator as a renewed assault. I took Sam on the balcony out of the perfume to wait for the cops. When the police arrived, Mom and Marcus were coughing from the perfume. The cops had to take statements outside because of the reek."

Irene asked, "Is that why you got a restraining order against you?"

"Yup. The peace bond happened from that. My mom charged me with assault. I charged her too. Luckily, the charges went nowhere but cost lots of money to get there. The peace bond was a dumb idea because they could not meet me to get Sam. I wonder where my intelligence came from. It was this incident that got me here, literally. This was when my lawyer told me I should volunteer to look better. It was also when things spiraled truly out of control, going very badly for me." Bea pulled her legs up onto the chair, hugging them so she was almost in the fetal position.

Cat said lightly, "Surely, it can't get worse?"

Bea did not react to Cat's quip. "After the incident, Marcus moved to his parents' house. As much as we were at odds, his company kept me saner. On my own, with the wreckage of the incident to clean up, almost no money, and my only hope getting custody of Sam, I was depressed. Both sets of parents pulled out all the stops to get Marcus as much custody as possible. Sabrina would intentionally be late to get Sam, making me late for work. I was told if I was late again, I would be fired. I left Sam on his own knowing she was five minutes away. She used it against me, calling me a bad mother in front of the judge. They used the perfume incident to say I had been abusive to Marcus. They said he was too manly to report it, so they had to. They used cheating as a good way to bring Sam's paternity into question, they even tested it. Somehow, they even found out about Princess…" Bea trailed off and pulled her legs up tighter, rocking. "I wanted to be able to live my life. I had to divorce Marcus to live my life. Yes, I made the divorce happen in a selfish, mean way. But they went scorched earth on me in the divorce proceedings." Bea started to sniffle and her eyes teared.

Irene found a tissue and handed it to Bea. "Stop if you want. We understand."

Bea rocked a few more times while crying, then dabbed her eyes with the tissue. She un-balled herself. She sat cross-legged and cross-armed. "The worst part was my pride. I had these idealist notions in my head. I would not fight for spousal support beyond six months, just enough to get settled and a better job. I didn't bring Marcus's sins into the fight. Even though, he was just as guilty of what lost me custody of Sam. Even when I was being held to the standard of a mother, a higher standard than a man, I did not try to even the playing field by being dirty. It was not fair. I was prideful enough to be fair. Even today, I must pay $442 of child support a month. I can barely afford this. Five years ago, when Marcus finished articling and started his career, he generously said I did not have to pay for it. But I still do. It is enough that I wouldn't be in debt right now if I took his offer. I won't take his offer. My pride won't let me. It's fair that I pay child support just as he would if I had custody, so I do. And I'm not even sure I wanted a kid."

"What isn't fair is that the man I worked my ass off to get through his first year of law school can use the divorce to smooth his way through school. Then he can slide into a nice career with a nice house, nice car, and a flat-assed childcare provider, or what he calls a wife, in three years. With each year his life gets better. Meanwhile, I can't get back into university because I can't get a student loan. I can't risk getting a different job because if something does not work out at the wage I get now, I'm homeless. Hell, I'm homeless if I can't get my debt paid off before the annual rent increase reduces my disposable income to nothing. My life after the divorce has, in small increments, become much worse. Yet, Marcus continues to rise. I'm so jealous of that. I'm smarter than him. I work harder than him. I'm more talented than him. I'm better looking than him... especially in a bikini."

"The first few years after the divorce, I worked three jobs: as a collection agent, as a server, and as a resentful bitch. But I could not pull myself up by my bootstraps, only burn out. Worse, during this time Marcus had changed. I was too resentful to notice. There were small olive branches that I broke without seeing them, like giving me more time with Sam, talking to me about Amy and his job, or leaving gift cards with Sam for us to use. Oh, and the obvious one, giving me a break on child support, that I didn't take. I took it all as him rubbing it in my face."

"It wasn't all me, though; this is when Sam started calling me 'Momma B' and Amy 'Momma A.' Amy and Marcus thought it was cute because I'm Bea and the biological mom. I heard it as I was the second mom, the lesser mom. I told them I did not want to be called it. They said, 'But it is what Sam wants to call you; we can't stop him.' I fumed, vowing revenge. At the same time Marcus was confiding in me that Amy was not getting pregnant. I told him if he loved Amy stick up for her when Sabrina tells you to divorce Amy for being infertile. He said, 'he learned his lesson.' I said, 'Three years too late.' This is when I started to teach Sam to call Amy the Barren-ess because she was barren." Irene put a hand to her mouth that covered a gasp. "Sam was at the age when he would pick up any word said and mimic it. I got so much shit from the Barren-ess for saying 'dumb fucker' in front of Sam. The little guy ran around for a month yelling it at cyclists – he so takes after me. Sam caught on to Barren-ess quickly. Amy thought it was cute. After a week or so, Marcus asked Sam why he wasn't calling him the Baron if Amy was the Barren-ess. Sam told his dad the truth. I got an angry call from Marcus with Amy in the background crying. Marcus demanded an apology. I demanded they stop Sam from calling me Momma B. They said that was different. Hearing Amy weep made me relent. Marcus and I came to an agreement: they would not call me Momma B, and I would stop encouraging Sam to call Amy the Barren-ess."

Irene said, "Bea, that was horrendous! That's way too far."

Bea responded, "Maybe it was but my life was ruined, and they were encouraging my kid to remind me of the rubble. I still feel belittled when Sam calls me Momma B. They have no empathy for that. It was tit for tat."

"But that is the worst thing you can say to a woman. It is so hurtful. I would never say that to my worst enemy." Irene squirmed in her seat.

Cat chimed in, "Sure, it's a harsh insult but really, how is it worse than supporting a mother's child to defeminize her by saying she is the lesser mother?" There was a long silence that got awkward. Irene consciously looked away from the two women. Cat clarified, "I'm not sure defeminize is the right word. I wanted to say the opposite of emasculation. I thought it was effeminacy, but it is not."

Bea sensed the generational gap. Bea said, "Effeminacy is more of a word for men taking on traditionally female traits. But you mean degrading or attacking one's femininity." Cat nodded. "That there isn't a word we know is the problem." Cat and Irene agreed.

"There is no doubt I went too far by calling Amy the Barren-ess. But that is where I was at that time. It was not right. I knew that. I should have been angrier at Marcus. Amy was probably on my side but there's no way I could see that. All I could see was her taking on all I was not, and I was jealous and resentful even though I didn't want those things. I had broken the marriage because I did not want what she had. But I'm also sure at some time in Amy's life she became aware that it was easier to go with the current than swim against the tide and accepted her role. That makes it harder for me to buck the tide. It makes me jealous."

Irene said, "How I hate this feeling of déjà vu. It is the same problem we had in the sixties, just more hidden. Equality is nothing if old traditions make it harder for those striving to exercise their rights than those happy to be subjugated by men."

Cat said, "Equal is hard to achieve when one side's archetype is based on having power over the other."

"It certainly is harder," Bea agreed. "Eight years after the divorce and I have a fifty percent chance of throwing hands if I was with Marcus for a day. So many things have to do with that. It is not all Marcus; his beliefs are a mirror of those around him. Even Sam has to do with that anger. Sam is such a great boy. I love him deeply. And I still think of who I would be if he had not been born. Then I remember, I'm awful for thinking that. Sometimes I feel that looking back at how things could have been different is written on my forehead for him to see. When I think Sam can see my thought of a life without him, I'm wracked with guilt to the point of tears. At the same time, I never want another child. And honestly, I never wanted Sam. Seeing Sam so happy with Momma A makes me think I should walk off into the sunset. Be a great aunty for him and give up on being mom. But I'm torn up inside by the feeling I will lose him again. Even participating in Direct Democracy gives me fear I will be pushing Sam out of my life."

Irene gave her opinion. "There is no reason you should feel that way, Bea. First: Because you've been with Sam when he was young, you will always be a big part of his life. Maybe not the center, but you will always have more of a connection with him than Amy. Soon he will be in his teens, and he'll be pining to get away from Marcus and Amy. You'll become more important. Second: Direct Democracy is real because of you. When it is over, regardless of Harold winning his seat, you will have tangible achievements to make your resume a winner. Think of the connections Derek has. At a minimum you'll be able to say, 'I organized old people into an internet army and have social media accounts with thousands of followers.'"

Cat reinforced Irene's opinion, "I have a niece and nephew. When I was in my early teens, I took care of them from when she was a toddler, and he was a baby. They see me as the Cat's meow. All the things Irene said Direct Democracy will give you are true. On a bigger level, I see Direct Democracy will fight political polarization and allow more diversity. The wedge issue will lose power because a person can vote on the wedge issue without adopting a party's entire platform."

"Irene and Cat, I like the way you think. I think in a very real way a little more democracy was all I was looking for in Marcus and my relationship. Instead, here we are trying to change Canada with an old white man's idea for an app... a good idea nonetheless." Bea raised her nearly empty glass. "Thank you for listening to me."

The three clinked their glasses. Cat said after the toast, "Thank you for sharing, Bea. Marcus totally gas-lit you. What kind of person would not listen to their partner on serious issues like having children? Then to have the families fuck you over is cruel."

Irene continued the support, "I'm amazed you can even see Marcus as anything but a giant dick." Bea snickered to herself about the giant dick comment. "I think we need another glass of wine to lighten the mood. Then I must go win another drink ticket."

The three women talked of nothing while having another glass of wine.

Bea and Cat left soon after. Cat's place was not far from the owls so they detoured to see Josie. In the last light of the spring evening Bea found Mister in a line of ponderosas pines. Bea introduced Cat to Cheryl the Owl Lady, who stood nearby. Mister flew into a cherry tree, looking as if he was hung up in the tree's small branches. Cheryl told Bea and Cat the gruesome details of Mister's attacking a bird's nest to get the eggs or chicks. Owlets need soft food. Bea was fascinated. Cat was horrified. Mister flew off into the sunset, back to the nest.

🦉 Owls, Doughnuts, and Democracy, by Jason A. N. Taylor 🦉

Before parting ways with Cheryl Bea gave her the Direct Democracy elevator speech. It was received well. Bea and Cat went their separate ways once out of the park.

13.

It was the first time in ages that Bea had taken an afternoon off for herself. She usually cashed out her year-end holiday pay to pay down more debt. Leaving work in a business casual skirt and blouse felt great. The outfit would have been better with heels rather than runners, but she was probably going to have to sprint home after the UVic Direct Democracy presentation. She was sure no one would notice her shoes. Besides, everyone she knew who looked at feet was a pervert. She noticed Mike do a double take of her when she left the office.

Bea took the longer bus route to the University so she could walk through Mystic Vale hoping to see an owl. Robin's alarm calls showed her what she thought was the silhouette of a harassed barred owl across the green gully. She wondered if the owl was the progeny of one, she saw here when she was in university. She walked through the Finnerty Gardens, noting that it was too early for the best of the rhododendrons. She reminisced fondly of one late spring night in the garden, hiding with a friend, dodging a security guard's probing flashlight, all but naked and secretly hoping they would be caught.

The room was in a building Bea had taken classes at and found it easily. Not long after a skinny, bearded man in a tweed blazer with elbow patches approached. Dr. Fridman did not look any different from when Bea was in his class. They re-introduced themselves, both saying how little the other had changed. He asked the question Bea was dreading, "What of your career?"

"I help people get out of debt. A credit counsellor." Bea was saved from digging further into the lie by a student trying to hand in a late paper.

The conversation thankfully moved on to how Direct Democracy got started. Bea told the short version.

"Before we get started," Dr. Fridman told Bea, "I should tell you. You'll have the last twenty minutes of our time and your Power Point slides have been added to the lecture stack." The casual air Dr. Fridman assumed set free butterflies in Bea's stomach. It seemed to be very little instruction for the first time in nine years that she would be speaking publicly.

Bea found a seat on the left side, three-quarters of the way back. The spot was perfect for checking out students. She tried to pick which one was who Ajay wanted her to meet. Cat said he was a computer science student so likely he'd be a loner and have a nerdy vibe. Her target would be sitting alone.

The first potential suspect was tall, sitting at the front, wearing a collared shirt and jeans with a stupid Bass Pro Shop hat covering feathered hair. Probably a hockey or lacrosse player who did everything aggressively, as if it was a competition. Something nice to know about and harness when needed.

Someone came in behind her, and the guy in the hat turned, revealing an acne-covered baby face. He was young enough that she might feel awkward though she did not, liking the thought of being called a MILF. The latecomer sat next to him. Bea surmised that she was his girlfriend by the close greeting they exchanged.

The next possibility was an Asian guy, sitting next to three women. Bea could tell he was the nice guy, too nice to exercise the crush he surely had on one of them. Bea felt certain she could help him build that confidence and would have a great time doing it.

The door at the back of the theatre opened again. Bea thought this might be the person, but it was another girl.

The next interesting guy was big, a teddy bear with chubby baby fat cheeks. He left a seat between him and the next person, likely reasoning that he needed an open side because he wrote left-handed on the next desk's notebook platform. Bea sensed it actually was because he was self-conscious of his size and feared the embarrassment of touching another person accidentally. She immediately desired to embarrass him by sitting in that seat and nuzzle into him when he accidentally touched her. She'd known guys like him; more often than not real people pleasers who could be fulfilling.

Bea abruptly sensed being leered at. She turned aside to just glimpse a leather jacket-clad arm a few rows back.

Near the front, on the opposite side, another loner had his hand up. A stereotypical nerd. From his style, Bea knew his question was going to be: 'will this be on the exam?' She was right. The answer from the professor being yes, his head bowed to his notes, writing furiously.

The noise of a falling binder somewhere behind diverted Bea's attention. She turned around, not caring how conspicuous she appeared. Behind and further to the left was an indigenous guy in a black leather jacket. Straight black bangs nearly covered one of his eyes. He was now staring so intently at Dr. Fridman that she had to assume he had been ogling her. She turned away then snapped her head back in his direction to catch him. Still, he remained gazing at the professor. 'It must not be him,' she thought.

Turning back, she caught the guy in the centre row checking her out. He was tall and lanky, with glasses and held a stylus above a tablet, ready to write. This was probably the guy. She stretched, head back, pushing her chest out, to give him a good view.

Bea closed her eyes as she stretched and opened them looking behind her. The indigenous guy gawked down her blouse. 'Maybe it is him,' she thought, smiling. She noticed the tall guy gazing at her also and was doubly happy.

"This will not be on the test." Dr. Fridman's declaration took Bea from her thoughts. "But I am pleased to introduce you to Bea Jensen, leader of Direct Democracy. One of the few…" He mimed air-quotes. "New… ideas in Canadian democracy. It proposes using an app to allow all constituents in a federal riding to vote on legislation. A throwback to Athenian Democracy, wouldn't you say, Bea?"

"Our inspiration for Direct Democracy was the historic egalitarian societies." Bright eyed, Bea answered as she walked down the aisle. "They polled their members for input on how to govern. Athens happens to be the one we speak of most in the West. But unlike Athens, we want everyone to participate."

"Indeed," Dr. Fridman drolly said. "Allowing the franchise to only land-owning men would hardly be considered democratic today."

Bea took Dr. Fridman's spot at the lectern and could now see that there were around fifty students present. "Thank you, Dr.

Fridman, for allowing me to be here today. I do have to correct your introduction, though. I'm not the leader of Direct Democracy. I lost that contest by one vote to former Progressive Conservative Member of Parliament Harold Gordon. The only party I've been leader of is a Voting Party."

The hand of the guy in the Bass Pro Shop hat shot up.

"Wow! Questions before the presentation. I'm flattered. What is your question?"

"Are you the Bea that started the Voting Party?"

"Yes."

"That's lit."

"Thanks." Just say beer, Bea thought, and poli-sci students will jump. "I'm honoured it has lasted so long..." Bea shifted, thinking. "Did you know if you are part of one of the major political parties but given the youth vote portfolio, your career is over?" She listened for slight murmurs from the crowd. "That's how much the big three care about the youth vote. YOUR VOTE!"

Some of the students shifted uncomfortably.

"How many of you have seen the *Canada's Other Pass Time* unicorn video?" Bea smiled as they all put up their hands. "How many of you know who was actually being interviewed?" Roughly half the students put up their hands. "So this entire poli-sci class on democracy saw that video but only half noticed that it was about politics? What does that say?" She could feel the audience was more than a little miffed at being called out. "The three big Canadian parties are right to not care what the youth think."

Bea let the audience grumble slightly as she paused for effect. "The unicorn interview was about politics, Direct Democracy, for those of you still in the dark.

Another hand raised above the crowd and a smartly dressed young woman stood. "I heard it, and I knew what they were talking about. Why isn't Direct Democracy discussed on mainstream media, not just podcast?"

"Excellent question. To me, the fact we haven't been recognized by the larger political news says people are not being heard, because people who are heard listen. If you felt heard, you'd be listening for your voice on Canada's Other Pass Time and other media and correcting them if it was not. For us at Direct Democracy, not being heard is the reason politics are becoming more polarized and more dangerous.

"For example, the election of the Orange Dumpster Fire President in the US is a result of people not being heard. Invariably his electorate will say, 'we need to drain the swamp, shake things up' because their lives are getting worse and traditional politicians have not listened to them. The loss of a person's political voice in Canada may not be as extreme as in the United States, but the less we're heard, the less democratic we are. Direct Democracy can raise the voice of the people." She knew invoking President Pussy Grabber would trigger disgust in most Canadians, particularly those who valued an education.

For Bea, this was more than telling these students of a new, old idea with a bland PowerPoint. It was an opportunity to get more than followers, it was recruiting soldiers for Direct Democracy. As antithetical to her cause and beliefs as it was, she channelled Mussolini's and Hitler's passionate, gesticulating oration to convert her missionaries. Emotion was what was needed.

Bea took the audience on an emotional rollercoaster. She could see they were angry. With the hook set she changed gears, telling the story of Direct Democracy. How Harold, an old white luddite man, by using the internet tripped over a new way of expressing a fundamental human need to be heard. Harold was like Homer Simpson, s.m.r.t. enough to see the potential of the idea and knowing the world turns on taking stupid risks. The class seemed to sympathize with Harold and his band of oldsters, in the same way they would Homer.

This, combined with the students' anger at the big parties' dismissiveness, made them ready to ride alongside Harold's tilting at windmills. She then filled them with warmth and cuddles by telling everyone in the room they could be part of Direct Democracy without having to change their political beliefs. The inclusivity was avocado toast to these Millennials and Generation Z, they ate up the idea of a political party with all the room in the world for diversity. When she finished the class applauded her without the professor's prompting.

Bea smiled widely, scanning the crowd, making eye contact with each person. She felt that many would volunteer for Direct Democracy. "Any questions?"

The Bass Pro Shop hat guy was first. "Do you want to join us after class for happy hour at Felicita's?"

"I could go for a beer."

"Right on!"

Bea pointed to the next person, the young woman who had asked about media coverage. "Is there an example of how the App for Direct Democracy will work? I really like the concept… like something where everyone has equal say, that's awesome. Can I volunteer?"

"I'm so happy to see your enthusiasm! Our website has a mock-up of the App. It's far from the final product. We need feedback on it. To volunteer just sign up on the website. Thank you in advance."

Bea did not want another softball question. The indigenous guy with the leather jacket had his hand half up. "You," she pointed. "In the leather jacket. What's your question?"

He looked about, as if Bea may have pointed at someone else. Then he said, "Is it a good idea letting every Joe Six-pack vote on all legislation?"

"I am so happy to hear this question." Bea beamed. "Right now, there's no qualification requirement for Members of Parliament. Just the perception that because a candidate is vetted by their party and won their campaign, they become qualified. We think the Direct Democracy system will diminish the risk of one nutbar getting elected and running amuck. A reasonable majority dilutes the extremes."

"Does it bother you that Socrates warned against Athenian Democracy, direct democracy?" Bea was happy the guy had another hard question. "He said the public was not qualified to govern."

"Amazing," Bea smirked. "A self-qualified old white man telling the average person they're not qualified to make complicated decisions. Did you know Socrates was also not big on writing? That's why Plato wrote Socrates' dialogues down. Socrates thought writing was inferior to discussion because you cannot question a book like you can a person. How far would we have gotten without writing?"

Bea let the question sit until the leather jacket guy moved again to speak. "We don't live in Ancient Greece," she continued. "Nowadays everyone gets a public education. More than 90% of Canadians have a high school education and nearly 70% have post-secondary education. We also have the communication system to get the information to people quickly enough to decide."

"Only about 60% of the electorate voted in recent Federal Elections," the guy said sarcastically. "How will you get these highly educated people to vote on every bill before parliament?"

"Maybe the reason people are unmotivated is because they're voting for an MP who might not support legislation important to them." Bea dialled down the surliness and said, "Keeping people keen to vote on all legislation is the biggest challenge. The app is designed to make it easy for a person to quickly determine their preference on the bill. It can be as simple as setting the app to vote the same way as your preferred party's platform. For those more invested in specific topics, they can be as granular as they want, all the way down to voting on every bill."

"That's not your biggest challenge..." He was smirking now. "Taking power from the powerful is. What politician will let Direct Democracy make them redundant? None. They will do everything they can to keep from losing their power. I hope Harold Gordon has thick skin."

"Oh, Harold can hold his own, I assure you." Bea furrowed her brow. "He was one of three Progressive Conservatives to survive the nineteen ninety-three elections. Even took a physical beating to keep his constituents on his side. Why would you say that he needs a thick skin?"

"Because a populist with no political platform – except taking power from the powerful – can only be attacked on personality."

"What do you mean populist? Direct Democracy is not some proto-fascist party like this red-hatted tomfoolery in the States."

"Look up populism."

Owls, Doughnuts, and Democracy, by Jason A. N. Taylor

A quarter of the class took this as a challenge, pulling out their phones. A very blond, bespectacled coed answered first, "There are three interpretations of it." She stared at her screen. "'Noun: 1. a political approach that strives to appeal to ordinary people who feel that their concerns are disregarded by established elite groups; 2. support for populist politicians or policies; 3. the quality of appealing to or being aimed at ordinary people.'"

With her head tilted up and to the left, looking into space, Bea considered the definition. "You're right. Mostly numbers one and three. Direct Democracy is a populist movement."

"The next biggest challenge is Harold Gordon." The guy in the black- leather coat sat forward in his seat, losing some of the smugness he'd had when Bea accepted his answer without argument. "He'll always be beholden to conservative ideology. Left-wingers will not likely follow an old Progressive Conservative."

"I don't see it that way. Harold has name recognition. Especially with the right, which is the group we need most. The left will join more readily, recognizing that Direct Democracy is about equality."

"You give the average voter too much credit. Why would an NDPer change to a party headed by an ardent Conservative? Why not just vote for the NDP?"

The very blond librarian woman added, "In an interview for *Libertarians on Guard for Thee*, Harold Gordon talks as if he is a conservative libertarian. He references his stance on old-growth logging and trade."

"What!?" Bea was taken by surprise. "When was the interview from?"

"It's new today," the librarian responded.

"I've not seen it." Bea cleared her throat. "If it is as you say, I will be lighting a fire under his derriere next time I speak with him." Bea slapped the side of the lectern as if spanking a baby.

Seeing Bea's consternation the very blond woman said, "I don't think it's a problem. *Libertarians On Guard for Thee* is really right-wing. I only watch it to know what the other side is saying. Few people with differing political views will watch it." She paused, watching for Bea's reaction. "And Harold did separate his views from the party's."

"Good to know."

"Any educated person will understand that Direct Democracy does not have a political stance…" the librarian changed the topic slightly. "Except for maximizing democracy. It is a defiant stance that will attract many people. I don't know if it will win. But I do think it will change every election after if it pulls more than a few percent of the vote."

"As in the 'Direktdemokraterna'." Smiling, Bea knew she had butchered the word. "Sweden's Directdmokraterna is the only Direct Democracy party we know of. It set the voting record all-time low with 0.08 percent of the electorate. I know we can do more. I know we can win. Come for a beer after this and I'll tell you how to help." The class took Bea's last statement as the unofficial 'class is over' signal and started packing up their books.

"If you want to win, you'll need the votes of the un-educated." The guy in the leather jacket spoke loud enough to be heard over the noise of the class. "To flourish, populism needs the stupid and uninformed, the people of Walmart." The class was stunned by his lack of political correctness, with many stopping what they were doing to see if anyone was going to correct him.

Dr. Fridman noticed the class's gaze on him but was not able to say anything before Bea stood tall and shouted. "I shop at Walmart!"

The guy hid his face with his bangs. Bea continued, "I would say populism needs all people to flourish," Bea continued. "And democracy needs all people to flourish." The guy got up to leave. "If anyone wants to talk more about Direct Democracy, come to Felicita's." Bea hoped the guy knew that was directed at him.

Dr. Fridman took the lectern. "Please thank Bea for discussing this novel party with us."

The class clapped briefly and then left as a group. The assemblage included the Bass Pro Shop hat guy and the mousy librarian. Bea kept her eyes on the receding leather jacket youth, resisting an urge to intercept him.

"Bea, don't worry..." Dr Fridman touched her arm and nodded after the subject of her gaze. "Mr. George puts his foot in his mouth often. He is used to rebuke. He is a smart, odd student. Computer science major but he seems to know a little of everything."

"Mr. George?"

"Yes. Raymond."

"Good to know."

"And thank you for presenting. The class was quite engaged. I do hope a few of them help with your cause."

"Thank you, Doctor. I'm so grateful. Will you come to Felicita's?"

Dr. Fridman leaned in. "Unwritten rule, professors never go to the bar with first year students. But thanks for the offer."

Bea thanked Dr. Fridman again then scanned for Raymond. She could not see him.

On the path toward the Student Union Building Bass Pro Shop hat and his girlfriend walked alongside Bea. "Dope!" He exclaimed. "I'm going to have beer with the creator of the Voting Party." He extended his hand, "Ethan. And this is Mia."

"Nice to meet you both."

Students walked by introducing themselves to Bea, only to say they had other classes and could not join. Ultimately less than ten formed the party.

Bea spotted Raymond at a bike rack and paused. "Ethan, you go ahead. I'll catch up in a minute." She jogged toward the bike rack where Raymond was putting on his helmet. "Hey, Raymond!" He did not respond and mounted a large electric scooter. Before she could close the distance, he was rounding a far corner. She gave up the chase.

The procession was easy to catch up with. "Do you know Raymond?" The very blond librarian asked.

"No. But I was hoping to argue with him a bit more. It was getting interesting."

"Oh, he's 'interesting,' all right."

"Do you know him? Ahh... what is your?"

"Joice. Interesting is right. I was in a group with Ray once. He always showed up late, argued about what the group had done, then left early. I even did his section, thinking he was not going to have it done. But he did get it done. And practically rewrote the two other sections that did not flow well, while not criticizing the two other group members' work. It was the best group project mark I've ever gotten. That's all I know about him; he likes to argue and is smart. And he rides around on that stupid electric scooter, like, get a bike."

"Huh, weird he did not want to come and argue some more. I think the electric scooters are pretty neat." Bea felt she was acting too smitten with Ray. She said, "I like bikes too..." Bea tried not to sound too cutting. "Just not the people who ride them."

"I think it would be more accurate to say Ray likes to be right in an argumentative way, rather than argue. You probably scared him off by arguing back." Joice finished her thought on Ray. She squinted. "I bike. What's your problem with cyclists?"

"Cyclists who follow the rules of the road are fine. But I've never met one that does."

To make Bea's point, a bell dinged behind them. The cyclist called, "On your left." The group, except for her, gave up the pedestrian walkway for the grass boulevard to let the cyclist pass. She pointed one arm up in the air at the sign telling cyclists to yield to walkers. The cyclist dodged her and said, "There's always one asshole."

"Yes there is," Bea replied hotly. "You!"

"I always give way for pedestrians," Joice said.

"I'm sure you do." Bea laughed.

Bea moved on to finding out who was in the group. She employed the FORDS method of inquiry: family, occupation, recreation, dreams, and social media, to derive information on her fellow drinkers. Her goal was to build a dossier like Herbert Hoover and organize Direct Democracy's minions with the efficiency of Stalin.

Joice was the first to be examined. She was far from her family in Ontario; her choice of university was probably based on such distance. Her parents thought she was studying something practical like business administration. Really, she had many courses that would add up to minors including economics, philosophy, and political science, but she was still searching for a major. Environmental science was her current passion, although she liked the idea of math better than the practice. She dreamed of making a difference, travelling, and living in a tiny home. Reddit, TikTok, and Twitter were her social media platforms of choice. On them, she was unabashedly Anarchist, Anti-Fascist, Anti-Zionist, Environmentalist, and Feminist. The obligatory Social Justice Warrior through and through. Ben Shapiro was her favourite target. She was so blond that her legs looked shaved until light illuminated the almost white fuzz. She was curvy. A Star of David peaked out of her top. Likely a good fit for Rich's wing.

Ethan and Mia were a high school Insta Couple. Bea had a hard time understanding if there was anything more to them than their clothes. Their families had suburban white picket fence houses in the Fraser Valley. Ethan was enthusiastic about beer to the point of posing a drinking competition with Bea. Mia was more interested in wine and taking pictures of the group in the company of the voting party inventor. Ethan was doing a degree in Health Information Systems and Mia was in Social Work. They took a course together every semester so they could share the university experience. This semester their common study was Canadian Politics.

Bea asked Ethan if he fished. His answer revealed that his Bass Pro Shop hat was strictly fashion. He played hockey, though. Mia's recreation was hiking, camping, and posting. Both dreamed of the perfect house, probably on Vancouver Island because the mainland was too expensive. They could not settle on whether they dreamed of a cabin to spend summers at or travelling abroad. Both scenarios would start with an amazing West Coast wedding, then three kids, two boys and a girl or two girls and a boy, it did not matter which. On Instagram, they had tens of thousands of followers. Bea could see them demonstrating Direct Democracy in cute Insta Couple posts. Something like the two of them putting up a Direct Democracy sign with Ethan's thought bubble voting for the pipeline and Mia's voting against the pipeline but still voting together. Bea sensed she had to win the beer-drinking competition to ensure this Insta Couple would be on board. She won easily.

Justin had two brothers and was from Campbell River originally. His Christian values were bright enough to shine through his 'I'm hanging out with snowflakes' filter. Joice triggered him. He should have been the person wearing the Bass Pro Shop hat. A patch of a buck that was the logo for Browning, the gun maker, was discreetly on his bag. He fished and hunted and showed Bea a picture of his raised truck with stickers of cartoon boy Calvin pissing on the DFO (Department of Fisheries and Oceans). "If we could just shoot seals and sea lions he said, salmon stocks would rebound, especially chinook - the ones the marine biologists say southern resident killer whales only eat, stupid whales."

Justin was proud of his truck, logging, and mining. He dreamt of living on the outskirts of a small town with acreage. Policing came up a few times when he talked of his career path. Bea could see him being a cop but not one she would want to meet. Politically, he dreamt of the Conservatives kicking J.T. out in the next election. He reminded everyone every chance he got that the Conservatives got more of the popular vote than the Liberals in the previous election. But he did concede that even the Conservatives did not take freedom seriously enough and had more back-room dealings than he liked.

To Justin, Direct Democracy seemed more grassroots and less corruptible than even the Conservative party. He had faith country folk would vote right if given the chance. His dad talked fondly of Harold Gordon, which created a healthy interest in Justin to know more about the party Harold would lead. Free speech was a topic he raised often, though Bea felt he was holding his true opinions back. Twitter was his favourite platform, but it was getting over-moderated. Bea knew she had to get him to Harold, sure he would become his henchman. Harold might even get to go fishing.

When Tyrell told Bea his name, she finally remembered her trainer's name. The student was a skinny, tallish young black man with a limp and slow, deliberate speech. She hated that her mind was trying to intuit his disability, speculating that it could be cerebral palsy, aftereffects of a stroke, multiple sclerosis, or even aftereffects of polio. She reiterated in her mind that she has no need to know or care. He lived with a large family. Political science was his major

Owls, Doughnuts, and Democracy, by Jason A. N. Taylor

even though he seemed too reserved to be in politics. He was excessively polite and did not talk ill or negatively of even those he disagreed with.

The others in the group said awful, vulgar things about the less-than-moral acts of politicians, but Tyrell did not stoop to that level. He would always stop before impugning the character of even a politician. He hoped to use his poly-sci degree to work as a faithful Public Servant, giving back to the people. When she heard him say this, she believed him. If only there were more honest people like him in politics. Walking and movies were his pastimes with over-the-top comedies his favourite. She thought inviting him to her house for a showing of *The 40-Year-Old Virgin* could be fun.

The only dreams Tyrell would allow Bea to know of were too mundane to be real. Literally, his sole dream was to work in any government position. Social media was a thing he did not understand or participate in. She could tell he was too polite to say he thought social media was full of idiots. She thought Irene would like him, but she hoped to investigate more while walking him home after the outing to the bar dissolved.

These five students stood out to Bea as the most likely to participate in Direct Democracy. The four or five others were more involved in socializing and drinking beer. She still took their names and beer when offered.

As happy hour passed, and drinks became full price the group began to break up. Bea was happy enough to get going, more beer would make her incapable of running home. She had everyone's emails and social media handles and her new, new crush, Tyrell, was leaving to walk home. She invited herself to walk with him.

Bea started the conversation: "Are you really interested in Direct Democracy?"

Tyrell walked surprisingly quickly on the tree-lined sidewalk. "Lobbying breeds corruption. All MPs are lobbied by interest groups." His words were delivered in a slow, intentional tone. "It seems to me easier for a special interest group to change minds than the entire constituency of a riding."

"You are that concerned about corruption?" Bea accidentally, on purpose, brushed against him.

"Bea," Tyrell paused, thoughtful. "Government should be striving for consensus. Corruption is the enemy of consensus."

Bea resisted the impulse to fill the pause.

"Politics should be the process of building consensus. Lobbyists convincing the public of an idea's merit is closer to consensus than an MP messaging one thing to the public while listening to the lobbyist in private…"

He got stuck again. Bea sensed that most people would fill in Tyrell's words for him when he stopped short of a complete statement. She waited.

"If companies must lobby the public," Tyrell continued, "to support laws that help the corporations, at least the people made the decision, not some MP in a back room." A short pause this time. "Melissa from *Canada's Other Past Time* said this at the end of your interview. I agree with her."

Bea yearned to 'lobby' Tyrell in a backroom but knew this was not the time. She kept striding with him, saying nothing for more than a minute in case he had more to say.

"J.T. was my favourite politician. I would have voted for him last election if I was old enough." Tyrell's face contorted during the pause. "When he went down to meet with the Indigenous protesters in the teepee on Parliament Hill and sat with them, I thought he got it. It was mostly PR but I thought it was truthful."

"I thought it was an honest gesture," Bea added. "But politicians." She lightly touched his arm.

"It was all politics. Junior's true colours came out with how he treated Jodie…" Tyrell paused, peering at Bea. "Wilson Raybould." He stopped walking, his head shaking, and turned to look at Bea. "I don't like saying this, Bea. They're the only words I have. J.T. treated Wilson Raybould like a piece of shit. I don't like saying that." He shook his head more. "SCN Lavalin have their claws into Junior so deep that he humiliated and bullied his closest ally."

"It was a dick move," Bea said unconsciously.

Tyrell started walking again. "When the Jodie thing happened, it showed me that J.T. cared more for power than empowering the disenfranchised. You might not understand this, Bea." For a few quiet seconds he made a face like he was going to admit something shameful. "People have bullied and humiliated me because I'm different. I dream of a time when that does not happen. But our Prime Minister does it."

In the subsequent long pause, Bea wished intensely to hug Tyrell. She contemplated trying to empathize by recounting times in her life when she was bullied but sensed they would be nothing to his experiences. She so wanted to take him home and love him, or at least lust him for a few days. She settled for patting him on the arm and leaning her head against his shoulder.

"I like Direct Democracy because it removes the onus of an MP to be morally perfect." Tyrell continued; his brow furrowed with thought. "No one can be morally perfect. An MP, elected to the will of his constituency, must uphold their honour all the time to remain seen as moral. A Direct Democracy MP must only show he is trustworthy to vote for what the constituency voted for."

"Huh, I hadn't thought of that."

A gurgling noise came from a raised truck decelerating to the lights in front of them. On the tailgate above and to the right of the truck nuts was a large sticker: Fuck Trudeau. "Tha... that...," Tyrell stuttered. "That is uncalled for. It is wrong."

Knowing Bea had to do what she was going to do, she said, "Get ready to take off." Then she walked into the street to the truck's passenger side and knocked on the window. She smiled and waved for the driver to roll the window down. He promptly hit a button and as the glass receded, she had a clear field to yell: "I want to fuck Trudeau too!"

The driver frowned in combined annoyance and mystification.

"He is so hot!" Bouncing to bring home her point Bea continued: "I want to fuck Trudeau. We should see if J.T. wants a threesome. I doubt Sophie is a swinger. Do you want to pitch or catch? You look like a catcher. That's good, I don't do that. However, I have a 12" strap-on I can fuck you with so you get some practice."

The driver hollered, "What is wrong with you, whore?"

"Nothing a threesome with J.T. wouldn't cure, honey."

"Get away from my truck, you cunt!"

"Fucking limp dick tease!" Bea's expression turned from mocking to angry. "The only balls you have are on your truck! Eat a dick!"

The light changed, the engine roared, and the tires shrieked as the truck took off. Seconds later its brakes squealed, and a crunch was heard as it lightly rear-ended the car ahead.

Tyrell's face mixed with terror and laughter.

Bea grinned back at him. "Let's take a detour."

They rounded the next corner at a speed-walker's pace. Away from the main streets, Tyrell's horror changed to giddy laughter mixed with coughing and spasmodic knee-slapping. "That was too much, Bea!" Gasping, Tyrell shook his head in disbelief. "I was worried he'd get out of the truck."

"Truck nuts wouldn't have done anything. Guys like that are too manly to fight a woman."

"Let's not do that again."

"You have my word, never again... at least not with you around."

They walked on, talking. The entire time, she wanted to ask him if the Little Guy from Shawinigan (Chretien) was his favourite Liberal leader now that J.T. had fallen from his grace and if he liked pepper on his plate. She bit her tongue. She had made the connection because of their similar way of speaking and walking. She would hold off until they knew each other better.

Approaching the spot where Bea should turn home, she hoped Tyrell would invite her over or ask where she lived. She had been walking close, patting his arm occasionally, but felt she might have to take control.

Out of nowhere, Tyrell started laughing. He said between guffaws, "It was so funny what you said to that guy in the truck. You remind me of Space Beth from *Rick and Morty.*"

"Rick and Morty?"

"It is a Sci-fi cartoon on Adult Swim. Space Beth is Rick's daughter." Tyrell struggled to describe Rick and Morty. His verbal stumbling manifested in a bunch of starts and stops. He finally settled on. "Space Beth is a brash woman saving the universe."

"Sounds like my kind of woman."

"I think you would like her. She does not take any... shhh aww... crap."

"Hmmm... interesting. Can watch it at your place?"

This stopped Tyrell. "My family will be having dinner and watching TV," he said, pausing. "*Rick and Morty* is on Netflix. You can watch it there."

"I have Netflix, we can watch it at my place." Bea smiled and winked. "Netflix and chill?"

Tyrell grimaced, stepping awkwardly away. "My family is expecting me."

Bea sensed his fear, and she wanted to assist Tyrell in overcoming it. However, she felt that if she did, she would break his heart so badly that it would not heal. So, she stood in the same spot and said, "It was great meeting you."

"Umm.. me too."

"It's fun talking with you but here is where I turn for my place."

"Okay."

"Can I put you in contact with Irene? She's Direct Democracy's resident Liberal."

"I guess."

"She's a nice oldster."

"Sure, please put me in touch. I want to be involved. Thanks for walking with me." Tyrell turned toward his destination. "Have a good evening."

Watching him stride away, Bea wondered if she was seeing an innocent person terrified of her strength or someone who might realize they missed an opportunity. Tyrell was likely too innocent for her. Perhaps it was the absence of social media in his life. She would not spoil this unicorn.

Feeling like Super Woman but probably acting like Space Beth, Bea found some less-than-concealing shrubs to take off her dress. She put it in her gym knapsack, not wanting to get it sweaty running home. In a sports bra and short bottoms, she knew she was super. With her hair in a ponytail, she started running.

Flying down the Gary oak-lined streets of Saanich, Bea tried to get home before her buzz wore off. At an intersection she saw, silhouetted in the setting sun, an electric scooter a hundred metres away and thought it could be Ray. She kicked up the pace but could not overtake. The only realistic way she would catch up is if he stopped.

The scooter slowed to a stop at what looked like a kiosk where wealthy homeowners hawked eggs, flowers, or homemade stuff at the side of the road. Bea slowed to a jog. At about thirty metres she saw that it was Ray. He seemed to be placing books from his bag into a little library. As Bea approached, he saw her and took off. She thought of yelling but reasoned that they'd not actually been introduced. She started running again, only slowing to take a picture of the books in the little library.

The scooter turned up the next street toward a steepish hill. She hoped she had more horsepower than the scooter. At the top she saw him on a dead-end side street placing books in another little library. She had to know what books he was leaving. Keeping mostly out of sight, she was on the verge of catching up when he zoomed back onto the main street across from her. He seemed to be ignoring her.

Bea could see the pattern now and had a plan. On his side all the streets were dead ends next to a golf course. She knew of a larger little library a few streets down that she had taken books from at the dead-end, visible from the main street. She would catch up with him at the golf course where the bark mulch running trail would slow him down.

Bea took a quick picture of his latest library then booked it back to the main street. She kept up but did not try to close the distance. As she thought, he turned down toward the larger little library. Again, he put books in, so she easily caught up with him. When he saw her, she waa three metres away, standing between him and the main street. With hands on her hips and elbows out, she called: "Hey Ray! What are you doing?"

Ray did a U-turn, only to be stopped by the trail. He circled back, stopping between Bea and the little library. "Have you been following me?"

"Yes. But not intentionally."

"That makes no sense."

"I agree, it doesn't. I happened to see you when I was running home. I wanted to talk with you after the class, but you took off."

"I didn't want to be around a bunch of drunken idiots," Ray snorted.

"Fair enough."

"What did you want to talk about?"

"Direct Democracy." Bea stepped smiling to the little library. "But now I want to know what books you've been dropping. Have you been corrupting the youth, Socrates?"

"Oh good God!" Ray shrilled over-dramatically in an outraged mother's voice. "He was putting books into the library. How evil!" Ray stepped into her view of the library.

Bea walked around Ray; eyes fixed on a red dust jacket. She pulled at the plump volume. "*Mao's Little Red Book*." She waved it at the houses around them. "You think these people put this book in this library?"

"I'm sure it was the people in the house with Buddhist prayer flags..." With extra sarcasm Ray said. "They're a great cover for Chinese Communist Party operatives."

"Really?" Bea made up reality to get to the truth. "I saw you put it in the little library." She was hoping he did. She thought it was hilarious.

"I put the Little Red Book in the little library. Call the cops or get off my back."

"I like your style." Bea smiled widely. "What other books do you return to these libraries?"

"Anything banned or controversial like *White Niggers of America. Lolita. The Communist Manifesto.*"

Bea winced at the use of the N-word.

"I've wanted to put *Mien Kampf* in them, but copies are rarer than gold."

"Have you ever seen a reader find these treasures?"

"No, but I love thinking of their thoughts. How would they look at their neighbours? Or what if little Sally brings it home and is now a Marxist? Would the parent confront the owner of the house the little library is in front of? Freedom of expression is messy! I can't wait to see a little library with a note saying, '**Please don't leave any controversial books**.'"

Bea laughed. "Or a list of books banned from the little libraries. I could see that making *CHEK News, Victoria Buzz*, and being the biggest thing on *r/VictoriaBC*." In an overly dramatic voice, she screamed, "Think of the children!"

Ray laughed too. "I think you should be quieter. The neighbours are watching." He head-gestured to a man watching from a window.

Bea thought it odd Ray cared that they were being watched but not enough to say anything except stare back with a fuck-off face. "Let's find more little libraries."

"I'm out of books."

"Damn. This looks like fun."

"Wanna smoke a joint?"

Bea didn't really want to, but she did want to find out who Ray was. "Ok." She strode ahead to the running track at the end of the street covered with a canopy of Gary oaks, believing she could feel his eyes on her ass. "Ajay said you could assist with voting security."

"He did?"

"Are you on board with Direct Democracy or were you being devil's advocate?"

Ray followed Bea, pushing the scooter. He took off his helmet and appeared to be trying not to be distracted by her ass.

"I'm going to reframe your question," he declared. "Do I agree with Direct Democracy? No. Not at all. It's childish. Giving the uninformed more ability to affect the direction of a country is folly."

A family walked past. Ray waited until they were out of earshot to continue. "In the States, the uninformed, or conspiracy people, have coalesced into the biggest demographic. This allowed that Trumpsterfire to get into office. They are totally captured by the rhetoric of the demagogue. Direct Democracy could be another way for this outcome by allowing the demagogue to bank on the perception that the uninformed people are acting on their own in a smart way. It's easy to empower dumb people to do things that hurt their cause by making them feel their dumb idea is smart. These uninformed people will become the loudest voice of Direct Democracy because they will be the people most easily pushed to action by social media targeting them."

"Sounds like another argument from Socrates," Bea countered sarcastically. "Beware of the orators whose only desire is power."

"Everybody desires power."

"That may be. But tell me why you don't agree with Direct Democracy, not what a dead European thinks."

"I wouldn't want minorities to get lost in the tyranny of the majority." A couple coming from behind made Ray fall silent until they moved on. "Before 1960 Canadian indigenous people had to give up their status to vote," he said gravely. "In nineteen forty-eight a parliamentary committee made the recommendation to grant them back full democratic participation. In nineteen sixty Diefenbaker gave them the vote regardless of status. Do you think nineteen sixty Canada was progressive enough to have fifty-one percent of people vote for indigenous voting rights? Given what I've heard of university students' comments on Indigenous students getting free tuition, there's no way the average Canadian riding would vote for Indigenous voting rights in nineteen sixty."

There was a short pause as a runner jogged by. "We need leaders who can envision enshrined rights for even the smallest minority. In a Direct Democracy scenario, the average person will not care for the very small minorities and only enemies of the minority will care to vote. Leaders who care for the good of the country are needed to keep Canada moving in the right direction. The majority does not always know the right direction."

"That's a good point. I hadn't thought of it that way. Or maybe I perceive it differently because the group I'm part of is not technically a minority. Women. We're struggling for equal footing."

"Okay..."

"Possibly, I'm naïve, but I have faith that the majority will do the right thing." Bea paused. "Particularly for the minority."

Ray nodded his head in agreement with her being foolish.

Bea struggled on: "If I had a view strongly against an idea like Direct Democracy, I would not be walking with one of its biggest supporters. Is Ajay your only reason for coming to the class? He thinks you are the computer security guru that Direct Democracy needs." She winked. "Or is there something more?"

Gobsmacked, Ray gawked at Bea, one eye covered by his black bangs. Then he stumbled on a root. Only his grip on the scooter kept him from falling. She had the feeling he had already fallen.

Shaken, Ray answered: "Ah, Ajay's my mentor. He did want me to meet you because I'm working on security and transparency for an indigenous voting app. I might not agree with Direct Democracy, but I do understand and respect what it could do. It might force parties to reevaluate how they engage with constituents. Hopefully, it pushes the traditional parties toward a philosophy of building consensus policies that benefit Canada as a whole, not just those of party ideology. I would like to see Canadian politics be less partisan and work more toward consensus like indigenous political systems do. Direct Democracy could also open the door for other political reforms like ranked choice voting. It allows for a person's vote to always be counted but does not take power from the politicians."

Bea was certain these great reasons for wanting to be part of Direct Democracy were not Ray's true reasons. She hoped a joint would help get to his root cause for being so interested in the party. "Weren't we going to smoke some weed? You promised me we'd get high!"

A family of at least three generations was passing as Bea spoke. The grandmother responded immediately with, "Well, I never!"

Ray waited until the granny was well away. "With Direct Democracy, you must avoid Liquid Democracy."

"You're avoiding getting stoned. You know it's legal. Light it up."

Ray did take out a joint but seemed reluctant as runners, families and couples strolled past. Instead of lighting it he palmed it and continued to talk. "Liquid Democracy is when a voter can give their vote to another voter they trust as a proxy. Essentially, by giving the proxy to the other person the proxy holder gets two votes, theirs, and the proxy... or more if the person is trusted. To my mind, this is the breeding ground for corruption. A person could build a power block that gets 'sold' to the highest bidder. If a person got enough proxies, they could be a de facto MP because they hold a large percentage of the electorate's votes."

"Isn't there some way to prevent that with app security?"

"App security and transparency will get very complicated. You cannot under any circumstances allow the exchange of votes."

"Our app will allow voters to align their vote with a party. Isn't this Liquid Democracy?"

"There's a fine line, but the difference is that the app allows the voter to vote as the party does... rather than the voter giving their vote to the party. The voters keep control over their votes with the app. Liquid Democracy has the voter give their vote away."

"Fine line indeed. Direct Democracy will have to put up some boundaries as to what parties or people are allowed to have their position on the app. Probably only the big parties."

Ray nodded in agreement.

Walking down the hill next to the golf course, Bea ran by a few of her ideas on ways to get Direct Democracy bigger online. Ray provided some tips on making bots. With his advice, she was certain she could make a bot to post information on Direct Democracy every time democracy was mentioned on Reddit. They also discussed gaming YouTube and TikTok algorithms. She loved that he did not patronize her as other techies would. Even Ajay would give her the gears when she asked questions, he thought were basic.

They walked past a ball diamond and came to a wooded area where the path over a bridge crossed a stream to the other side of the golf course. It was the last place to covertly smoke a joint. Bea slowed their pace to ensure no people would be close. Next to the bridge was a small trail probably used by kids finding frogs or unhoused people finding shelter. She pushed Ray down the path, helping with the scooter where branches crossed the path. Once past the underbrush, the area opened under large willow trees. The drooping branches hid them. Someone had put candles at the base of a tree, forming a little grotto.

Ray lit the joint, taking a couple of big hits and passing it to Bea just as he erupted into a coughing fit. She took a couple of shallow tokes. When his coughing mostly stopped, Ray said, "Some good shit, eh?"

"I'm not sure I'm feeling it," Bea giggled. "I don't smoke often."

"You sure seemed enthusiastic to do some."

"Well, I have to confess to ulterior motives."

"Huh?" He took another long toke.

"Forgive me, but... Are you actually going to help with Direct Democracy?"

Ray coughed out a 'Yes!'.

"Great!"

"Hack, cough cough... If you say so."

"We meet every Saturday at the James Bay Senior Centre..."

"Okay."

"Sometimes there's a meeting on Wednesday night for the old people to learn social media. You won't need that unless you want to help." Bea took the jay again, puffing more deeply. "Still not sure if I'm feeling it." She peered up the trail. "Did you hear that? Is someone coming?"

"It's someone on the bridge." Ray toked. "They won't be coming down here."

I hope not."

"My... cough... name is Trickster Raven."

"Cool... That's your indigenous name?"

"Yes. Given to me by Medicine Man Coyote Cliché on April Fools." His grave silence following left Bea dumbstruck. "NOT!" Ray laughed loudly. "It's not my Native name. It is my Reddit username and Gmail. I've had it since I was a kid."

The weed made Bea unable to get the joke. She said, "I'm sorry..."

"Nothing to be sorry about," Ray responded. "I'm not into hanging out at an old folks home telling them to turn the computer on and off again, assuring that no one is stealing their personal data."

Bea snickered.

"Plus, Ajay said I should keep arm's length because I could be perceived as providing a service to Direct Democracy. And that could mess with my project and Direct Democracy's finances."

"Oh yeah. Derek talked about that. What is your project?"

"I am working on an app for indigenous tribes to vote securely and transparently on tribal issues. It'll be part of my PhD."

"Nice!"

"Thanks."

"That's exactly what we're looking for…"

The blunt alien shape of a barred owl passed over them, wings roiling the smoke from the joint, and landed in a tree. Both stared at the owl, three metres away.

"Amazing! We must take a selfie." Bea found her phone and positioned it for the best angle.

Ray awkwardly leaned to get out of the picture.

"Move over here." Quietly, Ray stepped out of the frame.

Bea took a couple of shots. "These pictures are for me. I'm not putting them on the internet."

"Okay."

"You should take one with me. This owl wants us to take a picture with it."

Woodenly he moved closer to her.

"Are you afraid of owls?" Bea asked gently.

"No. I love 'em."

Bea took this as permission to put her arm around him. Ray stiffened into a statue, making it easier to drape herself around him.

"One of my favourite ironies is Hedwig from Harry Potter," Ray said. "A flame war was going on over how much of a TERF (Trans-Exclusionary Radical Feminist) J. K. Rowling is on this forum I'm on. Some Fanboy was trying to minimize her transphobic remarks 'cause Harry Potter is amazing, and the trans community was correcting the Fanboy. Then, out of nowhere, someone posts that there is a trans character in Harry Potter. Everyone else agreed that there wasn't one. But this birder posts that all white Snowy Owls are male. Hedwig, in the books, is a completely white Snowy Owl. Hedwig is male by biological standards. But Hedwig identifies as female. Hedwig is trans."

"That's awesome!" Bea laughed. "I kind of want to fact-check it, but at the same time, it's so good, why ruin it? Maybe it is our destiny to get it out there?"

"I've never doubted it. But I doubt many non-woke people would get it. Or they'd be hung up on birds having gender, even with all the gay penguins."

The owl let out a 'WHO COOKS FOR YOU!' Bea turned on the video to catch the next call. When she finished videoing, she turned to see Ray ogling her ass and midriff to side boob. Kittenishly she said, "My eyes are up here."

"I wasn't, ah… I was making sure the cherry from the jay was out. I don't want to start a fire."

Bea quickly flipped through pictures on her phone. Coquettishly, she said, "OK. I will give you that one. But what about this!?" She displayed one of the selfies in which Ray was obviously staring at her cleavage.

Ray was not catching on to the vibe. He took a step back, putting his hands out, palms facing her. "I didn't…"

The sound of people crashing down the trail made them both turn. A big man and a cute woman with cameras were making their way through the underbrush. The woman pointed her camera and said, "Owl!"

"Sorry," the man said to Bea and Ray, "we didn't mean to interrupt. There's a Barred Owl."

"What?!" Bea said with a fuck off tone. "There's an owl? I didn't notice. Maybe that's what that loud hooting noise was. I thought it was a monkey. Lots of monkeys in the area. But I see it now, right above our heads." Bea and Ray stifled laughs. "And you're big-time owl photographers?"

"More like small time." Apparently not noticing Bea's patronizing tone the man explained, "We take lots of owl pictures. We are *Cute*

Christa and Fishy Jay on YouTube and *The Real John Owler* on TikTok."

Ray picked up his scooter and started out of the bush. The mood broken; Bea followed him.

"You're Cute Christa..." She took names. "And Fishy Jay on YouTube. Right... I'll check it out."

"You can find us by searching John Owler on YouTube."

"I'll do that." Bea stepped after Ray.

"Have a good day."

Catching up at the bridge, Bea asked Ray, "I'm going that way, wanna walk with me some more?" His body language and abrupt exit told her the answer, but she wanted to be sure.

"It was nice meeting you. I kind of spaced on something," Ray spoke with eyes on his shoes. "I'm going to be late if I don't leave now."

"I had a good time."

"Great."

"I expect an email."

"Okay."

"Here's my address." Bea showed her phone.

"Got it." Ray tapped at his screen. "Sent."

"Good boy," Bea smirked.

She contemplated Ray's butt as he zipped away. Was it the weed or her that put him off? It was not clear. What was clear was that she had just put out interested signals to two guys, and neither turned out. She was feeling less like a MILF all the time. Seduction was so much easier when she was in university.

Bea forced herself to run the rest of the way home. Or at least to the liquor store a few blocks from her house. Then walk. A few beers before bedtime were the only way to hold at bay a slight headache.

At home she found Harold's most recent interview, watched it, and watched it again. Her fist increasingly punched the air the more times she viewed and the more beer she drank. Yelling at the screen she reflected that it was the Paulina Apartments, so no one cared about the noise.

The interviewer stroked Harold's ego by saying how good he was as an MP. When the bait was deeply swallowed, he asked: "Knowing of your great legislative experience and understanding of Canadian resource economics, how can you let non-experts decide policy?" Harold fell quiet for a few seconds, but the interviewer was ready with a follow-up provocation. "Sure, it's easy enough to let everyone vote on fluffy nonconsequential legislation. I think that's great for 'inclusiveness.' But are you, Harold Gordon, telling me you'll let Liberal, NDP, and Greens make resource decisions that impact small western Canadian towns?"

"It's not really time to go into the detailed mechanics of Direct Democracy," Harold blurted.

"Come on, Harold," the interviewer prodded. If Direct Democracy is different, then be different from every politician and be honest—like you were as a PC."

"As I said, the details have yet to be hashed out. But holy doodle… There'll be some legislation that will have to be left in the hands of elected representatives with particular expertise. If there are bills on Canada's natural resources and how they are used for the enrichment of Canadians, gosh darn it, I'm making that call." From that point on Harold's answers veered toward a conservative platform, with Direct Democracy a wet nap to wipe up all the lefties' tears.

'How could Joice say it was not so bad?' Bea thought. 'Probably because she saw this through the lens of left and right, a partisan struggle.' From the partisan perspective, having contradictory messages was more acceptable because one was at war with the other. All is fair in love and war. Bea knew this us-or-them style would not work for Direct Democracy.

Bea cracked another beer and sat down at her computer. She wrote:

Dear Harold,
RE: *Libertarians on Guard for Thee* interview

I was not impressed. Getting Libertarians to side with Direct Democracy should be as easy as shouting '**Freedom**'. But you fucked it up. You left them thinking Direct Democracy was the Natural Resource Extraction Party with a novelty voting app to placate the lefties.

The leader of Direct Democracy must be for Direct Democracy and nothing else. The feeling that a person could hold opposing ideological views on different topics is our bread and butter. For the leader to say anything different is heresy.

To keep the shit-fuckery that happened on *Libertarians on Guard for Thee* to a minimum, next meeting, I suggest we go over these simple talking points:

1. Interviewer questions the ability of the average person to vote. Reply: That question implies Canadians are stupid. Do you think Canadians are stupid? I do not.

2. Interviewer massages your ego by saying how great a legislator you are. Reply: My greatness is that I am, at heart, an average Canadian. That's how I voted so wisely. Now, I'm giving that opportunity to all constituents.

3. The interviewer asks about your political views. Reply: My political views don't matter. My belief in Direct Democracy is what matters. Allowing all people in my constituency to vote is my politics.

Saturday, we will work on tailoring these responses to better fit your style. In the meantime, please do not inject your politics into media interviews.

On a positive note, I presented Direct Democracy to a first-year Canadian Democracy class at UVic. We could have five new enthusiastic student volunteers.

Regards, Bea.

After hitting send Bea searched for *Cute Christa and Fishy Jay* and found their website. She quite liked the videos, especially the John Owler ones. With a YouTube account made for trolling, she left a bunch of awful comments and a copyright strike on their channel. They messed up her evening.

On her real YouTube account, she became Cute Christa and Fishy Jay's one-hundredth subscriber.

She went to bed thinking when it would be right to email Ray.

14.

Thursday was pretty good.

Any hangover Bea had was quickly gone with the application of strong coffee. Work went swimmingly, everyone she called was ready to pay up and easily persuaded to pay as much as they could. By the end of the workday, she had determined that she would not approach Ray until the following week. At home, readying for a run, she had still not received an email from Harold. She sensed that the longer Harold took to reply the less pissed he would be.

After her run, she received Harold's email:

Good day, Beatrix Jensen,

I find it amusing that you think by cutting down my great interview with *Libertarians on Guard for Thee* you can hide your lack of loyalty to Direct Democracy.

It is irredeemable that you did not inform me, the party leader, of the UVic Political Science invitation. How can I trust you if you cannot keep me informed of important opportunities? I cannot stand for my right-hand man going behind my back.

You then try to bury this disrespect in an email chastising me for conducting a great interview. The comment section of the *Libertarians on Guard for Thee* interview was subsequently full of converts to Direct Democracy. More than 25 commenters professed their intentions to join the party, 20 more than the five that may volunteer for us from your pathetic attempts to emasculate me by speaking in my place at UVic. If I had been at UVic that tally would be more than six.

Before telling me how to lead MY party, remember that I came up with the idea of Direct Democracy, and I have won every election I have contested. You are an amateur who could learn if you follow my lead. I expect to see you on Saturday to address this.

Honourable Harold Gordon, Retired

Owls, Doughnuts, and Democracy, by Jason A. N. Taylor

Bea would concede that her email was less than professional, but it did not warrant the vehemence of Harold's response. The message needed to be said. And the sooner it was said the better because a string of similar interviews would hinder them. What she had really not expected was that he would perceive her UVic activity as treasonous. She suspected he still assumed she sought to be leader. It should have been clear she did not want it. If Harold had done the presentation, she knew at least that Ray would not have been receptive.

Bea contemplated. Part of her wanted to blow it up, shake Harold by his lapels yelling, "Direct Democracy is not PC light!" But he was tall and old: with her luck he'd fall over, breaking a hip. The opposite course would be to prostrate herself, admitting guilt. She was sure she would not and could not do this. She felt strongly that she was right to go to UVic and right to criticize his interview. These supposedly treacherous acts were done to make Direct Democracy stronger.

Eventually, she decided that she should bring a bunch of doughnuts, apologize for the tone of her email, apologize for the UVic misunderstanding, successfully argue that her actions were right, and then they would work on talking points for the hard questions. She could admit that they both were hotheads, but premium doughnuts and coffee would ease them onto the same page.

Saturday was the type of spring day Victoria was made for, tulips and early rhododendrons bloomed. Bea got three boxes of doughnuts at Discovery Coffee as it was closer to the Home. She hoped there would be a few of the raspberry glazed left over. She loved them and they would save her a few breakfasts. The doughnuts had depleted her meagre disposable income.

The home was a hive of action. Karen was being overwhelmed by a group of university students politely waiting to sign in as guests. Bea saw Joice, Justin and Tyrell waiting with two other students she did not recognize. John, one of Harold's lackeys, was holding the door open for a delivery person with many boxes of Empire Donuts. Bea jogged in before the delivery person, getting the stink eye from John.

"Karen, I can sign these people in." Bea put her doughnut boxes on the front counter. "They're all here for Direct Democracy."

Ms. Anderson wandered around hoping a university student was one of her grandchildren. Bea asked her to get Irene or Wendy to come and help. Wendy came quickly, taking Bea's doughnuts and escorting the students to the lounge. Bea stayed at the front counter for a few minutes after ten AM to assist any stragglers. There were more than a few. Mia and Ethan accompanied four other students. Bea was impressed that eleven students had shown up, almost a third of the class.

With the students, there were more than thirty people for the meeting. Extra chairs were needed. Bea drafted Justin to help get more as he already had a spot to put his coffee and doughnut down.

With everyone seated, Bea saw that the room resembled a high-school dance, with students in a clump not mixing with the oldsters. Harold and his apparatchiks were at the head table in muffled conversation. Others were sitting in political groupings. She decided students needed to be formally introduced. She stepped to the head table.

"Finally, come up to apologize." Harold addressed her. "I know this is hard for you to do."

"We must apologize to each other," Bea spoke firmly but low enough not to have the room become aware that there was controversy. "That's not important right now. We'll talk about our disagreement later. Right now, we need to get the students to mix with our other volunteers. Follow my lead." Bea then strode to the podium and whistled so loudly that everyone stopped. "We have a bunch of new members." She pointed to the students at the back table. "Direct Democracy is an inclusive party. Let's break the ice and mix this drink. We are going to play political two truths and one lie." She explained the game and how the groups would be split into four members to two newbies. She made sure that Justin was in Harold's group to start. Then she mingled with the groups, injecting energy and controversy into those groups not engaged to the point of loud, joyful conversation.

Halfway through the Ice Breaker a peacock-suited Derek tentatively tapped his way into the lounge, making his way to Bea. "I did not know there was a party scheduled for today's meeting. I am underdressed for socializing."

"Relax, Derek. I presented to a poly-sci class at UVic the other day. The result is eleven enthusiastic volunteers." Bea gestured to the scattered unfamiliar faces. "The meeting wasn't getting them involved and Harold wasn't getting them interested either. I got them mixing with this Ice Breaker." She pointed at Harold, who was animatedly speaking with one of the students. "Even the old pissed-off curmudgeon is having a great time."

"I got an email from Harold regarding you being disloyal. I did not read the email. The subject line was treacherous. I dismissed it as an old man rant. However, I think I should have read it."

"The gist is that I went behind his back going to UVic and I shouldn't critique his interviews, either. Because giving honest feedback is not an acceptable trait in politics, apparently."

"Ah yes. Traditional non-communication."

"But I have a plan to smooth it over. I got doughnuts. I'll apologize for my part and we'll move on."

"I suggest you have me participate in that encounter." Derek glanced to the table with the doughnuts. "Did you get Empire Donuts?"

"No." Bea surveyed the groups. "Yonni's from Discovery. They have my favourite. Raspberry glazed."

"Looks like they are the favourite of a lot of people. Might not be any left."

"Crap! What time is it?" Bea checked her phone. "Phew... Forty minutes before I have to get Sam."

Bea whistled again. "Now that everyone's had a chance to meet, please find a seat with your new friends." She waited while everyone obeyed. "We use this part of the meeting to go over Direct Democracy business. Sorry to sidetrack our normal agenda." She gestured for Harold to join her. "But I think there's time to go over most of it."

Harold shrugged in his seat to say, 'Who me?' in surprise. Then he gave Bea the broadest politician's smile that said 'fuck you' behind his toothy grin. "Are you sure you're done?" His tone was joking but not. "That was great fun. I wouldn't want to spoil it with business."

"Unfortunately, it is time for business."

Harold sauntered to the podium and started with a review of the previous week's interviews and other activities. He talked up the potential for twenty-five new members from his great *Libertarians on Guard for Thee* interview. Bea had decided she would only call him out on content if he brought it up. He did not. He talked down her presentation to UVic, hardly acknowledging that around a third of the people in the room were there because of it. She had expected this and continued to sit on her hands.

Harold finally tabled the biggest news of the day. "Direct Democracy now has a colour. Young Morty is a retired graphic artist. He's come up with the perfect colour. Johnny, can you bring us the colour sample?"

John shuffled a large piece of cardboard to the front.

"Cerulean blue is a colour that evokes peace and confidence," Harold proclaimed. "Which is what Direct Democracy will bring to Canadian politics. It is the colour of the clear blue sky, symbolizing limitlessness to grow." Harold looked directly at Bea. "Finally, it has feminine attributes that highlight inclusiveness."

The crowd murmured. Bea heard mutterings that the colour was similar to Conservative blue. Harold's lackeys began to applaud, enticing the rest of the room to join in. Bea clapped a slow, mocking accolade that only Derek noticed.

"It is great to hear the enthusiasm," Harold celebrated. "Aside from the colour, we also have some preliminary designs Morty has come up with for the Direct Democracy logo." John picked up another large cardboard sign, turning it to show the members. Two D's with red maple leaves comprised the centre; below each D the full word appeared in small font. It looked like a Canadian Forces aircraft roundlet or hockey jersey logo.

Bea did a phone search for the Conservative logo. The font was similar, with the maple leaf in the middle of the large C. In smaller font, the word Conservative was under or to the right of the big C, like a roundlet or hockey jersey logo.

The chatter in the room was full of hushed words reflecting the DD-to-conservative similarities.

"Harold," Bea spoke up. "Do you not see the resemblance to the Conservative logo?"

"Ours is completely different," Harold said confidently. "First, the blue is cerulean, not navy. Second, ours has two Ds. Yes, they both use a maple leaf, but ours has two, and it is, after all, Canada's national symbol."

Bea stifled a laugh, but she did let out an exasperated, "Really?!"

"Yes really, Bea." Harold was losing his composure.

"The colour and style is too close to the Conservative's," Bea asserted. "People will be confused." The murmured tone of the crowd told her they quietly agreed.

Harold sensed the members siding with Bea. He stooped over the lectern, holding on, looking old and tired. "If you think the logo is too similar to the Conservative's..." Harold spoke almost wearily, "...raise your hand."

The vast majority raised their hands.

Harold sighed. "The members have spoken." He raised his eyes and voice to the back of the room. "Morty, it's back to the drawing board. Whatever the new design is, it should stand out in our colour." Harold glared at Bea. "Cerulean blue."

Arguing with Harold over colour was not a winning proposition, Bea let it go. She was mildly impressed or mildly infuriated that femininity was part of the colour consideration. 'Progress,' she thought.

Harold ended the meeting shortly after.

Before Bea could talk with Harold she was stopped by Tyrell. "Bea, the meeting was really interesting and fun." He paused. "All the people I met were great, especially, Irene."

"Irene is awesome." Bea checked her phone for the time.

"I don't want to hold you up too long…" Tyrell somewhat bashfully said. "But remember the other day when we talked about Jodie Wilson-Raybould?"

Bea nodded.

Tyrell took a book from his knapsack. "You can borrow my copy of *"Indian" in the Cabinet* if you'd like to read it."

"Thank you very much. I will read it." Bea took the book and stepped slightly away. "But I must talk with Harold. Thank you! And thanks for coming."

"The pleasure was mine. Cerulean blue," Tyrell chirped.

They laughed.

Bea found Harold sitting with the lads and Derek. Too late, she noticed that Derek seemed to be gesturing her away. She said to Harold, "We need to talk."

"I already heard that you don't like cerulean blue," Harold said. "It's too Conservative. Would neon pink be Liberal enough? Or chartreuse close enough to the NDP?" His cadre laughed and hooted.

"I only use neon pink hoochies for sockeye and pink salmon," Bea said smartly. "Chartreuse is a good chinook flasher colour."

The boys fell silent, unsure how to respond to the salmon fishing references.

"Holy doodle, she knows fishing too," Harold said. "Look Missy, I'm not here to spar with you. The only thing we need to talk about is your apology for being disloyal. Then we can talk about the chaos that happened today. Maybe we can salvage something good from it."

Bea took a deep breath. Then another. "I'm sorry I didn't tell you about the UVic presentation. The invitation was specifically for me. I know the Professor. I was not disloyal, everything I've done is for the benefit of Direct Democracy. You must apologize to me for accusing me of being treacherous."

"No."

Bea was floored. "What?!"

"I am the party leader and you're holding a book by a traitorous liberal asking for an apology. I'm not giving an apology to such a person."

Bea held it together, resisting an urge to throw the book in Harold's face. "You're saying I'm disloyal for having a book a friend lent me? Get a grip."

"Let's take a second to get back on the same page," Derek interjected. "Everyone here wants Direct Democracy to be successful. Bea, you've been on your feet since the meeting started; why not grab a doughnut and have a seat? We can talk."

Bea wanted to ensure she would hit Harold with the book. She swung her arm underhand like a softball pitcher, getting used to the weight of the ball. She decided to listen to Derek. She turned to get a doughnut, then saw that there were none left. She came back to the table. "They're all gone."

"John," Harold turned to his main lackey. "Where did you put those inferior doughnuts?"

"I threw them in the garbage, boss."

"You threw the three boxes of Yonni's doughnuts in the garbage?" Bea glared at John. "That I brought? $54 of doughnuts in the garbage?"

"Yes," John said, backing uneasily from the table, worrying for his safety. "Harold told me to get them out of here.

"I said get them out of here," Harold barked. "Not throw them out. I thought they were from Irene. We only have Empire Donuts at Direct Democracy."

"Where did you put the doughnuts, John?" Bea turned to Harold. "And you… and only you, come with me!"

"In the bin behind the kitchen's swinging doors," John replied.

Bea said nothing more. She thought of destroying the Direct Democracy website and membership list. Harold followed her into the kitchen where they located the three boxes dumped in the large garbage can. Two had their contents spilling out. Bea grabbed the one salvageable box, wiping off glaze so none would get onto her or the book.

Harold stood, appearing not to know what to do.

"Harold, I am done." Bea struggled to speak calmly. "I believe in Direct Democracy; I did everything to make it better... but I am done. I will continue to administer the website for two weeks, but if you have no replacement, I will send you the login info, and you can do with it what you want. I wish Direct Democracy the best. I will be voting for it in the fall regardless of your tomfoolery. Pass on to Derek that he was great to work with. Now, I must meet Sam."

Harold poked around in the garbage and found that all the discarded doughnuts were soiled. The sound of the doors swinging from Bea's departure ended his rescue mission.

Early to the meeting spot, Bea sat on a playground bench reading the Wilson-Raybould book. Immersing herself in the story kept her from thinking of Harold and Direct Democracy. Amy was slightly late dropping off Sam. Bea was content to read in the warm sun, distracting herself from Direct Democracy.

Sam ran up yelling, "Momma B!", arms wide for a hug. She hugged him. He took off to ride on the zipline. Amy stood by.

"Hey Bea," Amy said.

"Amy."

"Has Marcus talked with you about this summer?"

"He told me you're going to Ottawa for the summer."

"That's it?"

"Yup. Is there more I should know?"

Amy's fidgety body language told Bea there was more to know. "Yeah, the details... dates, places, that sort of stuff. Marcus has been really busy travelling. I'll make sure he gets that to you."

Bea thanked Amy and got back to the book while Sam played. Twenty minutes of entertainment was all the playground offered for him. "Momma B! I'm hungry. It's hot. Can we go to Beacon Drive-In for ice cream?"

"Not today. I have some doughnuts and juice." Bea's answer reminded her of the lost money and the juices she had to steal because of Harold. "Once we finish, let's go see the owls. Remember last year around this time?"

"Josie had owlets!"

Owls, Doughnuts, and Democracy, by Jason A. N. Taylor

"Not quite this early... but soon. I was thinking of how Mister would chase the squirrels around the nest. Remember that?"

"That was cool!" Sam saw a squirrel begging for nuts. He pretended to be an owl and chased the squirrel up a tree.

They walked to the nesting area. In late spring, the forest was an explosion of vivid greens from new leaves and shoots. They found the old owl lady near the nest. After saying hi, the owl lady showed Sam where Mister was and walked him around the area, pointing out all the owl-related sites. She showed him their food caches, pellets, and the remains from their last meal.

Bea took a seat on a little log fence across the chip trail, five metres from the nesting tree trunk. To keep her thoughts from dwelling on Harold and Direct Democracy, she read. However, she began to see similarities between the Justin Trudeau versus Jodie debacle and the situation she had just experienced with Harold. Regardless of Junior's rhetoric, he was in the game for power, his ethic being that with him in power, the world would be a better place. Jodie was in it to make the world better, period. Bea felt the same. Regardless of the fact that both J.T. and Jodie had good intentions, she was an outsider, someone who did not understand or want to understand power in the way politics-raised Justin understood it. J.T.'s understanding of power was dominant and existed many hundreds of years before Harold was forced to buy into it as all other political people had to do.

Seeing this relationship caused Bea great distress. It made her feel that there was no way forward, no better world. She felt the country had lost a chance for more democracy because she and Harold could not make Direct Democracy work within the traditional power structure. She tried watching Sam as a distraction but began to cry, knowing it was his better world that was at stake. She tried to hide her tears from Sam.

Sam came up and hugged her. "Are you crying because I'm going to live in Ottawa?"

"No, kiddo." Bea wiped her eyes. "And you're only going for the summer."

Owls, Doughnuts, and Democracy, by Jason A. N. Taylor

Sam went quiet, scanning for what Mister had started to track with his owl eyes. "Mister sees a squirrel bouncing toward the nest tree!" Sam pointed to a black squirrel crossing the chip-covered path toward the large dead Douglas fir with its top broken off. Josie's nest was in the broken top.

The squirrel stopped mid-trail. From a large maple tree, Mister swooped down silently, nearly brushing Bea and Sam. The squirrel bounded away, narrowly avoiding talons. Mister pulled up to land on a branch. The squirrel hid on the other side of a tree trunk at the same height as the owl. The squirrel's head pointed to the ground and tail to the sky. Mister peered left and right trying to locate the squirrel. Mister perched long enough for Bea to get out her phone. Mister launched off the branch, flying in a semicircle to come around the trunk with talons out. There was a clack and scrape, the squirrel fell from the tree. Mister hovered for a second and then dived, but the squirrel scampered away in the nick of time. Mister powered up and flew back to the branch over Sam's and Bea's heads.

Excitedly, Sam replayed Mister's squirrel hunt with sound effects and an inner monologue of Mister and the squirrel.

Bea played back her phone video and was shocked how good it was and how close Mister came to getting the squirrel. However, it was strange to her that they had never seen the owls eating a squirrel. They'd seen the owls eat lots of rats but no squirrels. She asked Cheryl the owl lady, "Do the owls ever get the squirrels?"

"During the day, rarely," Cheryl responded. 'It's more of a game. The squirrels try to raid the nest. Mister stops them."

'It is a game,' Bea thought. Maybe Harold and her were entwined in a similar game. He was following what he knew. She was forced to play because he could not change. It was as obvious as the scientific study that proved people are happier on weekends.

Some crows came to hassle Mister, keeping Sam entertained while Bea continued to read. The cry of a peacock took her head out of the book. Coincidently, the biking peacock was dismounting his road bike at the end of the paved trail. "Derek," she said coldly, closing her book.

"Nice day, Bea."

"If you say so…"

"I thought I might find you here." Derek looked around, smiling. "Hey Sam, where are the owls?"

Sam took him by the hand, showed him the nesting area, introduced Cheryl, and provided what Derek thought was a modern dance interpretation of Mister's squirrel chase.

"Thank you for giving me the grand tour. Can you excuse me? I would like to talk with your mother."

Derek took a seat on the log fence next to Bea.

"Are you here to convince me to come back to the party?"

"No. That is a choice only you can make. I did want to thank you for the amazing work you put in. If you do not return, Harold and I will be drafting letters of reference for you."

"Very kind of you."

"And I wanted to offer my services as a mediator if you would like to talk with Harold."

"Oh?"

"Of course, Harold would have to agree as well."

Bea was quiet, watching Mister. "I'm not sure I want to. It seems the conflict I am having with Harold is that he feels I am a threat to his power."

Derek nodded.

"It's funny," Bea laughed, "because by definition the leader does not really hold any power in Direct Democracy." Derek chuckled too.

"And even though I've made it clear I have no intention of leading, he sees me as a competitor. A threat, even. Wasn't it clear enough during the leadership election that I intentionally cast a bad light on myself to not get elected?"

"Yes. I knew it. Most of the members knew it." Derek paused. "Harold must have known."

"Just as I could do the math, Harold could too. Quite frankly, I think it scared the old Harold to compete with a woman having the support you did. That old part was more scared when you're not following the rules bore fruit."

"What do you mean old Harold? He's all old."

Derek pointed to the volume in her hands. "The part of Harold that learned the power politics you are reading about in that book."

"This is a disturbing story."

"It should be. It is a process whereby a man like Harold slowly forgets how to listen to his constituency with each election win. And every whispered Cabinet or leadership promise from PC insiders intoxicates him more."

"To me, that's not a good reason for me to come back." Bea sighed heavily. "It tells me that if I work to my potential and do not kiss his ring, I'll be fighting Harold at every turn."

"Perhaps."

"Why does it always have to be the same?" Bea ran a sleeve over her eyes, sniffling. She took note of Derek watching her intently. "Allergies," she lied.

"Bea, take a step back. Look at the big picture. It might help."

"Help with what?"

"Perspective."

"Please explain."

"The reason Harold got into politics is deep in his heart. It is the reason most politicians get into politics. He wanted to have his people heard, to bring views from the west coast to Ottawa. Then Ottawa got to him. Direct Democracy is the inevitable conclusion of what he wanted to do from the beginning. He started out ideologically conservative, but this was as much a reflection of how the West felt about central Canadian politics as it was his actual political stripe. When given the chance to think, and not challenged, he has always come down on the side of Direct Democracy."

"When not challenged, eh? In that case, I should stay away."

"Make no mistake, when I say challenged, I mean in the sense of being called out rather than reasoned with. Certainly, Harold does not always follow what is reasonable…"

"On that, we agree."

"…But he is good at correcting his course when wrong. Remember after the Unicorn video? How willing he was to practice Zoom?"

Bea nodded.

"The problem is that calling him out engages his power instinct... Any fear of being usurped and he becomes unreasonable—particularly when his yes men are around."

"John is a fucking assclown."

Derek poked fingers into his bike short pockets. "Before I forget. What John did was unconscionable." He handed Bea three twenty-dollar bills. "Take this."

"You don't have to, Derek. It was Harold and that idiot John." Politely, Bea tried with a half-ass effort to push the money away. She took it on the second offer.

"Direct Democracy is one hundred percent upside for you. We know how talented you are. And as I mentioned, if you really do not continue, Harold and I will be writing you glowing letters of reference."

"I'll keep that in mind."

"I will also be a personal reference for any of your endeavours. If you stay with Direct Democracy, win or lose, you will have skills at your disposal, a large network of helpers, and our backing. It is almost like getting a degree without going to school. There is no downside. Trust me, these kinds of connections matter."

"I'm truly touched...you're awesome."

"Would you like me to arrange a meeting for the three of us?"

Bea watched Mister for an awkward amount of time. "Derek, I was pretty close to throwing this book at Harold and kicking Johnny in the nuts today. I have never been so disrespected by people I work with. In fact, it felt like how Marcus, my ex, and the families treated me during the divorce proceedings. It's a win for Direct Democracy that I didn't go nuclear on the website and members lists. I wanted to do it..."

For the first time in Bea's experience, Derek looked dispirited.

"I'm not ready to make this decision."

Derek lingered for a time, raising other subjects of political interest. After a few more minutes of talking about Skippy, the new populist leader of the Conservative party, he mounted his bicycle and left.

Bea and Sam then went to get ice cream. In the late afternoon, the weather changed to rain, so they watched movies for the rest of the evening.

After Amy came for Sam, Bea emailed Ajay, Cat and Irene regarding her falling out with Harold. She included the correspondence from her to Harold and Harold to her. She needed to hear other opinions on the situation, knowing that she could be beautifully angry and lose her perspective in a dispute. They all got back to her quickly with similar responses: her email could get anyone's back up, but Harold's was worse. So were Harold's actions at the meeting. However, they felt taking Derek up on the mediation was the right thing to do.

Bea emailed Derek to arrange a meeting.

"Bea, you're looking chic today." It was the end of the shift; Mike had approached her between calls. "You've upped your fashion game lately. Big date?"

'Chic' would not be the word Bea would use for the grey donation bin pantsuit she was wearing. It was from a charity that helped women down on their luck get suitable clothes for job interviews. With less than twenty bucks until payday, she felt she qualified to partake in charity. She'd gotten the suit on Derek's recommendation to wear something professional for the mediation.

Irritated, she replied, "Not really your business, but no, I don't have a date tonight. And if I'm going to keep the good numbers up, I must get to the next call." She hit the dialler and watched Mike walk stiffly away.

The call was the last of the day. She was able to twist the arm of the debtor into paying an installment. She was killing it this month, nearer and nearer to her bonus. Once off the call, she rushed out to meet Derek. He had volunteered to pick her up since Harold wanted a meeting at 4:45 pm. It was Yorkshire Pudding night at the Home which Harold could not miss.

By Dallas Road, the wind was picking up; large, choppy waves crashed up and over the sea wall. Derek's place was half a dozen houses east of the Surf Motor Motel, just far enough from the ocean that sprays rarely touched the grounds.

The front of the house was windows, tinted for privacy. Inside the door were steps that ascended to a large living room with a bar and couches oriented toward the sea. Harold was sitting at the bar. Derek guided Bea to a seat at the other end. Bea and Harold greeted each other by name alone. Derek freshened Harold's drink and mixed Bea a Manhattan. They sat watching the water for a bit.

"Derek..." Bea broke the silence. "If I had this view, I would not need a TV."

"Do you see a TV in here?" Derek responded. "I have Harold to thank for this. He recommended I put in the big windows."

"It is a great view," Harold grunted, "but I wouldn't want it. I'd be jealous of every boat I saw fishing. It's going to blow a gale today. Not an evening to fish."

"I suppose we should get started." Derek spoke from the opposite side of the bar, the water view behind him. "Let's start by acknowledging how you are feeling about each other and why. Then we will look at the facts to see what valid concerns there are. Finally, we will see if there can be reconciliation. Who would like to go first?"

Harold rolled his eyes. "Ladies first."

"Don't 'ladies first' me. I'll go first because I deserve to go first." Bea sat up straight on the bar stool. "I feel like Harold thinks I'm a threat to his leadership. I feel that he wants me to show that I'm subordinate because of this. I feel he does not recognize the work I have put into Direct Democracy if it is not doing his bidding. I feel he wants a yes man, not an uppity woman, like his three stooges. I feel he is missing that this is a new and different race which will need different ways of running it to win."

"Calling my crew the three stooges is disrespectful," Harold blurted. "And..."

"I was not finished. I feel that I have to accept Harold and his cronies disrespecting me, like when John tossed my doughnuts in the trash."

"Holy doodle!" Harold tossed the money along the bar. "Here's sixty bucks to wipe your tears with." The money sat between them for a quiet ten seconds. "Is it my turn to say how I 'feel'?"

Derek gestured for Harold to speak.

"First off, feelings are BS. You are a threat to my leadership. You are a subordinate because I am the..."

"Harold!" Derek interjected urgently. "This is not how mediation works."

"Blow it out your ass Derek!" Harold blustered. "This is how leadership works."

Despite the heated exchange, Bea was distracted by waves hurling large logs against the cobble beach. A gust of wind shook the glass.

"When you prance around behind my back," Harold ranted, "messaging a different platform from mine..."

Bea had to object: "Direct Democracy does NOT have a platform!"

"... I look stupid," Harold continued, ignoring Bea's contradiction. "Playing childish games at our meetings and forgoing the agenda weakens us. And for what?"

Bea answered the rhetorical question, "To make eleven motivated volunteers feel welcome."

"POPPYCOCK! The disruption set back our agenda by a week."

"Whatever..."

"And poor Morty called out for his great work. For what? To make a bunch of basement-dwelling do-nothing gen-Z's feel included? No one should have to make them feel accepted, they should want to be with us. The only one worth his salt is Justin. Winning takes work, not games. If I had been at the University, I would have got twenty Justin's to join. Like I got twenty-five membership commitments from *Libertarians on Guard for Thee*."

"Time!" Derek held a hand between Harold and Bea. "Pause! Let me freshen your drinks and we will start again."

Bea downed the last of the Manhattan, then joined Harold, watching the storm grow stronger.

Bea pondered her new drink, seething inside. The big sip she took did not calm her. Cautiously she said, "Harold, before I decided to come to this 'mediation,' I used a tool I call the three-asshole rule."

"Do tell."

"Please listen to Bea, Harold. You'll get your turn for rebuttal."

"I asked three reasonable people if I was an asshole in this situation. They said I was an asshole if I didn't try to bridge this divide. All said my other actions were right, if not tactful." She gulped the rest of her drink. "I concede that I was not tactful."

"How big of you."

"But I will not subordinate myself to someone who is wrong. I thought Direct Democracy was about being more egalitarian. You're acting like a dictator." Bea stood up as a wind gust shuddered the house. "I will not follow you."

"Suit yourself, lady."

"None of those twenty-five potential members will ever join." Bea gave Harold one last glare. "Their comments were left by sock puppet accounts Ajay, Cat and I made. The score is eleven for me, nothing for you."

"Derek, thanks for trying." She took Harold's money and left.

Salt spray mixed with Bea's tears as she ran the Dallas Road path toward the Story Totem Pole and the owls. She was happy she did not get shoes to match the suit because she would not be able to run in them.

Spending time with the owls, even in a storm, was a way for Bea to delay going home. Still irate, the more time between now and getting to her computer meant a better chance she did not frag Direct Democracy's online presence. Despite her bitterness, she knew too well how important it was, though she knew there was little chance of the movement—online presence or not—surviving with Harold at the helm.

Douglas Fir branches fell around Bea, sitting by the nest. Douglas Firs shed small branches during storms to lose drag, keeping the entire tree from coming down. The maples, with their new leaves, made ominous creaking noises that she ignored. It was not an evening to be in the wilder, oldish-growth area of Beacon Hill Park. Even the unhoused people were finding safer places to camp.

Swaying maple branches blocked the owl nest from sight, but Bea saw an owlet head poke above the top edge of the nesting snag. Bright-eyed, she cooed aloud: "Oooo, Muffin get your dryer lint butt back in the nest. It is too windy for you." However, the little owlet did not listen. Luckily the wind direction was blowing Muffin back into the nest.

Bea had to share this with whoever would listen. She texted the picture to Rick and Cheryl. She even sent an image to Amy so Sam could see brave Muffin.

Spending time with the precious new owlet sent a warm strain of level-headedness through Bea. She knew then she would not sabotage Direct Democracy. Meanwhile, with a shake of her head, she realized it was stupid to be in the woods in a windstorm. She would have a ton of time to hang out with the owl family on nicer nights.

15.

Almost two weeks went by.

Life for Bea was going well. She was in a state of flow in her job, truly killing it, like the Canadian Women's hockey team versus the Europeans.

What made her particularly happy were interruptive emails telling of Harold's latest debacle. There had been nearly a mutiny at the Saturday meeting. Harold's lads had suggested that Direct Democracy should be less direct regarding economic policy, as in: The government's budget should not be decided upon by non-experts.

Morty changed the logo to a D within a D then a maple leaf, making it even more like the Conservative logo.

Harold signalled they were working on a platform, but the idea that issues like economic policy would be decided by experts caused great disharmony. The Tuesday social media meeting Cat hosted was not attended by any conservative-leaning Direct Democracy members because Harold poopooed it.

All this instilled an unabashed surge of schadenfreude in Bea. While sympathetic to her reasons for leaving, Irene, Wendy, Rich and others had begged her to come back.

But she had had more time to appreciate spring, read, and be with the owl family. There were two Barred Owlets in the nest, Muffin and Shakespeare. Watching these little puff balls peak out of the nest in the evening glow delighted her. She spent most evenings in the park and did not think of Direct Democracy.

The more Bea read of the Wilson-Reybould book the more she wondered how Jodie could see herself as much different than J.T. Both were brought up to be in politics. Their fathers were around the table for the drafting of the Canadian Constitution Act of 1982. They were groomed to make decisions for people, yet their jobs were to hear people and act on what they heard. Of course, both knew they had the ear of the people, but was their ear only hearing from their people? Jodie definitely felt J.T. was just hearing from the Liberal Elite and people that could keep him in power or kick him out. In her mind, the overall prerogative of the Liberals was to stay in power by listening to those who could keep them there. Was Jodie in a similar situation with her constituency and Indigenous power base but unable to see it because of her participation in it? Is not the act of representing a group of people in a democracy an act of partisanship? As the decision maker one must take a position that will necessarily be contrary to some of the people.

Partisanship was the argument for Direct Democracy. The most Bea would do to solve this problem was vote for Harold if the party still existed at election time.

Meanwhile, there was some thawing of Bea's relationship with Amy. Bea had gotten a flattering text while at work Thursday morning:

Hi Bea, Sam's been dying to see the owlets ever since you texted me last week. He loves seeing them. I love that you show him so much nature. I would like to take him owl-watching a few times more before we leave. Can you come show us where they are? Tonight?

It was odd for Amy to want anything to do with Bea. Amy had never suggested Bea see Sam at any other time than Bea's day. But Bea knew how tenacious Sam could be if he wanted something. Bea felt it was time to give Amy a chance, possibly Bea might get a free burger out of it.

Bea texted back: Tonight works. 6 pm at Big Wheel Burger on Cook? Sam loves it.

Nearly instantly, Amy texted back a smiley emoji: See you at 6 pm.

Mike caught Bea looking at her phone. She hid it when she saw him and quickly got back to calling debtors. He came up to her desk. "Bea, Terry and I would like to talk with you."

"I am just dialling a lead."

"Don't worry about the call." Mike put his hand on her desk. "Come with me." Bea followed Mike to a meeting room. Terry sat at the table, a folder in front of him. The sound of a phone vibrating on the desk could be heard.

Terry said, "Have a seat, Bea." Then turned to Mike and said, "Your phone has been ringing since you left."

Mike lunged to grab his phone before it vibrated its way off the desk. "Sorry, Terry. I thought it was on silent. I keep on getting spam calls. I even changed my number. But I have to have notifications on in case the wife needs something. She's not been well."

Bea covered her smile with a hand, though she knew a meeting with Mike and Terry in a meeting room was not good. Before anything else, Bea and Terry wished Mike's wife well.

"Bea, we've had a customer complaint." Mike cut to the chase. "We've thus determined that you've broken company policy on pressuring customers."

"Pressuring..? How?"

"Threatening to tell family members of their debt, calling workplaces, that kind of thing. Plus, your performance has been lagging..."

"I'm number one this pay period."

"...Your numbers have been down year over year for the past two years. And you've been taking more time away. This job must be your number one priority. Unfortunately, we must terminate you."

"But... Seven years and not even a reprimand. Then straight to termination?"

"It's policy," Mike muttered.

"What the fuck?! You know we all do what I am accused of doing, Mike. You and I shared tips on how to pressure 'customers' when you were on the floor. What chucklehead complained? I bet it was that basement-dwelling mouth-breathing day drunk, Andrew Chow. He runs a shady massage business from his basement. And you took his word? You didn't even ask your loyal employee what happened. Bullshit!" Bea kicked the table leg.

"Calm down," Terry said. "There's no need to take this personally. We got a letter from his lawyer...we had no choice."

"Don't take it personally! I'll remember that in three weeks when I don't make rent and explaining to my kid why I live in a tent in Beacon Hill Park. 'Sam, Mommy likes sleeping in the park with the owls. It's like summer camp. The creepy guy who smells like whiskey and piss is my buddy. He keeps me safe.' You have no clue. Just let me breathe a second, and I will calm down," She finished her sarcastic rant by shaking her head and leaning back in the chair. She sprung bolt upright. "I will not calm the fuck down."

"Here is your record of employment." Mike pushed a paper across the desk. "We can go get your stuff."

"Can't you just lay me off?" Bea begged. "Then I can get EI (Employment Insurance). I've paid into it long enough."

Mike grabbed a box from under the table. "Let's go."

In the hall, Bea stopped abruptly and put a hand on the wall. "I have to go to the bathroom. I think I'm going to be sick." Without a further word, she dashed to the washroom. She went into one of the stalls and plugged the toilet with toilet paper. Grabbing the boxes of tampons and pads, she left the washroom.

Mike was standing at her desk. "Mike," she leaned close in a near whisper. "I think one of the toilets is plugged. I'm pretty sure it will overflow."

"I better go check. Pack your stuff."

With Mike gone, Bea pulled out two reusable shopping bags to take the lunchroom coffee and snacks. At the supply cabinet she took a red Stadler stapler with the other office supplies. Finally, she grabbed the few items on her desk and the ergonomic mouse and keyboard, replacing them with standard ones from a vacant desk. Before Mike finished in the washroom she was gone. She felt no need to talk with any of her colleagues.

Every cyclist on her way home heard from Bea, whether obeying the law or not.

Bea did not need Knight Rider on patrol in front of her building today, but there he was on Kit sitting guard. Her anger towards him was sublime. Though he started a rant at ten metres distance, she overpowered him at five, yelling: "Fuck you! I'm in no mood to deal with your bullshit today." Her vehemence shut him up, saving her from going to jail for assault. He even gave her some of the sidewalk for her to pass on.

Survival mode took over at Bea's apartment. Dumping out the loot she took, Bea realized the effort was not worth it. She did not need extra paper, pens, stapler, or computer peripherals. The hygiene products were not ones she would use. She could get better at the women's health clinic. The coffee and snacks were the only things of value to her. She took stock of what she had. With the food she had taken, she probably had two weeks of rations, many meals consisting of a granola bar. She would Google community pantries and food banks. She counted her cash at hand, including bottles to return and any change in the couch. Under twenty bucks. Her last paycheque should cover another month of rent, internet, and phone, with fifty bucks extra if she reduced her debt payments to the minimum.

Bea needed employment quickly. Any employment. A resume was her next task. Finding out the ink in her old printer had solidified had her fantasizing about going *Office Space* on the evil device. Instead, she hoped a call to Karen at the Home might get her resume printed. If not, there was the depressing Jobs BC Centre.

She called Karen, who picked up after what seemed like a dozen rings. "Hello."

"Karen, it's Bea."

"Oh hi, Bea. What's up?"

"I got let go from my job."

"Oh!"

"I won't be able to make it this week… and volunteering is up in the air right now."

"That's awful!"

"Tell me about it."

"And I heard you had a falling out with Harold too. He's an old crank. He'll come around. Word is that there is a mutiny or coup afoot."

"Not my problem."

"What are you going to do?"

"That's why I called. I can't wait for EI. I've got a resume ready but no printer. Could I send it to yours?"

"Sure thing. Send it and I will print it. And if you need any small stuff like toilet paper, coffee, leftovers…" Karen listed off items Bea normally helped herself to. "Don't worry Bea, you'll bounce back. Everyone here loves you. Except Harold, he's been stomping around grumbling. He's the most jealous, petty man I've ever met."

"You're making my day Karen. I'll email you, then be there soon. Thank you kindly."

Before leaving home, Bea emailed Derek to ask for the reference letter he had promised her.

Tired and hungry, Bea left her last resume at a coffee shop and bar on Cook Street. More than ten applications handed out in the first afternoon felt like a good day. A few of the places gave her good vibes. She hoped they did not pick up her desperate, defeated aura.

With twenty minutes until meeting Sam and Amy at Big Wheel Burger, she took a break, reluctantly using her dwindling change for an iced coffee. The ambiance of Cook Street on a sunny spring afternoon lifted her mood slightly.

Walking toward Big Wheel Burger, she saw Sam and Momma A across the street, waved, and then joined them, chatting awkwardly on the way to the burger lineup.

Bea insisted on paying for the three of them, but Amy argued, Bea relented, and Amy paid for Sam and herself. Bea then acted surprised when she could not find her debit card and had no cash, achieving her goal to have Amy pay for her burger.

Ravenous, Bea tore into her double burger. Sam was almost as voracious. On the other hand, Amy unfolded her lettuce-wrapped chicken patty, cut it into pieces, then ate slowly. Bea stopped devouring her burger to offer, "Have some fries."

"I can't." Amy chewed deliberately five more times and swallowed. "I've got to keep on plan."

Bea's expression said 'why' so loudly that Sam had to answer. "Momma A has to keep in shape for Dad. She can't get flabby."

Amy went red. On other occasions, this would be Bea's queue to dig deeper, but not today. They continued to eat, talking about nothing. Amy even took a few fries.

They set out walking as the setting sun made everything better looking. Sam orbited around them, running ahead and falling behind depending on what interested him.

Sam's blurted disclosure about Amy's eating restrictions unsettled Bea. When Sam was out of earshot, she said: "I was shocked you called. We have not had a great relationship. And thanks for the burger."

"You forgot your card, it's no problem. Sam hasn't been able to talk about anything but the owlets. I thought he should get to see them before we go to Ottawa."

"Can I ask you something personal?"

Amy crossed her arms defensively. "I suppose…"

"Sam said that you can't get flabby. Is that true? What's that about? You're tiny."

"Kids say the darndest things." Amy sighed. "But it is true. I can't be heavier than a hundred and thirty pounds. It's in the prenup."

"Whoa..!"

"I'm not near that but I don't want to get near it… Sam overheard us talking about it."

"My god…"

"I think I'm too thin to get pregnant or stay pregnant."

"What the fuck?! How is that part of a prenup? Why would you accept that?"

"Please don't swear…"

"Sorry but…"

"It's pretty common in prenups these days. At least for a catch like Marcus." Amy visibly shuddered. "Gawd, I don't want to be fat either."

"Fuu…dge Amy! Please don't let Sam hear you guys talk about stuff like this. He can't grow up learning how to be a misogynist. What else does Marcus have in that slave collar around your neck?"

Amy stopped and looked Bea in the eye. "It seems pretty easy for you to say hurtful things like that."

"It's easy if it's true."

"Look, I married Marcus because I love him and he had the financial security I wanted. Not all of us are smart, talented, and can eat double burgers while keeping trim. It's not my fault you didn't want what Marcus has. I was not duped into the prenup. It covers things I consciously agreed to because they're my goals too. I don't want to be a fat ass. Or work. And I want children. What's wrong with putting that in writing?"

Consciously was the only four-dollar word Bea had ever heard Amy use. "I understand your choice," She lied. "But Sam's mind is not sophisticated enough to see why you made it. I don't want him growing up with that prejudice because it was 'okay' for his Dad. Just like you want to keep him from bad words, I want to keep him from bad ideas. I'd prefer him to be kept innocent enough not to expect a transactional relationship from the people he loves."

"I get it. I was feeling defensive. I didn't want Sam to hear that."

"Glad to hear you say that."

"I'm so lucky to have him in my life. If it weren't for Sam, the clause in the prenup about kids that Sabrina put in would have kicked in. But Marcus has shielded me…"

Bea hit her palm with her fist. "At least Marcus learned one thing from our marriage."

"What was that?"

"To protect his next wife from Sabrina the bitch."

"Oh, Sabrina is great when she takes me shopping. But she's the biggest reason I'm happy to move to Ottawa. Even with the winters."

"What do you mean the winters? Aren't you just going for the summer?"

"Oh gawd! Bea, don't shoot the messenger! I wanted to tell you in a better way. Actually, Marcus should have told you. But he's too afraid of you."

"He damn well better be!"

"So here I am telling you. I didn't want to just blurt it out." Amy cringed. "I'm sorry."

"Sam getting Senator's memorabilia at his birthday party. Marcus' new job and getting stuck in Ottawa…" Bea shook her head. "I should have seen it."

"Please don't be mad."

"Oh, I'm mad, but not at you Amy. What a cowardly dick. He's afraid of me… Hah, what a coward."

"We still want you to have your time with Sam."

"That's nice of you…"

"He loves you and you're good for him. We'll still be coming back to see Marcus's family."

"That's comforting..." Bea tried unsuccessfully not to be sarcastic.

"We don't really need your support payment so we thought we could use the money for an annual trip to see Sam."

"You will let me use my money to babysit Sam!" Bea's sarcasm dam burst. "In Ottawa! In the winter! While you're in Mexico! Great! Can I have the key to the liquor cabinet and a boyfriend over too?"

"Please don't overreact."

"How awesome, my time gets reduced to having to fight with Sabrina for Sam when he's here. And taking him to hockey practice while you sit on a beach. Everything I wanted from life."

"We were thinking the trip to see Sam could be to a holiday destination like Mexico."

Bea shook her head. "Don't talk with me for a few minutes. I need to let this settle in." Walking intentionally ahead of Amy, Bea cried quietly.

Amy let Bea cry on her own and pretended not to notice.

Sam reached the nesting tree first, watching for the little fluffy owlet heads to poke out.

"There's the nest." Bea pointed. "Go watch the owls with your kid, Momma A." Bea plopped down onto the fence.

"Thanks for showing me." Amy perched next to Bea. "Sam just loves owls. I want him to see them as much as he can. I want him to see them with you. Text me any time you have time before we leave. I'll bring him."

"That's kind..." Bea sniffled up a last tear. "I'll text you."

Amy held her arms wide for a hug.

Bea did not respond. "But not kind enough for a hug. Go watch owls. Let me be."

Amy did as Bea said.

After a time, Bea joined in. She reiterated to Sam all the things she knew about owls, hoping Amy would learn a bit so she could help Sam find them in Ottawa. When it was almost dark, Mister and Josie had a singalong that Bea, Sam, Amy, and a couple other owl people joined.

On the way back to the car, Amy asked, "How is Direct Democracy going?"

"What?"

"Marcus has been going on and on about it since Sam's birthday. I'm not political but I think it's a great idea. I'm voting for Direct Democracy and if Harold wins, maybe you'll get to Ottawa with him…"

"Harold and I had a falling out. I'm not part of it anymore. I'll still help but not in a way that will get me to Ottawa."

"That's too bad."

"Well, it's a long story…"

"Maybe you can patch it up with Harold."

"It's not looking good."

"I so like the idea of being able to vote for what's important to me."

"That's the idea."

"My Dad is a veteran. I want to support him, but Harper and now this Perrie P guy. What a clown. I also want to vote for the environment, Perrie P won't do that."

"I call him Little Pee Pee," Bea offered. "It suits him."

"Perfect!" Amy regarded Bea oddly. "Honestly, Marcus is totally envious of your political ideas. He's obsessed, even. Watches all the interviews. Shares them all over the place. Argues with his Dad."

"No kidding?"

"If you didn't resent him so much, I'd be worried." Amy paused, quizzical. "Do I have to worry?"

"God no! In fact, now that you've enlightened me, I might have to beg myself back in just to irritate Marcus."

"Don't feel you have to go against your principles…"

"Oh, and Direct Democracy was not my idea. It was Harold's."

"Marcus says he sees your hand in all the Direct Democracy messages."

Bea did not respond.

Amy brightened. "Can I ask you a girl-to-girl question?"

"I'm not a girl..." Bea's nose elevated slightly. "But I can answer as a woman."

"Did Marcus ever want you to dress up as Princess Leia? Every Halloween or costume party he wants me to go as Princess Leia, and he goes as Darth Vader."

"We did that at a costume party once," Bea lied. "But that was it." She told the obvious truth next, "He's always been a big Star Wars fan."

The lights on Amy's Range Rover flashed. "Do you want a lift home? It is getting dark."

"No. I want to walk and think. Thanks for the offer. Thanks for the burger. Thanks for being the messenger. This evening was mostly fun. I will be texting you." Bea squatted down, arms open. "Give me a hug!"

After Sam's long embrace, Bea stood to find Amy close and opened up for a hug. "Nope." Bea put out a fist for a bump, which Amy returned.

At home Bea went online, seeking to chat with Bubo or Babou71. Both were online. Both relayed reports of the chaos surrounding Direct Democracy. Then they worked on getting her to rejoin. She politely declined but volunteered to help with the third party.

Bea then told them of her awful day; Sam moving to Ottawa; the loss of her job. They offered to take her to dinner on Friday.

Dinner was at a vegan place Cat wanted to go to. Bea thought the meal was great, but the company could have been better. Cat was ecstatically optimistic that Bea's calamities were good omens. Sam going to Ottawa was a sign Bea had to stay with Direct Democracy. The loss of Bea's job was to give her the drive to make this new politics a winner.

"You need to be like Spock," Cat enthused, a mouthful of lentils altering her speech slightly. "Speaking truth to Harold's macho, emotional Kirk. Just work with the sourpuss and put aside your pride."

"We're more like Zapp Branigan and Kiff," Bea assured. "Anyway, I'm sure I won't be part of anything if Harold is the leader."

Attempts to change the topic were stubbornly rebuffed. Finally, in desperation, Bea asked about their relationship. That got them onto Bea's meeting with Ray. Bea told them the anticlimactic truth: the meeting was awkward and interrupted too soon, and she had not heard from him. Then Bea heard all about Cat and Ajay. She immediately suffered a long, drawn-out spiritual death from exposure to an excessively cute couple.

They invited her out for drinks after dinner. Bea went for one but needed to get home for an early start at job hunting. She was home to Villa Paulina before the Friday night cop car arrived.

Bea was woken by a call from Discovery Coffee for an interview at eleven o'clock. Glad that at least the crappy job market was good, she hoped if she got the job the intrusive thoughts of living in Beacon Hill Park would stop. The coffee shop had the typical hipster vibe. She donned a short flowery sundress and thrift store rescued Doc Martins, hoping it made her look right for the atmosphere. Unfortunately, she did not have a toque or Bass Pro Shop ball cap to round out the ensemble. She ensured she was well caffeinated and started walking. She could not help feeling this was a step back. Nearly thirty and interviewing to be a barista.

Fifteen minutes early for the interview, Bea sat in sunny Pioneer Park and wasted time checking email. It was interesting that just after telling Ajay and Cat about her clumsy meeting with Ray, there was an email from Ray. While reading it she was pinged with a text from Joice. Then an email from Rich. Followed by one from Irene. More texts from Mia, Justin, and Wendy poured in. Emails too. The gist of all this communication was that Direct Democracy had fallen apart. She felt sad but turned her phone off so as not to be distracted in the interview.

As soon as the coffee shop interview got going Bea felt like she would fit in. Her style was different from the baristas, but there was an eclectic mix of workers with cool being the only defining style. The manager liked Bea and let her know that she would hear from her soon, hinting at a possible training shift the next day.

Happy, Bea decided to forgo further job hunting. Instead, she would seek out the owl family. On the way to the park, she turned her phone notifications back on in case there was a call about the job.

Bea could not ignore the phone's explosion of notifications. Any Direct Democracy members with her phone number had texted. There were emails from all the regular members and some others. Even Harold and his cadre had contacted her. There were too many to read but the subject lines told her all she needed to know.

First there was the official statement from Harold that Bea had been purged from the party for disloyalty. Second, he dictated a platform that eliminated direct voting on economic bills. Bills he felt he was an expert on. Third, a motion that members had to swear allegiance to the party. Fourth, a decree that Morty's Conservative light logo was to be the official Direct Democracy insignia.

The first messages were from members who had left even before Harold had finished his proclamations. They were too upset with Bea being called disloyal. They urged her to fight back. They would stand with her. She was touched by their strong allegiance to her, but her mind was not swayed.

The next group of communications had to do with Harold's about face from actual direct democracy toward what they considered authoritarianism. Bea didn't think Harold was an authoritarian down deep, but he was playing the traditional hierarchy and authority game. Describing her as the ultimate power in Direct Democracy, the members beseeched her to put him in his place.

She felt pride but knew her conviction to Direct Democracy's ideals would not help the situation. The old way was entrenched.

Then there was a series of Harold and his lackeys rebuking her, accusing her of staging a coup. They believed this was her conspiracy and they demanded she call off her mutinous dogs. Simultaneously they said she would never succeed with her fiendish leftwing mutiny. What dogs? What mutiny? She was proud in a way, hearing how she was the reason Direct Democracy was crumbling, as she knew it would, without her. She knew the magnet that drew people to Direct Democracy was their deep yearning to be heard. Her only talent was not obscuring the message with her own beliefs.

When she got to the owl's nest Rich and Irene were there.

"How are the owls?" She asked, hoping not to have to talk about Direct Democracy.

"Mister delivered a Rat Brand rat ten minutes ago," Rich said. "Josie and the owlets have been hunkered down in the hollow of the tree. You can't see them, but you can hear their little screeches."

A steam kettle blew.

"Do you think the owlets will branch soon?"

"Cheryl said it was only a matter of days. Last year's happened on today's date, according to her diary."

"Branched..?" Irene was quizzical. "What does that mean?"

Bea and Rich spoke in unison: "Branching is..." Bea let Rich speak. "...When owlets leave the nest. It's a dangerous time. They can't fly but must leap to a tree. If they fall..."

They all looked from the top of the nesting tree to the branches of the maples three metres away. Then down the rest of the way to the ground, twenty metres below. All three knew the owlets' first leap might be their last.

"Bea, we know you've been kicked out of Direct Democracy," Irene changed the subject. "We want to talk with you, but you've not been responding to emails. Direct Democracy is over if we can't change Harold. Will you help us?"

Bea was quiet.

"Direct Democracy is worth fighting for," Irene continued. "Even if it's only use is flipping the bird to the traditional parties and getting us fat with doughnuts. To see young and old people like Tyrell and Morty working together is good."

"True..."

"But Harold is killing it. Please help us. With you, we can save it."

"Irene is right," Rich added his two cents. "I'm a cynical old socialist who sees social injustice and corruption everywhere. I trust Jagmeet as much as J.T., Liz, or Skippy because they're all players in the same game. I'll vote NDP with Jagmeet leading because he's my favourite player, but I would rather change the game. Direct Democracy is a way to change the game. Even with Harold's recent bullshit, I feel more kinship to Conservative him trying to make Direct Democracy work than the Socialist leader of the NDP. We have nearly fifty politically different people willing to work for it. It's miraculous. I want it to have a chance to fly. We need your help."

Bea had been eyeing the edge of the broken-off top of the dead Douglas Fir tree. She hoped an owlet would pop its head out and allow her to ignore her friends' appeals. She could see the owlets and Josie, they stayed in the nest. "I already tried to work it out with Harold. Derek arranged a mediation for us."

"Oh?" Irene was hopeful.

"Harold would only accept me as his lackey. Subordinate. He demands loyalty and can't separate his politics from Direct Democracy. You can see this yourselves: if the party is to win, it has to have an egalitarian structure and an obliteration of the traditional party platform. Direct Democracy's platform must provide people with the power to vote on bills in the House directly and only that. Harold cannot accept that and, in that case, I will not work with Harold."

"If I can put aside my disdain for that old codger," Irene pushed back, "you can too!"

"Direct Democracy is the least of my worries," Bea shot back. "Marcus is taking Sam to Ottawa permanently, something I learned on the same day I was fired. Sorry, I'm not into fighting an old fart over the heart and soul of Direct Democracy. All this drama doesn't make it worth me ending up homeless and unable to see Sam. So, you see, I have real things to worry about, like rent, or I'll get to hang out with the owls 24 hours a day…"

"Fine." Irene turned to walk away. "I tried."

Bea felt bad for being so harsh and resolved to apologize to Irene when the situation calmed down.

"Oh look!" Rich pointed. "Owlet! Wish I had my camera." They watched quietly for a few minutes. "I can't stand it," Rich whined. "Gotta get my camera. I'll be back."

🦉 Owls, Doughnuts, and Democracy, by Jason A. N. Taylor 🦉

Alone but for passersby, Bea sat reading *"Indian" in the Cabinet* and watched the owlets, hoping for a call from the coffee shop. After nearly an hour, she got a call from an unknown number. She got out a hello before being interrupted by Derek.

"Bea, I know you don't want to be part of Direct Democra..."

Bea cut him off. "So why are you trying to convince me to rejoin? I got fired. I need the reference letter you promised. Send it to my email!"

"Don't hang up!" Derek sounded uncharacteristically stressed. "Harold's in the hospital!"

"What?!"

"All I know is he was on one of his constitutional walks when he collapsed. His crew was not clear on what happened. He's in Royal Jubilee. I don't know how serious it is. I hope it's not his heart."

Bea sighed. "Is there anything I can do?"

"Not right now. I felt I needed to tell you."

"I appreciate it."

"If he's 'okay' and he wants to see you, will you visit him?"

"Of course. What do you mean if he's 'okay'? He's a tough old crank.

"I pray that's true."

"Spite will keep him going."

"Maybe so."

"Bet on it."

"In any case, I will be in touch. I will have your letter soon."

"The letter can wait."

"It's nothing... Take care, Bea."

Bea had never heard Derek so sad. She, too, was strangely sad and shocked but also touched that Derek thought she needed to know right away. She sat thinking how much better and more fun her life had been since meeting the cantankerous old codger. Every thought was tainted with two ambulances responding to Harold having a heart attack he would never recover from. She wanted to cry but without knowing of Harold's fate she would not.

Bea arranged to meet Sam and Amy to watch the owlets poke their heads up and Mister bring food. Meanwhile, her phone kept buzzing and beeping with news of Direct Democracy and Harold being in the hospital. Not long after Amy and Sam arrived, she got another call from a strange number. She answered sheepishly, "Hello."

An over-caffeinated voice stated, "Bea, it's Miriam from Discovery."

"Oh, hi Miriam."

"You sound down. Did I catch you at a bad time?"

"No... no." Bea relayed the story of her day. Miriam nevertheless wanted her in for a training shift in the morning.

"How come you're so important today?" Amy's eyes were wide. "The world seems to be contacting you."

"I wish the world was not."

Bea told the story.

Amy was excited. "Now you can lead Direct Democracy."

Bea gave her a Clint Eastwood-staring-through-a-low-down-varmint squint. "You know I can't. At least if I want to see Sam again. Marcus won't have it."

"What do you mean?"

Amy's question told Bea she was ignorant of her divorce situation. With a forced laugh, Bea said, "Oh, nothing... I was having one of those moments where I wanted to kill my ex." She smiled stupidly. "Divorcees think about killing their ex at least three times a day. I'm sure you feel that way sometimes."

Cautiously Amy joked, "I only wanna kill him once a week or so."

It was not long before Sam got bored, and they dispersed toward home.

Bea went to bed with no new news about Harold. The next morning, she woke early to get ready for her new job and consciously tried not to read her correspondence until on the way to work. She even avoided her phone for the time it took to sit on the toilet for a pee.

Derek messaged Bea that Harold had broken his hip but was otherwise fine. Harold wished her to visit him that afternoon, so she messaged Derek that she could go with him after two o'clock.

Serving came back to Bea quickly. The shop had a consistent flow of people, and the day did not drag. Derek showed up twenty minutes before the end of her shift, overdressed and looking like he had slept little. He got a large coffee and waited quietly in the corner.

Bea bought a doughnut for Harold. Though it was not an Empire Donut, surely any doughnut would be better than hospital food.

In the car, Derek opined: "God, I hope Harold learns from this. He must slow down. He's working too hard. I should have stopped him getting so involved."

"He is an old guy, all right."

"But he seemed to be getting stronger."

"Oh, stop it, Derek. Do you know Harold? Once his mind is set on something you can't slow him down. You told me that."

"I could have made Direct Democracy look like a farce and a fool's errand."

"Do you think Direct Democracy is a farce?"

"No. It is the most important political work I have ever been involved with. It challenges the worst behaviours created by our system. Currently, the system pushes all parties towards limiting political participation and increasing partisanship. The goal of the parties today is to invigorate a small but loyal group of voters by using wedge issues to make the voters feel that the choice of a party is a moral one. This causes the voter to have to accept the party on their side of the wedge issue even if other parts of that party's platform conflict with their views. All the parties need to do is stay true to the wedge issue and all other legislation won't lose them votes. But that is in the past."

Bea was quiet. God forbid abortion becomes an issue again. If it did all anti-abortionists would be on the party that sided against abortion. The same wedge issue was brewing with guns, coal, and oil. With Direct Democracy, the constituent could vote for their side of the wedge issue and then break with the party to vote on other issues, satisfying their moral need to support what is 'right.'

Derek was pulling into the hospital parking lot when Bea asked, "What do you mean in the past?"

"Direct Democracy is over. Even if Harold's able to run, I will not assist him. Without you or him running, it will not have a leader. Irene might be an accountant, but she will not be able to manage the campaign finances without me. It is done."

Bea agreed with Derek's assessment with her silence. Direct Democracy might well die in this hospital without having a chance to do all the good things it promised. Walking to Harold's room her sadness grew. "Maybe one of the UVic students can run?" Bea blurted.

"The only one with the charisma, intelligence and presence I've seen is you."

Bea felt a lump in her throat grow, wrongly attributing it to concern for Harold.

Down the hall, a voice boomed: "If you think Junior is a liar and Little Pee Pee isn't, the Doc fixed the wrong part of your anatomy!" There was a murmur while Harold reloaded his oratory. "Don't get me wrong, I'm more in agreement with the Conservative platform. But at least half of it is bullshit to get the religious types, Albertans and wannabe 'Mericans riled up. If the Conservatives strayed more right, they'd have to ask Adrien Arcand for directions."

Another old voice half as loud asked, "Who is that?"

"Learn some Canadian history! He was the leader of the National Unity Party. Otherwise known as the Canadian Nazis. He even ran after World War Two as a Nationalist."

Smiling and picking up their stride, Bea and Derek arrived at the room. Harold had been addressing two old men. In a far bed, another man was sleeping.

"Harold, what happened?" Bea asked. "How are you doing?"

"It was an inside job! I'm lucky to be alive."

"Huh?"

"John's got a thing for women with big... big... melons." Harold gestured. "And this lady was jogging on the other side of the road with a sports bra in need of new elastic."

"Oh..."

"She's bouncing down the road with John bouncing along too... until he stumbles forward on a curb, hitting Cameron on the scooter.

Cam inadvertently hits the throttle and has to choose between hitting Morty or me."

"You?"

"Cam made the right choice. A man with Morty's constitution would be a goner for certain. I fell hard, couldn't walk and had chest pain."

"Yikes!"

"To my good fortune, the ambulance shelter was a block away. There's a lot of pain but the doctor said I'll be fine… in time."

"Whew," Bea sighed genuinely. "Good to hear."

"But not in time for the election."

Bea fell silent.

"So, you'll be okay," Derek perked. "That is great to hear."

"It is, isn't it." Harold agreed.

"How is your heart?" Derek pressed.

"Beating like a Timex… takes a lickin' and keeps on tickin'. The chest pain was nothing."

Bea chimed in, "You're rather upbeat, Harold."

"The nurse was in with morphine." One of the old men said. "He was insufferable twenty minutes ago."

"I was insufferable because of pain…" Harold bit back. "What's your reason?"

The old man retorted, "I can see why you were stabbed in the back. Direct Democracy needs a candidate that doesn't wear his asshole on his face."

Harold laughed but stopped abruptly. "Good one, Gregory… but don't make me laugh; it hurts."

"Your speechifying hurts. So, we're even."

Maybe so…" Harold gestured to his guests. "We need privacy."

Bea and Derek looked at each other wondering how there could be privacy in a room with cloth partitions.

Harold continued, oblivious to privacy. "Who wants higher federal healthcare transfer payments to the provinces?"

Gregory and the other man raised their hands with Harold, voting.

"Come on Derek and Bea," Harold griped. "Hands up."

They raised their hands.

"That's the power of Direct Democracy," Harold proclaimed.

"It is a powerful idea," Gregory affirmed. "It's the only thing Harold says that I don't hate. He's even got Amanda, the nurse, on board. He intentionally drops things on the floor to get her to bend over. She knows he does it and still she's a supporter."

"Harold!" Bea admonished. "Stop being a pervy old man!"

"I can't help it. When she gives me drugs, I change. I say what I'm thinking. I fumble with stuff."

"How come it never happens with Alfonso, the male nurse?" The other man smirked.

Harold picked up a pen, winced in pain and dropped it. "Can you get that for me, Bea?"

"Stop being a dirty old man or I'm out of here."

Derek retrieved the pen, making sure to bend at the knees.

"Sorry, Bea. These drugs are powerful. I go a little wackadoodle. I say the strangest things. I can see why junkies love them" With small talk at an end, Harold spoke to the other patients, "Put on those noise-canceling headphones and leave us be." The two old men obliged, donning headsets.

Harold turned to Bea. "I'm apologizing for how I acted towards you. I couldn't see how much you personally held the party together. I was wrong to question your intentions. I want you to take over, be the leader of Direct Democracy."

"What changed?" Bea shook her head.

"What do you mean?"

"Why not run one of your lackeys? I'm sure they'd love a chance to be the leader of Conservative Light."

"I'll tell you one thing…" Stoned Harold ranted. "It is amazing how your perspective changes when you think you are going to die. As the ambulance was coming, I didn't think I was going to make it. I saw how Direct Democracy is bigger than me. I saw how I had surrounded myself with sycophants as every politician does. John, Cameron, and Morty are nice men, but I had them at my side to tell me I was right. That was wrong. I now see that Direct Democracy fell apart so quickly because I was only hearing myself. Seeing young and old people of most political stripes working for more democracy was great. But I got lost in myself. I had forgotten that when I first ran for office, I didn't finish work if there was a letter from a voter unresponded to. In the early days, before parliament began or ended, I would take a road trip through my riding, doing a temperature check and having coffee at every town with a greasy spoon. To hear the people. To bring their message back to Ottawa. Every year I was in office, though, less letters were answered. I had fewer lumberjack breakfasts. I don't know exactly what happened, but... we need to get the people's voice into Parliament again, Direct Democracy can do that. Unfortunately, it took a crippling injury to make me see that. But you... You, Bea, can take the baton and run with Direct Democracy."

"Harold..." Bea crossed her arms. "I find it very ironic you've rediscovered how important being heard is, but you haven't heard that I don't want to be the candidate. I can't be in the public eye. I intentionally lost the race because I did not want it. That's the end of the story."

"Without Bea to run..." Derek was grave. "I don't see Direct Democracy moving forward."

"Poppycock! There's no way Larry, Curly, or Moe could be the candidate," he declared, referring to his lackeys. "Irene is a possibility, but she'll have to tone down the man-hating. That kid Justin is a maybe... maybe a budding tyrant. Rich... too much of an old hippy. Ajay, too brown..."

"Harold, that's uncalled for..." Bea admonished.

"...I'm only being truthful, sweet cheeks."

Bea held her disdain, realizing Harold was too high to get through to.

"Cat would be great if she was ten years older and didn't actively hate children. How can a woman hate children? Oh God! I missed the obvious. Derek, you would be a great candidate. Of course, you'd have to overcome being a lawyer."

"There is no way I would be the candidate." Derek held out a hand. "Besides you need me as the electoral agent. No one else can do that. I cannot be both."

Harold fell back in his bed, gazing at the fluorescent light as if it was God. All the vigour in him left. He lay with his mouth agape and closed his eyes. If it was not for the rising and falling of his chest, Bea would have thought he was dead. "You're right Derek," he said weakly. "Bea is by far the best candidate. If Bea won't run, I fear the whole thing is over."

They were quiet for more than a minute, then made small talk until Harold got sleepy. Before losing consciousness, he begged weakly: "We can't let Direct Democracy die. Please reconsider, Bea…"

"I will reconsider…" Bea humoured. "And I got you a doughnut… but it's not an Empire Donut. Sorry."

"Any doughnut is better than what they have here. I couldn't even bribe the nurse to get me an awful Tim Hortons cruller. You are a saint, my dear."

Gregory and the other old man urged Bea to run, having obviously been filled in by Harold about the crisis of leadership. She grimaced and walked away.

Bea's second training shift at the coffee shop was in the late morning, time enough for an early run. Back home, a new barrage of emails and text messages buzzed from her phone. The email subjects were all along the same lines, begging Bea to come back. She was amazed that John, Cameron, and Morty were among those pleading. Harold must have cajoled all this into happening. There had even been a vote on the Discord that named Bea the next candidate for Direct Democracy.

The only email she cared to read was Tyrell's. His subject line was: My copy of "Indian" in the Cabinet. In the email he urged her to finish the book because it might help with her candidacy decision. He made no demands. It made her want to hug him and more, but he was too innocent for her. She squelched any further thoughts.

After work, Bea went to Beacon Hill Park, excited that she might see the owlets branch. When she got there the owlets were still hiding out, so she opened an *"Indian" in the Cabinet* to read while waiting for any action.

She got to the part that Tyrell had referred to. Jodie was saying strong words about how the system had to change, and partisanship had to decrease. People, especially indigenous people, had to have louder voices. What was good for Canada needed to be done, and that would not necessarily align with the party that formed the government's platform. Parties needed, at times, to stray from their platforms to do what was right and good for Canada. That was not happening in Canadian politics today. Bea agreed with everything JWR said.

Less impressive was JWR's half-assed solution to the problem; independent MPs who listened to their constituents. Jodie made a big deal of being the first Indigenous woman to win as an independent, but an independent is still just a representative filtering constituents' voices into decisions. It's not revolutionary at all but more like representative democracy-lite. The independent had the same problem of how to listen to all the people and whom to give weight to before casting their ballot. A big nothing burger.

Bea stopped reading before the end of the book. Thought of running swirled in her head as she sat on the wooden fence next to the owl nesting tree waiting for the owls to do something entertaining.

Then it happened, a "WHO COOKS FOR YOU" Call. Bea closed her book to see that like normal, Mister was on a branch some distance from the nesting tree nibbling on a rat for afternoon tea. Josie responded, the owlets pushing their way over the edge of the snag to see what was happening. Josie pushed by them, taking flight over to Mister. The couple kissed a few times while transferring the rat, then flew their separate ways.

Mister circled the compost pile to hunt another rat.

Josie took wings toward the nesting tree, perching in a maple a little ways from the nest. With the rat in her mouth, she was visible to the owlets. Josie started making a mewing noise Bea knew as the 'come here' call.

Sitting on the fence, Bea shot off a text to Amy. The owlets were going to branch.

The little steam kettle shrieked at their mother in the other tree. Brave little Muffin perched at the nest edge, stretching her wings and screeching. Shakespeare was trying to get some purchase at the edge, but Muffin had all the real estate.

Bea's heart raced with every gust of wind, scared they would fall.

The two little birds jostled each other to get the best position to see mom. Bea gasped as their rough housing ended in the owlets falling back in the nest, their squeals for food muffled as they tumbled out of view.

Bea's phone pinged, a text from Amy. She was unable to miss the accompanying messages begging her to come back to Direct Democracy. Bea was not used to having so many people on her side.

Shakespeare poked over the edge, looking small, curious, hungry and afraid. Shakespeare's steam kettle went off again, she ducked back into the nest. Bea wondered if Josie was struggling with not bringing the rat to feed her hungry babies.

With no owlets to watch Bea went back to pondering Direct Democracy. This time she focused on the fun she had. It was the best thing she had done since university – excluding a few moments with Sam and possibly a night or two with Marcus. Regardless of the goal of the party being achieved, making this absurdity work had been great.

Muffin took a turn at the parapet, wings boldly testing the wind. Josie mewed. Shakespeare's head popped up, surprising Muffin. Head bobbing in the direction of Mom, it was clear Muffin was working out different angles to judge the distance to the maple tree. It was Shakespeare's turn to be astonished. Muffin leaped into the air, flapping little wings vigorously.

Bea jumped off the fence.

Muffin flew more like a toy soldier with a parachute than a bird or a brick. The courageous falling owlet arced close toward the maple tree and mom but missed the mark, wings, talons, and beak flailing to try to make contact with anything. The owlet crashed into the leafy lower branches of the maple, clinging precariously to the canopy. As Josie's mews increased in frequency and pitch, Muffin hung by leaves, upside down, holding on by a talon and beak.

🦉 Owls, Doughnuts, and Democracy, by Jason A. N. Taylor 🦉

Bea stood recording the drama, phone in one hand and the other ready to cover her eyes if Muffin dropped. She was heartened by the fact that Muffin was likely now low enough not to be hurt by the fall, but she prayed the owlet would be able to climb onto solid branches.

Muffin struggled to climb to safety, leaves fluttering down, branches threatening to break with the strain. Finally, she ungracefully found her way to a thick branch and Josie flew down with the rat. Muffin waddled down the branch with wings out for balance to meet mom for some owl kisses and fresh Rat Brand rat.

Bright-eyed, with a silvery tear of joy rolling down Bea's cheek, she knew what she was destined to do.

Part 2

16.

Tuesday morning, Bea woke up, eyes gleaming.

The night before, Derek sent out an official email to the Direct Democracy membership, telling them Harold could no longer lead the party and that he was endorsing Bea to take his place.

Bea then sent an official email to all the members of Direct Democracy to say she was back and would be honoured to stand as their candidate.

Bea was genuinely excited, ready to use her newfound energy to organize the party's online presence.

The day was summer-like. Bea took her computer onto the deck. She was in such good spirits that the crows trying to eat the vomit of the semi-conscious neighbour passed out on the Paulina's lawn was only hilarious to her, if distracting. Cautiously, a crow would bounce up to the puddle of vomit only feet from the groggy person, grab a chunky bit, and caw in delight. The neighbour would moan. The crows would then caw and fly away in a panic. She laughed every time this cycle occurred.

The website for Direct Democracy was updated with bio pages for Bea that she would keep hidden until she was officially the leader. For the most part, the information was standard boilerplate stuff. She broke from tradition with a page she called Bea Accountable.

The Bea Accountable page was dedicated to preventing the coming attacks on her character. She discussed three of her most public foibles: her cyclist-shaming YouTube channel, her collection agent past, and the conflict with Knight Rider. For all of these things, she did a strange thing for a politician: she took responsibility.

She put a caveat on the Knight Rider section because Sam was involved, asking that videos with her son not be shown. It felt good getting who she mostly was out to the world. She hoped it would help frame her as a victim and be enough to discourage further investigation. She knew from reading about Teflon Bill that recovery from a scandal can bring in voters if done well. She did not want to admit to herself that President Orange Abomination was also an inspiration for how to turn the narrative of a scandal around to a benefit. She felt more than prepared. After all, this was local Federal Canadian politics; how much mud could be slung?

The next task was emailing Justin, Morty and Irene to see if someone could go with her to see Harold that night, meet to discuss the new logo, and somehow get to the Home for a free dinner. Before she had a chance to get into her running outfit, everyone had emailed back.

Despite the afternoon being so nice—a perfect time to get to the beaches to dip feet in the water—Bea stuck to her plan. She met Morty to discuss the new logo, sitting down with him in the lounge.

"I want you to know that Harold basically said what the logo was going to look like." Morty declared. "I even mentioned it was too much like the Conservative logo."

"Hey, Harold is Harold, I understand. Let's move forward. You're the expert, Morty. Make the logo. My only guidance would be that it be inclusive and shouldn't be linked to any other political party."

Morty furrowed bushy eyebrows and scratched his combover. "Hmm, not linked to any political party. I can't think of a colour that isn't politically aligned in Canada."

"That's a tough one."

"Eureka! What about a rainbow? All the colours because we represent all political views."

"That's the right idea, Morty. But the rainbow is used as the symbol of the LGBT2+ movement…"

"Damn… the Alphabet People already took it. It would have been perfect."

"Morty, 'Alphabet People' is derogatory."

"I heard it on the *Mark Levin Radio Show*. It's much easier to remember than LGQRD or whatever it is."

"It's patronizing." Bea shook her head. "And simplifies and misnames the person's gender."

"It does?"

"Just stop using it around me, ok?"

Morty nodded.

"Great. Be creative. Think outside of the box." Morty gave a thumbs up, taking a drawing pad and pencil out of his walker.

With Morty working on the logo, Bea found Irene to have dinner. The conversation was better than the food, but the food was free, so Bea was not complaining.

Cat joined them later on. She was hosting another Direct Democracy primer on social media. Tonight, Instagram with Mia. The goal of Cat and Mia was to get a net of followers who would always comment, like, and follow every Direct Democracy member and post. This would hopefully help game the algorithm. Bea preferred to stay but had to get to the hospital with Justin to see Harold. But the Direct Democracy crew arriving for the tutorial wanted to let her know they supported her. It began to look like she would be late getting to the hospital.

She texted Justin, who responded instantly that he could get her. 'How chivalrous,' she thought. She discreetly pocketed a tablet and joined the tutorial until Justin texted her. She easily identified Justin's old, lifted truck and jumped in.

"Thanks for this," Bea said, buckling up. "I like your Calvin-pissing-on-the-DFO (Department of Fisheries and Oceans) bumper sticker. But where's the 'fuck Trudeau' sticker?"

"Yeah, I wanted one." Justin didn't get Bea's sarcasm. "But my bro had one, and his truck was pissed on and keyed in Van. It's not worth the risk some liberal scumbag will vandalize Daisy. I didn't think you would be the fuck Trudeau type... thought you were a lefty."

"My family liked fishing until the regs got so complicated that you had to be a lawyer to keep a spring. And like every girl, I wanted to fuck Trudeau. I like guys who are into roleplaying." Justin leered at Bea until she said, "Daisy is a nice name for a truck... if you can call an F-150 a truck. You must be a skilled mechanic to keep a Ford on the road. You know what Ford stands for?"

"You a Chevy girl? Flipped Over Roof Down."

"Fix Or Repair Daily was what I was thinking. I'm more of a Ram woman, but I do like the bench seats."

Justin was having a hard time keeping his eyes on the road.

Owls, Doughnuts, and Democracy, by Jason A. N. Taylor

She was waiting for him to ogle her, getting ready to say, 'Eyes on the road buddy.'

"I can respect any girl that knows trucks. Maybe after we see Harold, I can show you what's under the hood."

"I know what's under the hood of a Ford, disappointment." Bea was done with flirting, she got to business. "I would like you to assist Harold with leading the conservative wing of Direct Democracy."

"The conservative wing..?"

"He's going to be recovering for a long time. Definitely, he won't be a hundred percent. Can you help keep him on track?"

"That's why I'm here. It's the Christian thing to do."

"Great. You'll need to work with him closely to keep connected with our meetings. Along with helping him understand our social media campaign. It'll be a hard task. He can be a handful. And he'll need Empire Donuts... he runs on them."

They stopped at the hospital Tim Horton's for doughnuts.

Harold's room was much quieter than last time, he was the only patient awake. "I hope you have doughnuts and good news," Harold said, frowning at Justin. "What's he doing here?"

"We'll get to Justin being here after we set some boundaries," Bea asserted. "Meanwhile, we have Timmy's and good news..."

"You're the Leader now. You say jump. I say how high."

"My campaign does not run that way but if you want it that way, fine. You just have to be willing to follow a few ground rules."

"Ground rules away." Harold bit into a glazed cruller.

"Number one: Every Direct Democracy candidate is neutral politically – I don't speak to positions. Number two: Direct Democracy members can hold whatever political positions they want, but they never ask the candidate to take a position other than what the constituency votes for on the app. Number three: We accept arguing on the issues but not personal attacks – if outsiders personally come after our members, they are fair game."

Harold looked up from his doughnut. "Holy Doodle, Bea! I understood the first point. But the other two, I don't know. Who is this person 'they'?"

"They, the non-gendered pronoun."

"Oh God! The drugs have made my mind soft. Gott's ya, it is PC bullshit. Didn't you say the candidate was not to be political? 'They' sounds political."

"It's respectful because the majority of the population is not gendered he, him, his, Harold."

"For as long as we've spoken English, we used he, him, his…"

"Oh, for crying out loud, I'm not getting into this right now. We've got other stuff to do." Bea pulled out the borrowed tablet. "A present for you. I'll hook it up to the Wifi because you seem a little too high to manage."

"Fine. What do you want me to do?"

"Be our mouthpiece for the conservatives in Direct Democracy. I've brought Justin along to assist you. Are you up for this?"

"Yes."

Justin and Harold formally exchanged contact information before the three of them shot the shit. After half an hour, Harold began to fade, so Bea and Justin found a reason to leave.

Justin offered Bea a ride home. She asked instead if he would give her a lift to Dallas Road. He revved his engine, excitedly heading to the beach and turned into Clover Point.

"Oh, I was hoping you could give me a lift up to Cook Street."

"I thought you wanted to watch the sunset and maybe see what's under the hood."

"I'm sorry, Justin. You misread the situation. You're a great guy, but we are too different. I entertain thoughts of hatefucking you, but we're now basically working together. I could be seen as exploiting someone from a position of power. It's not the right thing to do."

"I ahh…" Justin had turned bashful. "…Really thought you were interested in seeing the work I did to my truck."

"I must apologize again," Bea humoured. "Please show me, Daisy."

Proudly, Justin showed the modifications he'd made.

Bea acted interested, then politely said she must get going.

She could tell a thought was smouldering in Justin's mind. "I don't think Joice would like your truck…", and not resist adding, "But I'm sure you two would be fire together."

Owls, Doughnuts, and Democracy, by Jason A. N. Taylor

The owlets did nothing spectacular, but bobbed heads, attacked leaves and screeched. The usual. But their fluffy cuteness was worth the mosquitoes.

Bea knew the Saturday vote was all but decided. Still, she needed to make it feel like she was taking over decisively. Her speech was inclusive, short and to the point. She looked great in the mirror. She would pick up Empire Donuts on the way to the meeting to keep the tradition going. The doughnuts gave her an idea. Each person in Direct Democracy had a favourite doughnut. Harold's was Empire's. Yonni's were her favourite. If Irene and Cat had their choice, they would get the vegan Frickin' Delights. Rich was an Esquimalt Bakery fan. Then, of course, there was the mildly nationalistic Tim Horton's crowd. A small, persistent happiness inside her accompanied the idea that the different doughnuts represented diversity. This was what she was bringing to the party.

But how about the budget? Only the Timmy's were cheap, the rest were way more expensive. Bea felt the evil pull of her credit card, the one to maintain her good credit that she only used for her cell phone. Was this poetic idea worth pulling out the evil plastic?

Yes. Yes, it was! Bea called in orders from all the bakeries to deliver via UberEATS or Skip the Dishes. She saved money by stopping at Empire, Timmy Hoes and her coffee shop for Yonni's.

The doughnut load was awkward to carry but Bea was rescued by Mia and Ethan driving to the meeting, likely saving some of the cargo from being dropped.

"I'm set to deliver each member's favourite doughnut," Bea chirped, settling into the car.

"So cool!" Mia was enthused. "I can make the best Instagram and TikTok ever out of this! But don't let anybody have any doughnuts, until I finish getting some shots. Okay?"

"Sure. But..why?" Bea asked.

"There is no point in asking her," Ethan interrupted. "The "artist" will not show the finished product until it is done."

"Trust me, Bea, you'll love it. It will be delicious... pun intended."

The lounge was already half full, thirty minutes ahead of time. Mia and Ethan took on the task of intercepting the arriving doughnuts. Bea made sure the Zoom meeting got started.

As the meeting got underway, the lounge had at least forty people in it. Karen had to do a head count to ensure no fire code was broken. A dozen people joined online. An elegantly be-suited Derek took the podium to start the meeting.

Harold, in his hospital bed, took up the T.V. next to Derek to promptly start the meeting. "Welcome, everyone. Thank you for the well wishes. As you can see, I'm recovering. But I will not be well in time for the election. And…" Harold tailed off for a second. "…Before my accident, I must admit, I ah, I was not leading Direct Democracy well. I would like to change that today… put it back on track." The room applauded spontaneously. "We all know why we're here. To vote for a new candidate. A leader. Let's do that."

Derek took over. "Thanks, Harold. We are going to hold a show of hands for this election. Those online can either use the electronic hand or raise your hand on the video. Currently, there is only one candidate: Bea."

Some in the crowd clapped and cheered even though it was not the right time.

"Does anyone else want to throw their hat in the ring?" Derek paused for responses. "I don't see anyone in the room or online. For this vote, Bea needs a simple majority to become leader. a show of hands of those voting for Bea?"

The only people who did not raise their hands did not understand what was happening.

"Bea," Derek proclaimed happily, "you are the new candidate for Victoria and leader of the Direct Democracy party."

Vigorous applause ushered Bea to the podium as Derek stepped aside.

"Thank you, Derek, and thanks to all you out there." Bea cleared her throat. "Most of you know I was reluctant to do this. My reason was that by nature, any leader of a party with a true direct democracy platform is a leader in name only." Bea paused for effect. "You are the leaders of this party. I'm just here to ensure you get heard. To that end, I have some guidelines I will do my best to follow. I ask that you try to follow them, too. My guidelines are: Number one: Every political perspective is allowed – we value diversity. Number two: As your candidate I will be politically neutral – I won't speak to positions. Number three: Direct Democracy members never ask the representative to take a stand on an issue – the representative will only vote for what the majority voted for. Number four: We accept debate on the issues but not personal attacks, though if outsiders attack our members, they are fair game. Number five: We are the party of having fun. Nothing we are doing is so serious we can't laugh about it at the end of the day."

Bea paused to survey the room. "Can you get behind those guidelines?"

The crowd clapped in agreement. "Our next order of business is the Direct Democracy logo," Bea peered into the assembly. "Morty... can you come up?"

Morty was well-dressed for the occasion. He plied his way up with his walker while John followed with an easel and a well-hidden picture. "Bea asked me to find a logo that said Direct Democracy," Morty leaned over the podium. "Ancient Athens was the first known city-state to have a form of direct democracy. Athena is the Goddess of Athens. Owls are the symbol of Athena."

John pulled the cover from the picture, dramatically revealing a group of owls. Each was a different, bold colour, similar to the colours of other political parties.

Morty cleared his throat. "A group of owls is a parliament. Our symbol is the owl. The different colours represent the various political views within Direct Democracy. If you hold conservative views, your lawn sign will be a cerulean blue owl."

The membership murmured with discussion, not seeming to understand the idea.

Irene stood. "Let me get this straight... if I lean politically toward the Green Party, I'd have a green owl on my sign?"

"Yes," Morty said.

Tyrell stood next to Irene and started to clap. Irene followed. Then the entire room stood and joined in.

When the clamour subsided, Bea said, "I swear I had no influence over Morty's work here, but I love it!" Bea pretended to tickle the belly of one of the drawn owls. "To celebrate these changes, today's meeting will be more about coffee and doughnuts than politics. We have more than just Empire Donuts today. We have all varieties for all our different tastes." Again, everyone clapped.

"Before we attack the doughnuts..." Ethan jumped up and shouted to Bea. "Mia wants to get a few shots for an Instagram and TikTok post. Please, tell her if you don't want to be photo-ed picking up a doughnut."

The members posed and mingled with their coffee and doughnuts. Mia videoed, then found a corner to edit. Mia shortly brought the draft to Bea, who watched and was moved.

Bea re-took the podium and shouted: "Mia has made a video!" The crowd hushed. "We're going to stream it over the T.V. Then I want all of us to share the crap out of it. If you are not on Instagram, TikTok, or What's App, get one of your neighbours to help sign you up."

The video started with a shot of well-filtered Empire Donuts and chipper music. "Have you seen a more delicious doughnut?" Mia's voice-over was as seductive as a cruller talking to Homer Simpson. "The glaze is a technicolour dream. A more scrumptious doughnut you have never seen. Empire Donuts are in a class of their own."

Captions under the doughnut read:
Lower taxes
No deficit spending
Reducing the national debt
The Conservatives

A Yonni's doughnut next graced the screen, equally well-filtered. "Look at this gem: a raspberry cannoli doughnut. No artificial flavours. Moist, yet fluffy..." Even Mia's impression of Homer Simpson had sex appeal. "Just the right tanginess to make you go 'mmm, Yonni's doughnuts.'"

Captioned below:
Business-friendly
Socially progressive

Reconciliation
The Liberals

Nutella oozed out of the overstuffed next doughnut from Esquimalt Bakery. "Jelly doughnuts with raspberry jam or Nutella, maple bacon on Friday. Perfectly glazed, indulgent, but not pretentious. Esquimalt Bakery doughnuts, doughnuts that do not put on airs... the working person's doughnut."

Captions:
Housing
Strong labour protections
Anti-discrimination
New Democratic Party

The Frickin' Delights Donuts could be mistaken for Empire Donuts, their glaze was that good, but they were smaller. Four different delectable types were in the frame. "If you didn't know these doughnuts were vegan there's no way you'd taste it. Sure, Frickin' Delights Donuts are smaller than the others, but that leaves more room to try them all. Definitely the choice for a person working to save the world."

Climate change
Sustainability
Conservation
The Greens

Tim Bits started falling from a box onto the table in slow motion. "You can't talk doughnuts in Canada without Timmy's. There isn't a Canadian who has not craved a Tim Bit from time to time. They are like a little taste of heaven. All too often, by the time you get the box, the one you want is gone. They're not big enough to satisfy a true doughnut craving. But they are what every Canadian wants to see when they come to the table."

As the Tim Bits fell, phrases fell with them:
Healthcare spending, promised by all never enough
electoral reform, a campaign promise only
pharmacare, trumped by other priorities
affordable childcare, pushed down the road
abolishment of the Indian Act, too controversial for today...

The camera zoomed into an empty Tim Bits box. "Wouldn't it be nice if there were enough Tim Bits for everyone?" In the box, there was the statement:

One day after the election, all gone.

As the camera panned over all the doughnuts, Mia spoke in a more serious tone: "Imagine if you had to choose which doughnut you were going to eat for the next five years. All doughnuts get old and stale."

The changing filter on the doughnuts made them appear to wilt in seconds. Overlayed were sentences: Empire Donuts: Lack of transparency and austerity for the middle class only. Yonni's: Endless corporate scandals and cronyism. Esquimalt Bakery: The only chance for influence is in a minority government. Frickin' Delights: No realistic chance to gain power.

An AI filter decayed all the doughnuts to sad music.

The music then changed to a song of sunrise. The decay on the doughnuts reversed. The video brightened with dawning light.

"There is another way," cheerful Mia's voice smiled. "A new, old way. A way to have all kinds of doughnuts. A way for them never to go stale. A way to have your doughnut and eat it, too. Which ones do you want?"

The text on the screen read:

Direct Democracy allows you to vote for what you want.

People were shown nibbling on every type of doughnut. Finally, full-size Tim Horton's doughnuts took centre stage. "This way, we get actual doughnuts," Mia laughed. "Not bits." The silhouette of an owl, Direct Democracy's new logo, appeared with the name written in big, friendly letters.

The audience was split. The young got the message right away, as did some of the savvier oldsters.

Irene and Rich liked it.

Then there was Harold, looming large on the lounge TV screen, brow furrowed, looking like Big Brother. "Are we opening a doughnut shop!" With the volume loud, Harold unknowingly spoke with his mute off. "Have the young people gone whack-a-doodle? Good God! Where's the nurse... I think the drugs have addled my mind!"

🦉 Owls, Doughnuts, and Democracy, by Jason A. N. Taylor 🦉

Most of the group broke out laughing. Those who did not seemed as confused as Harold.

"If you don't get it..." Bea hurriedly spoke, "...don't worry, just share the video."

The crowd murmured for a moment.

"That's it for the official meeting." Bea paused, looking over the expectant faces. "See some of you at the Tuesday Social Media Tutorial."

A murmur of satisfaction took over.

"And finish off the doughnuts!" The group organically organized itself into smaller groups to share the video with all the different social media apps.

Derek nudged Bea. "Your first meeting as leader was perfect."

"Derek," Bea leaned close. "It's crazy. Here we are with Gen Z to Boomers all on the same page."

"Remarkable. A sign of your appeal."

Bea ignored the compliment and pulled out her phone. "I have to get a picture of us up here with Harold on the T.V." She took a selfie of the three of them. Harold's disembodied head stared cockeyed into the distance, unaware of Bea taking the selfie. It made the picture perfect.

After another coffee and doughnut, Bea left for the bitter part of her day. It was the last afternoon with Sam before Ottawa. She planned on keeping it low-key, watching the owls and strolling in the park.

The owlets and Josie were asleep when they got there. Bea suggested that because it was low tide they go down to Clover Point. They spent a couple of hours flipping rocks and catching little crabs. Bea lamented that there weren't the thousands of purple starfish that had populated the shore when she was young. They only found two. She had read it was because of a virus that caused them to dissolve, a plague with ocean acidification. She did not mention this to Sam.

At the Beacon Drive-in, Sam brought up what Bea had not wanted to talk about. "Momma B, I want to go see the owls. It's the last time I'll see them before we leave."

"Sure, Kiddo."

"Do you think the owls know us?"

"I don't know. I think they do. I've heard Josie make her mewing call, as she does for Muffin and Shakespeare when we're the only ones around. Why else would she call?"

They took their milkshakes to the owl nesting tree in the long June afternoon. The park was in full bloom.

The owl family was active. Mister had caught a rat. Josie was tearing it up for the two owlets.

The grossness enthralled Sam. Long strings of intestine had him talking of never eating spaghetti again. He made sure that anyone passing by saw the two little teapots shrieking owlets while Josie placated them with bits of Rat Brand quality rats. He was especially happy when passersby were either grossed out or interested enough that he could give them an owl lecture.

Watching Sam have so much fun kept Bea from interrupting him. She was getting sadder, and retreated onto her phone to check how Mia's video was doing. There was a ridiculous number of likes in the tens of thousands on Insta. The comment section was blowing up, too. Her favourite was: 'What did I just see? Was it a political ad? It was! For Direct Democracy! I want doughnuts.' The gist was of curious confusion. A curious viewer will be most likely to investigate further. The video was killing it on the other social media platforms, too.

Something in Bea kept her from basking in this success. She found herself scrolling through Instagram, something she never did; her relationship with these apps was usually all business. Today she was sucked in by emotions. Every post of a perfect, happy nuclear family having a picnic hit her in the heart. Scrolling through her photo gallery, she compared her family's real pictures to their touched-up ones. Her pictures did not compare; the Insta moms were better lit, filtered, cropped, retouched, staged, and captioned. She felt ashamed because her life was not like these women with their perfectly filtered family pictures. But she could not see that the difference in quality was in the photoshopping.

Three pictures caught Bea's curiosity, slowing the spiral of shame. They were of the Little Libraries where she had caught Ray planting subversive books. In the last picture, *Mao's Little Red Book* stood out, but there were no Little Red Books in the other two Little Libraries. She zoomed in to see titles. None stood out as controversial, but she vividly remembered seeing Ray put books in each one. He had admitted spreading banned books but where were they? She pored over the three pictures, not spotting anything new.

"Momma B, what are you doing?" Sam leaned on the fence.

"A boy I know left me a puzzle. There's something the same in each of these pictures." Bea swiped through each picture for Sam. "But I can't find any pattern. There should be some link between the books."

"Give me your phone," Sam took it gently out of her hand. "I'll figure it out." He walked aimlessly, scanning back and forth between the pictures. Not a minute later, he yelled, "I see it!" He leaned on the fence but hid the phone from her, smiling mischievously.

"Come on, show me."

"You have to answer a question first. Do you like this boy?"

"Probably... yes."

"Good, Momma A said you need to meet a boy."

Bea tried to hide her grimace.

"See..." Sam proffered her phone, pointing to an image. "Each library has the same two kid's books. *Jack (Not Jackie)* and *Red A Crayon's Story*." Sam indicated the books in each picture.

"You're right." Bea took her phone back to look more closely. "That's not the type of book I expected Ray to leave."

Sam bounced off, singing, "Momma B and Ray sitting in a tree. K-I-S-S-I-N-G..."

A quick Google of the books had Bea falling more in love. They were controversial and subversive. And oh, so right. Children growing up trans. So much more radical than Mao or Marx. Aimed at people young enough to change.

Bea reasoned that the Little Red Book must have been a plant, a distraction to draw a suspecting person's attention from the really rebellious reading. It was a preposterous plan, but there was so much style to having a contingency for being caught in an act that was not illegal.

Ray's book drops were an artistic way of changing the world. She loved him. She would arrange a date.

She found that she had forgotten to get back to Ray's email of more than a week ago. A lump grew in her throat, worried she may have turned him off. She emailed a light and cheery note, hopeful she was not too late.

Bea joined Sam, watching the owls. Josie was doing her best to get the fed owlets to practice flying. She would fly a few trees away, then mew to Muffin and Shakespeare. The owlets would scream, wanting Mom to come to them. But Josie kept her distance. Muffin was the first to fly the twenty metres, receiving owl kisses soon after landing.

This moved Bea. She started to sniffle.

"Are you crying because I'm leaving?" Sam asked.

"No. It's my allergies."

"You're lying. Momma A said I didn't have to cry because your new job will send you to Ottawa."

"How is a job at the coffee shop going to send me to Ottawa?"

"That's not your job. Direct Democracy is. Momma A is sure you'll win and go to Ottawa. Even Dad thinks it could happen." Sam walked over to Bea to hug her. "So don't cry."

Bea hugged Sam. "Dad thinks I could win?"

"Dad and Momma A argue about it. Dad thinks you would win if you gave it a hundred and ten percent and get a little lucky." Sam's voice wavered as if he might cry. "You will try your hardest to win? So you can come to Ottawa?"

Bea answered emphatically, "Yes, Sam, I will. I'll give it a hundred and twenty percent."

Pink light from the late spring sunset sifted through the maple trees. The owlets became more playful in the twilight, moving down from the tree canopy. Amy and Marcus came to get Sam. The owlets found their way to the ground, flying in the near dark between low branches and to the fence. Muffin and Shakespeare landed so close to Sam and Bea they felt they had to keep their distance to not scare Josie. The owlets were not as friendly with Amy and Marcus.

Bea asked Marcus, "Do you think I can win?"

Marcus quickly answered, "Yes." After a pause, he added caveats. Bea did not hear them. She knew his first answer was what he thought. Nevertheless, it brightened her sad day.

At Amy's prompting, Marcus brought up the potential to use Bea's child support for her to travel to Ottawa. If Bea did not win.

Sam and Bea had one last heartfelt but not tearful hug. Amy tried to be part of the moment but only got a fist bump.

Bea stayed alone in the grove with the owls until the only light was stray beams from streetlights and cars.

17.

Harold and Derek chatted on the Discord of an early election call.

J.T.'s Liberals had made hay on bills providing minimal emergency dental care for the poor and a childcare subsidy contingent on provincial matching. Tim Bits for the people. The job numbers were good, though, for crappy jobs. There was a surprise surplus. And the Conservative's Little Pee Pee had been caught pandering to hate groups with hidden hashtags. The time was right for the writ to drop.

Coming in from a morning run on the first true summery Saturday of the year, Bea prepared for a long, fulfilling day. She had two missions: Number One: Question Colleen Lauren, the incumbent Liberal MP, at the Moss Street Art Walk. Number Two: Make Ray fall for her on their date this afternoon.

On her bed was all the equipment she would need: Cute sun dress, check. List of questions to memorize for her guerrilla MP interview, check. Children's books on growing up trans and one copy of the Communist Manifesto, check. She pondered the books, hoping Ray would be impressed because she bought them on credit and was not certain she could get a refund. She glanced at her dresser for the receipts, check. Sunscreen, check. Water bottle, check. Condoms, check.

For a second, Bea wondered if it was presumptuous to bring condoms on a first date but remembered how much she did not want another kid. A snack for lunch, check. A matching backpack/purse just large enough for her supplies, check. Comfortable matching shoes… she did not have any. Only perverts looked at feet. Comfy runners were the shoes she picked. The chartreuse shoes only clashed with her dress, hat, and backpack/purse when seen together.

Ready for the day, Bea double-checked the meeting spot at École Intermédiaire Central Middle School, where they would coordinate the activities. It felt good to have a fun purpose, so she left home.

Owls, Doughnuts, and Democracy, by Jason A. N. Taylor

In the field next to the middle school, at the top of Moss Street, a group of 18 Direct Democracy members stood in a circle. There were seven UVic students, six oldsters, and three in the middle. Bea, Irene, Joice, Rich, Justin, and Ajay organized the group into flights of three. Bea, Mia, and Ethan had the main objective to interview MP Colleen Lauren. Four of the groups would get interviews from the crowd on how they would want their MP to vote on topical issues. Justin's group would do recon to find Colleen Lauren and keep eyes on her while Bea was alerted. Justin's group would also keep the four Direct Democracy interview groups from crossing paths with Colleen Lauren. They made a WhatsApp group chat for the overall mission and then went over the plan one last time.

"Hey..." Justin called for everyone's attention. "Harold and Morty had the idea of having shirts made with our new logo on them." He held up a blue shirt with the owl logo on it. "There's one for everyone. There's an equal number of the colours for the major parties. Sorry if you have to wear one that's not your political view." He looked at Bea, "We have a special shirt with a non-aligned colour for you." He held out a neon yellow shirt with the owl logo in black.

"Oh my God!" Bea scrunched her face. "Did Harold think I would be directing traffic? It's a high vis-vest." She pulled it on, grimacing as if she were biting a lemon. It was big enough to almost cover her entire dress. "At least it matches my shoes."

The group broke with a cheer. The flights went their separate ways. There were thousands of art walkers on Moss Street, the kind of event that had people asking about the matching shirts and getting the Direct Democracy spiel. To get to their area of operation, Bea, Mia, and Ethan strolled down Moss Street from the top of Fort Street hill, gazing at art and spreading their message.

When they got to where one could see all the way down Moss Street, Bea was awestruck. It had been years since she had been to an Art Walk, and she had forgotten how many people participated. The street was two kilometres chockablock full of people, staggering. Finding Colleen Lauren might be harder than she thought. At least Colleen's Facebook page indicated she would attend.

◊ Owls, Doughnuts, and Democracy, by Jason A. N. Taylor ◊

The trio meandered, browsing the kiosks on one side of the street to the other. Mia and Ethan used the stroll to get clips for their next Insta Couple video. Bea was drawn to every vendor with owl artwork. They all checked their phones regularly for messages. There was lots of traffic on WhatsApp but none at Colleen Lauren's location.

The surreal view of paragliders crossing the end of Moss Street over Clover Park meant the three were almost at the end of the route. They had not seen Colleen Lauren, nor had WhatsApp signalled where she was.

Bea reluctantly asked, "Do we have a plan B?"

Ethan shrugged his shoulders. "Walk back to Fort Street?"

"We could try to schedule a meeting with her," Mia said. "Or we could make our point by saying how she voted."

"Maybe."

"But an interview is better," Mia agreed.

"Okay," Bea sighed. "Let's have some water and walk back up."

As the three drank and put on more sunscreen, their phones pinged. "OH SHIT!" Ethan was the first to get the message. "She's on Fort Street. Justin thinks she might be leaving."

Bea shoved her bottle into her bag. "I'm going to run for it." Not waiting for Ethan or Mia to respond, she took off, dodging walkers in the street until she figured out the sidewalk had less traffic. Profanity, too, helped move people out of the way.

Ethan and Mia tried to keep up but could not.

Sprinting, Bea did not stop for the police-controlled intersection at Fairfield Road. She did not turn to see a reserve constable shaking a fist at her. The section after Fairfield was the busiest because of the weekend market; there was no way the police could catch her. Dodging and weaving through people slowed her, but not much. She was able to pick up the pace up the hill. At the Rockland Avenue intersection, also one controlled by police, she felt the right thing to do was stop. At least she might catch her breath but there was no way it would help dry her baggy shirt pits, wet from sweat.

She checked her phone. Justin relayed that Colleen's position was at a vendor less than a block from Fort Street at the end of the

Owls, Doughnuts, and Democracy, by Jason A. N. Taylor

Art Walk. Running again, Bea was soon out of breath and feeling like she might puke. She located Justin and Joice near the last two artists on Moss Street, making a be-line for them.

"Where is she?" Bea gasped.

"That's her over there." Justin pointed to a woman flipping through prints and laughing with the artist. "Don't take this the wrong way..." He lowered his gaze. "Bea, you're looking a little rough."

Bea took out her phone to breathily look at herself. Justin was right. The gigantic florescent yellow owl shirt hung like a smock with unflattering sweaty spots. She took off the shirt, but the floral dress was now damp and pretty much see-through, showing off her bra, underwear and happy nipples. Definitely not appropriate. With an involuntary whistle, Justin agreed with her assessment. Joice agreed with Justin, too, with a leer.

Bea threw the high-vis tent shirt back on. took the scrunchies out of her hair, pulled the shirt tight at her waist and used a scrunchy to hold it that way. "Joice, do the same with the shirt and this scrunchy at my shoulders. I can't reach there."

She held her hair as Joice worked and got Justin to fish a hairbrush out of her bag, not caring that he would likely discover the Communist Manifesto, trans kid's books and condoms. She laughed internally at what he might think of her. After a few damp brushes of hair, she felt this was the best she could do. "How do I look?"

Justin reframed from commenting.

"Uhm, you look great, but..." Joice did not want to point out the obvious.

Bea could feel the problem but used her cell phone to look at herself. She looked great, the perfect look for an after-aerobics-themed soft porn shoot. Her girls had to be seen regardless if the shirt was a tent or form-fitting. She chose form fitting.

"Who has the best camera on their phone?"

Joice replied, "I have the newest iPhone."

"You're the camera person. Let's go."

With Joice and Justin hurrying after Bea, they quickly caught up to Colleen, who was in a kiosk looking at an owl print. Bright-eyed, smiling and genuine, Bea strode up to their target. "Hi! Are you Colleen Lauren?"

"Yes."

"You're our MP for Capital Victoria, aren't you?"

Colleen nodded.

"Great! It's awesome to meet you. I'm Bea. This is Joice and Justin. We're doing an art project on democracy."

"I had a feeling you were together. The matching owl shirts. Why owls?"

"Owls are the messenger of Athena. Owls represent Athenian Direct Democracy."

"How interesting."

"May I have a few minutes of your time? We want to get more younger people engaged in politics."

"An interview?"

"If you have time."

"Sure..."

They spoke for twenty minutes.

Later on, Ethan and Mia caught up with them and viewed what had taken place. All agreed the interview had been a great success, with high-fives all around. Justin reminded everyone there was a beer garden with bands playing. They all agreed to go. Bea put up the boundary of one beer before she had to leave for her date.

After two free beers, Bea checked the time. She had to leave soon or be late. She messaged this to the group. Justin insisted that Harold would get her one more beer for the road. She did not resist... and could not help but watch Justin's tight ass as he went to get a beer.

Joice noticed. "Bea, Justin's been eyeing you all day. Buying you beer. Now you're looking at his ass. Get on with it."

"For a man, he has a nice ass," Bea said idly. "But he is not at all my type." She doted on Joice's soft curves for a long time after she finished what she was saying.

Joice received the drunken adoration as flirting. They talked shit while Bea drank her beer, and when her glass was empty, Bea said: "Thanks, everybody, for the great day! I have a date to get to..."

"If you get stood up," Joice called, "Text me!"

Bea waved, not catching what Joice had said.

Artists were striking their kiosks as Bea walked down Moss Street. A slight breeze from the water made the afternoon pleasant, if busy, on the walk to Cook Street Village. It was too pleasant to check the time. She detoured to freshen up in the Starbuck's washroom, then crossed the street to Mocha House. She saw Ray sitting outside with his electric scooter and coffee, gazing up and down the street. Everywhere but in her direction. Finally, she looked at the time. It was 5:23 pm. She was twenty-three minutes late.

"Hey Ray!" Bea called as she sat down. "I'm so sorry. I got tied up with Direct Democracy. We did a guerrilla interview with Colleen Lauren. It'll be great. Thank you for waiting. Do you want another coffee? I need one."

His intent stare made Bea discreetly make her dress more revealing.

"I'm good for coffee," Ray replied nervously. "I was worried you weren't coming. Particularly when you didn't email me back the first time we met."

"Oh yeah, sorry..."

"...But Ajay insisted I reach out. Let me get your coffee." Ray stood.

"'Reach out,' that sounded so like Ajay." Bea put her bag on the chair across from him to make him feel she would not leave. "I'll get my own coffee."

Bea had not been on a date since the divorce, but she had always been good at making guys feel comfortable. She started with the weather, a good topic on a sunny day. Then she moved on to how Ray got to know Ajay.

Ray was happy to tell of his relationship with Ajay. They'd met in his last year of Bachelor of Science in Computer Science. Ajay worked with the company where Ray interned. Ajay became his mentor for his masters. Through connections he had made with Ajay, Ray was now working to create a secure online voting system for First Nations.

They bantered on the potential for Direct Democracy's success. Ray believed real parties would drown Direct Democracy like unwanted kittens. The real parties would be pouring money into the campaign for Victoria Capital if there was even a hint of it making an impact. Bea conjectured that every extra dollar spent to quash Direct Democracy would do the opposite. Making Victoria Capital a battleground riding would only fuel the underdog's fire, and Direct Democracy was the underdog, she argued. She caught him when he posited it would end in unending character attacks, reminding him how much the 'Mericans loved the Dumpsterfire's Presidential scandals. The Tangerine Turd was on all media all the time because of the controversy, she reminded him. If the same trend happened here, Direct Democracy would get what it needed most: free media. And the underdog wins. She stopped arguing. He continued to stress his point.

With a shrug that was not noticeable, Bea let the shoulder of her dress slip off.

Ray's argument slowed as he noticed.

She wriggled the strap of her bra off with a turn of her head and a drop of her shoulder.

Mouth open, Ray could not remember his argument as her bra cup threatened to droop over to reveal a naughty bit in public.

"Uh Bea, your..." He pointed to her shoulder.

"See how the possibility of a little scandal can hijack the conversation?" Bea spoke without fixing her bra strap. "The more the big parties highlight the riding with money, the more Direct Democracy's in the spotlight." She pretended to slip the girl out. "Oops... she almost escaped." Bea adjusted the strap and dress.

Automatically, Ray turned his head down and to the side, covering his eyes with his bangs. "You didn't win the argument. You played dirty."

Bea found this extremely cute. "That's how you win at politics and have great sex."

Ray did not respond.

"Did you grow up on the island?" Bea asked.

"No."

"I've lived here my whole life."
"Where did you grow up?"
"Alberta."
"Alberta's a pretty big province… anywhere in particular?"
"Do you know Alberta?"
"Not really."
"Then how would being more specific be helpful."
"Studies prove…" Bea decided to make up a fact. "That getting to know your date is one of those things that lead to a stronger connection and a doubling of the chance of intercourse."

Ray snickered involuntarily, then crossed his arms and looked down, bangs covering his eyes.

She gave him a chance to respond, but his defences did not lift. She moved closer, elbows on the table. "Ray, in the very short time we've talked, I think I lov… like you a lot. I like your smarts and discussing things with you. I like your poetic way of putting controversial books in little libraries. I like your ninety's bangs and flannel shirts. I think they go well with my summer dresses. I love that there's an emo emoji that looks like you flipping your bangs out of your eyes. I like that Ajay respects you; that's a huge compliment. I want to get to know you. I know I can be a little too… Bea. You don't have to tell me everything. If you do, I have no reason to judge. Remember, I'm a twenty-eight-year-old MILF that works at a coffee shop, has minimal custody of her kid with only a political lark to keep her sane." There was a silence long enough that she had to fill it. "I also know from the way you look at me, talk with me, and what Ajay's told me, that you got a thing for me, too. Let's see if it works."

Ray uncrossed his arms. "Cold Lake." He flipped bangs out of his eyes and smiled. "Cold Lake, Alberta."

They both laughed. "I grew up in Esquimalt," Bea said. "When I was twelve, our class went on a field trip to the BC Legislature. All the weird idealistic sayings made me feel I wanted to work there. The only one I can remember is 'the virtue of adversity is fortitude.' It was like the building was aspiring to higher ideas and that made the people in it better. I wanted to be in government, and my teacher was sure I could get there. But every year after that, it became more unlikely. First it was parents that thought marriage and not education was the way for a daughter to get ahead. I had to fight with them to get a student loan. Then came my ex, Marcus, who seemed like a great guy but turned into Mr. Misogynist once Sam, my son, was born. Then there was the whole custody fight…"

Bea chuckled mirthfully. "Now I know why I remembered, 'the virtue of adversity is fortitude,' LOL!" She paused, feeling the conversation was getting too serious. "Enough childhood talk. Enough of how lame my family is. Let's go see some owls. They are my chosen family."

The evening was pleasant. People strolled to and from the beaches on Dallas Road. When they got to the small triangle of forest near the city works yard and the totem pole, only a few people were wandering the green leaf-shaded trails. The owlets had moved to a spot hard to see from the paved path.

Bea knew of a path that led to a better view of the owlets.

Ray wanted to spark a joint, and Bea hoped it would make him more talkative. The walk was enjoyable but with little conversation. He seemed overwhelmed as if he could not believe he was walking with her. His big stupid grin, which she loved, only reinforced this. It was like he was hanging out with his high school crush.

Once the weed smoking started, the fluffy bobbing heads of the murder muppets had them in stitches. Josie brought a rat to the voracious fluff balls. Muffin had them falling down laughing by pulling the rat intestines out like a magician with an unending handkerchief. Unfortunately, their laughter and the owlet tea kettle calls summoned other owl observers. It became awkward.

They left to sit on a bench overlooking the Salish Sea. It was hidden from the busy Dallas Road path by a brushy hedge. To the west, the sky was starting to grow more orange than blue. Most of the shoreline's rocky fingers pointing into the sea had couples sitting on them, watching the sunset. It was that kind of evening. Bea glanced down to the rocky point where Marcus had proposed.

Ray started to roll a joint.

Bea noticed a homemade tattoo of a male symbol with 'man' written below it on the underside of Ray's left wrist. "What's with the 'man' tat?"

"Aw nothing..." Ray shifted his arm to hide it. "I was a drunk teenager with a tattoo gun."

"Come on, let's see!"

Ray pulled up his right sleeve. His forearm, just below the elbow, held a West Coast indigenous-style raven. From its beak, in letters that did not look professional, it was saying, 'Not.' "I got the raven when I was fourteen," Ray said. "My family took me to the West Coast. I snuck off to get it. I could not believe the artist believed I was eighteen. I guess I have something of a trickster in me."

"Why is it saying 'not'?"

"I thought it was funny, and you can't change tattoos."

"How about the other ones?"

Ray pulled up the other sleeve.

Along with the male tattoo on his left arm were scars and burns Bea did not ask about.

"I was a pudgy teen," Ray admitted. "My friends called me a girl because I had man boobs. It really bugged me. A girl I had a crush on called me a girl when I asked her out. I got drunk and angry. I drew the male symbol and man myself. Teenagers are assholes."

"I can't believe anyone would mistake you for a girl. You're right, teenagers are assholes. Having been one, I know they work hard to find the hurtful things that make a person feel bad and then pick at them." Bea instinctively hugged Ray.

He did not resist, nor did he respond.

Bea tightened her embrace and tried to kiss him on the lips.

He did not reciprocate but flinched.

She got his cheek. "See, you're all muscley, bristly, manly."

If his skin tone could show a blush, it would have. He went back to rolling the joint.

"Ray, when a woman asks about your tattoos, it's only polite to ask the woman what tattoos, if any, she has."

"You got an owl near your ah... uhm... on your mons Venus."

"What!?"

"At least, that's what I think you'd have."

"An owl?"

"That would be so you."

"MEN!" Bea shook her head, smiling. "Ajay told you, didn't he?"

"You went out with Ajay?" Ray spluttered. "Yeah... Ajay? Yeah... Ajay... Yeah... that's how I knew. Yeah. I didn't ask, he told me."

"I know guys talk like that... women talk like that."

"I'd never ask that kind of stuff."

"It is all good. It's how people get better at intimacy without talking to the person they're sleeping with. Ajay loved my tattoo and thought it was the most creative thing ever. But I wouldn't really say we went out. More of a passing amour."

Ray passed Bea the joint.

"You know that's the first time I've heard a man use the term 'mons, Venus,'" Bea spoke, exhaling. "You get points for that, Ray. It's nice when a guy knows anatomy." Bea stood up. "Do you want to see it..?"

Ray nodded stupidly.

Bea pulled up her dress with one hand and her underwear down with the other, stopping before anything that would get a video banned from TikTok was shown. All that was revealed was bush. "Well, you can't." Bea chuckled. "It's late spring. The bush has all its foliage. The little owl is hidden." She used two fingers to brush aside some of the bush. "You can see the owl's little head. That's about it." She pulled her panties back up and let her dress down, then sat.

They smoked the joint as the sun went down. It was romantic, but Ray was too content to do more than hand holding. Very stoned, Bea was happy to let Ray be content. She had the strange feeling that he had a deep crush on her that was, in a weird way, holding him back from picking up what she was putting down. Absurdly, she thought he was acting like she would act if Rick Mercer had replied to her racy letter by taking her on a date. Of course, she was really high, so she giggled at her thoughts and the setting sun.

Out of nowhere, Bea yelled, "Oh crap!"

"What!? Cops?" Ray instinctually said, even though pot was now legal.

Bea reached for her bag. "I almost forgot. I want to go on a mission with you."

"What do you mean?"

Bea pulled out The Communist Manifesto. "I want to subvert young minds."

Ray let out a chuckle, flipped his bangs back and smiled.

Bea put the book down. "That's my distraction book. I caught onto you, Ray." She put *The Communist Manifesto* back in her bag and took out the children's books on transsexuality. "These were the books you were really planting. The truly controversial books of the twenty-first century. Maybe more scandalous in Cold Lake than James Bay... still," She looked from the books to him. "Let's go distribute them."

Ray was granite. He seemed to stare through Bea to the sea.

"Did you see a ghost?"

"I thought I saw a killer whale."

Bea turned to scan the orange-yellow sun-dappled ocean. "Did you see the direction it was going?"

"It was between that freighter and the little yellow boat." Ray stared down at Bea's books.

"Oh... as far out as the pilot boat and that freighter." Bea adjusted her gaze further out. "You have great eyes, and they look good too." For a few minutes, she watched the harbour pilot being picked up.

"I only saw a fin for a second." Ray remained gazing at Bea's books. "I could have mistaken it."

"It's totally possible. I've seen orcas out here many times fishing with my dad. It could have dived deep." Bea continued to search. After another minute, she turned to him. "I only see a sea lion over by Holland Point." She grabbed her bag and stood. "Let's go on our mission."

Dallas Road and the streets into James Bay were busy with the clip-clop of horse-drawn carriages, cars revving their engines to pass the horses, and lost cruise ship tourists.

Owls, Doughnuts, and Democracy, by Jason A. N. Taylor

In the purple light of the setting sun, Bea and Ray deposited books in little libraries. Bea became childlike and giddy, making a game of sneaking up to put a book in. Ray followed awkwardly, oddly chuckling at her. An old lady in the window of a nineteenth-century heritage house gave her the evil eye. She flipped the bird and tore off running, Ray following on his scooter.

Walking back from Fisherman's Wharf book-less, Bea worked on getting Ray to help her make a bot that would automatically post a Direct Democracy comment link every time a Redditor posted or commented on the Canadian election, democracy, or politics.

Ray could see the problem she was having but could not articulate it. However, he stubbornly tried, knowing she would get the concept if he could communicate it.

Bea was having a similar communication problem. She had not been able to initiate any more touch than the hand holding at the bench overlooking the beach. She could tell he had a deep crush on her by how his eyes were glued to her ass. Especially when she made a show of bending to look at all the titles in the little libraries. She just could not get him to go further. Was the six-year age difference an impediment to intimacy? Was it possible younger people today were not quick to get to bed? Could her personal experiences be out of the norm?

Distracted, Bea and Ray almost bumped into Cameron on his rascal, John and Morty following behind.

"Eh, slow down, you fool!" Morty called. "You're going to cripple our new leader!"

"It's too soon for a joke like that, Morty." John scolded. "Cam's broken up over putting Harold in the hospital."

"Bea... I mean, dear leader, I swear I was not trying to hit you," Cameron sounded sincere. "Did the Art Walk go well?"

"We got the big interview of Colleen Lauren. Tomorrow, it should be edited together. I'm sure it will be great." Bea looked over the group. "This is my friend, Ray."

They all politely exchanged greetings.

"What are you up to this fine evening?" Bea asked.

"I'm not going to lie," Morty confessed. "We're on a beer run."

"No wonder you were in such a rush. Ray, get out of the way of these young men. They need beer." Bea stepped off the sidewalk, pulling Ray with her.

As Cameron passed Ray, he whistled and said, "Nice wheels. I wish I could still handle a hot-rod scooter like that."

Ray grinned widely at the old man. "She can do over forty kilometres an hour."

When the old men were out of earshot, Ray confronted Bea, "You're the new leader of Direct Democracy?"

"Yeah. Harold broke his hip. The membership wanted me."

"When were you going to tell me?"

"Uhm, first date... and I thought you'd know anyway. Does it matter?"

"I don't want to go out with anyone who could be in the public eye."

"Who'd you murder? Promise I won't tell."

"I really like you..." Ray stopped moving. "But I have reasons why I don't want to be on social media or in public. Going out with a leader of a political party breaks my boundaries."

"We're going out? Did I miss our first kiss? And really, calling me a leader of a political party is ridiculous! It is so absurd that if I posted it on *r/technicallythetruth*, it would get a million upvotes. I'm the leader of a party with one candidate in a country where an election has not even been called."

"Direct Democracy might not be big now, but what if it grows?"

"I feel you're being just a little paranoid. I'm not going to ask why you don't want to be around a public person. It is your boundary. But I'm not exactly a public person. Even if Direct Democracy was successful, this is not the United States. Canadians don't get crazy about politics like 'Mericans do."

"Or is it that they don't have a dumpster fire to watch?"

"Are you implying I'm a dumpster fire!?"

"No. No. Not at all. The media is always waiting for a shitshow. A fringe candidate with a weird platform could be the clusterfuck they seek. Trump did not make the media. The media made Trump."

"Look, you can call me a clusterfuck waiting to happen, but at least give this a chance until the shit hits the fan. Because I really think you're being paranoid. I mean that in the most supportive, positive way. I've had a really great evening so far. Even with the failed assassination attempt by Cameron."

"What?"

"The guy in the scooter knocked Harold over. He tried to do the same to me. In a world where I'm a public person, that was an assassination attempt." Ray was confused. Bea shook her head and continued. "Nothing. Let's pick up at you like me, and we're having a good night. Or am I too public for you?"

Ray scratched his chin, contemplating. "It has been a great night. Ice cream would make it better."

"Lead the way."

They walked downtown with the cruise ship throngs. Government Street was packed with meandering visitors. Bea did her best not to push through the shambling mob; pretty sure Ray would find it off-putting. All the ice cream shops on Government were packed. Near the Bay Centre, they stopped to listen to Darth Fiddler, a violin-playing busker dressed like Darth Vader. She humoured Ray by acting entertained but she did not find any novelty in the costume. She'd seen way better performance art featuring Vader. They decided to keep walking to the sketchy Dairy Queen close to her place.

There were no seats open, so they took their dipped cones to go. Bea directed Ray toward her place, walking slowly as tourists. Both were starting to feel the long day of walking across Victoria. At Blanshard and Hillside, they were less than a block from the Paulina in the late spring twilight.

"I'm over there." Bea pointed to her building.

Ray pointed up Blanshard. "I'm near UpTown."

Bea decided that, if Ray had not caught on that he could invite himself to her place, she was too tired to give any more hints. "Are we going our separate ways?"

"I had a great time. I want to go out again."

Bea sensed Ray was wavering on whether to kiss her. She took positive action, planting an unexpected kiss on the lips. Unfortunately, he was trying to say something, and they clinked teeth painfully. Both recoiled, hands to mouths.

"Aw shit, that hurt..." Bea screwed up her face. "Sorry for the bad timing. I had a great time, too. I want to go out again as well."

"I was going to say I'm out of town for the next few weeks."

"No problem. When you're back, we'll go out." Bea paused, waiting for a kiss. When it did not come quickly enough, she said, "Ray, this is a warning. I'm coming in for a kiss goodnight." It was a quick kiss on the lips that had Bea feeling like a teenager.

They two went their separate ways, Bea resisting the urge to turn back and drag Ray to her apartment. She distracted herself with her phone messages. Mia would have the interview video ready for all platforms on Sunday morning. Then, the different politically affiliated voter groups would edit the video for their audience. With customized messages, a large group of members sharing the content, and Mia's Instagram fame, the message was sure to find a broad audience.

At home, sitting feet up, Bea scrolled through TikTok's political videos. She hoped through this half-assed research she would find the content to break the algorithm. Mostly, she felt herself getting stupider, which was ok on a Saturday night.

The phone pinged with a message. It was from Joice: How was your date?

Bea: It is 9:45 pm, and we're texting.

Joice: LOL

Bea: It was good. But they weren't picking up what I was putting down. Maybe I'm out of practice.

Joice: Wanna chat about it over coffee tomorrow? We can watch and share the interview, too.

Bea: Sure. I work at noon. 11 am at Discovery on Blanshard.

Joice: It's a date!

Bea: Two in a week. LOL

It was a hot morning for Victoria. Bea dressed the part in a sports bra top and tennis skort. The only people on the street were waiting in unending lines to get tables at trendy brunch places. She arrived at her coffee shop to see Joice already seated outside. She waved before getting a complimentary coffee.

Bea became aware of Joice checking her out and did the same when walking back to the table. Joice had a wispy light dress on that was tight in the right places for her curves, which made Bea want to cuddle.

"Why don't we go sit on the grass by the playground?" Be suggested. "It has good shade and government WiFi. Mia's posted the interview. I can't wait to see it."

They sat in the shade of a large Gary oak and sat close to share the view of Joice's large phone.

To 1990s cheery television show music, a collage of pictures from the Art Walk introduced the video.

"Is that the 'Eye on Springfield' song?" Bea asked.

Joice did not respond.

Ethan did a great impression of The Simpsons' Kent Brockman delivering "Tonight on Eye On Victoria. Bea Jensen compares how Member of Parliament for Victoria Capital, Colleen Lauren, voted vs. the Art Walkers."

With the music fading, a black screen zoomed out to reveal Bea's shapely, nipply, tightly constrained, bouncy chest with shades of the 'Eye on Springfield' opening scene. The camera zoomed out until her entire body was seen in the gigantic traffic control yellow owl safety shirt. Bea shook her head at how nipply she was. "I don't know why they do that when I run."

"You bussin, I love it."

Bea shrugged, not getting the young word.

"Bussin." Joice squished her large breasts together to emphasize her cleavage. With a giggle, Joice concluded, "Tits sell."

On the video, Bea introduced herself as the leader of Direct Democracy, and MP Colleen introduced herself. Then Bea asked her first question, "What's the job of an MP?"

"My job is to listen to constituents, regardless of their party," Colleen answered with a wide smile. "Then I act on their behalf in

Parliament. That's one of the reasons I'm here at the Art Walk, to hear people."

A hair metal band guitar solo screeched, and the scene cut to Art Walkers, followed by Brockman's voice: "Victoria Capital constituents, did you want a pipeline?" The screen flipped quickly through interviews, and the citizens stated their political leanings and that none of them wanted a pipeline.

Another guitar solo, and Brockman said, "Does Colleen have an excuse?"

"Hmmm, the pipeline…" Colleen's brow furrowed. "It was a hard decision. I supported the Prime Minister's choice. He had what was best for Canada in mind."

The riff played, and Brockman responded, "What was Colleen's job?"

The clip of Colleen describing her job played. "My Job is to listen to my constituents regardless of their party." A whan waaw sound effect played.

The intro sound played with more b-roll from the Art Walk for a second. Bea took centre stage again, asking, "How did you vote on defence?"

"Sovereignty is important to every nation," Colleen asserted. "My grandfather served. The Liberal budget provides for a strong Canadian Armed Forces that meets its commitments with honour."

Another guitar riff broke the scene with a voice-over of Brockman saying, "The survey says!"

Canada's Pacific Fleet is in the Victoria Capital riding. Its constituents were not unanimous in the desire for more military spending than the Liberals had budgeted. But it was a supermajority. And the voters in support were of every political stripe.

The whan waaw sound effect played while Colleen's self-described job description was repeated. "My Job is to listen to my constituents regardless of their party."

The same pattern repeated for Indigenous Reconciliation; the vast majority were unhappy Colleen voted for a bill they thought was half measures. For health care spending, all voters felt Colleen did not do her job by voting for the budget that was devoid of a spending increase. Housing, no one was happy with the action the Liberals had taken that Colleen, following party lines, had supported. Proportional voting, a strong majority from all parties wanted this bill to pass, Colleen voted with the Liberal majority to kill the bill – Tim Bits indeed.

A final guitar riff ushered in Brockman one last time, "Can we blame Colleen for not listening to her constituents?"

The sound effect of a ruckus crowd yelling "yes" answered.

"Hang on!" Brockman rebutted. "It's not Colleen's fault. It's a system that's only set up to listen to the constituents once every four years or so. Then, the MP gets to go to Parliament to party with their Party. In the time between elections, listening to the voters means going to events like the Art Walk and reading letters from the type of people who write letters to MPs."

Colleen smiling and waving at the Art Walk was followed on-screen by Abe Simpson writing a letter and shaking his fist at clouds to illustrate the point.

"The tools are not in place to hear the voters in our modern democracy."

The shot of Bea's bussin' top zoomed out from the black of the owl to the full view. "Direct Democracy solves the problem of being heard. It gives constituents the opportunity to vote on all legislation. No longer will constituents in west coast ridings have their voices fall on the deaf ears of a politician more concerned about the Party line than the damage a pipeline could do to our sacred coast." A snip of Colleen and other Liberal MPs in a conga line flashed on screen, and then a broken pipeline spewing oil played on screen. "Have your say! Support Direct Democracy." An owl with outstretched wings blackened the screen with instructions on how to contact Direct Democracy.

"WOW! That was good." Bea exclaimed.

"Yeah. Let's get sharing." Joice tapped on her phone to share the Instagram Reel to TikTok, Facebook, Twitter, Reddit, and YouTube. Multi-tasking, she looked up and asked, "What went wrong on your date?"

Bea multi-tasked, too. "Nothing bad happened. Overall, it was a good first date. But it did not end up where I hoped it would."

"Where did you hope it would end?"

"In bed. But all that happened was an awkward end-of-the-night kiss I had to initiate."

Joice giggled. "You move fast."

"It has been a while, but I know what I want. Plus, it was a long date... like four hours. They seemed really into me, too." Bea stopped tapping her phone and turned to Joice. "You're their age. Is it a generation thing?"

"I don't think so. I'd be down with hooking up on a first date if I was into the woman. Maybe it was a consent thing. I've met a few women who demand explicit consent. Like they say exactly what's ok and must be sober when they say it."

"That could be it. They're a pothead. We were stoned pretty much the entire date."

Joice leaned onto Bea's arm so that side boob and side boob met each other. She made eye contact with Bea. "If you're feeling out of practice. We could practice together?"

Bea leaned into Joice, moving her arm to embrace her. Then she thought about the situation. She pulled away.

"What's wrong, Bea? It was only a first date; you wouldn't be breaking any commitment to her."

"That's not the problem. I would not tell him. It's none of his business."

"Oh, him. I thought you were gay." Joice scooted a few centimetres away. "Sorry, Bea."

"That's not it. I'd love to have some fun with you, but I'm the leader of Direct Democracy, and you're a volunteer. There's a power imbalance."

"You're joking!"

"No. I said the same thing to Justin..." Bea spoke as much to convince herself as Joice. "It's not right to fuck around in a workplace. If it ever came out, it would look bad."

"Ew! Justin. But I can still fantasize... right?" Joice batted her eyes.

"Do what you have to do, girl."

Bea's work shift came too soon, but she slung coffee and doughnuts nonetheless, doing her best to avoid the phone. She silenced it and hid it away to keep it from temptation. During her break, she finally took a look. An overwhelming wave of notifications, likes, comments and shares were blowing up her social media. She did not know where to start. Instead of monitoring the feed, she read her dozen or so texts. Most were from Direct Democracy members texting the success. Shockingly, Marcus congratulated her on the interview. But the one she keyed in on was from Cat: Check out your Twitter post. Colleen Lauren called you out.

On the interview's Twitter comment thread, a blue checkmarked account, @ColleenLaurenMPVictoriaCapital, commented: This is what politics has come to: disingenuous mud slingers trying for the gotcha video. I should have caught on when I was asked for an interview from an art group promoting democracy. LOL. I guess you got me. But it is pretty easy to cherry-pick responses to show any result you want. It is clear that's what happened here.

Bea responded, @BeaJensenDirectDemocracy: Hi Colleen, it was great meeting you. Direct Democracy is a new party; sorry I was not clear... New to this ☺. Here are all our interview responses (linked). But don't take our word alone; check out the third-party polling (linked). It's for BC, but you get the gist. Which of the 70% of voters that did not want a pipeline were you listening to? Or is the poll wrong? Is there an enclave of pro-pipeliners in Oak Bay that you listen to exclusively? ☺

During a quick washroom break, Bea checked her Twitter comment. It was getting lots of likes and shares. Best of all was the reply from @ColleenLaurenMPVictoriaCapital: "enclave of pro-pipeliners in Oak Bay," what does that mean? Are you accusing me of corruption?

@BeaJensenDirectDemocracy: I was merely pointing out that my statistic could be wrong because of a large group of pro-pipeline supporters somewhere in Victoria-Capital. Having no power or experience within government, I will leave the discussion of corruption to the experts, the Liberals. ☺

Back on duty, Bea sneaked glances at her phone between customers, gleefully waiting for a reply. It didn't take long: You're obviously not an expert. MPs are not in Ottawa to 'party' with our caucus like your video implies. It takes dedicated, serious people who want to make Canada better to hold office. MPs do serious work.

Jumping in the conversation was @HaroldGordonHonorableMemberRetired: Holy Doodle Bea, you know Colleen's been to Ottawa because of the manure she spews. An untrained monkey can do the job better than most MPs. I did it for half as long as Colleen's been alive with no degree. And I worked on NAFTA, the biggest international trade agreement of its time. All it takes is a man willing to sell prairie oysters at a sushi stand.

Colleen let Harold's reply go. But after Bea's shift ended, there was a notification from @ColleenLaurenMPVictoriaCapital: Your video is a misrepresentation of how the system works. It wrongly simplifies complicated issues, many of which do not get voted on individually in parliament. To suggest I did not listen to my constituents because I voted differently than the majority in my riding is ridiculous. MPs must take into consideration what is best for Canada.

@BeaJensenDirectDemocracy: You defined your job as "to listen to my constituents regardless of their party." Our Art Walk polling and BC-wide polling done by a third-party company found you did not listen to your constituents. As a Direct Democracy candidate, I will always vote the way my constituency tells me to in Parliament. That's my one and only promise. ☺

@ColleenLaurenMPVictoriaCapital: Good luck.

Over the rest of the evening, Bea checked her phone regularly. She hoped for another response from Colleen but did not get one. The repartee had gotten a huge amount of attention. Bea wanted to partake in more Tweeting but surmised that a smart person in the Liberal party must have told Colleen there was no winning by giving a platform to your no-name opponent.

18.

Bea had turned her phone notifications on in expectation of a call from Sam, which, when it was over, left her feeling sad. She went to bed early, and at some time after 5 am, the notifications woke her up. A group message with Harold and Derek confirming and counter-confirmed that the election was as good as called. CBC reported that Junior had been seen going to Rideau Hall.

She went for a run in the warm early morning, then ate a light breakfast, watching CBC coverage on the big election issues. The housing crisis was highlighted. She watched from the washroom, which kept her from fixating on the highly mildewed, probably mouldy corner near the bathtub. The Power and Politics clip distracting her was a discussion of the big parties' leaders' housing situation. She laughed at it sarcastically. She found it especially rich when Evan Sullivan commented on the modest Gulf Island home of the Green party leader as if any home on Saltspring was modest.

Silverfish scurried from the light as Bea stomped her feet at them when she got her running shoes. She was happy she got two with one stomp. She opened the door lobby and mailboxes, nearly running into a neighbour.

The neighbour held up a letter. "Have you seen this? Along with the annual rent increase, the landlord is making us pay for heating."

"No." Bea opened her mailbox.

The letter was clear. Over the summer, the heating, which had been provided by a boiler with radiators, would be changed to an electric baseboard. The cost of the electricity would become the tenant's responsibility. The projected cost varied. What did not vary was that the landlord would get the two percent rent increase and pocket the cost of heating the apartment with the boiler.

The only thing Bea loved about her apartment was cranking the heat in the winter. Next winter, she would be poorer doing that.

Enraged, Bea had an idea. She narrated the Instagram Reel:

"The Canadian Housing Crisis. Do the leaders of the big parties care?" Newspaper headlines of the leaders caring about housing stacked up behind Bea.

"All of the big party leaders try to say they understand the problem. They act like populists."

"What is a populist? A person, especially a politician, who strives to appeal to ordinary people who feel that their concerns are disregarded by established elite groups."

"Does J.T. experience the housing crisis like you and your family do?"

"Justin lives in government housing. He owns other houses. He can couch surf at the Aga Khan's anytime he wants. Maybe he passed out on a chesterfield while working as a ski instructor but that's his closest experience to the housing crisis." 24 Sussex, the Prime Minister's official residence, pictures of his other properties, and a tropical island supposedly owned by the Aga Khan filled the background. J.T. in blackface was overlaid on the Aga Khan's island's beach.

"Little Pee Pee must at least forgo the government housing? He does try to say he is for cutting waste. But he lives in Stornoway. For shame Little Pee Pee, prior populist Preston Manning at least made a statement by not moving into such grandiose digs." A picture of the official opposition's house, Stornoway, was in the background. "Worse or better... I'm not sure. You rent out your investment properties. Are you a good landlord? If you rent, you know that was a trick question... good landlord, funny stuff."

"This one surprised me. The most socialist of the bunch, Jagmeet, is rich by anyone's standards. He owns houses in the lower mainland and land in India. I guess it is laudable to fight for the rest of us while not needing the changes for oneself. But the housing crisis must be pretty abstract to you." Again, pictures of the NDP leader's properties flashed behind Bea.

"The closest to reality is the Green party leader... oh, you know who. She has a small townhouse by the pier in Sydney. Really just a little thing. Oh... and a tiny cabin on Salt Spring Island where literally no one wants to live." An idyllic picture of Salt Spring Island added to Bea's sarcasm.

"And yes, there's the leader of the Bloc. But I'm in Victoria. Meh."

Owls, Doughnuts, and Democracy, by Jason A. N. Taylor

"Then there is me. I'm Bea Jensen, leader of Direct Democracy. I don't have the money for a gym membership. But I keep fit and safe by running through my crappy neighbourhood." A video of unsavoury characters, unkempt yards, and graffiti-marked murals played. "I won't show my building, but it is similar to these. Yes, I rent." Her video showed dilapidated four-story apartments with 'no vacancy' signs on them. "It's a toss-up between a cop car or a person in a mental health crisis being out front of my building. YAY! A cop car. Well, yay for me. The person in a mental health crisis is probably not getting any help from the cops." A bouncing video of a parked cop car played. The video cut to coming into her house. "My furnishings are humble but functional. It is a combination of street corner castaways, dollar store decor, and clearance items from Zeller's, Target, or Bed, Bath, and Beyond." Bea panned the camera around her neat but shittily appointed apartment. "Come see the spongy corner in my washroom. I would like to get the landlord to fix it… but I'm also worried about renoviction because that happened to the building down the street." She pressed on the black, hopefully, mildewy but probably mouldy spongy corner in her washroom. A picture of an apartment advertising newly renovated suites flashed on the screen when she said renoviction. The camera then walked back to the kitchen table. "The best part is the notice I got today. Heat, which was included in the rent, will be my responsibility next winter. And the rent is increasing! WTF!" The landlord's letter zoomed in. "You would think there would be a rent decrease as they don't have to pay for the energy for the boiler. Nope! The landlord gets their regulated two percent increase and the bonus energy savings. Probably $60 a month in the winter."

The video turned to a photo of Bea in her sweaty running outfit, beautiful and well-lit, on a hill with sunshine filtered through Gary oaks. "I understand the housing crisis. I am living in it. I shop at Walmart and the Dollar Store while being ashamed I must. I am one of you."

"Unlike Justin, Little Pee Pee, Jagmeet, and the rest, I don't pretend I have an answer to the housing crisis."

Owls, Doughnuts, and Democracy, by Jason A. N. Taylor

"But I do have a different way of doing politics. I want to give you the one thing we were promised by democracy: a voice in the process. As a Direct Democracy candidate, my mandate, if elected, is to do one thing: vote in Parliament for what the majority of my constituency has voted for on the app. That's it."

Bea's picture vanished, replaced by a screen shot of the app. She showed how simple the app was to use. "Using the Direct Democracy app, constituents of all political alignments will be able to vote on bills before Parliament. It is as easy as answering three questions, or you can vote on every bill."

The video changed to the scene on the hill. "My promise to you is that I will always vote for what the majority of my constituents vote for on the app. No flip-flopping on pipelines. No reneging on money for health care. No decisions on housing made by landlords or owners alone. I promise to listen to you." Eyes sparking, Bea turned into the sun with the light glinting on her sweaty hair and skin making her look angelic. The picture became bright white with light. A silhouette of the Direct Democracy owl took the frame as the video ended.

Bea did not find an imperfection in what seemed like the hundredth view of the clip. It had been more than two hours of editing. It was as close to perfect as it would get. And she would have to leave for work now, or she would have to run to get there on time. She posted it to Instagram. Walking to work, she pushed it out further on WhatsApp, TikTok, Facebook, Reddit and the rest. On WhatsApp, she alerted all the members of Direct Democracy to share the shit out of the post.

Harold and Justin collaborated on the Conservative message. Daisy, Justin's truck, pulled into a parking spot on Dallas Road. Justin's voice-over said, "Hi, I'm Justin… frig, not that one." A censored Fuck Trudeau sticker flashed quickly in the video. "I am from up Island, but I live here now. It's hard to fit in as a Conservative in this city." Daisy's big tires barely squeezed between the lines of the parking spot. Justin got out in work boots and a Browning ball cap. In the background, an out-of-shape running group trundled by. "People here have different values. Care about different things." The camera panned to the line of electric cars and chargers taking the best parking spots with no trucks. "I know my voting for the Conservative candidate in Victoria Capital will be drowned out by the majority. At least, it will be if I vote Conservative. There is another way."

"I can vote for Bea, the Direct Democracy candidate. Direct Democracy is committed to giving every Canadian in the riding an app to vote on bills going before Parliament. The candidate would then vote for what the majority voted for in the riding." A picture of Bea in sweaty running gear graced the screen. The video changed to different clips of Justin talking with people. "Because when I talk with Liberal and NDP voting Victorians, I find that they may not share all my views, but they do share some. For example, Conservatives, Liberals, and NDPers in Victoria Capital are for increased defense spending, changing immigration requirements, and limiting foreign investment in property, yet the governing Liberals did not pass bills to support these issues. A Direct Democracy candidate would provide another vote for these Conservative issues in a riding that frankly will not be in Conservative hands after this election. But who am I to listen to on this?"

The picture changed to one of Harold and Justin talking. Harold addressed the camera. "If you're a Conservative on the Island and you don't know me, holy doodle! I am Harold Gordon. I won four elections for the Progressive Conservatives and was one of three PCs to survive '93. This Direct Democracy thing was my idea. It is what we need on the West Coast to get our voices heard in Ottawa. It is time to try something new because we have not been heard the old way."

The tact taken by Irene and Tyrell with the help of others was different. It started with graphics and excerpts on what the Liberal platform is and what it has accomplished. Things like universal health care, same-sex marriage, the student loan system, the Canadian Pension Plan, the Constitution of Canada, and the Canadian Charter of Rights and Freedoms. The music for this was O Canada but played by a small band, not loud enough to be overly patriotic. A picture of a big tent reinforced the computer narrator's statement that the Liberals are the big tent party.

Then, the picture shattered with the sound of breaking glass. But this is what the Liberals stand for now. Headlines from newspapers spattered the screen, including WE Charity, SCN Lavalin, the Aga Khan trip, other opulent hotel stays, interference in RCMP investigations, concealing Chinese interference in the last election, cultural appropriation, and blackface. The sound behind this montage was a well-sung, if wavey version of Happy Birthday, changed to Happy Scandal Day by Irene. When the line "and many more" was sung, the screen read, "Really, there will be many more."

The clip changed to pictures of a new digitally animated big tent. The computer narrator read the captions, "There's a new big tent party. It includes every Canadian. It promises less corruption and fewer scandals. Direct Democracy does this by giving the people in a riding an app to vote on every bill before parliament." A quick demonstration of the app was followed by further discussion of how corruption would be harder without a politician to buy. Bea's image was taken from the first video where she looked like Athena. An owl silhouette finished the video.

Mia had something completely different. It was almost hard to see it as political. The reel started with her walking up to groups of twenty-somethings at an outdoor party in the golden hour. She was looking west coast radiant in a one of a kind yellow makers dress with the smile of a cherub. As she walked around the different groups, each one had a person spouting off a political view with the others in the groups agreeing. Little animated signs marked each person in the group with the political party they represented. All the groups were made up of people from the same party. None of them mixed.

Mia was different. She went from group to group, smiling, talking, and laughing. She did not have a sign. Once she had been to all the groups, she turned to the camera that had been following her. "I want to participate in politics, but I do not want to be my politics. Direct Democracy lets me do that." Information on Direct Democracy followed with Bea's picture overlaid.

Not all groups under the Direct Democracy banner were as social media adept. Rich's TikTok dragged. Rich painfully described how the app worked. For those with knowledge of who Joe Walsh is, Rich's stoned cadence was at least funny. It did not engage the viewer's resentment that the NDP has never won an election. It hardly set up how Direct Democracy would empower federal NDPers to have power without winning the riding. Worse, for the group that most identified with the common person, populism was not part of the pitch. It did not even have a picture of Bea. Rich did get some great shots of the owl family in but there were only so many owl ladies that voted NDP.

Joice's was an anarcho-feminist nightmare or gem, depending on your perspective. She wore a Guy Fawkes mask and a purple leotard with black leggings. She spun in front of a flag split diagonally in half, with one side black and the other purple. She shrieked, "Anonymous! Powerless! Anonymous and powerless! Revolution! Revolution! Revolution! Rev..." On about the tenth spin, she crumpled her way to the ground without falling, truly dizzy. "Hang on. The room is still spinning. Too much revolution." She got herself upright. "Let's try this again." She slowly started to spin. She weakly said, "Revolution! Revolution." She collapsed on her knees with her long blond hair covering her face. She lifted her head and flipped her hair out from her face. "There's got to be a better way to crush the system. Revolution is making me sick." She took off the mask. She pretended to wretch. "We need something different. Something to give everyone a little more power." She stood, putting a hand above her eyes like she was looking at something in the distance. "What is this?" From off screen she grabbed a child's telescope and looked off in the distance. Cropped to a circular picture, Bea's sweaty image from the interview with Colleen Lauren took the screen while she sang out of tune, "Look over there! Direct Democracy!" She dropped the telescope. She started dancing un-rhythmically to no music. "The evolution we are looking for. With it, the women in a riding can vote on every bill before parliament. If they come for our reproductive rights, we can outvote them." She danced out of the camera's view, still singing. "All of our little power will be more than theirs. We will destroy the system." She wheeled a workbench to the center of the frame. "We will have the power. Their nuts will be in a..." She paused to put two walnuts in the vice on the workbench. Out of key and extremely loud, she sang, "VVVVVIIIIIICCCCE!" She spun the vice's handle. "And we will squeeze! And squeeze! And..." There was a crack as the nuts cracked. She giggled loudly but acted demure. "And we will win. Viva le revolution! We will be equal. Democratic. Thank you, Athena." She used a clip from the first Direct Democracy video outro with Bea, Athena, and an owl.

Canadians for Greater Democracy was the official name for Ajay and Cat's third party. Their new social media propaganda started with a family on a long road trip. Playing on the family's car stereo was the Tragically Hip's Bobcaygeon. The dad asked, "Who votes to stop at the next gas station?" The family voted. The video then showed a myriad of situations in which Canadians vote, like kids deciding what movie to watch, who's buying beer, what restaurant the group should go to, and who's going to be the designated driver. A narrator said, "Canadians vote on things because it is a fair way to decide. Dare I say voting is to Canadians as apple pie is to... you know who." A procession of headlines highlighting the progress of Canadian democracy from the British North America Act in 1867 granting rich white people the vote to the Wartime Election Act and Military Voters Act expanding the vote to some women and minorities in 1917, to all Asian Canadians gaining the vote in 1948, to 1960 when First Nations could vote without giving up their status, and the final affirmation of the right to vote in 1982 with the Canadian Charter of Rights and Freedoms. A black and white picture of the Canadian Parliament assaulted the screen with J.T. pointing at someone, yelling, "You cannot have it!" The narrator said, "The 'it' was the promised electoral reform that was part of Junior's last election platform and this one too. But it is not just the Hair Style that does not want Canada to expand democracy with electoral reform like proportional representation. All the parties have electoral reform on their platform, but none will do it. Why? Because it is easier for them to stay in power with a less democratic process. You heard it right; less democracy is what they want. Less democracy means more lies, more scandals, more corruption. Make them change by voting for the only party whose platform is based on giving you the chance to vote directly on every bill before Parliament. Your vote will at least push the old parties towards the electoral reform that a whopping sixty-seven percent of Canadians want. Be Canadian, vote for more democracy." The narrator's last rant was accompanied by a montage of Canadiana to evoke the little patriotism in the Canadian soul. Then, there was a quick outro of Athena with Bea's face morphing into an owl that flies off. Bea decided she would steal the "Be Canadian" line from Ajay and Cat.

Bea watched the videos during her break. As the shift dragged on, she found ways to share, comment on, and reference other Direct Democracy content, search for the video hashtags, and watch each of the videos again. With each action, the social media algorithm's metrics positively biased Direct Democracy's content. The rest of the Direct Democracy membership was also doing the same. These actions drove a cascading wave of virulence.

Direct Democracy also paid for views on all the platforms they could because the real algorithm is money.

These actions cause Canadian for you pages on social media to be awash with Direct Democracy content.

Creators outside of Direct Democracy got in on the frenzy.

Joice's TikTok masterpiece caused a convulsion of feminist, anarchist, anti-anarchist, anti-feminist, anti-leftwing, anti-interpretative dance, pro-revolution, pro-conspiracy, pro-capitalist, incel, Jordan Peterson, anti-Jordan Peterson, fascist, anti-fascist, and every other fringe group to freak out. They used her content as the centre of rants assaulting her position. At the centre of every TikTok railing against her was the Direct Democracy message, a message being heard. Some of the content creators were asking what Direct Democracy was, wondering if it was a good idea.

Conservative creators were using Irene and Tyrel's admission that the Liberals were corrupt to make hay with their viewers. But Justin and Harold's video was used similarly, too, with Liberals and NDP highlighting the lengths to which Conservatives will go to win.

Owls, Doughnuts, and Democracy, by Jason A. N. Taylor

The message of Direct Democracy was passed on subtly to the viewers from other parties.

The nickname Little Pee Pee, Bea had coined for the Conservative leader, started to take on a life of its own. It was bound to take off; it was so much better than Skippy. The hashtag Little Pee Pee went viral, with left-leaning content creators running with it like a child with scissors. The other side took notice, too. "Fuck Trudeau" comments sprouted like mushrooms after the first fall rain. Bea responded to as many of them as she could with, 'Make sure to wear a condom, bring some lube, and form an orderly line.' Bea did not care to read any of the responses to her remarks.

Bea had every intention to respond abrasively to Liberal stooges, NDP chuckleheads, or shills for the Green party, but she could not find any. Then, just as she finished her shift it happened on Twitter. Little Pee Pee, or more likely his social media manager, attacked her: Is Direct Democracy's platform name-calling? It may have worked in the schoolyard. It does not work in the real world.

Bea was elated. She'd got Little Pee Pee's goat. She did a happy dance, grabbed another coffee and thought of a response: 'LOL! Little Pee Pee, I couldn't find your party's platform either... all I found was lots of divisive language and spew about removing gatekeepers. What's a gatekeeper? You don't even seem to know. Direct Democracy is our platform. We keep it simple.'

Little Pee Pee's account hit back quickly: Letting people vote on bills in Parliament directly is ridiculous. Nothing will get done.

Before responding, Bea took screenshots for future use. She posted: A person in your position believes the average person won't get anything done given the chance to vote in Parliament, DISGUSTING! You are with the party that says the Canadian budget is like a household budget. Sir, do you actually think a person who must shop at Walmart and the Dollar Store to make ends meet is not smart enough to vote in Parliament and move Canada forward? All the MPs in the Legislative Assembly currently get nothing done. Or at least nothing that Canadians want.

Little Pee Pee's stooge took some time to reply. In the meantime, Twitterers began seeing the thread, helped by Direct

Democracy members and Bea. Finally, there was a response from the stooge: Conservative Canadians don't need the hassle of voting on every bill. That's what his representative is for.

Bea was giddy and loved this. She instantaneously tweeted: It was a YES or NO question. Little Pee Pee, do you think a person who must shop at Walmart and the Dollar Store to make ends meet is not smart enough to vote in Parliament and move Canada forward?

Little Pee Pee's account: I will not respond to name-calling.

Bea: That's a politician's way of saying NO! For shame, Little Pee Pee, your dangly bits are as small as your tally whacker. Little Pee Pee, please grow some and answer the question: Do you think average Canadians would move Canada forward if given the chance to vote in Parliament?

Little Pee Pee's account: I will not respond to name-calling.

Bea: Little Pee Pee can't trust Canadians enough to answer yes to the question. How repulsive!

Little Pee Pee's account: Name-calling is not acceptable. I will not respond to it.

Bea shot back by linking a video of Little Pee Pee in the House of Commons vomiting an ad hominem-laced tirade at Junior. She added: You expect J.T. to respond to name-calling in question period? It must be that some people in Canada are more equal than me. Man of the people, pft! More like Little Pee Pee of the Elite. Believing some Canadians are better than others, what a vile way to think! Totally un-Canadian. Disgusting that he lives in government-subsidized housing.

Little Pee Pee's account: I will not respond to name-calling. You are probably funded by the People's Republic of China.

The Honourable member Harold Gordon jumped in: Pierre, I am not calling you names. I am a Conservative through and through. I bleed cerulean blue. I am a retired MP. I am not funded by the Commies. Peer to peer, answer the question: Do you think average Canadians would move Canada forward if given the chance to vote in Parliament?

Bea squealed when she saw Harold's post, taking screenshots. She could not wait for the response, but there was none. It was not long before Little Pee Pee's posts were deleted.

Dancing with excitement in the coffee shop, Bea pushed out the story with screenshots over What's App. She told all the Direct Democracy members to tell the story of Little Pee Pee's Tweets. Tell the world that Little Pee Pee does not trust Canadians to decide on bills before Parliament.

Bea's Twitter account was given a three-day suspension. Adding fuel to the fire, she added screenshots of the ban for the others to cry bloody murder over. There were definitely some behind-the-scenes shenanigans for her to get censored, even for a short time, on Space Karen's Twitter.

The Direct Democracy free-range Troll Farm got to work growing crops of discord. The pollen of disgust at the reaction of one of Canada's mainstream politicians caused an allergic reaction to Little Pee Pee's party. The revulsion was superficial, like hay fever; it did not cause real sickness. The internet sniffled and scratched with irritation at Little Pee Pee's disregard for Canadians' intelligence, but the blood-brain barrier between the mainstream media and internet content was only pierced by the local cable network. CHEK News ran a lighthearted Direct Democracy human-interest story that turned the controversy into a lighthearted ribbing of Pierre by a loveable party of local jokers.

Though Bea was disheartened by the smallness of the TV piece, the oldsters were ecstatic. Harold and Irene did their best to lift Bea's spirits. They assured Bea that the little spot was a big win and that everyone on the Island watched worker-owned CHEK News. But Bea knew the 'everyone' they were referring to was over sixty.

On the other side, the youngsters were talking of the internet success. The Canadian internet was ablaze with discourse over Bea's trapping Little Pee Pee and her subsequent ban. They were sure this would rocket Direct Democracy into orbit like a billionaire with a spare electric car and a desire to remake a scene from Heavy Metal.

Ajay and Cat sites were not in the stars but did see Direct Democracy taking flight.

However, Bea saw their internet virulence as similar to the branching barred owl's flight, close enough to how a rock flies to mistake it for one. She was supported in her view by a chat with Ray or

D-man: Kira B, it's the guy on the scooter. Bubo gave me your handle. I got some code for you. For the Reddit Bot.

Kira B: Thanks D-man ☺. We need to get the message out. I didn't think you played hockey.

D-man: Yeah, hockey.

Kira B: Did you see our instant of controversy?

D-man: Yes. It was entertaining. You did a good job getting him or whoever it was to say that. It didn't get to any real people. A waste.

Kira B: I like to think it was Little Pee Pee but I'm sure it was a lackey, now demoted to minion.

D-man: If DD is going to win, it needs to be in the mainstream.

Kira B: Our social media is great. It has caught lots of people. Derek is pleased with the steady growth of small donations. But those people aren't voters in Victoria Capital.

D-man: Your trolling of Little PP will make the big parties shut you out. That is their best tactic. Control the media.

Kira B: We can use some money to target Victoria Capital with our Instagram, TikTok, and YouTube.

D-man: That's a start. You need to force the mainstream media to see you. Make a scene at a debate or something. Live action will get you on TV.

Kira B: Yeah... I can do that. LOL! Are we going out when you're back?

D-man: Yes. Next week. Where do you want to go?

Kira B: Let me think about it ☺. I gotta go right now. I'm getting pinged by half of Direct Democracy. Thanks for the code.

D-man: See you next week.

Bea got back to working on the campaign's social media. She typed out a message to all members that they should bombard anyone they knew in the riding with Direct Democracy propaganda.

Owls, Doughnuts, and Democracy, by Jason A. N. Taylor

It was pushed out on What's App. She contacted Derek to find out where they could get lawn signs. She looked up the debate schedule. Finally, she started reading the emails coming into her party email.

The first one was not worth reading. The picture said a thousand words. It was something the sender should not have been proud of. At least he should have used forced perspective to make it more imposing. She would have kept anything that gave a sense of scale out of the picture, but the sender was not so wise. A beer can in the background made it look thin and short. The lighting was bad. Rolling back the foreskin would have made it look less like a chicken neck after its worst day. Still, it was the first dick picture she had received in years. As creepy and inappropriate as it was, she did get a slight rise from it. She wanted to thank the man for trying, even if the attempt was feeble.

Googling the dick's email address, Bea set out to find out what she could about the prick. Information on him was easy to find; in less than two minutes, emails from his contacts had come into her possession.

Bea clicked the reply button on the pecker's email and added the newly found contacts. Then she typed: Aw! Thanks for the picture. At first, I thought it was a Slim Jim, but pepperonis don't have turtlenecks. How cute! I could almost imagine you making me squeal with that massive member, but my imagination is not that good. Frankly, I don't know anyone with an imagination that good. Buy a truck with a lift kit, its a good replacement for what you're lacking.

Bea's finger hovered over the left mouse button... Something told her this was a bad idea. After all, she was the leader of a Federal Canadian Party, expected to act with decorum. True, she was contemplating how to make a media splash which likely would push those boundaries. But as much as she wanted to reply, she knew deep down that she should not directly attack the dick-pick sender. It went against who she was, but she resolved not to whack these tally whackers. She closed the email, the hardest thing she had done for Direct Democracy.

19.

The Home was busier than ever when Bea arrived. It was a big Tuesday night. Direct Democracy was launching two offensives.

The first was distributing their signs to as many members as possible, then to plant the rest on open ground. It marked their first foray into ground game politics. Most of them did not think highly of signs and pamphlets in a social media world where likes are easy to count. Harold's nagging on the topic did not help either. Like all emphatic, repetitive, patronizing, grandpa-knows-best grumbling, his holy doodles on the topic only helped move it squarely into a procrastination zone. The viral moment was thus broken with underwhelming media coverage.

The second was how to break into the wrongly named Local All Candidate's Debate. Direct Democracy had not been invited. Worse, mainstream media polling numbers had stopped at the top five parties, with an 'other' category for all the little parties. This lumped Direct Democracy in with non-winning parties like the Communists. This was especially frustrating because the overall category had numbers twice as high as in previous elections, higher than the last-placed Peoples Party of Canada. Bea had an idea to salt the town hall-style debate with Direct Democracy questioners to make the other parties look bad. Bea, like every good politician, knew that being able to frame the question is more powerful than being able to answer the question.

Before they could take on these missions, however, a more immediate problem came to light. Irene and Wendy were arguing with Fred. The argument was over the room. Fred was adamant that the Bridge game could not be interrupted. A group of people in the middle of the room played cards, while at the far end, half a dozen Direct Democracy members assembled signs. At the door, Irene confronted Fred: "We're here every Tuesday night. Let us in."

"It is our room," Wendy added. "Shift it!"

Fred pointed to the schedule on the door. "No one has booked the room. We're here first. We got dibs." Fred spoke in an annoying upper-class British accent. "There's a ton of money riding on that game."

"Irene, let me talk with Fred..." Bea stepped between them and addressed Irene. "We'll need a second room today; can you and Wendy look into that?"

Grumbling, Irene and Wendy shuffled off.

Bea turned to Fred. "All our signs are in there. We need to put them together. You're only using the other end of the room. Can a few of our members join the ones already in there to complete the signs?"

"The game is a serious one, Bea. There could be trouble if it's interrupted by noise."

"There are already three people making signs and not disturbing the game. A few more won't cause any problems."

"I don't know."

Bea rolled her eyes, "Fred, nobody's entitled to the room. Karen will side with the biggest group. We are the biggest group. Take the compromise. We'll keep quiet."

"Ok Bea..." Fred's voice lowered conspiratorially. "If you can distract Warren and Dorothy, there's $20 in it for you?"

"Sorry Fred, we said we'd be quiet."

From down the hall, Harold bellowed, "Fred! Tell those card sharps to take their game out of our room!" Harold waved a piece of paper. "I've signed it out!" He walkered his way to a few feet from Fred and waved the paper again.

Fred squinted his eyes like Clint Eastwood. "You have made an enemy."

"Harold," Bea intervened. "Fred and I came to a compromise!"

"Compromise foo-ie! The room is ours. Take your gambling somewhere else, you scallywags." Harold walkered his way past Fred.

Bea made herself scarce while Harold acted like an ass, not a good move on his part. Karen had turned a blind eye to Direct Democracy's use of the lounge, though it was not a group officially recognized by the Home's Residence Council. The Blue Bridge Club, which was a play on BBC, the Victoria Blue Bridge, and Blue Blood, was an official group. Like any pseudo-governmental volunteer organization, the Home's Residence Council was petty, officious, and insular. Upsetting one of the Home's Residence Council recognized groups was a sure way to lose any good will or leeway Karen might grant Direct Democracy.

When Bea got back from the washroom, the kerfuffle was winding down. Irene gave the retreating BBC members the evil eye. The BBC members glared back at Irene.

"You missed it, Bea," Wendy explained. "Harold and Irene booted the BBC out in the middle of the game. All bets got called off. It was brilliant!"

"I'm sure it was. Now let's get organizing."

The group with the signs did not need much assistance. Justin had taken the initiative. On a map, Harold outlined spots where signs could be posted legally. Bea left them to their work.

With Joice, Rick, Tyrell, and others, Bea sat down to outline her plan. It was simple: Have the members ask questions about Direct Democracy, and then Bea turns the answer into a platform speech. Bea was serious; though the plan was simple, the execution would take Ocean's Eleven-level skill.

To keep from being late Bea was running to the debate, hot from physical exertion and from Victoria weather. She went over her speech as she pushed to go a little faster, stopping her run a hundred metres from the school. Not late, but far from early. Her phone showed half a dozen texts inquiring where she was. She replied quickly, then held her hands over her head in a futile attempt to dry her pits. Worse, her crotch was equally wet, looking like she wet herself. Using her phone as a mirror, she got her hair looking good with some teasing.

She changed focus to her part of the plan.

The venue was an un-air-conditioned middle school gymnasium, stiflingly hot, even with industrial fans. There were a few local television cameras, like exactly three. About a dozen other media types, from local bloggers to the Times-Colonist political columnist, rounded out the attendance. An optimistic count had the crowd at nearly two hundred. Underwhelming.

Owls, Doughnuts, and Democracy, by Jason A. N. Taylor

On the optimistic side, the question queue was filled with Direct Democracy members; only four were unknown to Bea. She joined it.

The debate started with the candidates shaking hands politely with the others on the platform. All shone big smiles. They cordially answered one another's questions. The moderator hardly had to call time. There was little passion. The discussion was a combination of abstract national policy and the candidates talking up their values. The crowd seemed happy with the bland answers. It was a very Canadian start to the debate.

That changed with the first audience question. Joice was up first, starting civilly, if loudly into the microphone: "Colleen Lauren, you voted with your party to buy an oil pipeline. Around seventy percent of voters in Victoria Capital do not want one. How does this fit with your stated duty to listen to your constituents?"

"Canada spans six time zones," Colleen replied. "Thirteen provinces and territories. Bordered by three oceans. Doing the best for Canada sometimes means putting the greater good of the country ahead of a particular region's desires. Besides, there are safeguards in place to keep a disaster from occurring if a pipeline is completed."

"When the southern resident orcas die of starvation!" Joice's shrieking did not need a microphone. "Because of an oil spill that destroyed chinook salmon habitat. You not listening to us makes us guilty for your decisions. I will be culpable because you, as my representative in parliament, did not let the voice of seventy percent of your constituents be heard. I voted for you. My voice was not heard. I will have to say to my daughter, 'Dear baby doll, I'm responsible for the extinction of the orcas because I trusted Colleen Lauren.' FOR SHAME! YOU BROKE OUR TRUST! WE WANT TO BE HEARD!" Joice kept ranting even though her mike had been turned off. "DIRECT DEMOCRACY WILL LET ALL OF US BE HEARD! VOTE DIRECT DEMOCRACY!"

"Please, be respectful," the moderator spoke over Joice. "This is a civil debate. QUIET! PLEASE!"

A security guard stepped up to escort Joice out. She let him lead her until she got to the exit. "WE WANT TO BE HEARD! VOTE DIRECT DEMOCRACY TO BE HEARD!"

Butterflies flew around Bea's stomach. They had decided that Joice's performance needed to be disruptive, but she might have gone too far.

A couple of minutes later, the moderator said, "We understand how passionate everyone is. Please behave civilly. We will renew our audience questions." The security guard was repositioned next to the microphone.

The other candidates got to answer Joice's question. The Conservatives wanted a pipeline funded privately through tax incentives. The others were against the pipeline. All the candidates took shots at the Liberals for buying the pipeline and halfheartedly at Colleen for not voting against it, throwing pebbles at the glass house, knowing they would never break ranks with the party line.

The next question was from a rambling elderly person who meandered around the topic of health care. The non-Liberal candidates repeated their party's platform. Colleen blamed the Provinces for ineffectively using the money given to them by the Federal government. She mentioned the Liberals' willingness to work with the Provinces if they could all agree. It was Canadian healthcare politics as usual: blame the other guy and do nothing.

Justin swaggered up to the microphone. "I'm Justin; in my heart, I'm Conservative. I'm also realistic, I don't believe Mr. Lee is going to win because Conservatives have not won in this riding for thirty years. But there are topics of agreement that the majority of Victoria Capital voters agree on regardless of their party preference, like defence spending. The majority of Victoria Capital voters want more. Will the candidate who wins this riding vote against a bill that is bad for the Canadian Forces?"

"The Conservatives have always been strong on defence," the Conservative Mr. Lee replied. "But let me say... I don't understand why a young man like yourself would have so little faith in the party you identify with."

"I have faith in small-c conservativism. But this riding will not go big-C Conservative. Particularly with a leader who is seen as divisive. Being realistic and pragmatic, I would rather see those positions I share with the majority moved forward than not to be heard at all."

"Fair," Mr. Lee said. "But I urge you to volunteer for us. We need more young Conservatives."

The other candidates answered with boilerplate responses a la: 'Once in office, we listen to all our constituents.' As the Green party candidate parroted the previous candidates, Justin accidentally on purpose tapped the microphone. It made an awful noise, catching the attention of the bored crowd. Justin held his hands up, looking innocent, "Sorry, I didn't mean to hit the mike. But these responses don't give me faith that these candidates will care a lick about their constituents after the election. I'd like to pose this question to the Direct Democracy candidate, but she isn't on the podium. With Direct Democracy, I would have my vote heard as a Conservative. It would be tallied so that whatever the majority voted for would win. I'd get a Conservative say, even if my party has not won the riding in thirty years. I wouldn't have to trust a politician's vague answer to make a five-year commitment to their party…"

The moderator intervened, "Only parties that got more than five percent of the vote in the last election are invited to this debate."

"With all due respect, Sir, that's flapdoodle if I ever heard it," sounding like Harold, Justin strove forth. "Your poll lumped all the low-polling candidates into the 'other' category. The other category has a collective ten percent. That is more than any previous poll by seven percentage points. The other category is essentially Direct Democracy."

"Well," the moderator said. "That's one way of looking at it."

"A competing poll has Direct Democracy at six percent," Justin insisted. "Come on now. Please add the Direct Democracy candidate to this debate format."

The dozen Direct Democracy members in the crowd led the rest of the audience to applaud Justin's declaration.

Next up was Tyrel, speaking deliberately with the crowd, respectfully intent on what he had to say. "I, like many citizens, am concerned with the scandals these parties are caught up in. The Liberals have SNC Lavalin. The Conservative's illegal contributions. All the parties have strong connections to donor groups: Conservatives and Liberals to industry, NDP to Labour, and Green to NGOs. The common thread is parties listening to special interest groups rather than voters. What are you going to do to stop the scandals?"

The moderator indicated that Mr. Lee, the Conservative, could answer first. Mr. Lee quipped, "Maybe the Liberal should answer first. They're the experts." Some of the audience chuckled. "Seriously, this is a Liberal problem. Mr. Poilievre set a high moral bar for our members and expects the same from his MPs."

"No party is perfect," Colleen rebutted. "The only reason the Conservatives don't have scandals to point at recently is because they have not been in power. Unlike the Conservatives, the Liberals are willing to abide by and welcome the guidance of the Conflict of Interest and Ethic Commissioner."

"What do you mean no scandals for Conservatives?" The NDP candidate, Chad Farhan, chimed in. "The leader of the party includes dog whistle hashtags in his YouTube videos for Men Going Their Own Way, a misogynistic group. And he unashamedly acts American with fake filibusters in the House of Commons…"

Mr. Lee interrupted, "Our leader is fighting for your rights, too! If it were not for Liberal excesses, he would not have had to speak on bills for hours on end. Bills on which, for the most part, your party sides against the Liberals."

The moderator brought the debate back to the topic for the Green Party candidate, who had little to say on Tyrell's question.

"None of the parties here have a concrete way to address scandals," Tyrell asserted. "To me, it seems scandals are created by special interest groups. If the riding's constituency decided what the MP would vote for in parliament, like in Direct Democracy, there is no room for political manipulation by special interest groups."

The crowd supported Tyrell with wild applause. There were shouts for the Direct Democracy candidate to be put on stage.

"Thank you for your contribution," the moderator said weakly. "We would like to remind those posing questions to pose their question, then let the candidates answer the question. Please, no follow-up statements."

"Sorry." The crowd clapped as Tyrell walked off.

Other questioners asked about the housing crisis and wildfire response. They were answered by the federal candidates with a deferral to provincial authority.

Then it was Irene's turn. "This hall is only half full. To me, that says people don't believe they are heard by their representatives. Rank-choice voting or proportional representation can give people a greater voice. What are your party's positions on voting reform?"

The Green and NDP candidates wholeheartedly supported voting reform. The Conservatives did not see a need for change, and the Liberals were ridiculed by all for breaking their promise to implement it.

When Colleen Lauren began to speak, Irene spoke louder, admonishing the MP like a grandmother. "No. No. Deary, you lost your chance to answer when Junior did not follow through. Any answer you give is disrespectful. It's best to be quiet. And I've been a Liberal longer than you have been alive." With the crowd on Irene's side, the moderator let Irene continue. "The parties on stage only want to use voting reform as a carrot to keep your vote. None of them will follow through. If you want to be heard, Direct Democracy is your way because you tell the representative how to vote!"

The crowd spontaneously cheered Irene. The moderator ignored calls from the party staff to cut the microphone. The people had spoken.

Irene left the podium. The crowd died down. The moderator called for the next questioner, warning that the debate time was nearly over. The woman said, "I think the leader of Direct Democracy is behind me in the question line. I think we would all like to hear from her." The audience agreed loudly. The woman stepped aside for Bea to take the podium.

Bea glowed from finishing her run in the hot gymnasium. Her sweaty hair looked great, irritating every woman in the overheated gym. She stood at the podium, a stunning sight, even with a sweat-stained pit and wet crotch. "Hi. I am Bea Jensen, Leader of Direct Democracy."

Spurred by the Direct Democracy members, the crowd responded, "Hi, Bea! What is Direct Democracy?"

"In the ancient Greek tradition of Athenian Democracy," Bea began dramatically, "Direct Democracy gives people the power. It grants the individual the ability to vote on all bills before parliament using an app restricted to the riding's constituents. As the MP representing my constituency, a simple majority decides how I will vote. That is my one responsibility. You decide. Not the party or me."

The audience hummed.

"For example," Bea continued confidently. "Many polls have shown that sixty percent or more of Victoria Capital do not want a pipeline. If we had Direct Democracy, your Member of Parliament would not have voted for the pipeline."

The crowd agreed loudly, clapping with a cheer.

"That is a simplistic view," Colleen Lauren interrupted. "One representative's vote would not have turned that decision."

"You silenced these people's voices by voting against it!" The crowd gasped at Bea's vehemence.

"The House of Commons did not vote on the pipeline," Colleen insisted. "The government moved forward on its own for the good of Canada."

"Even worse!" Bea was pounding the air. "The government doesn't care about your voice. They don't care about democracy!" She turned to gesture at the spectators but mostly to stand in the range of the cameras. "If these talking heads cared about democracy, this debate would be attended by many more than the hundred or so political junkies and elderly citizenry stewing in their own juices on a Friday night in an un-air-conditioned gymnasium." She scanned the crowd, making eye contact with as many of them as she could. "If you cared, the room would have air conditioning, the debate would not be on a Friday night, and the atmosphere would not be high school jockstrap! Your only goal is to activate the base and exclude the middle with divisive minority wedge issues. Why do you think J.T. didn't move forward with proportional voting, even with a strong majority in favour of it?" Bea turned to her enthusiastic supporters. "Because they don't want you to have the power!" The crowd roared.

Colleen stood, shaking her head. "Let me speak!"

Owls, Doughnuts, and Democracy, by Jason A. N. Taylor

The Conservative Mr. Lee bolted from his seat. "Let me speak!"
Bea gave him a dismissive eye roll that said, 'If you have to.'

"It's great to see a young person so passionate for democracy," Mr. Lee spoke as the crowd quieted. "But enthusiasm is hiding your naivety. We have a representative democracy because a representative is needed to make decisions the working man does not have the experience to make. The majority cannot investigate, research, get feedback or weigh options the same way a representative can. There is not enough time in the day for the average man to do what the MP does."

Turning back to the crowd, Bea's sarcasm reached new heights: "The person from the party with a leader that compares the federal budget to a household budget is now telling us we are not smart enough, do not have enough time or are unable to search out the right facts to vote on legislation."

The crowd grumbled loudly.

"Please!" Bea shouted over the rumble. "Give the people credit! The tighter the budget the harder it is to balance. We all have tighter household budgets than Canada's and we can handle it. I guess the one thing a voter can't do that a MP can is let a lobbyist glad-hand the MP into siding with special interests?"

The crowd roared angrily.

Mr. Lee tried to dig himself out of the hole. "I did not say voters were too stupid to make decisions on legislation…"

"Your answer implies it," Bea cut him off. "The people are not stupid!"

The audience hissed at the Conservative.

"Direct Democracy has not been practiced in modern times because the technology to implement it was unavailable. And because some people don't believe their fellow citizens are smart enough, it's still fighting to come back."

"Moderator…" the NDP candidate spoke up. "Can I ask the Direct Democracy candidate a question?"

"Oh…" the moderator was slightly surprised. "Yes. You certainly can."

Chad grinned like his meme-sake, "Ms. Jensen, it seems much of your party's platform is based on this voting app. How can the public trust it's security? What type of verification does it use?"

"It has end-to-end encryption over an API with token exchange handshakes and two factor authentication on the users end." Bea waited a few seconds. "Does that answer your question, Mr. Farhan?"

The NDPer hummed and hawed for a long time.

"Can I assume from the delay that you don't know what I'm talking about?" She waited again as Chad looked more awkward. "Let's just say it's security is beyond the level that a federal candidate can understand."

The crowd laughed loudly.

Big party staffers waved frantically at the moderator for a time out.

Finally, the moderator arose. "I'm being told that the debates time is up. I would like to thank our candidates." There followed the obligatory thank-yous to the four candidates with each candidate then thanking the moderator. "Most of all," the moderator concluded, "I would like to thank our enthusiastic audience."

The crowd yelled: "What about Bea?!"

"Oh, I forgot Bea, the Direct Democracy candidate… Thank you!"

Bea responded with a bow. "You're welcome, everyone!"

Bea wished for nothing more than to bask in the glory of her dominating performance with Direct Democracy members but was intercepted by local media. They wanted to get a few clips of her for the nightly news cast. She gave them a brief synopsis of Direct Democracy as the sun went down, highlighting her great hair, beautiful smile, race car curves and sweat stained pits and crotch.

Bea got a text from Ray, making the night even better. He was back in town. She responded: When do you want to go out?

Ray: How about Saturday?

Bea: Tomorrow? It is a date!

20.

Saturday morning, Bea sashayed to the Home in a little floral summer dress that threatened to show butt cheek. However, it never did. She reviewed the debate in her head; Direct Democracy had been lucky. Things had fallen together rather than apart. Content with the performance, but knowing they could not swagger too long, she let herself strut.

At the Home, Wendy was at the front counter. "Hurry up, Bea. Harold bought doughnuts, but there are so many members; if you don't come quick, they'll all be gone."

The lounge was standing room full, many of the people unknown to Bea. A large folding table was cluttered with doughnut boxes from Victoria's finest bakeries. Harold was shooing people from the last Yonni's raspberry glaze. "Holy doodle, woman!" He called to Bea. "You'd think this was a police convention. Take this doughnut before the mob gets it. If I had a cane to wave, I could have saved more. I can't shake this walker around; it just looks sad."

"Thanks for saving this one. Let's get to business."

"Business!" Harold scoffed. "It's time to celebrate."

"Did all the other candidates pull out of the race? I didn't think so. We'll celebrate for as long as it takes me to finish this doughnut and coffee."

Derek made his way through the crowd. "Harold, there are no doughnuts. Wasn't that your job?"

Harold grumbled incoherently.

"That was some spectacle last night, Bea." Derek gestured with his coffee. "Good job."

"It was good but could have been better. We'll debrief when I'm done with this doughnut."

In five minutes, Bea strode to the front of the room and called for quiet. It took a full minute, but the room of almost eighty quieted and found seats. Nearly twenty had to stand.

When it was as quiet as it was going to get, Bea spoke, "How many of you know who Scotty Bowman is?"

Confused, most of the men nonetheless perked up to say they did.

"He was the best hockey coach ever, with a philosophy that it is the process that matters. For example, He would be happier with a team that lost following his system than won because of luck. He always worked to improve." Bea found it funny her dad told her this but never followed it. She was happy she remembered it, being one of the only good things he said.

"Direct Democracy won yesterday because we got lucky. My lines were not inflammatory enough, but I was lucky the candidates bit. My clothes were sweaty. My hair was a mess." Most of the women in the room gave her the stink eye because her hair was great, even sweaty after a run.

"I'm going to write a script to practice my message before the next event. Can someone help me with that?" A few hands went up. "Joice, Irene let's talk after. To keep from arriving sweaty, I'll work on leaving earlier so I don't have to run." She scanned the room. "Who'd like to go next?"

Only Tyrell raised a hand. His honest appraisal of what he could do better got a few others to join in. After twenty minutes, most of those attending the debate had reflected on their part and decided on improvements for next time.

Bea moved the meeting to the smaller political groups to spin their individual message like Clotho and the Three Fates would one's life. The jam-packed room hummed with discussion.

Bea's phone started humming with texts from Ray and, of all people, Marcus. She did her best to ignore them, but it only worked for Marcus's. The crush had her unlock the phone, scan the message notifications, then lock it again. She did this many times; basically, she was looking at her phone all the time without reading the texts.

The assembly was laser-focused. So much so that no one acknowledged Karen when she poked her head in at eleven thirty. Bea saw but kept her head down, not wanting to disrupt the flow. At noon, Karen came in and squeezed her way to Bea's table.

"Bea, there's a group booked for this room at 12:30," Karen said sheepishly. "Please have it ready."

"Sure. We'll do our best."

"Karen," Harold piped. "Our LARGE group is in the middle of an important session. Can you be a doll and see if they can use one of the smaller rooms?"

"I'll ask." Karen filtered her way back out of the full room.

A few minutes later Karen was back, led un-courteously by Fred and Dorothy pushing their way to the front. With a two-fingered physical education teacher's whistle, Fred got everyone's attention. "Quiet! Karen has something to say."

"Your meeting is in contravention of the Home's bylaws," Karen said nervously, not looking anyone in the eye. "There's an over-capacity that breaks the fire code. Plus, the meeting is over its allotted time. These infractions are two of the three warnings Direct Democracy will get before it's sanctioned."

"Tell them what the sanction will be," Dorothy insisted loudly. "It's your job to do that."

"If there is a further violation, Direct Democracy will forfeit room privileges."

Harold stood up, "Holy Doodle! Karen…"

"Harold, be quiet!" Bea shouted.

Harold was stunned.

"Sorry, Karen." Bea was conciliatory. "Direct Democracy apologizes for breaking the rules. In future, we'll limit our attendance numbers and finish the meeting on time. Can everyone help get the room ready?"

The members started clearing the tables, moving furniture back and leaving.

"This is your final warning," Fred shouted a parting shot. "Any more violations, and you're out!"

Dorothy glared at the seething Harold.

Luckily, Harold's lads could read the writing on the wall and walkered him out, diverting his malevolence toward Fred and Dorothy.

Irene and Wendy were almost as upset as Harold. Bea kept them from Fred and Dorothy by getting them to help with the clean-up.

Blue Bridge Club members shuffled into the lounge, scowling while Bea and a couple of the younger Direct Democracy members finished ordering the chairs.

The remaining Direct Democracy group was small enough to use another common room, but they found it lacked a TV, the chairs were uncomfortable, and it was cramped.

"This room will not do." Harold blurted what everyone was feeling. "We need a bigger space. Even the lounge was getting too small but someone better book it anyway."

Bea volunteered, intending to talk with Karen. She found the manager trying not to be seen in the office. Bea knocked softly, "Can I come in?"

"Oh, Bea, yes. I'm happy you came. These oldies are just like teenagers. Fred and Dorothy were holding a vigil at the desk, trying to get me to kick you guys out. And I was sure Harold would tear a strip off me like he did the other day."

"I'll tell Harold to be nice."

"I hope he'll listen."

"I'm the leader. He has to."

"We'll see."

"Meanwhile, can I get the room schedule?"

"Here it is." Karen handed Bea the binder. "You're not going to like it. The clubs have pretty much booked the lounge until the end of the election. Harold and Irene got the Council so riled up you're lucky to have any time."

"Hmmm…"

"Direct Democracy has great energy. I fought for you. But they wouldn't listen. All they see is Harold and Irene being asses and young people stealing the silver."

"We appreciate your advocating for us to the Council, Karen."

In the janitor's broom closet, the core group of Direct Democracy's oldsters squeezed in for Bea to pass around the room schedule. Everyone came to the same conclusion.

"To be honest, we need a real office." Derek reasoned. "Irene, how is our war chest?"

Irene let the group know the money situation.

They began to research. The consensus was that an office had to be near the Home. There was a building nearby, but it was on a side street with little walking traffic. There was an option downtown with tons of foot traffic near Colleen Lauren's office and on bus routes, but Harold sternly eschewed the bus. The third option was right in the middle of James Bay's business area, but it was the most expensive and smallest.

Narrowing the list took most of the afternoon. Derek, Irene, Harold, and Bea scheduled visits over the next week.

There was still one big problem from Bea's perspective. "It's great that we'll have an office, but none we've seen can seat our numbers."

"It's Democratic to have everyone involved," Joice quipped.

"Come on." Bea sighed. "Someone must have an idea where we can get a space for bigger meetings. One big meeting on Saturday is not enough. Think outside the box."

They had been in the small, cramped box too long to think outside of the box. Derek said, "That's our homework. Thanks for working overtime on this." The core members parted ways.

Bea realized she would be late for her date with Ray unless she wore what she was wearing. Being late for their second date was not an option. Her outfit was fine, but she wanted to be as fresh as possible. She petitioned for a ride from Derek, who was happy to give Bea a lift.

On the way, they discussed what having an office meant. There should be paid positions. Bea would get paid for party activities.

As always, there was a cop car outside the Paulina.

Ray had suggested a restaurant near Uptown Mall, close to his house. Bea liked that the restaurant was handy to his place. She checked her phone. It was a few minutes before they were to meet. Looking at herself in the Fast Fashion store mirror, she adjusted her yellow sundress so that going to his place was more likely. She knew the teenager who held the door for her would have taken her home. As she turned to give the boy a look that would earn his girlfriend's wrath, she was distracted by a text.

It was from Marcus. Bea ignored it. At the restaurant, she did not see Ray, so she checked her phone. She was exactly on time. Marcus texted twice more. Before she could get to them, she saw Ray roll up on his scooter. She put her phone away and walked out of the restaurant.

"You're looking good," Bea stood close enough for a hug.

"I'm happy to see you." Ray took a slight step back to get a better view. "You look great."

The Imperial March played. "Sorry," Bea got a lump in her throat. "I never get calls." She glanced at the screen. "It's my ex... Oh God... I got to take this. Something might have happened to Sam."

Ray gestured for her to take the call.

"Marcus, is something wrong?" She could hear crying in the background.

"Bea, it's Amy, did you read the texts? Never mind. Sam is having a total meltdown. He's homesick. Wants to see the owls and you. Is this a bad time?"

"I am on a date, so... Yes."

"Can you talk to him?" Amy pleaded. "Please."

"Ok." Bea covered the microphone. "Sam's homesick... give me a minute, would you, Ray?"

Ray nodded.

The background droning cry changed into a snotty sniffle, finally resolving into Sam's wet, shallow breath. "I HATE it here, Momma B! I want to go to your house! I want to see Josie and Mister and Muffin and Shakespeare!"

Bea had to hold the phone away from her ear as Sam howled.

Ray pretended not to hear.

"Kiddo..." Bea assumed her most calming tone. "Josie and the owlets are doing great. But I'm out with a friend right now. Can I video call from the park tomorrow?"

"NNNNNOOOOOO!"

The cry that came out of the phone had Ray and other passers-by turning heads. The noise died down into a hyperventilating splutter.

"Sam, I want to see the owl family, too, but I'm more than an hour away if I walk."

Sam's crying drowned Bea out.

"I can double you." Ray caught Bea's eye. "We can be there in fifteen minutes."

"Kiddo," Bea yelled into the phone. "Ray's giving me a lift to see the owls. I'll phone Momma A when we get there!"

Ray unlocked his scooter while Bea texted Amy.

On the scooter, Bea grabbed Ray around the high waist, grinding him close, telling herself it was necessary to grind on the scooter.

Ray zipped to the park, obeying only those rules that did not slow them down. He used sidewalks and bike lanes. They were halfway there before Bea did not fear for her life. Once comfortable, she moved her hand lower on his waist, trying to cop a feel. But whenever she got too close, he moved her hands back up. His coyness only made her more smitten. She made a note to address the consent issue early in the evening.

They reached the end of the pavement in the Douglas fir and maple grove where the owl family's nesting tree was. A murder of crows cawing grew louder as they approached. There were more than twenty crows speckling the canopy, flying occasionally, cawing insistently.

Bea had often seen crows mob the owls but did not delay calling Sam. She scanned the crows to see where they were pointing at or swooping, knowing that would be where the owls were. Ray was gawking uneasily at the murder, not seeing the owls in the chaos.

"Amy put Sam on." Bea smiled at Sam's red puffy-eyed, snot-nosed face. "Can you see me, kiddo?" She received a weak, sniffly nod. "I'm going to turn on the front camera and video this. The owls are getting attacked by the crows. See, there's Josie keeping the crows from the owlets. Whoa! That crow hit her!"

"Leave Josie alone, crow!" Sam yelled through the phone, sounding more angry than sad.

To her left, Bea heard the sound of an owl's beak clacking. Muffin was being harassed low in a tree. Bea aimed the camera at Muffin. In unison, Sam and Bea yelled, "Get, crow!"

The crow attack continued. Muffin clicked her beak at crows swooping from behind, and feathers ruffled from the fight.

The first sign that Josie was flying was the crows squawking in fear. With a puff of air from her wings, Josie glided in, taking aim at a crow behind Muffin. She passed by with a dozen crows scattering before her and the rest following. Shakespeare drove away the last of the invaders, alighting next to Muffin.

"WOW! Should we follow Josie or stay here?"

"Josie!"

Bea jogged off, recording the way to a crow-engulfed horse chestnut tree near Queens' Pond. She crouched under, ducking the lower branches. Josie snuggled into leaves, her back to the thick canopy, head darting around to keep eyes on the crows. Again, to no avail, Bea and Sam hollered at the nonchalant crows.

One crow, probably emboldened by the others, hopped close behind Josie, inadvertently trapping itself amid a thick screen of interlocking leaves. Josie turned and launched, talons first. The crow was quick, bouncing back into the canopy, but did not get away from Josie's second attack. A miserable cawing screech came up. Thankfully the dying crow visual was mostly obscured by Josie.

Josie flew down under the canopy with the crow hanging from a talon, brushing Bea with a wing.

"Oh my God! Did you see that, Sam? Josie brushed me."

"No, she didn't!" Sam giggled like a deranged child from a horror film. "That was the crow's wing!"

"Ew!"

"That was the best!" Sam was no longer sad. "You got it on video. Josie totally tricked that crow." The two of them marvelled over the experience as Bea came out from under the tree.

Ray discreetly took hits from a pot pipe he kept out of the phone's view.

Bea and Sam talked on their way back to the scooter.

Near the nest tree, Bea stopped to record Josie feeding the owlets.

Ray kept walking to unlock his scooter.

Bea and Sam discussed how gross the feeding was. The crowfoot was too big for Muffin to swallow. It protruded hilariously from the owlet's mouth.

Ray watched the Addam's Family values scene from ten metres away, directly under the owls. Muffin shook its head to dislodge the crow's leg. The severed limb bounced from Ray's head onto a shoulder, then the ground. Bea and Sam let out an instant 'ew gross' chorus, followed by maniacal laughter.

Ray did not know what hit him until he saw the crow's part on the ground. Then, like a B-movie starlet, he let out a high-pitched screech.

"Sam, that's my date." Bea trained her phone camera close to the shocked Ray. "He's the one with the book puzzle. Thank him for bringing me here. We would not have seen Josie and the owlets without him. His name is Ray."

Sam thanked Ray. Ray waved awkwardly, smiling and stoned.

Watching Ray do his best to chat with Sam pushed Bea into a place she thought was love but could have been obsession. Regardless, she loved the feeling and found it so adorable she let Ray flail with Sam for a couple of minutes.

But all good things come to an end. Bea aimed the phone back at herself and said goodbye. Sam said a tearful goodbye. Amy thanked her for ending the tantrum.

They decided on a new restaurant with a patio on the other side of the park. Scootering over there, Bea tried again to get handsy with Ray. Her wandering hands were moved back as soon as they strayed.

On Bea's third attempt Ray stopped the scooter. She was ready to apologize. He pointed to a sign that read **Beacon Hill Bandstand**. He said, "Bea-con... Bea-Con... like Comic-Con." Giggling at his joke like Beevis.

"Worst joke ever."

🦉 Owls, Doughnuts, and Democracy, by Jason A. N. Taylor 🦉

There was the god-awful noise of what dinosaurs must have sounded like. From the Douglas Fir trees near the amphitheatre, Great Blue Herons erupted from their nest. Behind them, Crows chased an Eagle.

"Let's not go under the herons," Ray said. "I don't want to risk getting shit on." He pointed to the pavement white with guano.

They parked the scooter to walk around the bandstand. Bea jumped onto the amphitheatre stage, yelling, "Direct Democracy welcomes you to Bea-Con!"

Ray's expression said she needed to explain. "You gave me the idea to use the bandstand for our Direct Democracy meetings. Bea-Con is here!" She ran down the edge of the stage, jumping off like a rock star.

After zipping through annoyed parkgoers, scootering to a waterfront bar and grill on the Inner Harbour, they were lucky enough to get an outside seat.

"I'm so grateful you helped Sam," Bea said. "It was very nice."

Ray smiled and shrugged.

Bea gulped and steeled herself. "Before we go further, I want to say you have consent. Anything but butt stuff is ok. Condoms, of course."

Ray wordlessly looked away and found his glass of water.

She read this as a disappointment, not bashfulness. "Butt stuff is not off the table. It needs some preparation. And it is only our second date."

Ray choked on his water, coughing so much that the wait staff approached. "I'm ok. It went down the wrong tube. Cough... Cough... I'll be fine." He got up to go to the washroom.

Bea took the opportunity to order drinks. Double Singapore Slings should get them in the mood.

Ray returned soon after and they talked about nothing while Bea waited for liquid lubricant. The bar was slow, but the drinks did eventually come. Bea clinked her glass to Ray's and took a long pull on the straw.

He looked at the drink skeptically, sniffed it, then took a tiny slurp. "Does this have alcohol in it?"

Owls, Doughnuts, and Democracy, by Jason A. N. Taylor

"Is the sea salty?"

"I don't drink."

"Oh, I'm sorry..." An awkward second passed Bea had to fill. "I didn't know. I thought since you toked... I can drink it." A loud admonishing voice in her head reminded her to assume is to make an ass of u and me. "Maybe, before I make any more incorrect assumptions, you should tell me who you are."

This opened Ray up. He told her of growing up with adoptive white parents and had little bad to say of them but nothing great either. They did eventually support him in whatever he did but didn't know how to help him in his efforts to find his biological family, of whom he knew nothing. He had no connection to his Indigenous roots, though was desirous of one. His adopted family did not know how to make a connection to his Indigenous roots. He described interminable feelings of never fitting in.

As he spoke, Bea wanted to hold him. The best she could do was say how she was sorry, empathize, and shed a tear. She secretly rejoiced that she did not have troubles like his. But as tear-jerking as his confession was, she could not help feeling something big was left out.

From the crowded walkway along the restaurant's patio, someone shouted what sounded like, "It's that DD chick! From the double D party. What's your name?"

"What a jerk-ass!" Bea said to Ray. "Catcalling in this day and age."

"I think he means DD, like Direct Democracy." Ray gestured. "He's calling you,"

She turned. The man was wading through tourists toward them.

"You're the Direct Democracy girl. I saw you on TikTok. I hardly recognize you without spandex. I love the idea of voting directly on issues." He fiddled with his phone on the other side of the patio fence. "Can I get a selfie?"

"My name's Bea." Bea put on her best politician's smile. "Not the Direct Democracy chick. You can have a selfie if you share it on your social media."

The guy and Bea chatted, taking several selfie shots and videos.

Ray ensured he was positioned out of camera range. Eventually, the guy promised to join the party and get his two friends to vote Direct Democracy.

"Do people recognize you often?" Ray asked.

"No. This is the second time. First time in public. The other was at the debate." Bea followed up with, "Are you concerned that I'm too public?"

"Yes. I'm willing to risk getting in the background of some of your fan's selfies but I'm not getting on stage with you. I can't be part of a Direct Democracy campaign promotion or defend you from attacks on the party. Consider me the apolitical boyfriend."

"Boyfriend. I like that." Bea took out her phone and held it up for a selfie. "Don't mind me. I must update my Insta with the big news that I have a boyfriend." She turned to face the lens full-on. "Friends, I have big, giant, news! I have a boyfriend. He's handsome but too shy for social media."

Ray squirmed, uneasy.

"I'm joking!" She laughed and kicked him under the table.

"How is your debate ambush doing?"

"Great. The Direct Democracy Army has made dozens of versions. The most views are on Reddit...hundreds of thousands on r/Canada, so a huge amount is not from Victoria Capital. The TikTok and Insta posts are more targeted. They have tens of thousands of views and likes. The YouTube videos are doing well, too." Bea wielded her phone, scrolling to examples of the Direct Democracy propaganda. "It's hard to tell the entire reach because we have so many different channels, but every political party in Victoria Capital has its parallel Direct Democracy group. Our biggest challenge is breaking into the mainstream media, but our Reddit and Twitter threads have gotten a few articles with online media like Victoria Buzz. It's happening."

"How would you measure the influence of such a diverse campaign?"

"The best way is the argumentum ad hominem ratio in the comment section." Bea scrolled through the comments on a highly viewed thread to find the choice burns. "Aw this one's so middle school: Sweaty Betty because I'm sweaty from a run. It started a theme with BOBea, BOGYN, and Pee Bea – I kind of earned that one for Little Pee Pee. Then some misogynist starts in with red tights; you can't tell if it is sweat or period."

Bea noted Ray's discomfort but could not help herself. "I find it hilarious that he just says, period. Using period blood is too disgusting? This led to OBBea – for the tampon company. And some boomer commenting if the saltiness of my words wasn't proof enough that I was on the rag, my bloody tights were. There's a bunch of red dots and pants emojis. So uninspired."

Bea broke into maniacal laughter.

Ray sat wordless.

Calming to a spluttering giggle, Bea said, "I've found the best. The moi..." She laughed out loud again, unable to read the comment. "Ray, you read it." She turned her phone to him.

Ray peered at the phone. "The moist choice, Bea from Direct Democracy, has everyone up in a lather." He fell silent as it was clear Bea could not listen to him over her laughter.

Hiccupping and teary-eyed, Bea did not notice Ray's agitation. "Oh! I love this one too. Camel Toe Karen." Noting Ray's sombre expression, she pulled herself together. "There's approximately one ad hominem attack on me every five comments. That's a great ratio. It means the message is getting out of the echo chamber to the haters and the converts."

"How can you laugh at that misogynistic bullshit?" Ray spoke heatedly. "It has me livid, and I am not the target."

"It's the internet. Anonymous trolls aren't real." Bea tried not to sound too patronizing. "They can't hurt me. In fact, their animosity shows we are getting to them."

Ray sat back, arms crossed, bangs over his eyes.

"A lot of the comments are nice. Look this one praises my great tits and happy nipples, even naming them. Glass Cutter and Poky."

She pushed her chest out all nipply and said, "Which one is which? Is this Poky or Glass Cutter?"

Unable to resist, the melting Ray smirked. "The left one is Poky."

"What really pisses me off is that I can't hit back at the dicks that drop in my DMs."

"What do you mean?"

"I'll show you." With quick taps, Bea showed the picture.

"What the fuck?" Ray reeled back. "Gross! Who thinks a DP (dick picture) is 'okay'?"

"I want to dox and shame him, but the leader of a party can't." Bea smiled impishly at Ray's sudden interest. "I can at least do the first part and find out who he is. I'll send you the email." She diligently poked at her screen. "It could be Little Pee Pee's; the size is right."

"Okay, got it." Ray stared intently at his phone.

"It is a race! Go."

So intently working on their task, they ignored the waiter's enquiries.

"I've got his name, address, Facebook, and Twitter details," Bea said after five minutes. "Can't believe the D-bag has a girlfriend." Bea showed the girlfriend's picture.

"That's pretty good. I've got all that. She works at Ardene's in the Bay Centre." Ray turned his phone to her. "Here's his whip." DP's car was an old Civic with an irritating muffler, racing decals and stupid spoilers. The photo was his profile picture on a Civic forum.

Bea noticed something in the photo that Ray did not. She took down the Civic forum name.

"He's in college, taking university transfer courses. But he's not the greatest student." Ray continued describing the DP's life.

Bea formulated a plan, recognizing the twilight background of DP's car picture. It was not far away. The people in the background were dressed up for a weekend night out, many holding ice cream cones from the shop nearby. Her mental algebra suggested the picture was taken on a summer evening before DP picked up his girlfriend from the mall. Bea had a sudden urge to get ice cream.

The rest of dinner took on the tone of a normal date. Good food, lots of eye contact, wine for Bea, some laughing and footsie under the table. When it came time for dessert Bea was emphatic: "I'm not ready, yet. Let's walk, smoke a joint, talk, then get ice cream." The walk involved hand-holding, light touch, and pecks on the cheek that evolved into a quick French kiss or two.

Eventually, they sat on a bench outside the Bay Centre, eating ice cream in the evening twilight.

Ray's eyes narrowed, focusing across the street. "Funny. That wasabi wagon looks like Mr. DP's car."

Scanning the lined side street, Bea smiled. "It is DP's car. His girlfriend should be coming out of the mall any time. I think this is the staff exit. Get ready to video me."

Bea had finished her ice cream when the girlfriend appeared. She sprung from the bench, moving quickly. "Excuse me!" Bea called in her politician's booming voice. "I would like to talk with you about Nord VPN." Stunned, the GF stopped as Bea approached. "It can help your boyfriend or you surf the internet without giving everyone your IP address."

The GF was puzzled. "I don't play video games."

"With a real IP address anyone with skill can find out who you are."

"I don't need what you're selling…" The GF turned to walk away.

Bea moved in front of her and held out her phone. "I think this is yours."

Not seeing the picture, the GF replied, "Thanks, but I have my phone."

"Oh no. I didn't mean the phone. I meant the little thing in the picture. Your boyfriend must be quite the sniper to keep you satisfied with that baby gherkin."

"What kind of sicko randomly shows dick pictures to women on the street!"

"Your boyfriend sent me this picture."

"You're a lying bitch! Get out of here!"

Bea smirked, "See the tattoo on this wrist, it matches your boyfriend's sleeve." She switched photos. "You can see it here on Facebook."

"What! Let me see that!" A look of recognition crossed the girlfriend's face as she noted the distinctive tattoo.

Bea did not notice the boyfriend getting out of his car to open the door for his GF – such chivalry. The GF sprinted toward him and shrieked: "Tyler! Did you send that picture!" She feebly swung her bag at him.

Tyler sidestepped the bag and ran to Bea, ramming into her with a two-handed shove.

As her phone flew from her hand, Bea stumbled, falling to the pavement. "You're on camera asshole." She jumped back to her feet. "That's assault!" She moved to retrieve her phone while Tyler did the same.

Ray ran in and swung a haymaker to the side of Tyler's head, sending him crumpled to his knees.

The girlfriend stepped in, crying, "Don't hit him! He's hurt!"

Tyler held his head, moaning.

Amped up, phone in hand, Bea shouted, "That's what you get for sending random dick pics, mother fucker!" She noticed Ray had disappeared and a crowd was gathering. She took off in the direction with the least people.

Far enough away from the Bay Centre, Bea texted Ray but did not get a response. She remembered his scooter was chained up near the restaurant and ran to the spot. It was gone when she got there.

Bea texted Ray again, but a reply did not come. Walking home, she was certain she had wrecked the relationship. She was too Bea for relationships to last. Her internal monologue discussed Ray as if he were her long-time partner. All the cognitive behavioural therapy questions she used to make her reality more objective could not make her monologue understand it was a second date. She was near tears and nearing her apartment when her phone pinged.

Ray: Was DP ok?

Bea: Dazed and confused but ok. You got a great right hook. ☺

Ray: I am sorry our date ended like that. It was my fault. I went too far. I had a great time before that. Talk soon.

Bea: What are you talking about? It was all my fault. Let me make it up to you or at least apologize in person. Where do you want to meet?

No response came after the message, though marked as read.

Bea: I'm sorry I got you into this. I should have told you what I was going to do. DP deserved it.

Again, there was no response. Bea typed, 'I love you,' on the text but remembered it was a second date, so she deleted the text.

Bea reverted to her normal routine. Shitty sleep; run; check Direct Democracy's media; off to work. She cut her run short, fearing her encounter last night might be online. From her memory, Ray was the only one recording. It happened in the street, so it was unlikely a mall CCTV camera got it. And she was certain that DP would not risk talking with the cops. Thankfully, Bea did not find the encounter online. If she had, she was sure she would not see Ray again.

But Bea's bad cyclist YouTube Channel had been found and was stirring up a shit storm on Direct Democracy's social media. Knowing it was inevitable this would happen Bea had gotten out ahead of it, listing it on her Bea Accountable page. Nonetheless, she would fight the fires, hoping it would fan the media flames in favour of Direct Democracy.

Bea spent an hour stitching together videos for Insta and TikTok in response to irate cyclists, sure that nothing would placate them. Cyclists are the most entitled people on earth. Trying to rationally respond to their comments was impossible. Instead, she highlighted how she was being victimized by attacks that had no relevance to Direct Democracy's political stance. An MP for Direct Democracy took their orders from their constituents. If legislation that affects cyclists came before Parliament, it would be the constituents that decided its fate, she pointed out. She counter-argued that posting links to the videos on her accountable page showed honesty. Truthfulness was the main quality a Direct Democracy MP needed. The Direct Democracy Army parroted her message with every post.

Bea was not sure if the explanation she was presenting was landing with the audience. What she did know was that the cyclists would never get off their high horse, and as unyielding as they were, the heat from the flame war brought more attention to Direct Democracy. That was the goal.

The online sparring kept Bea from obsessing over Ray ghosting her. His last text was definitely an 'it is not you but me' message. She wished she did not have the false hope of his last line, 'Talk soon', knowing in her heart that wasn't true. Still, all along the walk to work she hoped each social media alert would be his text, a text she told herself was not coming.

Just before Bea got to work, she did get a text, from Derek: Congratulations on angering Victoria's cycling community. Is it possible to meet me at my place this afternoon? It is a good thing.

Bea: Offending cyclists is like shooting fish in a barrel. See you around 4:30.

The shift went quickly, and Bea headed to Derek's in what felt like no time. Afternoons like this were why she loved walking. The streets of James Bay were full of happy people. It was warm enough to consider swimming in the Pacific, but puffs of cool breeze said the water would be cold. It would be the type of evening to share with a boyfriend on the beach.

The blue Direct Democracy sign on Derek's boulevard made Bea smile.

Derek opened the door as Bea turned into his walkway. "Wait there. I will get it from the garage."

She took a seat on his front steps, where the Dallas Road people-watching was amazing. The sound of the garage door opener got her attention.

Derek rolled an orange electric cargo bike in Bea's direction. "This will solve your arriving at political events drenched in sweat."

"Oh God, no!" Bea squealed with a gigantic smile. "I'm not going to the Darkside!"

"You certainly will."

"Derek, you can't be serious. This is too much. Is Direct Democracy paying for this?"

"No. It is a gift to a friend. I bought it for myself a couple of years ago, but I like riding for exercise." Derek kicked the stand out and placed the bike before Bea. "Also, orange is not my colour."

"Take it back to the store."

Derek regarded her oddly. "You can ride a bike, can't you?"

"Of course, but… Are you sure?"

"Yes. Take it for a spin. I think the seat is the right height."

Bea stood and gripped the handlebars.

"Let me get you a helmet." Derek went back into his garage.

Bea straddled the bike. "I don't need one. It'll mess up my hair…" She fingered the controls. "This is awesome! With the racks on it, I can do deliveries as a side gig." She sped off down the road, helmet-less.

Helmet in hand, Derek went to the top of his stairs to watch. Bea zipped along, half on the bike lane and half on the street, following rules only she was aware of. He took out his phone. Bea wheeled back into the driveway, smiling widely as Derek recorded her first E-bike experience. He was not sure if her delight was because of the ride or the thrill of cutting off a horse carriage"Try watching for other drivers next time," he called to her.

"I'm only modelling the behaviours I see of other cyclists." Bea got off and took a step back, admiring it. "Are you sure I can have it?"

"On one condition…"

"Yes…" Bea cut Derek off, rolling her eyes. "I will wear a stupid helmet."

"That's not the condition. You must upload any video of you riding badly to your bad biker channel. Your first upload is on our Discord."

"That's a great idea, Derek! It'll get more people watching. I'll even change the Bea Accountable page to have a 'report on my biking' button."

Bea's phone pinged. It was Ray. I'd like to meet. Do you have time tonight? She stared at her phone for thirty seconds.

"Did something serious happen?" Derek asked.

"I… uh… had a date yesterday. It ended weirdly. He texted me back." Bea was still looking at her phone. "I kind of called out a guy for sending me a DP. The guy pushed me. Ray, my date, laid the guy out. Then took off."

"Guys that send unsolicited dick pics deserve to be smacked."

"That was my sentiment."

"Is Ray worried about the police?"

"I don't think so. He has the guy on video pushing me."

"Wise move."

"Yes. He's strange in a good way, but I think he's mad at me. He doesn't like being in public." Bea spoke while texting Ray.

"Ray does not want to be public. You are a politician." Derek chuckled. "Opposites attract."

"Yeah, our relationship might be doomed before it's even just a fling."

Derek sobered. "If he is concerned about the police, I know some lawyers."

They spent the next half hour getting Bea familiarized with E-bike care and maintenance. Derek carefully showed her how to lock the bike securely, charge the battery, and properly operate the controls. She left with a very heavy set of locks in the front rack and a helmet on her handlebars. Ray had suggested they meet near Bea's place. She took the long route, quickly coming to love the E-bike.

She rode down the sidewalk to where Ray was waiting.

"Nice wheels!" He whistled as she pulled up. "Where did you steal that?"

"Derek gave it to me."

"Wow. He just... handed it over?"

"So, I wouldn't arrive at political events soaked in sweat." Bea dismounted. "I can understand why you are upset with me. I didn't mean to trick you into that situation. I didn't think it would go so far. Please give me a second chance. I really, really like you."

"I'm not mad." Ray looked downward, bangs over his eyes. "What you did was fine. I knew where you were taking me. I'm upset with myself. I went too far. I have problems with anger. That was a huge trigger for me. You did not need help. And even if you did, I didn't need to fight the guy. I'm lucky he didn't hit his head on something. And he's lucky he didn't meet me three years ago. He'd be in the hospital, and I'd be in jail."

"But he isn't, you aren't, and we know for next time." Bea went to hug him, but he took a step back.

"Yes. I was lucky. I wanted to curb-stomp him. He disrespected you. I felt the same way with all the trolling comments you read me. I also wanted that selfie guy at the restaurant to do something to piss me off so I could smack him."

"Ok..." Bea felt like crying but knew she would seem crazy if she did. "We don't have to go out in public. I'll just keep quiet about the trolls..."

"I can't control myself," Ray blurted.

She looked to the sky. "What are you saying?"

"I'm not ready for a relationship. Especially with someone who gets attacked so much. It'll only get worse as the election goes on."

Bea wiped a wet sniffle away. "We don't talk again?"

"We talk when Direct Democracy needs my security expertise during the campaign. But that's business. And after the election."

Bea sniffed, teary. "I'm not happy with this. I am not sure if I understand. But I can accept it. Can I get a hug?"

Ray stepped forward and hugged Bea. "I have to take off." Ray stepped onto his scooter. "But please do me a favour?"

She nodded dumbly.

"Wear your helmet."

Bea laughed weakly.

Ray clipped on his helmet and scooted away. She carefully donned hers and rode off.

21.

Hidden away in the new office, Bea inspected her hair. She could not accept comments that it looked fine after a helmeted bike ride. It felt like a hockey player's mullet, the last thing she wanted. She ran her brush through it a few times and was pleased at her coiffure's return to normal.

Bea was not naturally vain; she knew she always looked good, but today, the vanity told her she was a little nervous. The CBC election coverage people sought an interview in front of the Direct Democracy office. Nerves were perfectly normal for her first real mainstream media interview.

Leaving the washroom, reality hit amid extreme activity. A dozen acolytes put up signs, moved in second-hand furniture, drank coffee and ate doughnuts. Justin had even found a hide-a-bed sofa. The storeroom was filled with rainbow signs. Walls and windows were adorned with the owl campaign image, like a lame Andy Warhol knockoff. She strode out to the street to get a full view of the business front. Harold and Derek were supervising Justin and Ethan. Mia recorded the progress for further propaganda videos.

The building had an 80ss strip mall vibe with parallel parking in front. It was between a realtor and a Chinese restaurant. It was on Toronto Street, slightly off five corners, in the centre of James Bay's quaint retail area. It was amid a grocery store, pharmacy, coffee shops, pizza place, pub, community centre, liquor store, and weed store. Nearby stood one of the little libraries where Ray and Bea had deposited illicit books. Best of all, the Home was only a couple of blocks away.

Proud and happy as ever, Bea took pictures of the scene, too wrapped up in the situation to see a car cautiously come to a stop a few metres away. When a second car arrived, social pressure caused the first driver to sound a happy, 'beep, beep'. She huffily turned to flip the bird. "Fffuuu... Ajay! Cat! Come see our office!"

"It looks awesome!" Cat called. "We'll find parking. Be there soon."

The Direct Democracy banner was only hung after a hard-fought battle between Harold and a laser level. The light-emitting tool lost the fight, but no one could tell. Then Derek shepherded the membership into various poses out front, cajoling Ajay to take the photos. The pictures would be part of an update to the website and be shared on the Discord for use in organic propaganda.

Afterward, Bea was eager to talk with Ajay, separating him from the group. "Where's Cat?"

"She's getting doughnuts." Ajay paused with a smug grin. "I can't believe you have a real office."

"Right! The banner is a little janky, but it is the best we can do. Things are going well. We're securely in fourth and knocking on the Conservatives' door."

"Starting that electoral reform group was such a good move."

"What group?"

"There's another third party that's been touting Direct Democracy to pressure the mainstream into electoral reform."

"There is?"

"Really, you've not heard of it?"

"No. I've been focused on our actions."

"Let me show you." Ajay whipped out his phone and showed Bea the webpage for the new third-party group, Canadians for Electoral Reform. On closer inspection, the group was not new. What was new for the group was an article stating that Direct Democracy could pressure the government into electoral reform if Direct Democracy does well. Further, it stated that Direct Democracy was a more radical version of what they were for, and both groups had democracy as a core value.

This blew Bea's mind. "That is so awesome!" She took a few minutes to push this news out to the Direct Democracy membership.

Cat joined the conversation with a big box of Yonni's. "So, Bea, what's up with you and Ray?"

"I really, really like him. I'm sure he feels the same. But there was an incident that ended our last date…" Bea told them the details. "We're off until I'm less public." She rolled her eyes at this. "I'm hoping his reasons are true. Yet… I can't help feeling it was a classic, 'it's not you, it's me' kind of thing. Which, according to him, it was." She laughed unhappily.

"Ray is a great, strange guy," Ajay said. "I can confirm he is almost obsessed with you and has been for a while. Life has given him lots of challenges, not just his family but other mental health stuff. Don't push him; he'll figure it out. Direct Democracy needs his skills." He took the box of doughnuts from Cat. "I'll put these with the others."

When they were alone, Cat said, "I talk with Ray a bit. He's totally into you. I can tell you the anger management problem is real. He gets a seethe toward anyone who slights someone he considers a friend."

"That's a relief, I guess," Bea responded. "How come he's standoffish to touch?"

"I don't know. I get an aura of uncomfortableness in social situations. When talking abstractly, it goes away, but when talking about feelings or people, it gets really strong. I thought it was from smoking pot. Then I saw him sober, and he was way worse. He does open up. I've found it takes time."

"Ajay said Ray's been obsessed with me for a long time, what?"

"Ray showed me some of your old performance art videos."

"Did he mention what video?"

"It was of you reading a love letter to some Gen X comic on the CBC and condemning Harper's Conservatives for wanting to roll back same-sex marriage. Ray was fascinated that a high school girl was so outraged. I was not that woke in high school."

Bea threw her head back. "OMG my love letter to Rick Mercer! That was so wrong. I was sixteen, and he's gay!"

"The Gen X comic on CBC?"

"Yes. And I'm all dolled up in... Well, you saw."

"Oh! That reminds me of dick pics." Cat blushed. "That came out wrong."

"It always does. For me, anyway."

"Ray said the guy he hit sent you a DP. We can help with that. A webpage dedicated to the Dicks of Direct Democracy..."

"... To dox the assholes!"

"Right! Give the DP's name and pics to Headwig on the Doxed dark website."

Owls, Doughnuts, and Democracy, by Jason A. N. Taylor

"YAY!" DP's dominated Bea and Cat's chat until Cat and Ajay excused themselves ahead of the interview time.

Mia took control of the interview setting, marking where Bea should get the crew to set up. She directed the diverse Direct Democracy membership to look busy in the background. She insisted that the B-roll include Bea with her e-bike, talking with oldsters and youngsters, pushing the diverse grassroots origins of the Direct Democracy narrative.

After all the stage directions were given and the CBC van found parking, Mia gave Bea one last pointer: "Stay away from politics!"

"But I'm a politician!" Bea said, laughing. Mia laughed, too.

CBC anchor Ian Hanomansing introduced the segment in a voiceover montage of Bea helping youngsters and oldsters do fake tasks like straightening signs and moving furniture., "A truly new idea in the second oldest profession, politics, is rare. Direct Democracy is a new party based on a novel way of acting on an old idea. The Direct Democracy party promises to give all constituents the opportunity to vote on all legislation. But there were reasons direct democracy went out of fashion in the city of its origin, Ancient Athens." The camera switched to a radiant Bea in a floral dress, standing next to her bike. "Let's talk with the charismatic leader of Direct Democracy, Bea Jensen, to see what has changed. Good afternoon, Bea."

"Same to you, Ian."

"Can you tell us the story of how Direct Democracy started?"

"Thank you for having me on this lovely afternoon." Bea smiled broadly, telling an abbreviated version of the Direct Democracy beginnings.

"That's the most original origin story for a political party I've ever heard." Ian furrowed his brow. "You've caused frustration among our writing staff. Our standard set of positional questions doesn't fit. Let me show the audience. Where does Direct Democracy stand on health care?"

Bea smiled, shook her head, and chuckled honestly, "I don't know. You must ask the constituents of Victoria Capital. In Direct Democracy, we leave politics to the people. Politicians can't be trusted with politics."

"I believe that will be your answer to any policy questions." Ian changed tack. "Direct Democracy is a revolutionary way of looking at our representative democracy. Why does Canada need that change?"

"A recent Angus Reid poll found 56% of Canadians." Bea spoke seriously, "More than half don't trust the government to act in their best interest. Two-thirds of Canadians say they don't believe they can influence political decisions. Sixteen percent think a strong leader who does not bother with parliament or elections is favourable to democracy. This sentiment is three times greater for men eighteen to thirty-four and is growing at a frightening pace. Voter turnout is stagnant at around sixty percent. Canadian politics are becoming more divided with the adoption of populist tactics from the south. These indicators show the results of what modern representative democracy has been moulded into by the traditional parties. The parties want to make a group of politically zealous party members and a larger group of disenfranchised voters too apathetic to be involved in politics.

"The Democrats and Republicans in the United States are the best examples of this. Parties that once had many representatives with views that overlapped now only have a few. With this growing division the distrust in government, feeling of not being heard by the government, and most alarming desire for authoritarianism are on the increase. In the States, there has been a dramatic increase in the number of undemocratic executive orders because of legislative gridlock. Trudeau has been criticized for acting similarly, but the causes are the same: reduced democratic involvement and increased political polarization.

"Noam Chomsky said that the assault on democratic governments' credibility is the best way for the undemocratic forces – authoritarians, corporate interests, special interest groups – to reduce the citizens' involvement in directing government. However jaded one feels about our democratic system, Chomsky is right. Voters have no input into the decision-making of a protofascist authoritarian, a corporate board room, or an eco-terrorist group. But citizens can vote to affect how they are governed in an empowered democracy.

"If the attack on democracy continues with reductions in voting and increasing political polarization, the non-democratic forces grow stronger. We have seen this with Trudeau not following through on proportional representation. And Pierre, Little..." Bea stopped herself with two quick coughs. "Poilievre using populism to make a group of wedge issue zealots. The zealots are so blinded by the wedge issue Pierre has free rein on all other issues as long as he stays true to the wedge issue. The Conservatives will never repeal abortion laws in Canada, but the carrot will always be dangled for Pierre's followers to chase. Keeping them politically motivated.

"Another way of looking at the lack of equity in democracy is that our current representative, Colleen Lauren, touts reading all the emails she gets from constituents. But you can be assured the Vice President of Irving Shipyards – one of Victoria Capital's largest employers - has her cell phone number. The more apathetic constituents in her riding, the fewer emails she reads from them, and the more she can focus on her phone calls.

"Democracy drains the swamp. It makes it harder for authoritarians, corporate interests, or special interests to have an outsized influence on what the people actually want. Direct Democracy is the purest form of democracy because it gives each of us the ability to vote on our future without it being filtered through an elected representative. Advances in technology have made Direct Democracy possible again and a natural progression for more equity."

Ian commented, "I find it interesting that you use 'draining the swamp' while at the same time chastising the American way of doing politics. Is this contradictory?"

Bea lit up. "The belief that the political landscape is a swamp is a true sentiment. Evidence and experience show that the public must be skeptical of the system because it is not acting in their interest. Direct Democracy's response to that valid concern is opposite to President Orange Ass Hat or any other fake populist. Our goal is to give people the power."

"Bea, I see your passion but please, reframe from profanity."

"Sorry, Ian. President SA Orangutans is hard to speak about politely."

"I think most Canadians can agree more democracy is a good thing," Ian continued. "But can there be too much? For example, how will Direct Democracy form a government? There is much more to running a government than votes in the legislature."

"I am so glad you can see Direct Democracy with a chance to make up Canada's government; however, I am our only candidate running in this election. Certainly, many things the government does would need to be adapted for a Direct Democracy-led Canada, but that is too far in the future to worry about today. The goal of Direct Democracy is to show it has a place in our representative democracy. Once that's established, we'll work on the next goal."

"Direct Democracy has been criticized since it originated in Ancient Greece because it allows the layperson to make decisions they are not expert in."

Bea sighed with exasperation. "Ian, that sigh was not for you. It was for the hypocrisy of this argument, particularly in today's context. MPs do not have a test or set of qualifications or education they must have, but because they're vetted and elected, we're expected to let that slide. Politicians are continually talking of common-sense policy, policies we can all understand. They typically compare the Canadian budget to a household budget. The actual writing of the laws and policies is done or should be done, by those with evidence and experience, subject matter experts. Those voted into power are not the subject matter experts they claim to be because the questions put before them are too broad and numerous for an MP to understand as an expert would. The last time I looked, not every MP was an accountant, yet they all voted on the budget. Parliamentary decisions are essentially made by a group of lay people trying to frame the laws and policies in the simplest terms possible so they themselves can understand them.

"A great government is one where the laws and policies put forward for the representative to vote on are simple and clear enough that the layperson can understand them. Our population has more education than at any other time in history. Canada leads the G7, with fifty-seven percent of the population having post-secondary education. Canadians can make these decisions.

"Any politician who questions the ability of their constituents to decide correctly on a policy either does not have faith in the people they represent, thinks they are stupid, or is beholden to special interest groups. Complex legislation and voter apathy make our government less transparent. The less clear the parliament's decision-making, the happier the politicians are. With fewer eyes on them, MPs have more latitude to abuse the power they have. Direct Democracy will force transparency because the laws and policies will need to be written as clearly as possible."

"Bea," Ian became insistent. "You paint a rosy picture. However, all of what you have discussed is hypothetical. There's no real-world example."

"No real-world examples..?" Bea queried pointedly. "You mean, MPs listening to interests other than their constituents? Or being deeply over their head when voting on legislation? Please, what government are you watching?"

"You talk much of voter apathy, But it's the elephant in the room. How would constituents stay motivated to vote on all legislation?"

"Honestly, most voters will not vote on all legislation. Most voters will preselect what direction they want to take using our app. For example, if you were in favour of Conservative fiscal policy you would set up your app to mirror that. However, everyone will have the ability to change their vote up until a few hours before the vote in parliament."

"I'm sure our viewers are happy to hear that..." Ian refocused. "But you're dancing around the question. How do constituents stay engaged? Direct Democracy asks for a far greater time investment for the citizen."

"It's my belief that people, when given the chance to participate, will."

"That's optimistic, given the voter turnout numbers..."

"...But you're right, we don't know how much engagement there will be. However, we do know there will be greater voter engagement because, in the past, voters were basically out of the loop after the election... Oh, I forgot... We can email our MP."

Ian chuckled. "One of the flaws that caused direct democracy to fall out of favour in Ancient Athens was that it was cumbersome. The time it took for a decision to be reached was long. What's different now?"

"We don't need to assemble six thousand Canadians to vote..." Bea took out her phone. "Everything can be done from a smartphone. The App is easy to use. Voting is instantaneous."

"We all know apps can be quick and easy to use, but what about security? The United States is rife with reports of electronic voting fraud. Is this asking for trouble?"

"Ian," Bea rolled her eyes. "None of the U.S. allegations have been substantiated. Look at who they're coming from: President Dumpsterfire and his ilk." She became serious. "Direct Democracy's App has bank-level security. Do you trust an App for your banking?"

"Yes."

"Exactly. Further, any fraud would have to change so many individual votes it would be very labour intensive and easy to find. Direct Democracy will need less money and resources than other parties, money that can otherwise be used for IT security and third-party oversight."

"The other parties have customs, etiquette and standards of conduct regarding participation in government." Ian put on his most neutral face. "Direct Democracy is novel; how can the voter trust you to do what you say?"

Bea broke out laughing.

After a few awkward seconds, Ian had to quip: "Is there something funny off-screen?"

"Ian," Bea spluttered. "That was the funniest line I've heard in a long time because, in my view, politicians have a duty to be truthful with their constituents. Yet, politicians and liars are synonymous today. The lying politician cliché is the result of broken representative democracy. When a politician must change their position because of their party or changing reality, they are deemed a liar. Throw in all the truly deceptive tricks: corruption and desire to win rather than better society, and lying politicians become a truism."

"Direct democracy is the answer to the lying politician. A Direct Democracy representative holds no political position. That's the people's job. As a Direct Democracy representative, I am and will be truthful to a fault. I've already demonstrated this on social media. Our website has a page dedicated to my mistakes, Bea Accountable. Being honest is one of my qualities, even when it is not to my benefit. That's my commitment to Canadians."

"Aha…" It was Ian's turn to let out a chuckle. "Bea Accountable has already stirred up the ire of cyclists. How do you intend to address this truly Victorian controversy?"

"I'm a cyclist now." The camera panned over Bea's bike. "I have no problem calling myself out on my YouTube channel if I bike badly. There's a bad one out there already."

They both gave television chuckles.

"Do you have any parting thoughts?" Ian regarded Bea seriously. "We have thirty seconds."

"Whether you think Direct Democracy can succeed or not, a vote for Direct Democracy tells your MP you want to be heard and have more say. It opens the door for other more democratic options like proportional representation. Something the J.T.'s Liberals promised us… but lying politicians."

"Thank you for telling our audience about Direct Democracy. It was very informative."

"The pleasure is mine, Ian. Remember, a vote for Direct Democracy is a vote for yourself." Bea put on her bike helmet, got on her bike, and rode down the sidewalk.

Ian smiled. "We will be sending Bea a video of her riding on the sidewalk."

Later that evening, the old guard of Direct Democracy and other residents sat with Bea in the comfortable chairs in the Home's lounge to watch the interview on the big screen. Everyone applauded.

"Bea did great until the end," Harold spoke to the entire room. "What kind of politician does an obviously wrong act on TV? Madness, woman!"

Boos were directed at Harold.

"Stay in the past, you old coot!" Irene screeched. "Bea knows what she's doing. Show him what you're doing, Bea."

Bea cast the tablet to the TV. and connected to her bad cycling YouTube channel and the clip. Comments flooded in.

"Pappawheelie," Bea read loudly to the elderly crowd. "I am so conflicted. Do I applaud the truth or chastise the horrible channel?

Rokhan: OMG! A politician telling the truth. I'd let her ride on my sidewalk if you know what I mean. Wink emoji. Cappuccinobiker: Bea is a bitch! Reply to Cappuccinobiker from Spandexhighs: You're angry because Bea caught you running a red. And there's a link to the video. CrazyCatMan: A cycle hater and honest politician, ppprrrrreeefect. Westcoastlifer: What! WHAT! What am I looking at? Direct Democracy has my vote."

"By the Baby Jesus' foreskin!" Skeptical Harold sorely grumbled. "Those are all Bea's bots and sockpuppets."

"Blow it out your ass, Harold!" Irene retorted. "It's obvious Bea's plan was genius. Give her the win. Jealousy is ugliest on an old man."

"I think Rokhan is Ajay or Cat." Bea smoothed the situation over. "And it's easy to look truthful compared to today's politicians."

Owls, Doughnuts, and Democracy, by Jason A. N. Taylor

22.

Bubo: It has happened! ☺
Kiria B: What has happened?
Bubo: You should know. I'm not telling you. ☺
Kira B: I know you are trying to have fun but I'm just finishing managing DD's media and it is 1 am.
Bubo: PollingCanada/federalcurrent/byriding/victoriacapital.ca Look at the polls!
Kira B: Thank you. I will look in a few minutes.

Before getting to Ajay's link, Bea focused on wrapping up what she was doing, certain that whatever milestone Direct Democracy had surpassed was not major. When she finally clicked the link, she was proven wrong.

Direct Democracy was third in the polls for Victoria Capital. The details told an even better story. The Conservatives and Greens were in a virtual tie, separated only by their margin of error. Direct Democracy was five points above the technically fourth Conservatives. The potential for error meant Direct Democracy's secure lead might be two points. The NDP was technically leading Direct Democracy, but also within the margin of error. Direct Democracy was tied for second in the riding if the margins of error aligned. She would not say it out loud as she did not want to jinx it.

When Bea squealed for joy, stamped her feet, and danced around the apartment even after downstairs thumped on the ceiling. The only reason she stopped was to message the Direct Democracy world. She was up until morning, glad she was due at the coffee shop early. It would be an eight-or-more-cup day.

By daylight, Bea's instructions to the Army of Oldsters had saturated the media space. Meanwhile, Bea Accountable was spinning up the fan for the shit to hit. Social media stooges from the slighted Conservatives and Greens started hitting back. TikTok and Insta for you pages were full of Bea's Knight Rider harassment, or Canadian Karen, as she was newly nicknamed. Facebook feeds rehashed memes aplenty modified for this new outrage.

Harold's Conservative leaning feeds caught the first winds of controversy. Cat and Joice got something from the Greens. They sent Bea videos of Canadian Karen that evening with concerned messages. seeking direction on how to put the fire out.

Bea did what any honest person would, sharing the content with the caption, 'Yup, that's me. Canadian Karen, LOL! Knight Rider is an asshole. Keep pictures of my kid out of this.' She spent the rest of the night door-knocking with Tyrell, avoiding social media.

Oversleeping the next morning, Bea found herself rushing to work. She only made it on time because of her new bike and willfully ignoring the ridiculous number of phone notifications.

The weekday morning at the counter was busy with the morning coffee crowd. Bea received more furtive glances than usual from younger customers. A phone-fixated regular customer who looked like she ran into a printing press was glancing between her phone and alternately ogling Bea from the back of the line. Normally, she would just leer from behind her friends. At the counter, Bea glimpsed what she was watching: the video of Knight Rider and her. The line was too long for Bea to chat with her at the counter, but she improvised. "I love your ink."

"I got this one on the weekend," The woman replied, rolling a sleeve.

"That other one is from your DM picture to Lainey. She liked it. Too bad she's off-dating right now. Hey, it's busy now, but I want to know more about your tats," Bea confided. "My break is at two. Meet me outside?"

Shocked, the woman's mouth dropped open.

"I'll take that as a yes. I'll be over there." Bea pointed.

Uncomprehending, the woman did not turn.

"Here's your coffee." Bea gestured for her to move along.

The woman left the store. Bea watched her high-five a work friend and used two fingers on each hand to exaggeratedly slick back her hair, starting from her eyebrows to ears, then sashay away.

A few minutes before two o'clock, the woman arrived, trying and failing to look casual.

Bea left to meet her. "Hi, I'm Bea."

"Samantha..." The woman appeared ready to cry and run away. "Is this really about tattoos?"

"I do love your tats," Bea assured. "And one day, I want to get another owl. But no."

Samantha's face hovered between hurt and excitement. "Okay, then what?"

"When you were in line, what were you watching on your phone?"

"It was a TikTok of you getting into it with a jerk in a scooter. It was funny, but I didn't get it."

"Show it to me."

Samantha fumbled to find the clip, taking an awkward minute, having trouble focusing with Bea's cleavage so close.

The likes were at ten thousand. That was not surprising to Bea. What was surprising was that the video was on a nonpolitical TikTok and was one of the many altercations with Knight Rider combined with a video of a woman putting on makeup. The woman dabbed on foundation while discussing if it was right to call Bea a Karen, pointing out the reasons why one would give her that designation. Then the clip changed to one with Sam in it. Bea gasped, covering her mouth. The TikToker moved on to her eyeliner, pronouncing that calling Bea a Karen was uncalled for, Bea being a righteous momma bear.

"The scooter guy deserves it," Samantha said. "He hit your kid. I would have smacked that faker out of his chair." Samantha pretended to throw an elbow.

Bea noted the hashtags. "How did you find this?"

"My Mom sent it to me. She's buck wild for conspiracy theories. Lately, she's been sharing memes of you all over Facebook." Samantha's expression changed. "Are you into conspiracy stuff? It's totally cool if you are. I kind of like astrology and crystals." She smiled coyly. "I'm an Aquarius."

"No. I'm not into conspiracy theories. They only help obscure how we are getting fucked in plain sight. People who believe in conspiracy theories are literally idiots because they consciously exclude themselves from participating in democracy – why participate in a rigged system? Idiot originally meant a private person, as in a person who does not take part in politics. That was until Pussy Grabber in Chief found that conspiracy theorists are a great and untapped demographic. I'm not into astrology or crystals, either. Can you show me your Mom's Facebook page?"

"Sure. I hate President Small Hands. The conspiracy stuff is funny, but I don't believe it. I don't let astrology or crystals run my life, but they're fun, and like most gay women, I like them. So... you know."

Her mother's Facebook page was dominated by crazy conspiracies. Everything from birds being fake to the flat earth, 5G controlling the population, UFOs, anti-vax, and Trudeau is a lizard person. Some conspiracies were apparently beyond acceptance: White replacement theory, holocaust denial, and the parental right anti-LGBTQ2+ agenda. These Samantha's mom railed against.

"It is good your mom is on your side."

Samantha laughed sadly, "Mom knew I was gay way before I accepted it."

"I'm happy you did," Bea smiled at Samantha and winked. "It suits you." Samantha blushed.

Samantha's mom's Facebook showed comments referring to Direct Democracy as the last hope, a way conspiracists could be heard. That is if Direct Democracy was not a CSIS (Canadian Security Intelligence Service) operation to infiltrate and discredit the conspiracy theorist.

Bright-eyed, Bea wondered if Direct Democracy needed a conspiracy theory wing. Of course, it did not. An official Direct Democracy conspiracy theory branch would turn the true believer off—that's what CSIS would do. The group needed to be organic, growing from within the movement and not linked to Direct Democracy. Bea was certain she had found the Q, or in this case, S, to disseminate Direct Democracy into the conspiracy realm.

Samantha continued scrolling through the conspiracy world of her mother with Bea directing until one of Bea's co-workers reminded her of the time.

"I've got to get back to work. Here, take down my number." Bea flashed her phone at Samantha. "Text me your Facebook name."

"Are we..." Samantha was meek. "Dating?"

"LOL! No. But we are going out. Can you meet me tonight in James Bay?"

"Sure."

"Near the Thrifty's. Six pm."

Exploding into tremendous happiness, Samantha barked, "It is a date!"

"Yes. It is a date." Bea looked around. "No friends nearby... High five?"

Ecstatically, Samantha and Bea high-fived. From behind the counter, Bea saw Samantha use two fingers on each hand to exaggeratedly slick back her hair, starting from her eyebrows to ears, as she had done in the morning. Samantha strutted off to work.

Bea's machinations on the Deep Direct Democracy Conspiracy kept Bea from ruminating on Sam's video going viral with #CanadianKaren. Conspiracies are so much more fun than realities.

After work, Bea biked from the busy rush hour downtown to the laid-back traffic of James Bay, with its meandering tourists and the clippity clop of horse-drawn carriages. Beginning to hate the carriages more than cyclists, despite it all she was at Head Quarters in no time.

"About time you got here!" Harold bellowed. "Holy doodle, woman, we are in a crisis! Direct Democracy has dropped to fourth in the polls. The internet is calling you Canadian Karen. And I'm not sure what that means. But I'm pretty sure it is bad!"

The hodgepodge of different styles of discarded chairs that furnished the office were arranged in a circle. Bea took the last seat and was immediately uncomfortable, squirming in a squeaky chair.

"When you're the last one here, you get the shitty chair," chided Irene.

"Karen is a term," Bea spoke while looking at Harold, "for the type of white woman who would ask to see the manager for no good reason. The Conservatives and NDP are calling me Canadian Karen because they're scared, and it's kind of consistent with the Knight Rider video. But it's backfiring, putting our content on the feeds of non-political people. I saw it on a make-up TikTok. The bad press is nothing compared to the boost getting out of the political social media bubble gets us."

"But the Conservatives just overtook us," Justin asserted. "From our Conservative Direct Democracy groups' reactions, Canadian Karen is having a negative effect."

Rick frowned. "All the views in the world can't make up for you looking like you hate disabled and elderly." Rick panned his gaze around the room. "We know that's not true. But does the internet?"

"The makeup TikTok specifically said I was not a Karen. When people see Knight Rider hit Sam, they'll be on my side. But that doesn't matter," Bea argued. "What matters is that they get exposed to Direct Democracy."

Mia chimed in, "I think Bea and the group are right..."

"Such Gen Zed bull!" Harold interrupted. "Everyone gets a trophy!"

"Let her finish, you swine!" Irene shot back. "You're the only Karen here, you old blowhard."

Mia continued, unfazed, "I think we as a group need to extend the reach of the videos by defending Bea. Anywhere the Canadian Karen hashtag is used. Bea should not defend herself."

"That's a great idea, Mia. It keeps me honest. I'll be less likely to dig myself deeper because God knows I want to let it fly... especially at Knight Rider! And everyone will see oldsters and people with disabilities defending me. A great message." Bea put a hand to her mouth. "That was the most cynical, jaded thing I have said. Oh no! I'm becoming a politician."

Joice broke out laughing. "I've got our new slogan. Trust Bea, she's not a politician. We can use her caption when she shared the video saying, 'Yup, that's me.' It gets the truthful message out."

The group got their phones and tablets out to spread the message.

After a while, amid a lull in activity, Bea announced: "I've found another group of people we should reach out to..."

Derek cleared his throat. "Bea, can I have a moment before we move on?"

Bea nodded.

"This is a hard question... Are you fine with Sam being in the videos?"

There was a silence.

"Derek, I hear what you're saying. The videos have been on YouTube forever, so lots of people have seen Sam and me. Of course, I'm not happy with it..."

"But they did not know Sam or you," Justin pointed out.

"True. But if they wanted to, they could find out. I don't think anyone will be vindictive or vile enough to single out Sam." Bea was getting the evil eye from the group. "For God's sake, he's in Ottawa. Sam knows I'm crazy; he can blame me."

"You should know better!" Wendy berated. "People on the internet are assholes. Kids at Sam's school will be jerks."

"You're a person on the internet."

"Dear, I learned from the best!"

"Wendy!" Derek stepped in. "Bea did instruct us not to share videos of Sam. That was the prudent thing to do. Can we all agree that we did not think the Knight Rider video would go viral?" Derek waited for nods of agreement. "I think we need to do more to ensure the videos do not go mainstream. Is there anything more we can do?"

Bea was first to respond, "We can't ask to take them down; I'll look like a liar. Besides, it would only cause copies of it to pop up everywhere, like mushrooms. The best we can do is ask the owner of the original to blur Sam's face."

"Derek," Harold piped, "can we send out an old-school press release? Or contact any media we know?"

"Yes, we can, Harold"

"The best way to influence the internet is through shame," Mia added. "We can make it unacceptable to share children's photos."

"Do we have any other ideas?" Derek gave a few seconds for responses. "I think what we have come up with will help. Let's move forward."

Again, there were minutes of determined texting as the assembly shamed anyone who shared Sam's image.

Then Bea shared her newly acquired insight into the conspiracy crowd and discussed ways of getting the Direct Democracy message to the conspiracy fringe. Joice and Rick self-identified as listeners of Coast-to-Coast AM and other conspiracist outlets. Thus, they were put in charge of Operation Freedumb, spreading memes to post on Facebook and eventually to WhatsApp messages from S.

The group was interrupted by John at the front desk. "Bea, there is a young lady here to see you. Her name is Sandra or Sandy?"

"You mean Samantha. Tell her I'll be there in a minute. Everyone else, get door knocking."

As the group broke up, Bea intercepted Joice. "I promised Samantha a date. She's the one out front with platinum hair, a blue work shirt, and Carhart pants. You're going to take her out. Take her door knocking. I'm pretty sure she's your type. Even better, her mother has a huge, truly gigantic following among Canadian conspiracists, like tens of thousands of friends on Facebook. I think you can make her into the next Q from Qanon or, in this case, S."

"If she has tattoos and Birkenstocks, she's my type. Please introduce us. Please!"

Bea led Joice to Samantha, who was looking around the Home nervously.

"I thought we were going on a date," Samantha pleaded. "Is this a cult? That whole circle thing and multi-coloured owl signs are really strange. Are you some weird Born-Again Christians? If it is your thing, cool. But I'm not into any Seventh-Day Adventist type scene."

Bea fake laughed. "You don't look like a virgin, so you have nothing to worry about. We only sacrifice innocent souls."

Samantha's blank, round face reddened as she tried to decide if Bea was joking.

"I kind of didn't tell you the entire truth. I wasn't inviting you for a date with me. I wanted you to meet Joice. Samantha, I think you and Joice might find each other interesting."

"Hi Samantha," Joice led with her cleavage. "Nice to meet you."

"Bussin... um ah..." Samantha blushed. "I'll be bussing to Langford. I don't know why I said that. I say lots of weird stuff. I got a little bit of mental illness. When I'm anxious, I say too much."

Joice's hooked Samantha's elbow. "I like what you said; it's honest. Let's go on our date." The smiling duo stepped to the table with the pamphlets.

Bea sat with Derek and Harold. "Any update on the Bea-Con Hill Bandstand?"

"Yes," Derek said. "We can rent it for a weekend day over the next month. Saturday the first week, Sunday the second week, Saturday the third and then back to Sunday the fourth week. Monday of the fifth week is the election, which was great timing because the last Bea-Con was the day before."

They went over the donations, sign count, and door-knocking numbers. The door count was not higher. Members reported that if a person knew the gist of Direct Democracy, the discussion would end. This was not good. The best results occurred when the members were able to get an emotional response by hooking the voter.

Bea finished up her evening by contacting the owner of the Knight Rider video, asking them to blur Sam. She hinted that the blurred video could be monetized. The owner got back quickly and was fine with the request. The evening felt successful.

Joice was having a good night, too. Her Instagram had a photo of two pairs of feet. One set of legs was highly tattooed, and the feet soaked in a recycling bin. Jersey Shore was on television. In the background, a big-leafed monstera plant drooped over a sculpture with feminine curves. The caption read, "Chilling with a new friend ☺, after knocking on a hundred doors."

Not long after Joice's post, Bea got friend requests from Samantha and Mom.

Bea went to bed satisfied with the day, the week, and everything that had occurred since Harold had the idea for Direct Democracy.

At around five in the morning, the oldsters started pinging Bea's phone so much that the flashing light woke her up. Half-awake and needing to pee, she picked up her phone on the way to the washroom so she could find out about the barrage of notifications.

Harold's What's App message blew Bea away. Toronto's national newspaper, *The National Post*, ran an editorial by Dex Duffy denouncing Direct Democracy. She squealed and jumped up. The headline was, 'Direct Democracy jeopardizing the traditional Canadian system - left coast Canadian Karen wants to execute Socrates again'.

Reading the editorial through laughter was nearly impossible:

Direct Democracy jeopardizing the traditional Canadian system - left-coast Canadian Karen wants to execute Socrates again

National Post Editorial writer Dex Duffy;

It is easy to listen to the rhetoric of the Direct Democracy party and hear in it equality, diversity, and populism. It truly sounds good. Rhetoric is meant to persuade people to agree with what might not be in their best interest. Connecting the idea of Athenian Democracy with today's Direct Democracy party is worse than rhetoric; it is sophistry. It is true that 'we' in the West owe much to Ancient Greece; however, we ought to know the wheat must be separated from the chaff. For example, we do not own slaves. We do not have the same acceptance of young boys and men having sexual relationships. We do not force Olympic Athletes to perform naked. We do not have direct democracy because our world is too complex to run without competent leadership that has the time, education, and ability to deliberate over national issues that are too big for the busy average Canadian to ponder after working his forty-hour week, taking the kids to hockey, and getting involved with the community.

Not to mention that the leader of Direct Democracy is mistaking the myth of owls being wise when biologists know owls are some of the dumbest birds. This is the Dunning-Kruger effect, the thing that makes Karen feel smart. It is causing the 'group think' that is Direct Democracy.

Athenian Democracy, from those who participate in it, reads like a tragedy. It is a litany of failures, mistakes, and misdeeds that ended in Socrates's execution.

Accounts from the time tell that Athenians participating in Direct Democracy were all too ready to prefer personal accounts to actual evidence. I love great stories and gossip, and when I want some, I talk with my friend Sally. When I need to know facts, I do not rely on

Owls, Doughnuts, and Democracy, by Jason A. N. Taylor

Sally; God loves her; I go to the source. Is relying on personal accounts a good way to potentially take a nation to war?

Plato and Aristotle criticized Direct Democracy for allowing the people to make decisions that only benefit themselves because people are selfish. Consider the pipeline J.T. bought. I am not a supporter, however, Justin tried (and failed by not going far enough) to decide for the benefit of all Canadians. To tree-huggers in BC, the pipeline only supports big oil and its investors. To socialists, the pipeline is corporate welfare. To real Canadians, it is a small step in the right direction to more jobs and a thriving Canadian economy, with strong, stable corporations contracting our vital small businesses. Can direct democracy make selfless, hard leadership decisions like the ones we need our leaders to make to strengthen Canadian industry, including oil and natural gas, enough to employ all Canadians who want jobs? I can tell you Albertans do not want British Columbians and Ontarians making those decisions for them.

Then there is the tyranny of the majority. We like to think that the majority is always right. That is not the case. If the majority made all the decisions for Canadians, we might find out that the beliefs in equity, inclusion, and diversity are not held by all. We might have to confront that it can be the majority that does not want equality for the minority. Would we have the same drive towards human rights if the majority held the reins?

I could continue writing on the arguments against Direct Democracy, and I would if I were paid by the word. But I do not need to make any more arguments because Plato has written three of history's greatest books with arguments against Athenian democracy: *The Republic, Statesman*, and *Laws.* When one of the greatest thinkers in history writes three books on why something is wrong, do we need to try it again?

Then there is the most pernicious concept of Direct Democracy that goes against what Canada stands for. Direct Democracy takes the leader away from our ship. Our representatives are at the helm of Canada because a ship without a rudder is directionless. Policies made by our much-maligned politicians are – as much as I hate to admit this – well thought out, considering more than what a Mercurial population wants for the good of the country. Is this perfect? No. I make a living criticizing all politicians and ridiculing those who are defective and corrupt. But all our leaders have a direction, a right to strive for. Bea Jensen says she does not have a direction for Canada. Either Bea is a nihilist – the last thing Canadians need in office, or she is hiding her true agenda. Leaders only become leaders to lead. What is her agenda?

If, indeed, Direct Democracy is an honest attempt at changing government, Bea has not done her homework. Her answers to fundamental questions regarding forming government are, 'We will figure that out when we get there.' Lady, this is not a road trip. Canada cannot crash on a chesterfield if all the hotels are full. What the Prime Minister and Cabinet do is not easy to parse into individual referendums for the people to vote on. Is Bea going to have a plan, or will her true colours come out when she has power? Remember, power tends to corrupt. Absolute power corrupts absolutely.

Millennials in politics are a good thing, but only if they can understand the perspective of their constituents. We oldies might be set in our ways, but we do have perspective. We have been young. We understand more of life than the young. For example, I realize that an App for voting is a great way to discriminate against older people. Bea and the youngsters at Direct Democracy must not have had a calculator to do the math that most Boomers will not be able to use the App regardless of simplicity. Will Direct Democracy provide a teenager to Boomers for voting on the App? Or is this another example of the way Bea discriminates against old people?

If this article is the first time you are learning of Bea Jensen, you might not get why I would accuse her of the worst act a person can do in Canada: discrimination. It is because of the linked video of her acting as a 'Leader'. I will not describe the atrocity in detail. Watch the video. The video is of Canadian Karen heckling and name-calling an old disabled person with her child in tow for no good reason – not that a good reason is possible. The internet has minimized her role by calling her a Karen, which is a strange term that minimizes vile behaviour by making it seem funny. This is the worst of many socially unacceptable acts Canadian Karen partakes in, such as yelling at cyclists, trolling other political candidates, and caring so much about our political process that she shows up to a debate in a sweat-soaked running outfit. She tells us her personality does not matter because she will only vote as the constituents tell her to. She claims she is being truthful by telling us of these atrocious acts. And she is; she has a truly abhorrent personality. No politician is an angel; however, she is hovering around purgatory, if not lower. She definitely fits into politics down south and not in Canada. Do we want a discriminatory Karen as a leader in our country?

(The video of Bea and Knight Rider is linked at this point in the editorial.)

The questions I have posed are not rhetorical - unlike everything Bea says. Every Canadian must ask themselves these questions. It is not hyperbole to say that if Direct Democracy wins the one seat that Bea Jensen is running for, Canada's political system will never be the same. We will have forsaken prudent, respectable leaders for a Karen and a mob. Remember, Direct Democracy is the political system that murdered one of history's greatest philosophers. Is that a system Canadians should emulate?

Bea messaged the Direct Democracy Army: LOL! A man with eyebrows longer than his hair saying I'm out of touch with the Canadian people! This is great. We have done something right to get an editorial from Dex Duffy. Please respond, repost and ridicule on all platforms early and often. It puts Direct Democracy on a National level. Let's keep it there.

Irene responded immediately: Begrudgingly, I must give the glory to the Honorable Member. Harold has been trolling Dex Duffy since the beginning.

The group gave Harold the praise he deserved. Harold responded with an insufferable ego-ridden message.

The sun had fully risen on another beautiful day by the time Bea finished Dex's editorial. She went for a morning run, ten kilometres at full speed. It felt good sprinting past Knight Rider without engaging him. He had been unwittingly useful, but she did not want to push it.

Bea heard her phone play the Imperial March while still in the shower. She rushed to answer, getting there just before it went to voice mail. "Hello! Don't hang up. I'm putting the phone on speaker. Wasn't Duffy's article awesome? Direct Democracy is on the national stage! Amazing!" There was a long silence. "You called about the Post's article, right? Or did something bad happen? Sam is okay, right?"

"Sam is fine," Marcus said. "How can you see that article as a good thing? On days like today, I think you must be a psychopath. On one hand, you're asking how Sam is, and on the other, you're celebrating a national newspaper article that links a video of you, a grown woman, coaching her son to mock a person with a disability. What kind of person does that? It's narcissistic to care more for your popularity than your child's safety. What you are does not matter. What I do know is that our arrangement is over. I will not be saving your minuscule child support for you to come to Ottawa. It's not even enough to pay for the therapy Sam will need over this. How do you think other kids will treat him?"

"What? I got the person who owned the video to blur Sam's face. I checked myself. We told the media not to show Sam's face!"

"Dex Duffy's article had a link to a video with Sam and you harassing an old man on a scooter."

"Dex Duffy is a fucking asshole! We told the media not to show his face! I couldn't control that."

"I not going to argue with you. You had control. You didn't put Sam first. You better start acting like a mother, or I will be taking action to get full custody of Sam."

"What does that mean?"

"Stop hurting your son by playing at being a politician. Quit Direct Democracy. You are only going to cause Sam to be bullied. Not to mention, it puts me in an awkward spot. My employer will need me to explain what my crazy ex is doing. You know Dex Duffy is the mouthpiece of the oil patch. His words go a long way, and I represent the natural gas industry."

"I'm the psychopath! You're threatening to take Sam away because of the paranoid delusion that Dex Duffy will blacklist you because of me. That makes no sense. I'm not giving up the little life I have for your paranoia. Sam is strong enough to deal with people who would bully him. Those people will bully him and others, regardless of the reason. You are one of those people!"

"Bea, I will repeat myself this last time. Quit Direct Democracy so Sam will not be pulled into a shit storm. If you do not…"

"Don't threaten me, Marcus. How can you think it's right to dictate what I can do? You are such a sellout. I wish I never wrote papers for you. You wouldn't have gotten through uni. I will fight."

"Remember how well fighting worked last time." Marcus hung up.

Bea threw her phone against the wall and fell onto the couch, crying. Eight years on, and Marcus still had power over her.

23.

The peacefulness of the owl grove did nothing to calm Bea, the antics of the steam kettle Muppets not helping. She was trapped again, blackmailed. Or was she the unfit mother, not protecting Sam from the cruel world. She sat crying intermittently next to the owls. Josie even seemed to coo at her soothingly, but she could not hear.

Bea's phone, now with a crack in the screen, rang. The caller ID read Derek. She answered.

"Bea, have you seen the Direct Democracy email? The national news stations want a reply to Dex Duffy."

"Marcus is pissed at me. Duffy's article linked a video with Sam's unblurred face in it. He reneged on a deal for me to come to Ottawa. He threatened that if I continued with Direct Democracy, he would fight for full custody."

"That seems extreme."

"I'm a bad mother. I didn't really want a kid. And I love Sam. I didn't want him to get involved. That's one of the reasons I lost the leadership race. I didn't want to ruin his life." Bea cried.

Soothingly, Derek said, "Cry, it is a good thing. I don't think this is as bad as you feel it is right now. Sam knows you love him. Sam knows you are… uhm… entertaining…"

Bea moaned, "Crazy."

"Maybe, but in a nice way. What I'm saying is that he knows who you are and has always loved you for it. Sometimes, he'll be embarrassed by you. Sometimes, he'll get ridiculed for who you are. Sometimes, he'll get in trouble for defending you. But that's partly how people grow to be better."

"That's easy for you to say. You're awesome with kids. I'm sure yours see you as a God."

"That is not true." Derek took a deep breath. "I knew I was gay when I was a teen. I got married to my wife knowing. Jenny knew, too. We accepted it. I wanted children, and a beard was the way to have a more normal life then. I did not want the controversy of fighting to be a gay man with kids. When they were young, we did everything to make them have a great childhood. They had a great childhood. When the youngest one left for university, I came out. My wife and I did it in what we thought was an honest, considerate, compassionate way. It destroyed all the trust we had with our children. Do they still love us? I think so. They say they do. But they do not let me close anymore. If it is not a holiday, I am not in their lives. The relationships are forced. If I had the chance, I would have rather – if even possible – brought them up experiencing the discrimination and antipathy I would have gotten as an out man than to lose their trust forever."

"Oh, God. I'm so sorry. And so selfish not to have asked." Bea continued to sob.

"No need to be sorry. You're not selfish. The thousands of people wanting you to make Direct Democracy win can easily distract a person from their own life. That's not selfish. Direct Democracy is right for those people, for Sam and for you."

Bea sniffled, "I will do my best to believe you."

"Let's meet at the office to organize the response to Mr. Duffy."

A committee of Derek, Harold, Irene, Mia, and Cat worked with Bea on talking points as CHEK, CTV, and CBC crews set up outside. Mia also wielded a camera.

The time came. At a music stand for a podium, Bea got lost trying to read the cards. When she did focus on the first point, 'I understand your concerns,' it felt like appeasement to her. Angry tears began to flow so that she could not read the flashcards her committee had prepared. A crow began to caw. Then another. She remembered Josie and the mob of crows. Weepy, she knew what to do.

"Thank you for letting me speak." Her voice was cracking but firm enough to be clear. "Everyone wants the horrible Canadian Karen to apologize for treating an old man in a scooter badly." She wiped her eyes with a dress sleeve. "However, I will not act in the way you want me to. I own my actions toward this frail old man, Michael Knight. He terrorizes my neighbours and me by posting accusatory, defamatory signs in our building. He leaves our doors insecure in a bad neighbourhood. He assaulted my son. I loathe him for this. I righteously treat him like a jerk. I will not change until he does. Go talk to him and see if I'm credible. If you want to know who I am to respectful people, ask my volunteers."

"The only behaviour that a Direct Democracy candidate must have is honesty." Bea paused. "Honesty, like I am demonstrating now by telling you what I actually think."

Bea stopped again to wipe away tears. "I am trying to hold it together because I am the victim here." She looked into the sky, closing her puffy red eyes. "I put my lowlights on the Direct Democracy webpage to show who I am. I asked only that my child's picture be blurred. Dex Duffy and his cronies at the *National Post* linked a video with my boy's face on it. A line even internet trolls did not cross. But Dex and the dicks in the Mainstream Media fucked me."

The video bleeped the bad words, but every Canadian could use their hockey fan's lip-reading skills to understand what she said.

"Dex and his moneyed Mainstream Media handlers showed an unblurred picture of my son. Because of this, my ex has reneged on an agreement for me to see my boy in Ottawa. If I do not quit Direct Democracy, my ex has threatened to challenge my limited visitation rights. Dex, a one-time wannabee Liberal politician and current corporate stooge, has truly fucked me."

"Knight Rider is not the victim. Dex is not the victim. The internet people clutching their pearls at my antics are not the victims. I am the victim. I am the one having my family's life dragged into public view when it literally has no bearing on my promises as a politician. I am not pledging to be the rational representative of my constituency. I am pledging to do what my voters say. That's it. It is what my opponents are afraid of. I am the victim."

Bea sniffled, then smiled wryly. "Direct Democracy must have pissed off someone in power, the elite, for a tool like Duffy to hammer down on me. Direct Democracy must have made the elite afraid. Why is a Black Media Empire newspaper getting an oil patch shill fake populist writer like Duffy to write a hit piece on a single candidate party? Why has Dex, a noted populist who constantly talks of how people of the heartland are being mistreated by their sophisticated city-slicker politicians, changed his tune to, 'people must have faith in their superiors, the political leaders, the elite?' A message completely contrary to Dex's normal rhetoric of government bad, people with corporate resource sector jobs good.

"Mr. Duffy has accepted Plato's and Aristotle's argument that the elite are better than us; therefore, they must lead. The people paying Mr. Duffy conveyed their view nicely. It was a flowery, 'fuck you, you are not smart enough to decide on policies that will affect your life.' Direct Democracy scares the elite; that is why Dex 'accidentally' linked an unblurred picture of my kid. I was victimized by the elite with this editorial because the elite are afraid of us. And they should be!

"Why are the elite afraid of what has made Canada great?" Bea's voice rose defiantly. "Because they have spent almost two hundred years making the political information space around our representative democracy one owned by the elite. It does not matter how democratic our government institutions are if the information our decisions are based on is manipulated by the elite.

"Like Dex Duffy editorializing against a one-candidate party. The goal the big parties, with the assistance of the elite, have striven for is to lull most of Canada's population into political apathy with parties becoming more and more alike while nurturing a rabid base activated by wedge issues. This creates the performative political world we are in today, where our view is diverted from what matters to dumb issues like J.T. doing vanity shots in South Asian clothes. Tactless? Certainly, but it has no influence on the job of prime minister.

"Conservative supporters are so close to the truth of Canadian politics when they ridicule Justin for being a drama teacher. What better background for performative politics? J.T. is good at finding the dramatic that keeps the Liberal base engaged. Think of the contrived PR coup when Junior sat in the teepee occupying Parliament Hill. Every white person felt great, but the Indian Act remains. Little Pee Pee taking off his horned glasses, pretending to get his boots dirty, talking like he buys Double Doubles daily, and saying common sense is his inner drama teacher pandering to his base. Jagemeet's best performance must be when he lets a crazy

Karen right-winger yell at him while he sends love her way. You can bet the NDP practiced for that eventuality for months before his chance to shine.

"No wonder that World Wrestling Entertainment veteran down south, President Trumpsterfire, has done so well activating his rasslin' fan base with his imbecilic word salad. Professional wrestling is performative politics and our friends to the south have mastered it. But don't forget Canada has a storied history in wrestling, Brett, Owen, and the rest of the Hart family are Canadians.

"The problem Direct Democracy presents to politicians is that it takes the performance away from them. There's no need for me to be anything but honest. In the immortal words of Dr. Frankfurter, *I will relieve the cause but not the symptom.* I will be the performer for Direct Democracy. Remember, my antics are an act to keep Direct Democracy in the spotlight so my fellow Canadians can exercise democracy and keep the elites at bay.

"If we do not force the system to be more democratic, the elite will continue making politics into cringe entertainment. Something that makes for easy laughs on late-night T.V. but leaves the average person feeling icky. With less democracy, the elite will dominate decision-making in Canada. Politics will become an even dirtier word. We need Direct Democracy to clean the ickiness of the elite's swamp. Then we can feel good about participating in our political system."

"But this is also about me. Dex Duffy and his puppet masters' have caused me to have one purpose: to win. It's the only way I can see my boy. Dex has taken my child from me. I will do everything I can to get to Ottawa for my kid's first hockey game. Fuck you, Dex! You fucked with the wrong Canadian Karen! The people of Walmart and I want to see your manager! I will not let Dex and his puppet masters fuck us anymore." The double middle finger Bea gave to the camera would be blurred, but everyone could tell what Bea was holding up.

In Bea's mind crow feathers were fluttering down from the music stand. She was plucking a dead crow named Mr. Duffy and about to feed her internet army with it. The crow's head dropped to the ground, mortifying the onlookers.

The camera people stood with the same stunned looks as the core of Direct Democracy members assembled behind them.

"That's a cut, right?" Harold glanced around to see if the cameras had stopped filming. "A little off script but great! That gas bag Dex Duffy deserves every word. Calling them the elite was brilliant. Bringing in the family bit is a gamble that I think will pay off. And there's nothing to lose since that chowder head threatened custody of your kid. A few too many f-bombs for my liking, but I think that language will engage the young people."

"Thank you, Harold." Bea nodded toward the office. Dex should not have shown Sam. Let's finish him off."

The group assembled for the follow-up communications blitz. Bea provided Joice with a copy of her pre-prepared response to Dex, advising her to disclose it to Samantha's mother as quickly as possible. Joice was to make it sound like a government informant leaked a brief intended for CSIS, the Cabinet and the elite.

Mia was tasked with getting the ire of Instagram moms up by alleging Sam was intentionally left unblurred to force Bea to quit.

Irene worked on more testimonials from oldsters touting Bea's volunteering benevolence.

Harold continued to troll Dex, directing Justin to have Direct Democracy Conservatives condemn him and the media tycoons who endorsed the attack.

Cat started creating videos on the destructive power of performative politics.

Bea worked with them all to increase the emotionality of their posts.

The group had Bea's response to Dex Duffy's article ready well before it was to air. To ensure it was not edited, Mia scheduled Direct Democracy's YouTube Channel to premiere the video an hour before the T.V. news did.

Less than ten minutes after it was released, Bea's phone played the Imperial March. She was expecting this call. "My video must have landed the way I expected. You called me before you could watch it three times, amazing. That makes my day!"

"What is wrong with you?" Marcus yelled. "Psycho bitch! You'll never see Sam again!"

"Marcus," Bea raised her voice but did not yell. "You went nuclear by threatening to take one hundred percent custody. Serious people act on threats as if they are real."

"You are so naïve. I hope you said 'I love you' to Sam the last time you talked with him. Dumb cunt."

"You played your threat cards. I still have mine. There's lots of stuff I've kept hidden for the sake of Sam. Things that will ruin you. If I never get to see him again, why would I need to hide them?"

"You wouldn't. It would ruin you, too."

"I spent the last eight years with my life in ruins to see Sam. Just watch me."

Marcus hung up. Bea smiled, feeling good that she had gotten to him.

"I knew it," Harold grumbled. "Bea's a closeted Liberal, quoting Pierre Elliot. 'Just watch me.' Those are the strongest words ever said by a Canadian Prime Minister. By a Francophone Liberal. Holy Mackerel!"

Irene chimed in, "Remember the second strongest, 'For me, pepper, I put it on my plate,' Chrétien, another Francophone Liberal. Chrétien, choked a protester out too."

"How could I forget the Shawinigan Handshake! Stop rubbing it in. I can't help that the Liberals are hated so much they must act tough."

"Didn't J.T. win the boxing match?" Bea couldn't help needling Harold further. "Between him and senator sexual assaulter?"

Mumbling too quietly to be heard, Harold distracted himself with his tablet. After five seconds of unintelligible muttering, Irene and Bea broke out laughing.

24.

Finger hovering over the enter button, Bea was conflicted. She wanted to know where Direct Democracy stood in the polls. Her spat with Dex had gotten millions of views over all the media channels but she worried it would eventually trend negatively. What if the truism that all press is good press was not true? The number of emails she had to forward to Hedwig of Dicks of Direct Democracy suggested her Dex response cleaned up. She sent nearly ten times the number of dicks as the first CBC interview – that's a lot of dicks, but they still did not measure up to a meter stick.

Too nervous to check the polls, Bea entertained herself on the Dicks of Direct Democracy site. She liked how Hedwig had doctored the photos with the addition of scale, always unflattering. In a collage around the person's dick pic were pictures from the dick's social media with captions that cracked her up, like 'Now you know why my truck is so big.' After viewing the pathetic packages and the people attached to them with their lame lives, she felt strong enough to review Direct Democracy's standing.

They were tied for second. Bea had to admit that tied for second was a bit of a fudge. The NDP and Direct Democracy's margin of error overlapped at the NDP's bottom and Direct Democracy's top. One had to squint to make the two parties appear neck and neck. That was not the entire story. The Conservative and Green numbers had fallen off with Direct Democracy seeming to have eaten up their losses.

Saturday's meetings had become an open if organized, what-worked-and-what-did-not strategy session. Doughnuts were secondary and socializing was kept to a minimum until the end, when members broke into canvasing pairs. The meeting noise was loud enough that Harold bought a gavel to call order. With a flurry of banging, he brought the meeting to order.

The first topic of business was waning door-knocking engagement. Ethan pulled up a graph showing the dates and average time for the door-knocking conversation. It was getting less and less, being less than a quarter of what it was when they had started the campaign. Ethan gave a few hypotheses such as better knowledge of Direct Democracy, voters experiencing election fatigue setting in after a month of campaigning, and canvassers being better at giving their spiel. Regardless of the reason, there was less engagement. Ethan overlayed another graph showing engagement numbers at a better position than at the start of canvassing. Ethan said, "These numbers are from Justin and Tyrell last week."

"You're telling us J.T. has the best numbers?" Bea snorted. "Really..?" She looked around and saw that no one else found it funny. "Not a chuckle?" She slumped in her seat.

"Justin, Tyrell," Ethan ignored Bea's comment. "Can you show us how you got this great engagement?"

Justin spoke first. "Tyrell and I got accidentally paired last week when our normal partners could not show up." He gestured to the room. "We tend to pair up with others of our political persuasion. I go with a fellow Conservative, and Tyrell with a Liberal. But Tyrell is a Liberal, and I'm a Conservative. We found playing good cop and bad cop worked well. For example, imagine Tyrell and me knocking on Harold's door. Start with our normal script, Tyrell."

Tyrell pretended to knock on an imaginary door. Harold pretended to use a peephole, then unlocked ten deadbolts. The door opened, and Harold stood glaring with crossed arms. Tyrell said they were from Direct Democracy and asked if he'd wanted to know more about their party. Harold humoured them, nodding, but ended the engagement after Tyrell's one-minute information dump.

Tyrell addressed the crowd, "That's a typical door knock. We get across what Direct Democracy is, and a polite homeowner takes a pamphlet. Now, we will do the good cop, bad cop.

Harold hammed up imaginary deadbolts to open. The script was the same until Tyrell asked, "Is that your electric car, I love it." He pointed at an imaginary car.

"Egad! I wouldn't be caught in that lithium crystal contraption. You can't drive it in the cold."

Justin jumped in. "Are you a Conservative supporter?"
"Yes."

Tyrell said, "A vote for the Conservative in this riding is wasted. The Liberal or NDP candidate will win. Get ready for a higher carbon tax and gas prices. You'll want the EV."

"Blow the carbon tax out of your ass!"

"Your vote doesn't need to be wasted. Direct Democracy will let you vote as a Conservative would. Even the greenies here would vote for another carbon tax."

"Don't sign him up," Tyrell interjected. "It's obvious he's with Skippy to the end."

"Give me that handout and tell me about Direct Democracy," Harold thundered, pointing. "The Liberal can wait on the property line."

Justin and Tyrell followed up by giving topics that could prompt the good cop, bad cop talk.

Next up was Joice, presenting a meme with what looked like a bad cartoon of Princess Leia recording the R2D2 hologram message. The caption read, 'Help me Forty-four, you're our only hope.' The crowd murmured in confusion.

The reference to Princess Leia and Star Wars sent a shiver down Bea's spine. She sat still, hoping this was not a connivance she would be revealed to be a part of.

"Conspiracists love codes," Joice explained. "They're stupid, so their codes are obvious. D is the fourth letter. Forty-four is Direct Democracy. We have become the party of the conspiracists because Direct Democracy can overthrow the elite. The conspiracists have determined it was the Canadian Shadow Government that ordered Bea's son's face shown because Direct Democracy is a threat. The Canadian Shadow Government is run by Conrad Black, technically a Lizard person. The Shadow Canadian Government is made up of Lizard people like Shadow Governments of all the New World Order States." The membership was more confused.

Bea breathed a sigh of relief. It was not the intrigue she had been worried would leak.

Joice decided it was going to be easier to tell members how to engage with the conspiracist than to detail the conspiracist worldview. She gave the group instructions to use the code word

Forty-Four instead of Direct Democracy, to make posts vague enough to allow wide interpretation, and to use terms like elite, globalist, New World Order, and Lame Stream Media. S was their secret weapon in this community. S, Samantha, had become the Q to the Canadian conspiracists. Joice and Samantha had created S to disseminate conspiracies so that Forty-Four could be the solution. S surreptitiously dropped the Direct Democracy propaganda on Samantha's mother's Facebook, where it was devoured by the conspiracists.

Joice had a warning: "You can't spell conspiracist without racist. Be careful not to parrot coded racist messages. The ideas of globalism, New World Order, Lizard people quickly dissolve into otherism, scapegoating, and white supremacy. Do not use or share posts with 14 words, 1488, ACAB, Blood and Honour, Protocols of Zion, Not Equal, Lying Media or Rothschild. These are just some racist code words. There are hundreds. I can't list them all."

"It's probably best if you don't use or share posts from conspiracists unless you're sure the content is not racist. Stick to our messages. Or don't share anything."

There was confusion on every face. The oldsters were particularly bewildered.

"Thank you, Joice," Bea said. "The last agenda item is Bea-Con. I hope to see you all at the Beacon Hill Bandstand for our first rally. I know it might rain. If it does, it will be a welcome summer rain. Please drop by. It'll be fun on a summer's evening. There might be a rainbow."

Harold turned to Bea to see if that was all. She nodded. He banged the gavel. "That is all the business on the agenda."

Derek stood. "I have a notice from Elections Canada I must convey to the membership. In the last week, there has been a spate of vandalism against Conservative signs. People have been taping pictures of shirtless Harold on them."

Bea broke out laughing; the group followed suit. "Derek, I'm not sure I understand what you're saying. Do you have a picture?"

"No. However, the description in the email is a shirtless Harold Gordon."

"What malarky!" Harold roared. "Elections Canada is defective. Why would someone at Direct Democracy put my stunning visage on a Conservative sign? Holy doodle, talk about conspiracies!"

"Seriously..." Bea composed herself. "If anyone here is doing this, please stop." She could not resist. "But get a picture of your work first." Everyone laughed.

Harold banged his gavel. "Order! Order! The meeting is not adjourned!" The membership quieted. He banged the gavel again. "Meeting adjourned!"

Leaning over to speak into Harold's ear, Bea said, "You have learned much from Internet Comment Etiquette, padawan."

The following Saturday's meeting started with Bea reviewing polling data. The polls had fluctuated but not in a meaningful way; Direct Democracy was third, with the NDP's margin of error slightly overlapping at the bottom with the top of their margin of error. Again, there was a noticeable reduction in voters for the parties under the top three.

Ethan, who had some background in statistics, was quick to point out that what they were seeing was not necessarily statistically relevant.

"There are three kinds of lies!" Harold shouted. "Lies, damned lies, and statistics."

Bea-Con was next on the agenda. Bea stood up and tried to look and sound like a bloated Orange Orangutan with a combover and Secret Service protection. "Our crowd was the biggest crowd to have ever assembled on the Capital. It was so large that a satellite had to be used to get it all in one picture. It made the million-man march look like a hundred people." She and the members laughed. "Despite the torrential rain we had a great time with maybe forty people over the evening, almost all members. We did learn a lot. Direct Democracy's platform does not lend itself to long speeches on policy. We need to make Bea-Con more of a party than a political rally. It needs to be fun, like with music, dancing, and food. Direct Democracy is the Party that parties.

"The rain was actually a blessing. A band sheltered in the bandstand with us, jamming. We had a great time. They offered to play at the rest of the Bea-Cons.

"Rich thinks a political costume theme would be fun, possibly with an impersonation contest. Talk with Cat, Mia, Ethan or Rich if you're interested in playing music, performing spoken word or standup, or if you can help with food. We have fliers to post at the doors. When messaging about Bea-Con, stay away from the political. Keep it festive."

Justin was granted the floor. "A new controversial video of Bea has come up."

The bottom dropped out of Bea's stomach for a second.

The video came up on the T.V.: Bea had the stolen bike with a hipster in front of her. The woman behind the camera was yelling, "Murph, should I call the police?" The hipster is civilly asking Bea to check the bike. The kid can be heard screaming that the bike is his. Bea responds bitchily to the hipster, arguing until the hipster flips the bike over to show the markings he made. Defensively, Bea told him she bought the bike off Craigslist for Sam's birthday. Bea backs away from the hipster. The hipster flicked Sam's birthday card toward Bea and then took pity on Bea, telling his wife not to call the cops because Bea's child was not getting a gift.

Bea closed her eyes, thanking the cosmos; it was not the video that made her stomach drop.

Justin informed that video was on a Conservative Twitter feed, yet to get shared outside of the Conservative bubble.

Glancing toward Harold, Bea saw an angry old man. She then scanned for Irene. Irene would not look her in the eye. She instantly remembered she had not been exactly honest with them. She stood up. "I must apologize to the original members because I was not truthful. I told you Sam's birthday present, the bike, was stolen. It was stolen but not from me. I bought it from a shady person and did not want to know where it came from. I let members Irene, Harold, Derek and others believe the bike I bought for Sam was stolen from me. It was not. I was not strong enough at the time to tell you the truth. I am sorry. I hope I can make it up to you."

Owls, Doughnuts, and Democracy, by Jason A. N. Taylor

Irene left the meeting.

"How do you want us to spin this Dear Leader?" Harold said acidly.

Irene's leaving caused Bea to sniffle, unable to hold back tears. "Give me a minute, Harold…" Derek handed her tissues. "I didn't mean to hurt my family. I'm sorry." She wiped her eyes. "We don't spin it. We tell the truth. Getting the bike from a Craigslist ad was a lie. I, a desperately poor mother, approached a shady person to buy a probably stolen bike for her son's birthday to make her feel like a good mother. I did not question where the bike came from. I gave the bike back, losing my kid's birthday gift and the money I paid for it. I was wrong for doing what I did, but I did it for the rightest reason, love." She paused to wipe her eyes again. "We share it outside the Conservative forums. We message that the Conservatives want to smear us, but we are truthful. We counter with Little Pee Pee's and the other leaders' scandals. They're bigger and more immoral than a misappropriated bike."

"Bea…" Harold now sounded less outraged than concerned. "I may have sounded sarcastic, but I was serious. For your sake, we should spin this."

"In today's world, the truth is spin." Bea sat down with nothing more to say, wishing to smooth things over with Irene but knowing she could not leave.

Next on the agenda was Mia, noticing that on the other parties' websites there were no policy statements. She displayed the parties' pages. The Liberals had links to accomplishments that were hidden by Canadian flags, good-looking diverse people in visionary poses, and the gorgeous Hair Style PM. The NDP was similar but with orange replacing red, more diverse people, Jagmeet, and their policy stories at the bottom in small font. The Greens page was disturbing, not for its lack of policy but because the pictures of the co-leaders resembled a May-Autumn relationship photo shoot with gray-haired May thrilled to be with her sugar baby, complete with awkward touching. Finally, the Conservative page was devoid of policy. Little Pee Pee was in front of a crowd of people holding signs reading: common sense, powerful wages, powerful savings, lower taxes, with a smattering of province-specific slogans. Mia shared a picture of the Conservative page without Little Pee Pee, it looked like an ad for Zellers, Dollar Store, or Walmart, not a political party webpage. All the links on Little Pee Pee's page were attacks on the Liberals, most were personal attacks on J.T.

"There's one other party we must view." Mia put up Direct Democracy's webpage. "Ours. It's the only website with the entire party platform on the first page. Amazing! We must let the voters know this. I've made a video that will be on all the usual apps. If you want to use parts of it for your own content, the Discord has all the clips."

Cat stood to explain that at the national level, the election was becoming very close. Many polls suggested a minority government. Pundits and poll watchers put their money on a minority government, likely with the Liberals and NDP. But a Conservative and NDP minority was a possibility, too, with one occurring in recent history. This was great news for Direct Democracy. If the government was a minority, an MP controlled by the people could make a difference. Propaganda promoting a minority government must be a priority for Direct Democracy. Canadians for Greater Democracy would be messaging the power and benefits of a Direct Democracy MP in a minority government, too.

In bigger news, Cat displayed the webpage of Canadians for Greater Democracy, a third-party advocating voting reform and proportional representation options like ranked-choice voting. She highlighted an article on how Direct Democracy could pressure the government into proportional representation as a compromise, recommending that readers from Victoria Capital vote for Direct Democracy. Canadians for Greater Democracy was the second, third party advocating Direct Democracy to assist with electoral reform. Again, Cat gave directions on how to share, promote, and propagandize the proportional representation angle.

Ethan had the last new business. Victoria Buzz had run an article on Direct Democracy voting security. They did not have evidence that voting would be insecure but did conflate the wacko and unsubstantiated electronic voting machine controversy in the US with like concerns in British Columbia. The conclusion Ethan drew was that Direct Democracy should get ready to defend the security of its voting app. The media did not need proof to run a newsworthy article.

Bea agreed, especially because it meant she had a reason to see Ray again.

Before Harold could bang his gavel to adjourn, Derek had an urgent addendum. "Elections Canada sent me a picture of the sign vandalism. Bea, can you put up the picture?"

"A warning to those who are sensitive," Bea cautioned. "You may want to look away." She allowed a few seconds pause before clicking on a picture of a shirtless, wrinkled Harold Gordon. Hands behind his head, grinning widely, sitting with the sunny Salish Sea behind him, he was wearing wraparound sunglasses and little else.

"Thanks, Bea," Derek said. "The warning was prudent." He turned to the members. "Whoever is doing this, stop. It is not funny." Derek and the members disassembled into laughter.

"Why would I have my pictures attached to Little Pee Pee?" Harold stood up, glaring at Derek. "No one in their right mind would want to associate their likeness with Little Pee Pee. I am offended. I am the victim of shenanigans!" He banged his gavel.

The members conversed as they left the lounge.

Bea shimmied and squeezed through to look into the dining room and other areas. She did not see Irene. She went back to the lounge, scanning the room for Cat. "Hey... Do you have a minute?"

"Bea, why did Irene stomp out of the meeting?"

"When I told Irene the bike I got for Sam was stolen, she arranged a tour of the Raptors to make up for it. I let her believe it was stolen from me, but I bought it from a crackhead in my apartment building. It was a shitty thing for me to do. I have no excuse."

"I'd be angry, too."

"Can you help me?" Bea stared at the floor, feeling like a teenager. "I want to apologize. I think she's in her room, but I'm sure she won't answer the door if I knock. I'm begging you to come with me. I know, it's totally high school. I can't stand that she's upset with me."

"Ok. I'll help." Cat sighed. "But I don't think this is necessary. And if there are strange noises like buzzing or moaning, I'm out!"

They went to the third floor, and Cat knocked on Irene's door. "Who is it?"

"It's me, Cat. Do you have a minute?"

Bea changed places with Cat.

Irene opened the door. "YOU! I am so angry at you. How could you lie to us? You want us to tell the world how truthful you are, but you lied to us. If you told the real story, I would have helped you anyway."

"I am so sorry, Irene. I was scared. I had no money, no gift, and I didn't know I had the friends… family I have now. It wasn't right." Bea started to sniffle. "I'm not perfect."

Irene turned back into her apartment. The door closed automatically. Bea began to bawl.

The door opened. "Apology accepted." Irene held out a box of tissues. "Dry your eyes. I want to get a drink."

The three of them found seats on a sweltering patio and ordered cold drinks.

Irene asked, "What did I miss?"

"Not much," Cat assured. "Mia has a new spin for Insta. It talked about the possibility of a minority government and a new third party that endorsed us. What else was there, Bea?"

"Ethan's concerned security will be an issue. Oh! The Election Canada complaints." Bea got out her phone to show the shirtless Harold picture.

Irene said, "What?" Then leaned in to see.

"Don't expose her to that!" Cat grabbed at Bea's phone. "It's bad enough we had to see shirtless Harold."

"Thank you, Cat," Irene said, not looking at Bea's phone. "I don't need to see it. I can't believe people do things like that."

Bea put her phone away. "Harold's pic is tame compared to what Direct Democracy gets."

"How do you mean?"

"Dick pictures. Lots of dick pictures. There have been fewer since Ajay and Cat started '*Dicks of Direct Democracy*.' Ajay and Cat amaze me with how heartless their doxing of the dick-pick senders is. They're ruthless."

"It's not Ajay or me," Cat explained. "Hedwig is Ray. I wanted to help him, but he insisted he should run the site alone. He didn't want me to get found out."

"Do you think Hedwig was emasculating those dick-pick senders for me?" Bea did not need to see Cat nod to know the answer and loved Ray for it. "Did Ray ever tell you that Hedwig is transgender? In Harry Potter, Hedwig is a pure white owl. Only male Snowy Owls are pure white. Hedwig is a 'her' in the book."

"We've talked about Harry Potter a lot, but he's never mentioned Hedwig being trans. Can an owl be trans?"

Bea wondered if Hedwig, trans children's books, a shyness to touch, tattoos, and Ray had anything in common. She was certain she loved him.

"If a goose can be lesbian, an owl can be trans," Irene added. "And who is Ray?"

"Ray is kind of a student of Ajay," Cat explained. "Ray's helping with IT security for the Direct Democracy App. The three of us hang out and game from time to time." Cat smiled slyly. "But most of all, Ray is Bea's crush. And he is hers. They're so cute together!"

"First, you lied to me," Irene bristled. "Now I'm in the dark about your new beau. Bea, I thought we were friends!"

"Irene, I've only gone out with Ray twice. And he likes to be private. In fact, he's called it off until the election is over."

The Lounge room at the Home was more rambunctious and filled with doughnuts than it had been for a Saturday meeting. For once, Harold's extreme gavelling for silence was necessary. He pounded away for ten seconds, yelling, "Order! Order! For Christ's sake, order!"

When the group quieted, Bea spoke, "It sounds like you've heard the new poll. Direct Democracy is technically in second!" She paused for the cheering. "You deserve a doughnut, coffee, and pat on the back. This is amazing!" There was another wave of cheering. "Ok! Ok! That's enough for now. I said technically because the NDP is within our margin of error. And we are not first yet. With your help, we will be!"

Harold allowed the cheering until he saw Karen pop her head into the room. He banged his gavel. "Order! Get back to the agenda! Joice is up first."

Joice stood. "The good news first. Conspiracists are rushing to Direct Democracy. The bad news is you can't spell conspiracist without racist. Vice News has done a story highlighting the fringe groups supporting Direct Democracy. The reckless report found one Neo Nazi from up Island and a few Communists in Victoria. This fuckery has been eaten up by local radio call-in shows, and Conservatives are flocking to it like good sheep. I'm sure it will get bigger.

"Denouncing the extremists in the party is the traditional way of dealing with this problem. Commander-in-Chief Wide Body Combover and MAGA in the states are the only people in mainstream politics not to condemn Racists!" Joice spat. "We can't have racists in our party."

The members howled in agreement.

"We don't need the support of commies or fascists!" Harold hollered.

Irene, Justin, Tyrell, Wendy, Cat, Rick and others added their hate for hatred in loud, ironically incoherent defamatory statements.

Standing, Bea shouted: "I don't care for extremist groups or hate!" She waited for the crowd to calm down. "How many of us in this room hate extremists and hate groups?"

Every hand went up.

"How many of us think hateful people should be denied the vote in this election?"

Everyone glanced about to see what their neighbours were doing.

"Remember, this is a safe space. You will not be judged."

A few hands went up, but when more did not, the few tried to hide their vote from everyone but Bea.

"Let's say Election's Canada did deny the vote to haters. How would they identify them?" After ten seconds of unconstructive crowd mumbling, Bea continued: "There is no way to exclude the haters unless they act criminally. Unfortunately, they're part of society. Direct Democracy is about finding areas of agreement among diverse groups. There is always a middle ground between the extremes. Extreme groups must be able to participate in direct democracy for our party to be truly equal and inclusive."

The membership did not entirely take to this, but the few arguments raised were not strong enough to deny Bea's logic.

"Democracy is equity and inclusion, even for haters!" Bea yelled. "I feel your anger. I have your anger. Anger is fear. But we don't have to fear if we participate in democracy. Direct Democracy must allow haters, but that does not mean haters are to be welcomed. Remember, Direct Democracy does not have political positions. We're simply working to be more directly heard regardless of our political beliefs. That does not mean a Liberal, Conservative, or National Socialist Nazi can take our platform because we do not have one. The majority on this issue is the direction we go."

The crowd buzzed. Bea paused before adding: "That said, we will not accept hateful symbols attached to our logos and party materials."

"Bea, I understand what you are saying..." Though seething, Joice nevertheless modulated her voice to be authoritative. "The people of Walmart will not! I'm not willing to sacrifice my work to be seen supporting hate. It won't matter if it's right to allow the hateful in if we get seen as collaborators. Direct Democracy must denounce Nazis!"

"One does not collaborate with Nazis if they participate in democracy," Bea asserted. "Fascism is always antithetical to democracy, even when democracy has fascist minorities within it. It's the corruption of democracy that leads to fascism. MAGA and Corporate Democrats are moving the States toward fascism because of moneyed interests holding sway over politicians. Hitler may have been elected to the Reichstag, but the normalization of political violence by fascists and communists had already stolen democracy from Germany in the nineteen twenties. Empowering individuals to have an actual say in their governance, even if a few are Nazis, is how to fight extremism. I have a plan to show this to the people of Walmart. I'll need everyone's help at the next Bea-Con to execute the plan. Who's with me?"

Everyone raised their hand.

Bea outlined the plan, which required the immediate contact of all media.

Cat revealed her next video masterpiece. It asked the question: "What is harder to understand, a person's character or how to vote on an issue?" The aesthetic was an infographic, dialogue captioned in large script with words highlighted as spoken. The boldly coloured graphics were inter-spliced with photos of the people discussed: "On the one hand, Canada's leaders are obviously acting in a role. Justin's a drama teacher. Little Pee Pee pretends he is a man of the people but has only ever had a government job, hiding his true nature, expecting the voter to trust he'll stay in character. What characters are our leaders playing in front of the elite? Is it the same character they play on T.V. news for us? To vote on an issue all one needs are the facts. Facts are tangible. Facts do not need to be trusted. Facts are facts. If a person is given the facts about an issue, they can decide. How come our political leaders say it is easier for us to choose a representative based on the character the candidate has created rather than vote on a question with facts that do not change? Have you ever been burned by a disingenuous person? A person playing a character? A traditional politician, perhaps?" The leaders of the normal parties flashed by. "Do not vote for a politician's promise, and we know how good that is. Vote to make your own decisions with facts. Vote for Direct Democracy."

Everyone clapped and cheered. Harold granted a short break for the members to share the new propaganda.

Ethan was up next with more questioning of the security of the App. News organizations beyond Victoria Buzz were messaging short pieces on the issue. There had even been a suggestion that before the election, a test of the App's security should happen, like a debate on the technical side. Bea wanted to touch, get in touch with Ray, so an action item was made for security testing of the App.

The final speaker on the agenda was Justin. "There are three new videos coming up on Conservative channels focusing on Bea. We'll call them the good, the bad, and the ugly."

Bea's hands went instantly cold. She turned pale and felt nauseous.

"The good is an interview of Michael Knight, Knight Rider, the guy in on the scooter, that shows him as a wingnut. The bad are old videos of Bea doing dumb political stuff and reading a love letter to some GenX comedian, Rick Marcer... Mercer."

Bea held the bottom of her chair, worrying what the ugly was.

"The ugly," Justin continued casually, "is a recorded call of Bea working as a debt collector, threatening to tell the poster's girlfriend about his debt."

Bea, relieved, laughed loud enough to get Justin's attention and cause a "Well, I never" from the crowd.

"What's funny, Bea?"

"Sorry, Justin. And everyone. You probably won't find this funny because you've never been a debt collector. It is a shitty job. I'm going to assume that the video is from a basement-dwelling drunken troll who sexually harassed me in calls he did not post." Bea was not one hundred percent sure this guy sexually harassed her, but she was sure enough. "Again, we must not shy away from it, but we must pull out the parts that matter to our message. And that is..."

Bea cleared her throat. "Number one, I do not deny this. It is who I am. I will be this honest when I am doing my job in Parliament, voting for what the people of Victoria Capital tell me to."

"Two. Don't hate the player; hate the game. I had to do my shitty job the way it's acceptable to do in the industry. You may hate debt collectors, but it's a job, just like a lying politician."

"Three. I collected debt to get myself out of debt and provide my child with some luxuries, like a stolen bike. The job slowly got worse to the point that a single mom could not save to honestly purchase a boy's birthday present.

"All our jobs are getting shittier, but J.T.'s is not. My only option for a good income was the dodgy business of debt collection or other seedier, more socially unacceptable jobs. I did not have the option of political party stooges like Little Pee Pee or ski bum, I mean instructor, like J.T. I am the victim for having so few options, in a Canada where we were promised we could be anything."

"Four. The troll cherry-picked this recording. He sexually harassed me during the call, pretending to masturbate, breathing heavily and asking how I liked it." Bea paused. "'How I liked it' meant how I liked getting fucked."

The membership gasped.

"This small-handed drunk was not the only pissant who acted this way. Many did. And I was doing a job. I was a victim."

The crowd was too shocked to say anything.

After the pause, Bea pulled them back. "Look, I was rash on this last point. I don't have proof of what happened. You're all free to say what you want. It is what it is. When people feel attacked by a debt collector, they act badly... please go with the first three points."

Bea knew all four points would be messaged just as she knew this particular troll did not sexually harass her, even though many did. He deserved it for taping their calls. She hoped Hedwig would be listening too. Of course, she knew he would because owls have great hearing.

"That is how we should deal with the ugly," Justin concluded. "Basically, the same message as the previous scandals. I think we should share the good as much as possible. And the bad is pretty funny and shows Bea's honesty, so point that out. Do you have anything else, Bea?"

"Bad..?" Bea rolled her eyes. "My early videos are bad? I will have you know YouTube was only a few years old when I made those 'bad' videos." She jokingly fingered air quotes. "I was a pioneer."

Justin did not argue.

Harold asked for any final business.

Bea reiterated the plan for the next Bea-Con.

Harold banged his gavel.

"Harold," Derek interjected, "there is another complaint from Elections Canada. It is directed at you. Frankly, I do not know what to say. However, I do know that I would not want to see this pasting of shirtless old men's pictures on political signs become a trend. Please stop."

"Three white horses in a mud puddle is not a dirty joke. But this is!" Harold was indignant. "I'm shocked you are accusing me of putting my pictures up on signs. See this walker? I'm using it to throw Elections Canada off my trail. Elections Canada can blow it out their ass!"

"I was not accusing you. We do not want to see this as a trend. Do you want to see other shirtless pictures taped on our signs?"

Harold smirked a dirty old man grin. "I wouldn't mind Colleen Lauren's picture taped to our signs."

"You dirty old man!" Bea jumped from her seat. "Bang that gavel and take your perversion somewhere else!"

The meeting broke up amid boos and hisses.

Bea found Harold. "That was funny. But I had to yell at you."

Harold smiled. "I know how it works, boss."

25.

Every tree on a trail crossing, bike lane crossing, or corner within three blocks of Beacon Hill Park bloomed with colourful owl-printed signs, welcoming one and all to Bea-Con.

QR codes, printed maps, and arrows gave the directions. Cedar hedges and caution tape cordoned access to the bandshell. The side near the eagle's nest was open for partiers to enter. Tables with doughnuts and coffee were at the top of the small hillock in a grove of Douglas Firs, 50 metres in front of the bandshell. Direct Democracy members handed out coffee and doughnuts. Over four hundred people with all styles of dress and some in political costumes were milling around the coffee and doughnuts. The crowd was engaged by Direct Democracy members. Reporters' cameras sprouted like mushrooms after a rain, positioned by Mia to film the Bea-Con spectacle in the amber glow of a late summer's afternoon sun. The DJ and Jam Band had the sound system playing groovy trance loud enough to have people walking funky but not so loud as to drown out conversation. In front of the bandshell, Bea was arranging a group of members dressed as famous politicians.

When the light was nearing its most ethereal, filtered through Douglas fir and cedars, Mia, in Crooked Clinton dress, signalled Bea.

With gleaming eyes, Bea opened Bea-Con: "Welcome! Welcome! Welcome! I am so happy to see you at Direct Democracy's Bea-Con."

She allowed a few seconds of the obligatory applause.

"We're the party with a simple platform. We let you vote so Direct Democracy can be the Party that parties." She let the coffee and doughnuts partiers cheer. "Let's get this beautiful night started with a demonstration of what Direct Democracy is all about! Pump up the volume!"

A funky instrumental version of Steelers Wheel, *Stuck in the Middle With You,* began to play. The line of costumed politicians at the bandshell started to dance. On the far left, Joice gyrated as Karl Marx with a spectacularly lush beard. To the right was Samantha as Trotsky, goatee just as lavish. Next was Tyrell as Martin Luther King. Rich was Tommy Douglas. Irene did a great Crazy Bernie. Ajay was

Jagmeet. Harold and Justin dressed as Liberals Ti-Pet (Pierre Elliot Trudeau) and Junior. A young Crooked Hillary and Moose Jaw Mulroney, Mia and Ethan were there too. Right of Ethan but claiming not to care for terms like right and left, was Morty portraying the horned rimmed glasses wearing, apple eating, Little Pee Pee. Dutch, The Gipper, or Reagan's head was on the shapely body of Cat with his stuffed chimpanzee co-star Bonzo on one arm. Almost at the end of the right side was Fishy Jay in the prisoner orange jumpsuit Don the Con was sure to wear in the future. Don the Con held a large pickle jar with Tricky Dick's head floating in it. Cute Christa was dancing nearby in Klan Mom Margie's garb. Finally, furthest to the right was John with a shiny bald head, frowning and gesticulating vaguely Italian but with very offensive body language, pretending to be Mussolini.

The music got to the part where the singer should sing, 'Clowns to the left of me.' Instead of the original lyrics, Bea belted out: "Commies to the left of me, Fascists to the right, Here I am, stuck in the middle with you." When she sang 'Commies,' the five communists in attendance ran a Soviet flag down the aisle, beckoned by Marx and Trotsky. Two skinhead fascists came to join Mussolini. Both groups exchanged gestures of enmity.

Bea signalled for the people to stay apart as she barked: "Communists! Fascists! Stay where you are. We don't want a fight. We don't welcome you!"

The crowd roared in support. "But to be democratic we must let you participate." She smoothed her voice into a conciliatory coo. "If you follow Canadian laws, you can participate in Direct Democracy... but we do not accept your political views."

The song got to Bea's part again: "Socialists to left of me, Social Conservatives to the right, stuck in the middle with you." This time, much larger groups of partiers, maybe a hundred lefties and more than fifty-ish on the right, ran down to their sides. She added, "On the left, this includes everyone from Martin Luther King to Jagmeet Singh. On the right, it's from President Dumpster Fire to Little Pee Pee... of course, both don't 'get' left or right. We know where they stand, just left of Mussolini. Please don't try to argue with your neighbour across the political spectrum gap; you're not going to change their mind. Some friendly advice: if you ruin holiday dinners with your politics, please stop trying to educate your family. Stick to hockey."

Clapping along with the music, Bea shouted, "Liberals to the left of me, Fiscal Conservatives to the right, stuck in the middle with you."

Over a hundred and fifty people took their places almost in the middle of the line, uncertain where to stand.

"Crooked Hillary, the Trudeau's, Bryan the Cadillac Candidate, they're all so similar. It's hard to figure out where you are when the leader is a little left on Monday and kind of right on Wednesday. Just find a spot that fits. Chat with your neighbours; they're a lot like you."

Bea put a hand over her eyes, mock-trying to see something far away. "Commies to the left of me, Fascists to the right, stuck in the middle with the politically unaffiliated." She waved in the last less than a hundred people to come down the hill. "Come as you are. No need to join a political party. We don't demand you conform. Find a place to dance. Direct Democracy welcomes everyone. We're here for the party."

Bea grooved to the music as the group settled in. "Direct Democracy's been getting flak from the Mainstream Media for 'harbouring extremists'." Air quotes were fingered around harbouring extremists. "How many extremists are participating in Bea-Con?" Shouts of numbers under ten were called out by the line-up. "Seven. Let's see how seven extremists can manipulate Direct Democracy. Raise your hand if you vote for the issue. Increased spending for health care? Who's for increased health care spending?"

It took no time for all but a few of the crowd's hands to raise. The votes were a little thin between Little Pee Pee and President Small Hands, still most were raised, including the fascists.

As sarcastically as possible, Bea screamed, "OH NO! An issue communists and fascists agree upon. What to do? We must not support anything communists and fascists support; it is wrong!" She assumed a mocking tone. "Mainstream Media, and yes, Vice News is mainstream, does not understand Direct Democracy is not pushing a political agenda. Therefore, even the unwelcome communists and fascists can participate in Direct Democracy to be heard but not dominate."

"Let's see what happens when Direct Democracy gives the constituency a chance to vote on a communist bill. Who supports nationalizing the means of production? The government will own the factories, set production and distribute goods created from the labour of the worker to maximize social welfare. Raise your hand if you want to seize the means of production."

Only eleven hands rose.

"Come on! Put your hand up! We need like two hundred more votes to seize the means of production!"

"Mainstream Media..."She looked down, shaking her head. "This is how Direct Democracy would work if a communist bill came before Parliament. Direct Democracy is everyone finding the middle that fits. For example: remember when one sexy Prime Minister of a centrist party bought a pipeline?"

J.T.-Justin waved and yelled, "The Liberals did that for the good of the country... Alberta's part of the country even if they're jealous of my good looks and stylish hair."

"Shut up, Junior!" Bea cut him off. "We all know who you are. Who wants to buy a pipeline? It's so new it's hardly built. It'll be so great with all the cost overruns. Show of hands for the pipeline?"

A peppering of hands mostly in the right but not fascist sections went up, possibly seventy-five. Definitely not enough for a majority.

"If BCers were asked, we would not have voted for a pipeline," Bea declared. "Even our Liberals and fanboys of J.T. hardly voted for the pipeline. But we own one."

The mock voting continued on a variety of topics. Subsidized housing got support from over fifty percent of the right wing. The left-wing added enough to make it two-thirds in favour. Regulating tech companies with near monopolies got above fifty percent support from a broad spectrum; the libertarian right was opposed. Eliminating the Indian Act got overwhelming support from end to end. Proportional representation had pockets of dissenters throughout the left and right but was supported by more than fifty percent.

Bea primed the voters for the next demonstration. "The political parties in Canada, like most other countries with representative democracies have found the way to get elected is not to find common ground. The Bloc, Conservatives, Greens, Liberals, and NDP want you to see the world like this. Who wants to see strengthened language laws?"

Most people looked confused, but tens of hands were raised.

"If we were in Quebec, that would have slayed. But it makes the point that the Bloc is only about Quebec. Let's try a better one. Who wants more parental rights, like a school having to get approval for a child to go by their preferred pronoun?"

"Canada is a country of Common Sense," Morty shook his apple, shouting. "Moral people who know what's right! School should not indoctrinate children." Hands near him shot up but only a few raised to the left of the Cadillac Candidate.

"Amazing, only those with Little Pee Pee's worldview are in support." Bea loaded on the sarcasm. "The support stops exactly where the Liberal supporters start. I wonder why this is?" She paused for the crowd to ponder. "Let's try one for the Liberals. Who supports the carbon tax?"

"Remember," Junior Justin piped up. "We have exempted rural home heating oil. If my numbers don't go up, we'll expand it to pickup trucks."

Some wags jeered him. Some hands were up on the extreme left, but not all. A bubble of hands was raised in the middle, starting at Jagmeet but reducing toward Crooked Hillary. At Moose Jaw Mulrooney and to the right, no hands were up.

"The Liberals claim to be the big tent party but aside from picking up a few leftists, their tent ends where the true right starts."

"The parties want us to be divided into three groups. Politically active for their celebrated cause or the wedge issue, hopefully catching a group of supporters larger than their opponent's supporters."

'Celebrated cause' and 'the wedge issue' elicited Little Pee Pee yelling: "Parental Rights! Think of the children."

Little Pee Pee's cries were challenged by J.T. shouting, "Climate change! Think of the children."

Bea gave a pause for J.T. and Little Pee Pee to make their points each time the celebrated cause or the wedge issue was said, and then she continued. "The next group is politically active for the opposition, hopefully lower than their support. And the largest group is politically disengaged. The politically disengaged is the most important group because the larger it is, the more the party can create a rabid following that will always vote for them, regardless of the issue. If the key demographic always votes for the party, the party can vote and act the way it wants on other issues if it maintains the adherence to the celebrated cause or the wedge issue."

From behind a hedge and behind the line of politicians but in front of the media's cameras, the monocled monopoly man appeared, laughing and pointing at the voters. Conrad Black was half hidden behind a tree making Mr. Burns' excellent gesture with his hands in a spot similarly easy for the cameras to see but behind the politicians. Galen Weston was next to Black with a sign advertising butter; he was, of course, raising the price for no good reason.

Bea pointed to the elite. "The elite behind the parties do not want us to be active in politics beyond the celebrated cause or the wedge issue because they want to be able to influence the government more than we can. It is antidemocratic for a small group to exercise power over a larger one. Canada's representative democracy has turned into this. Tech monopolists, media moguls, grocery oligarchs, and resource extraction company CEOs quash agendas that are good for us but eating into their profits."

"Direct Democracy makes the celebrated cause or the wedge issue less powerful by allowing us to vote on all topics before the government. With Direct Democracy, we can vote for or against issues beyond what the parties and media want us to care about. To take a page from Little Pee Pee's book, it is like a family. The kids in a family may want to make the trip to the mall, all about the toy store and sugary cereal aisle, which is what the ad men of the elite aim for. The toy store and sugary cereal are the celebrated cause and wedge issue. A good parent knows that they cannot let their kid's bluster stop them from buying the essentials. Direct Democracy is the smartphone that distracts the kids from the toy store so the parents can keep the household running for the benefit of the entire family."

Shafts of sunlight that had lengthened during Bea's demonstration now faded with the setting sun. It was time for the party to start. Bea yelled into the mic, "That's enough politics for one night. Let's get this party started. Direct Democracy is a vote for yourself! You owe it to yourself to vote for Direct Democracy!" The partiers duly chanted.

As the chant and music faded, Bea made a barred owl call into the mic. "WHO COOKS FOR YOU COOKS FOR YOU ALL!"

Bea spotted a long-mustached Louis Riel wandering in the crowd. She jumped off the low stage to catch up with him. "What brought you here, Ray?"

"I beg your pardon, good lady. You have mistaken me for another." Ray bowed with one foot slightly in front of the other. "Louis Riel, Madam. I came to partake in your rebellion."

"I would hardly call Direct Democracy a rebellion. Nobody's going to be executed for our revolution."

"You say that now, but the fascists and communists look ready. Marx and Trotsky are half-assed communists. Where's Lenin and Stalin?"

"I wanted Stalin and Hitler." Bea rolled her eyes. "Samantha was willing to dress up as the Man of Steel since she didn't know who he was, and the moustache was cool. And I had to talk Mussolini John out of being Hitler. He even wanted to sing some Nazi song, Springtime for Hitler. John said some Jewish director wrote it so it's 'ok'. Mia objected because of taste and TikTok's algorithm would bury our content if we mentioned the Moustache Man. You can't use Hitler. TikToker only uses 'The Moustache Man who un-alived six million people.' I wanted Mao or Winnie the Pooh, Xi Jinping but China. Fucking TikTok! Damn your algorithm!"

"How much does Direct Democracy spend on TikTok promotions?"

"I think we only spend money on the official TikTok account. It's not much, like fifty bucks a video. Mia keeps us on the good side of the algorithm; that's why I couldn't have Hitler. It's the bot accounts that get the views."

"Direct Democracy is killing it compared to the other parties. Direct Democracy's TikToks get one hundred times the views of the other parties. That can't be from Mia's skill and bot accounts alone."

"Are you saying the Chinese Communist Party is supporting Direct Democracy?" Bea laughed. "A one-candidate party? Why would they support a democratic movement? Pray tell."

"Yes. The CCP, just like Bunker Grandpa in Russia, doesn't care about politics if the outcome is disruptive and sows distrust. What's changing a factor in the algorithm to them?"

"Great. Now I must worry about the upcoming W5 exposé on how Direct Democracy was infiltrated by Chinese Communists. I can imagine getting questioned by CSIS for my role. LOL. Was that why you came here, or can we start going out? Or can I go out with Louis? You could take me for a ride, I love the moustache."

Uneasy, Ray adjusted it. "My boundaries still apply. Ajay and Cat dragged me to Bea-Con for the spectacle."

"Was it everything you expected and more?"

"Yes. It was powerful. It felt like a cross between a sermon and a rave. You could almost apply your arguments to the democracy we have now. Participate in democracy, and the monkey business will be less. Is every Bea-Con like this?"

"No. This was the most preachy by far. We were making a point on extremism in Direct Democracy. The others have been just as fun, but the message was much shorter."

"What was with the owl call?"

"There's a pair of barred owls roosting in the cedars. I saw them before the rally. I thought it might be cool if they called back. But they didn't. Are you going to dance with me, Louis?"

The two of them danced. Bea did her best to bump and grind, but the event was family-friendly, and Ray did his best to keep it that way. Then they mingled. Bea doubled back to her friends for their impressions of Ray. It was obvious to all how smitten Bea was. Her friends told her Ray was smitten with her, too, but he was hiding it.

Bea asked Ajay and Cat again for background on Ray. Ajay had nothing more to say. Cat repeated how funny it was he never brought up Hedwig being trans with her and how vicious he was on the Dicks of Direct Democracy website.

"Louis, I would love to stay longer," Bea said after an hour. But I must leave. The members are going to spend the night working social media. I'll need your help with App security soon, like next week. When can we meet?"

"Ah… yeah…" Ray struggled to answer. "Next week is not that good."

"That's sucks. The election is a week after that. There have been stories doubting the security of the App. We'd like to put them to rest." Bea did her best to look alluring. "Can you find time? Day or night works for me."

"Showing the App is secure won't change someone who's concerned."

"Probably not, but we need to do everything."

"Tuesday evening and night. Be prepared for an all-nighter."

"Thank you, Hedwig!" Bea pounced, hugging Ray tightly. "I love how you shame my enemies. You'd better be prepared, too. Ready for anything." She did not kiss him but wanted to.

Walking at Harold and Morty's slow pace, the Direct Democracy crew moved to the office.

"Your friend dressed like Louis Riel…" Harold spoke to Bea. "He's an Indian, right?"

"Harold, you know better than that. Use the right term, Indigenous. Yes, he is Indigenous."

"Isn't an indigenous guy dressing like Metis cultural appropriation?"

"Some questions are better left unanswered."

"How can I learn if you don't answer my questions?"

At the office they re-shared the coverage the mainstream media aired with their critique and commentary. If the message did not conform to Direct Democracy's message, the source would be attacked. However, Mia's direction of the rally and media made the editor's decisions easy because the best shots were the ones Mia set up to make Direct Democracy's point. The meeting was over quickly because the Mainstream Media toed their line this time.

Bea easily twisted the arms of Irene, Joice, and Samantha to get drinks with her. She wanted to ask the three queerest people at the party what they thought of Ray.

It was unfortunate that Derek was not at Bea-Con; Bea wanted his gay opinion of Ray, too.

26.

A week before the election, the count of Direct Democracy signs on Bea's running route was the highest she had seen, but it was not one of their signs that brought her to a stop. It was the unicorn, Harold's shirtless picture, taped to a Conservative sign. She stopped to snap a picture while laughing. She had to think of the best way to show this.

Bea continued her morning routine at home, checking the poll numbers. After the last Bea-Con, Direct Democracy had moved into a true second place. But the success of a strange first-time party polling well in a federal election was not something she was patting herself on the back for today. Though it was a great achievement, winning was the goal. Winning was the only way she saw to see Sam and the only way to vindicate all the mud she had raked. She had, after all, used Sam as a political pawn when the chance came up.

The thought of Sam caused a burst of melancholy in Bea. She had not talked with him for almost a month. It weighed on her. She had a cry before getting dressed for a big day.

Showered and dressed, Bea double-checked her bag. She poured everything out on her bed to make sure the evening's accoutrements for her all-nighter with Ray were at the very bottom. To augment Bea's collection, Joice had offered Bea a sanitized marital aid with straps, but the only attachment Joice had was a tentacle. Bea declined the offer; she did not want the hassle of trying to explain why she had it or that it was borrowed. Sheets for the hide-a-bed and change of clothes went in to cover Bea's accessories. Then, Bea's spartan makeup bag. Finally, a second bag with Bea's laptop because there was every possibility Ray and her would do some work.

With the election closing in and Bea ever able to provide a great sound bite, the media came to her. After her shift at the coffee shop, she met them at the usual spot, in front of a totem pole at the edge of the provincial legislature grounds. It had good lighting in the afternoon. Usually, there was a slight breeze that ruffled her sundress occasionally but did not mess up her hair. Today, Bea was wearing an unusually formal outfit. She had a second-hand blazer with a matching skirt. The CTV reporter asked a warmup question, "How come you're all dressed up?"

"I didn't have glasses to take off, like Mr. Pee Pee," Bea answered flippantly.

The *CHEK* reporter asked a softball question. "The polls suggest a minority government is a strong possibility. What is your take on that?"

"It's great for Direct Democracy. A minority government makes your vote that much more important."

Next was the inevitable question from the dogged *Vice News* reporter: "Direct Democracy says it does not welcome extremists, but they can participate. What does that mean?"

"For eff's sake!" Bea exclaimed. "Not welcome means unwelcome. Like not receiving the person nicely. Like me talking with you. Dumb reporters like you are not welcome, but we have freedom of expression in Canada, and you can participate. That is what it means. Will you be asking me what 'is' means too?"

"I don't think that answers…"

"… You don't think. Next question."

The *Vice News* reporter tried to talk again.

"Psst!" Bea closed her hand three times, shushing before the reporter shut up.

Global News took its turn. "Are you aware there is a website called Di… ah… 'male anatomy' of Direct Democracy? It reportedly doxes and shames critics of Direct Democracy."

"Yes. I am aware of Dicks of Direct Democracy. It calls out people who send dick pictures. I don't know how you misconstrued 'critical of Direct Democracy' with sexual harassment. Sexual harassment is not criticism. Is critical thinking still part of the journalism school curriculum?"

The reporter gulped, then asked uncertainly, "Do you know who's running the website?"

"No. It's none of my business, but I thank whoever it is. People, especially women and the LGBTQ+ community must deal with sexual harassment like this whenever they're in public. We shouldn't have to. I love the person or people behind this. Thank you, Dicks of Direct Democracy."

A CBC reporter asked, "There are concerns that the Direct Democracy App is not secure enough for voting?"

"Before thinking of the security of our App, ask what else we use the internet for. EVERYTHING! Banking, shopping, music, TV., phoning, directions, doctor appointments, yet somehow, it's not secure enough for voting. Our App is as secure as any others. But to prove our security, two days from now, we'll have a beta version for people to try and hackers to attack." Bea paused, looking over the assembled journalists. "That's all the questions I can answer today."

"One more question, please," the *CHEK* reporter called. Bea nodded. "Why should Victoria Capital vote for you?"

"They're not voting for me; they're voting for themselves. Direct Democracy gives them the vote on every bill before parliament. Besides that, the government needs to listen to the people. A vote for Direct Democracy forces them to." Bea smiled as the cameras stopped recording. "Really," she joked. "I need an easy government job that pays well with travel to Ottawa so I can see my kid."

The group exchanged small talk, and the reporters were glad Bea had provided an entertaining interview.

She would have liked to stay and talk, but she was in a rush to get to the office before Ray got there. She had to clean the office, couch and sneak sheets onto the hide-a-bed. Then she moved some tables and found a couple of monitors and functional chairs to make a suitable workstation.

While the three members at the office's call centre did not notice Bea's labours, Irene did. "Tidying up for when your beau comes over, eh," she snickered. "Don't worry, deary, I'll stick to my side of the office."

Slightly before six, Derek arrived to help Irene make sure Ray's invoice was accounted for. When Ray arrived shortly after, Bea greeted him with a handshake. "Nice to see you, Ray."

"A handshake?" Ray was expecting a hug. "That jacket looks great on you."

"I'm working," Bea said coolly. "This is what I wear to work. I've got workstations set up for us. Why don't you see Derek and Irene about your pay? Then we can get started?"

Working out Ray's payment, Irene said loudly, "While I never! Bea, make sure Sam goes into IT. The pay is great."

Bea made sure her skirt was higher than it should be when she sat down. She sat on the right side of Ray so that an accidentally unbuttoned button on her thin white blouse threatened to show a free-range boob.

Meanwhile, Ray visibly checked out Bea's legs. Noticing, she rolled her eyes, pulled her skirt down and crossed her legs. "We're here to work."

Ray to check the App, knowing that Bea's work would be good. He was amazed at how good it was, showering her with compliments.

"I followed your instructions," Bea said. "It was easy."

"I estimated this would take a couple of hours. You're fine..." Ray stopped talking when he saw the open button and Bea's nipple.

Bea stretched, pushing her chest out. "My eyes are up here!" Quickly, she buttoned up.

"I was saying your fine work has saved us an hour."

"I am happy you think my work is great, Ray. I'm flattered you like how I look. But we are now working together. Technically, I am your boss. Whatever our past was, today, we are colleagues. Colleagues do not mess around. It's a serious boundary. I said the same to the two volunteers, Joice and Justin, looking to date me. Please, keep it professional."

"Is it 'okay' for me to have a toke, boss?"

"As long as you can get the job done."

Ray shuffled out the door, then returned, reeking of pot. Bea put her jacket back on when she saw his eyes linger.

They worked together on the script to send to the secure network Ray had made for Indigenous Tribes. Creating the Application Programming Interface (API) was tedious work, but Ray knew his network well, and Bea was a quick learner and great at interfacing.

"It is nine o'clock," Irene looked in on them. "My shift is over, and the phone canvassers have gone home. Don't do anything I wouldn't do."

Bea and Ray immediately got back to work, heads down, until the clock neared midnight.

"I need caffeine and food," Bea broke their concentration. "I'm going to the convenience store. Do you want to come?"

"No. We're close to testing the API. Can you get me an energy drink and Zesty Mordants?"

Beaver Buzz energy drinks and Zesty Mortdants in hand, Bea passed perpetually rolling hotdogs. She had an idea but wondered if the sacrifice would be worth it, she only had one white formal business blouse. She decided to get the hotdog, putting heaped amounts of ketchup, mustard, chilli sauce and cheese whiz on it. It was threatening to spill, but that was the idea.

Back at the office, Ray called out: "The API is ready to test. Do you want to have the honour?"

"Such a gentleman." Bea submitted the first ballot. The data was received. A response was given. The dashboard on her App registered the fake ballot as the only vote for the bill. "YAY! It worked!" Bea shrieked.

"Yup. Now we need to do a few thousand cycles to ensure it's ready for the demo beta testing."

"A few thousand! Tell me you're joking?"

"No. But I have an app to automatically run the test cycles. It'll take around thirty minutes for a batch of a thousand."

"I'm done with office chairs." Bea left her jacket on her chair and took the food and drinks over to the hide-a-bed couch. She opened her drink and sipped it but waited for Ray to eat the hotdog. When he was sitting crunching on chips, she started taking big bites out of the hotdog. She made noises that did not at all sound like she was eating a hotdog. With him watching her choke down the hotdog, she accidentally squished the overflowing toppings out the end and onto her blouse. "Shit! It's my only good blouse." She leaned back to keep the glob of sauces from running down off her left breast onto the rest of her blouse. "There're paper towels over there." She pointed with her hotdog holding hand. In her other hand was the Beaver Buzz energy drink. She could not put either of them down because the coffee table was out of reach.

"I'll get them." Ray jumped up quickly, grabbing the paper towels. A dilemma confronted him when he returned. The glop was squarely on Bea's hard nipple. He held the paper towel out dumbly, paralyzed.

"Ray, my hands are full. Wipe it off for me."

Ray did so as gently as he could. Still, the slight feel he copped was electric, and it made him glow.

When Bea felt he was getting too comfortable, she said, "I did not ask for a massage!" He recoiled instantly. "I need to soak this." She put the food and drink down and ran for the sink.

"Is there anything I can help with?"

"Thank you. No."

After a couple of minutes, Bea came back into the office area, arms crossed to cover her nipples. But the side-boob view was awesome. Ray was struggling not to stare.

"Have you seen my jacket?"

Ray glanced around, then shrugged in response.

She noticed it on the office chair. "Oh, there it is."

Ray responded, "I need to smoke a joint."

Bea giggled to herself as he left, happy her desire to interface was unfolding as planned.

By the time Ray was back the first batch of tests were done. They scoured the data for errors. There were none. They started a second batch of tests, heads down on other work while the second batch ran. It worked correctly with no errors.

While doting on Ray's focused, gorgeous to Bea, face reflected in his computer screen at two in the morning, Bea noticed a news feed story notification with her picture on it. "Ray, what's that news feed? The one with me on it."

"I aw... want to say this in a way that's not creepy. It's part of a database I have that tracks how much media Direct Democracy and you get. Please understand I did this to watch how you're doing and not for some nefarious reason. You probably have something similar." Ray did not look at Bea when he said this.

"Oh, please, Hedwig, I know exactly what your reasons are." Bea ducked in toward Ray to give him a peck on the cheek but remembered they were still working and disengaged. "I'm flattered. Show me."

With a few clicks, Ray brought up the database. He started with the dashboard, a page full of charts and graphs with every metric Bea could think of and some she'd never seen.

Most interesting to Bea were the measurements of Direct Democracy and her broad-spectrum media coverage compared to her competition. The first indicator showed dots and circles representing the amount of Mainstream media coverage the individual or group has. The dots were captioned with the names of her competition in Victoria Capital.

She did not recognize the name attached to the pencil-end-sized circle next to her rivals.

Ray explained it represented the non-party leader candidate with the most national coverage, a wingnut Conservative in Ontario. A dime-sized circle was the leader of the Green Party. Bea's name was above a loony-sized circle. The three bigger circles were the NDP, Conservative, and Liberal leaders. The next indicators showed the entire social media reaction history for the parties and her competition. Again, Direct Democracy was fourth to the NDP, Conservatives, and Liberals. Ray clarified that it was not worth putting her local opponents on this indicator because they would be microscopic.

The final indicator showed a breakdown of media coverage which was initiated by the actions of the original party, versus coverage in response to Direct Democracy actions. For those challenging her for Victoria Capital the pie graph showed small slices of content initiated by the party, but the vast majority was content responding to Direct Democracy.

By all these measures, Direct Democracy, a one-candidate party, was in a class by itself.

Bea was gobsmacked by the data.

"Direct Democracy is dominating media," Ray said. "And please take this as a compliment; it's because you're playing Trump's game in a Canadian way." He stopped for a reaction. "The righteous victim."

"Comparing my campaign to President Tiny Hands." Bea was sarcastic. "Well, I never!" She tossed her hair forward and said breathily, "You are so smart, and you get me totally. Too bad we work together."

Ignoring Bea's moves, Ray clicked to another page with a line graph on it. "You've been using controversies to overwhelm the media. Your view that all media attention would only increase Direct Democracy's message is proving true. I've got a graph that shows it."

Five lines tracked the major parties and Direct Democracy's poll numbers for Victoria Capital starting from the time Ray met Bea. Circles of various sizes were identified by the legend as Direct Democracy's media campaigns or controversies. The larger the circle the greater the event reached. The graph was near real-time; it had the interview she did yesterday afternoon and the latest poll numbers that had Direct Democracy firmly in second.

Ray described how the events the circles represented impacted Direct Democracy's poll numbers. He showed that traditional campaigning tactics, like the social media campaign, interviews on independent, and interviews on mainstream media, corresponded with a steady but shallow rise in the polls.

Controversies that shone a good light on Direct Democracy had more dramatic effects than traditional campaigning. Ray pointed to examples like the ambush interview of Colleen Lauren that pushed Direct Democracy from nowhere in the polls to registering a percent. Bea's populist TikTok and flame war with Little Pee Pee's lackey took Direct Democracy into the few percent range. Crashing the debate made Direct Democracy a contender to the four major parties. All of them caused an immediate uptick. But the effect of Direct Democracy's positive controversies died quickly when opposing parties stopped sharing the story.

Controversies that made Bea look bad were the best for Direct Democracy, Ray explained. The bad cyclist channel was the first bad controversy, not big enough to demonstrate the effect, but its reach as a story was as big as any of the good media. The Knight Rider affair was the next bad controversy; its circle was at least four times the size of the biggest, good controversy. The poll numbers after Knight Rider took an immediate dip for a day or so, then shot up. The same effect had occurred for all the bad controversies with Dex Duffy and the Bea-Con Conspi-Racist circles blotting out much of the other media. Even Bea's most recent interview had a large circle because the comments had rubbed the media wrong. The reason behind the amplification of Bea's bad controversies was that the rival parties shared the stories, hoping to hurt Direct Democracy instead of making voters learn of it. Furthermore, Bea's truthfulness with her righteous victim act caused voters to see the hypocrisy of a party telling voters to trust their representative while attacking the character of the leader of Direct Democracy, a party that does not rely on the representative to make any decisions before parliament.

"Ray, I love what you've done! I love even more that you're so unaware that you think other people could make a dashboard like this. You do not cease to amaze me. You totally have figured out why Direct Democracy is doing so well. I know we're working, but I think I love you."

Ray's nonresponse to Bea's declaration suggested he was overwhelmed. She dialled it back. Pointing at the increased pole numbers after Bea-Con, she asked, "How come Bea-Con Conspi-Racist is the biggest circle but the least increase in poll numbers?"

"I don't know the exact reason, but it correlates with the overall growth of Direct Democracy in the polls. As Direct Democracy has grown, the size of the controversy must be bigger to get the same effect as the previous one. My hypothesis is that most of the increase in the polls is from voters who are new to Direct Democracy – as in, never heard of it. Each scandal exposes more unaware people to Direct Democracy, reducing the total number of uninformed voters in Victoria Capital. Thus, the outrage of the controversy must be greater to reach the last ignorant voters in Victoria Capital. For example, if the Bea-Con Conspi-Racist controversy got national coverage resulting in a two percent increase in polls for Direct Democracy, to guarantee a similar bump, the next scandal must be at the international level."

"Oh my god. I must reach the ignorant, the stupid, the people of Walmart to win." Bea's two-in-the-morning brain thought out loud. "I am the female version of the Pussy Grabbing President. Can the stupid make the right choice for all of us? All of us deserve to be heard."

"In the nicest possible way, yes, you are like the Pussy Grabbing President. No, they can't."

Bea squinted her eyes at Ray. "We will see."

Ray laughed. "But seriously, the Pussy Grabbing incident is a great example of my hypothesis. It was a month before the election and should have tanked Trump. It was the right combination of over-the-top outrage that stopped Democrats from voting because a man like that could never win, while Trump's righteous victim act empowered boomers, who thought that their 'boys will be boys' identity was threatened, to go to the polls. Nothing activates voters more than attacking their identity. That's the entire reason Trans has become such a hot topic. Nothing hurts an insecure man's identity more than his being attracted to a 'fake' woman. And the Trans community is small enough that they can use us as scapegoats. Why do you think a can of beer with a trans woman on it can cause an alcoholic hillbilly to destroy beer? The same hillbilly that wrings spilt beer sponged off the floor into a glass and drinks it to look cool on TikTok. Yet, a picture of Dylan Mulvaney on a can of beer makes it too dirty for the hillbilly to drink it."

Bea saw Ray's distress. She put her arm around him for a half hug. "This is an authorized work hug." He smiled a big smile. She stopped hugging him. "Do you think Direct Democracy can win?"

Looking at the screen, Ray replied, "It is too hard to call. If the average rate of growth from the polling is taken, Direct Democracy will probably fall just shy of winning. However, there are lots of variables that can't easily be accounted for, like voters who identify with a party in a poll but vote for Direct Democracy, one of the other candidates shitting the bed, you shitting the bed, or a big controversy. The best way to make a victory for Direct Democracy most likely is a huge scandal in the next few days. Do you have any we've not heard about?"

"I'll check my scandal calendar. Damn, the next one is not until after the election."

They chatted about nothing until the next testing cycle was done. Again, no errors were found.

"The results we have are good enough to move to the beta launch," Ray said. "But I'm concerned. This has been going too well. Normally, there are at least a few bugs to fix. Are we that good?"

"Yes. You are paranoid."

"I want to do another test with some changed parametres." Ray was already modifying the scripts.

"Fine... I need another Beaver Buzz. Do you want anything?" Bea left to get them more energy drinks, making sure all the buttons on her blazer were buttoned.

Bea decided to walk an extra block to wake herself up. This brought her by the alley of the strip mall with the convenience store, Subway, Discovery Coffee, and pizza by the slice. Silhouetted by the light of the moon was the shape of an owl. She thought it was an owl scarecrow. But it moved. She watched the barred owl that could have been Mister or one of the pair by the bandshell. It was unlikely to be Josie; she would probably be with or near her owlets. The owl swooped down into the pitch-black void next to a dumpster. The sounds told her a rat was being dispatched. The owl took off, flying down the alley to the street, and went right by her. She was sure it glanced at her. A good omen.

When Bea got back Ray greeted her. "Bea! Good news. No errors. I have one more short cycle I want to run. If it's good, we're done."

"What does 'we're done' mean?" Bea handed Ray his drink and unbuttoned one of her jacket buttons.

"It means we can move to the real-world beta testing." Ray and Bea clinked cans.

"Yes, beta testing can begin. But what does it mean for us?" Bea fiddled with the next blazer button. Ray seemed not to be picking up what she was putting down yet.

"I guess it means we're done for the night. I'm amazed how fast we did this. I was expecting to work till dawn. It was only nine hours." Ray spoke while working intently. "If the political thing doesn't work out, I can get you IT work."

"I can't believe you don't know what it means when the tests are complete." Bea unbuttoned another button.

Ray remained engrossed in the work.

"Why don't you get some fresh air and have a smoke? I can finish this."

Bea was on her last button. She was certain Ray must be aware of what she was doing. She could see her reflection in the monitors, and he could see it too. She asked one last time, "Ray, tell me you know what else ends when the testing does? Like between us. You and me."

"Bea, can you give me a few minutes? I need to concentrate."

"Oh, okay." Bea took her Beaver Buzz to the couch. She fell back on the couch with her jacket open, showing her midriff and line of cleavage but still covering her breasts.

"It is done," Ray called. "We are beta test ready. 'Being done' means we are no longer working together." He looked at her slyly. "It was obvious. But you deserved your own medicine."

"Jerk! Come over here. Kiss me."

Ray did as Bea said. After a long kiss that somehow did not disturb her jacket's strategic position, she pulled him onto her. He resisted, sitting down on the couch and trembling a little. He said, "Bea," but could not say more.

Bea sat up to meet Ray eye to eye. "Ray, I understand the kids' books in the Little Libraries, Hedwig, and the tattoos. I don't need you to explain any of the whys. I know you are the man I want to love. I might need to know some hows. Sex should be like the Special Olympics; lots of fucked up noises and faces, with everyone a winner. Let's be winners."

Nervously, Ray said, "I'm not sure I'm ready to be in a relationship with you."

"Be in the now. Let's talk about the future in the future. You need this. I need this. Let's do this."

"But..."

"I love you. There are no buts." She kissed him.

Ray laid her back on the couch but stopped abruptly, backing off.

Bea opened her jacket in hopes of being ravished.

He said, "But..." She put a finger to his lips. "But the lights."

"Yeah, the fluorescent lights are hideous. And people might see us. I'll get them."

Bea used the interruptions to unfold the bed and get her bag of tricks.

Adult situations ensued.

At the break of nautical twilight, Bea and Ray were in a post-coital cuddle with little stamina left. Bea felt it was comfortable enough to ask, "How long have you had a crush on me?"

"What?"

"Ajay said you had a thing for me before we met."

"I was a teen when I saw your Star Wars video. I instantly loved it. The message was so bold. I got it immediately. It shows my truth and the truth of all the weak. You are so sexy in it. I still watch it. I love your other videos, too, but that one does it for me."

Bea silenced him with a kiss, then squeezed. "I'm glad you understand. I'm happy it turned you on. I watch that one from time to time. It is the most artistic thing I've ever made. I love it. Everyone should watch it. I want it to be out there forever. I didn't know how true the message was at the time. And I will never be Princess Leia again."

"I understand."

"Tonight was great. Next time, if there is one, I'd like to have a device with straps. I was going to borrow one from Joice, but hers was a tentacle. I wasn't sure you'd be cool with that."

"Tentacle fine. Borrowed! Disgusting!"

"Sanitized, of course."

"You're a barbarian, but I love that about you."

They fell asleep with the late summer's sun growing brighter.

The jingling of keys, working of the lock and door woke Ray. He roused Bea. Grumbling and the sound of a walker scuffing along the floor told them Harold had opened the office. They looked at each other, hoping Harold might not see them, but it was inevitable. Ray did his best to cover them up. Harold's gaze was at the floor as he neared them. Harold looked up. "JESUS MURPHY!" Harold stood gawking. Bea giggled. Ray pretended to be invisible.

"I forgot to get coffee..." Harold announced. "I need a strong coffee." He turned, redirecting his walker. "I can't believe I forgot coffee. I'm going to be fifteen minutes late." Louder, but to no one. "Fifteen minutes, that is how long it will take to get my coffee."

Bea broke out laughing.

Ray donned his clothes, unable to see the mirth in the situation.

She put on her clothes, stripped the hide-a-bed, and then packed away her equipment.

He nervously fidgeted.

They left.

Holding Ray's hand, Bea, still giggling, led him to get coffee.

Ray said, "I don't want to bump into Harold."

"We're going to Starbucks. Harold never goes there."

Bea was recognized in the coffee shop, which earned her a free coffee and kudos for taking on the establishment.

Ray hung back, awkward with the situation.

"Where do we stand?" Bea asked once they were seated. "Last night was awesome. This morning, I get the same awkward feeling from you as on our last date."

"Last night was great. I was more comfortable with you than I have ever been. This morning is different. I wanted to hit the person in the store that identified you, for no reason. I don't like that they like you. I'm terrified they'll find out... who I am. I feel like everyone is trying to pry into my life when I am around you."

"That is a problem."

They sat quietly as the sun warmed them and the coffee cooled. The Imperial March muffled from Bea's bag. She scrambled for it.

"Bea, you did it again," Marcus seethed. "You used Sam as a pawn. It's not a threat anymore."

"All I said was I would like to see my son in Ottawa," Bea responded as neutrally as she could. "That is hardly using Sam. Stop harassing me with calls. Do what your little mind tells you is right. I'll be in Ottawa to see Sam when the new session of Parliament starts. Hopefully, I won't have to tell too much of the truth to get there. Remember, you have much to lose when the truth is told."

Fuming profanities rose audibly from the phone's speaker as Bea mashed the end call button. She looked up at Ray. "Now where were we?"

"That was your ex?"

Bea nodded.

"It sounds like you must win. A big salacious scandal framed the right way could put you over the top."

"Agreed." Bea changed topics. "But what about us? Did last night change anything?" There was a long pause. "I'll be sad if it didn't, but I understand."

A woman walking into the shop pointed to Bea. "Canadian Karen! LOL! I'm voting for you." Bea waved politely but turned abruptly back to Ray.

"The hair on my neck stood up when that woman called to you. My boundaries stand. I need to be more secure with myself before being so public."

"Can we smash in private?"

"Let's talk after the election," Ray placated.

Bea was sure that after the election, the discussion would not change.

"Are you going to vote for me?"

"No. I don't believe the people of Walmart have my interests in mind. I would like to think the majority will do what's right for the minority, but I'm a realist."

"What if I do that thing again? The thing I did in bed." Bea drew satisfaction from Ray's embarrassed reaction.

🦉 Owls, Doughnuts, and Democracy, by Jason A. N. Taylor 🦉

They talked and had one last kiss before he got on his scooter, and she got on her bike. She stopped at the park and sat with the owl family, having to feel some feelings before work.

At home, Bea sat down at her computer, ensuring her VPN was on. She signed into a sock puppet account on a Liberal Facebook Group. She toyed with posting a link and then posted the link. She had to win.

27.

A few hours later, Bea's phone rang, flashing Irene's caller ID. Could bad news travel that fast? She took a deep breath before answering. "Hi Irene, what's up?"

"You caused a huge scandal!"

"I did?"

"Wendy yelled, 'Well, I never,' so loud people on the street looked to see if we were okay. Morty feels violated. In his own words, 'it was like having a prostate exam.' He almost had a heart attack. None of the oldsters will ever sit on that chesterfield again. And all the other chairs are so uncomfortable."

Bea played dumb. "What are you talking about?"

"Your large device got caught in the hide-a-bed. Morty felt a lump in the cushion. Wendy helped him investigate. They found it." Irene paused. "Umm, the ah, purple, you know…"

"Oh my God! I thought it was something else. I'm so sorry!"

"Deary, don't apologize to me," Irene cracked up. "I found it hilarious. The others are traumatized, but they're so old the memories won't last. I've hidden it away in your desk. They don't know it was your thingy. I am sure you will get questions. Make something up."

"Still, Irene, I apologize. I didn't want you to have to deal with that. Harold came in early. We had to rush. I missed it."

"Harold found you two in bed!" Irene let out a cackle. "He said nothing. Not that he would. How can the day get any better."

The next afternoon at the office was for beta testing of the App but Bea arrived early with a rented steam cleaner. She cleaned the couch and made a point of sending out a WhatsApp message to the membership verifying the chesterfield had been sanitized.

Derek showed up and helped Bea take the steam cleaner back. The stars of the beta test arrived shortly after. Morty, Wendy, Cameron, and Ms. Anderson were there to show anyone could use the App. They were ringers. Mia had coached them to act surprised and shocked at the simplicity even though they had performed the operation often during its development.

Bea saw the four Computer Science students Ajay rounded up awkwardly standing around outside, Ajay having not given them the exact suite number. Bea saw them and showed them in. This was the real test. Bea had confidence in Ray's work. These students would get schooled.

Not long after, a few reporters and camera people arrived too. Bea encouraged them to talk with the testers. The oldsters using the App played up their digital ignorance. Morty told the reporters of the time he called a 1-888 number for Microsoft, but hackers took his personal information. Ms. Anderson asked a camera person if the tablet was broken when its screen went dark because of inactivity. Cameron and Wendy said they never used the computer without the assistance of a grandchild. The reporters were amazed at how quickly these technophobes figured out the App.

Meanwhile the Computer Science students were not making any headway but were certain a breakthrough was near.

When the oldsters were finished demonstrating the ease of the app, and before the students had given up, Bea got a message from Ajay: Liberal vloggers are sharing the Princess Leia porno video!

Bea breathed slowly and deeply. She had been fearing this, knowing that if it did not come out, it would be the Sword of Damocles hanging over her head for the rest of her life. It was the leverage Marcus could wield at any time to make her behave. Now, it was out and could no longer surprise anyone. As worried as she had been, she was happy the cat was out of the bag. After all, she was not ashamed of the video. Quite the contrary, it was art. She loved it.

Ajay: Should we do something? We could limit its spread... maybe.

Bea: No.

Disengaged from the scene at the office, Bea's cynical thinking was fixated on dispersion of the video. How widely the video would be shared? How quickly was it moving? Would people get it?

Thirty minutes later, Bea got another message from Justin: I can't say this nicely. There's a porno of you on Conservative Reddit. +10k upvotes in the last two hours.

Bea: OMG! They found it. WHAT AM I GOING TO DO!

Minutes later, multiple members of Direct Democracy messaged of the impending catastrophe.

Mia stared at her phone, slowly mouthed, 'Holy fuck!' And swiped the screen to close the video. She came over to Bea. "Ah…" Mia kept her voice down. "There's a porno of a woman dressed like Princess Leia that the internet says is you. Its going viral."

"I know. It is me. I don't know what to do."

"Maybe you should sit down." Mia walked Bea to the couch. "I'll get Derek and Irene."

In the few minutes it took Mia to relay the message to Derek and Irene the reporters started getting messages.

A reporter immediately walked toward Bea like a shark smelling blood in the water, phone in hand. "Is this you in the video?"

Bea glanced at the beginning of the video. She was dressed as Princess Leia. She was enticing someone not yet seen by revealing naughty bits. She could not respond. The reporter persisted. Other media people smelled the blood and moved into a semi-circle around her.

"Yes!" Bea broke. "It's me! It is me! I am Princess Leia!" She pulled her legs up onto the chesterfield curling up. "Now go away!" She began to bawl.

Bea's crying caught the ears of the oldsters. Wendy charged into the group screaming, "Get away from her!"

Wendy's small body did not move the group, but Cameron's scooter bearing down, horn honking and knocking over chairs in his wake did. He roared, "Out of my way or you'll get run over! My scooter's drawn blood before!"

Cameron parked between the reporters and Bea. Morty and Ms. Anderson solidified the barrier, obscuring the camera sightlines. Wendy sat downside the still rocking and weeping Bea. Derek led Irene and Mia into the gaggle.

"Bea has no comment on this." Derek called. "You are welcome to continue covering the beta test. You are not welcome to question Bea. This is private property."

Owls, Doughnuts, and Democracy, by Jason A. N. Taylor

They hustled Bea to the privacy of the backroom where Bea regained some composure. "Irene, Mia, Wendy, thank you. I was overwhelmed. I need a few minutes..."

"Take the time you need," Irene responded. Her sentiment was echoed by the others.

Bea retreated into the washroom. So many feelings were tied up in that video, the most viewed production Bea had ever made. It was art. It had great pop references. It commented on today's unequal society. It had caused a stir when it first came out on Porn Hub. Over a million watched it in the first year. Certainly, it was reposted all over the internet. It would always be there, why would she remove it? She loved it. She would never take it down.

It forced her to get a paternity test. It was the evidence used at the divorce proceedings to take Sam from her. It was used to make her ashamed of herself. It was proof she was a bad mother and, therefore, a bad person. She never found out how Sabrina found it to use against her. She protected it by not implicating Marcus. It was only a threat to Marcus and not to Bea. She loved it, happy with the views her modicum of fame would garner it. She wanted people to see her art.

But it was also a time bomb that kept her terrified it would explode every day since she'd accepted leadership, worried Direct Democracy would be hurt by the shrapnel.

It was something Sam could get teased for, an awkward conversation with him that would have to happen in the near future. Not to worry, she was good at awkward conversations.

It was right to plant the video; she felt better having put it out there. She was in control, wiping away tears. She would let the shame others heaped on her go by showing the world how she saw the video.

Bea sat with her phone on the toilet viewing the video on Porn Hub. It was going viral again. Fifty thousand views since she last checked. The page was slow, suggesting the server was straining. She giggled with glee, thinking of all the people watching her and getting the message. She got off her throne, freshened up and left the washroom.

"Irene, are there any reporters out there?"

"I think there are. We can go out the back. Or I can see if Derek can shoo them away. What do you want to do?"

"I want to talk with them."

"Are you sure?"

"Yes."

None of the media had left. Bea addressed them: "I am Princess Leia in that video. I will talk with the media about it tomorrow. I am disheartened that my opponents feel it is necessary to continually attack my character. It is obvious that my past has no bearing on the duties I will perform as an MP for Direct Democracy." With that, Bea turned to leave the office.

The media followed, asking questions that she did not acknowledge.

Biking away, Bea reviewed the scene in her mind. The reporters had a clip of her breaking down then finding strength to respond. And now finally her taking off defiantly. Just the underdog message she sought. She rode the rest of the way home randomly yelling at cars and pedestrians.

At home the many emails and messages suggesting every course of action from blanket apologies to attacking the media to finding and doxing the person who shared the video did not distract her. She was happy she used a VPN. She messaged the membership to arrange a meeting that night. Then she went for a run to burn some energy and time.

At the Home that night, Karen was getting barraged by members of the Blue Bridge Club. With the lounge room schedule in hand like a shield Karen insisted: "Harold booked the room fair and square."

"Harold doctored the schedule," Fred argued. "It's fake!"

Bea passed wraith-like by the scene, making sure not to get involved. She stopped outside the lounge listening to the tone of the room. "Are you sure she's coming?" The voice came from one of the newer members Bea did not know. "I wouldn't show up if I just burnt the party down."

Owls, Doughnuts, and Democracy, by Jason A. N. Taylor

"Bea is tougher than cat shit and twice as nasty!" Harold thundered. "She'll be here. But what's with that defeatist attitude. Bea is the reason we have a chance to win. Have some respect!"

Taking her entrance cue, Bea strode in. After a collective gasp the room fell quiet. Using her phone to quiet the TV. she strode confidently to the podium. She took nearly a minute to meet the eyes of each group member. "Do you know why I was attacked?"

No one spoke.

"Because we're winning. Direct Democracy is a threat to every party's status quo. This lowliest of blows is their last and most desperate attempt to stop us."

Bea paused to dab wetness from her eyes. Irene put a box of tissue on the table for her.

"I knew this was coming. Those of you who have been here since the beginning will remember my disclosure at the leadership election. I highlighted my disqualifying baggage because I knew this video was out there. I been waiting for it to come out every time Direct Democracy gained ground in the polls. Now it is out, I am not going to quit."

"Are you delusional?" The same unfamiliar member Bea had overheard, challenged her. "Direct Democracy has fallen five points since yesterday. We're only a half a point ahead of third place."

"We're going to use the attention to win."

"There's less than a week to go."

"There's time. Let me show you."

The oldsters collectively gasped, preparing a 'well I never' as Bea waved her phone to cast to the TV. what they expected would be the porno. Sighs of relief were heard when Ray's graph came up.

"What our competition doesn't know is that our voters can separate scandal from our message. Here are the poll numbers and my scandals." With a hand, she traced the data over the duration of the scandal. "Notice the pattern; Direct Democracy dips with the onset of scandal, then it recovers to a higher level in about a week. The bigger the scandal the larger the rebound. We will win.

"My ex has told me he will fight for sole custody of Sam over this video." Bea grabbed a tissue to dab her eyes. "This attack is extremely personal and negatively life-changing for me. I have been victimized by our opposition. I could lose my son over this. We must win."

Starting with Harold and Irene, then Derek, Joice, Wendy, Justin, Cat, Rick, Tyrell, Mia, Ethan, and the rest began to chant. "We must win for Sam!"

When the chant died down Bea continued, "The plan is simple. Tonight, and tomorrow until the press conference, defend me in whatever way you feel is right. Most of all, share the shit out of all content related to the video, good, bad, or ugly. When the press conference occurs, share it as widely as possible. Remember, our gains in the polls might not show up until the weekend, which will feel very far away. Then we must up our ground game and make the last Bea-Con the biggest yet."

"Bea…" Derek stood up. "We are all worried about you. I must ask for the group, are you 'okay' to keep going?" Nearly half the crowd murmured.

"Thank you for asking. No. I'm not okay, but I will keep going because Direct Democracy is that important. Direct Democracy is worth it. You are worth it." Bea sniffled for a second. "I didn't want this to come out. I'm happy if people watch the video but I don't expect you to or for you to like it. For anybody needing to talk with me about your feelings on this, I'll stay. Tomorrow I will be sharing a 'sanitized' version of the Princess Leia video that explains its importance."

"Ajay has investigated the account that shared your video." Cat stood, speaking authoritatively. "It seems to be a sock puppet account used to disseminate Direct Democracy messages to the Liberals. It was probably someone in Direct Democracy."

"Cat…" Bea smiled uncomfortably. "I understand the desire to find a Judas, but the reality is if it was not one person it would be someone else. The best revenge will be winning."

The group resumed the "'We must win for Sam.'" Then slowly filtered out of the room. Many gave Bea support and consolation but, in some cases, sought an apology from Bea for not coming forward about the video.

Bea made sure to consult Cat, Joice, Mia, and Ethan for help with the press conference tomorrow. When the planning was over, she pulled Cat aside. "Please tell Ajay to stop looking for who posted the video."

"Oh?"

"It won't be helpful for any of us." Bea winked. "If it came from one of our group the internal conflict would hurt us."

"Oh! I get your meaning."

The office was filled with more reporters and cameras than at any previous press conference. The borrowed lectern from the Home stood in front of the borrowed big screen T.V., both strategically placed for the cameras.

Bea did one final check of her outfit, hair, and makeup amid the steady drone of the press outside. She texted Harold to check the mic and TV and watched as he walked to the lectern.

"Test... test," Harold tapped the mic. It made an awful noise. "Holy doodle! The mic is working. Can you see the screen behind me?" The camera people said no. He signalled the blinds closed until the camera people said yes. "You on the left; your camera is outside the line; move it to the right." He waited as the camera was moved to the other side of a tape line. He looked at the door to the back of the office.

Bea gave him a thumbs up.

"Beaver Biscuits!" The press focused on Harold. "I know your ilk cross boundaries for a living. However, anyone who does not follow these rules will be 86ed like a logger the day after payday. Bea will be making a statement. You will not interrupt her. She will not take questions. The conference is over when she says it is." Harold paused amid murmurings. "Most of all, don't act like swine. This is a sensitive topic. When there is quiet, we will start." Harold left the lectern.

Bright-eyed, Bea, in her dark suit with a short skirt, waited a good thirty seconds before walking to the lectern looking powerful and fabulous. Star Wars fans would recognize her Princess Leia cinnamon bun-like braids. Once she knew all the cameras were on her she signalled for the video to play.

A bigger-than-life-size image of her in a sexy, revealing white toga-like dress appeared. She had the cinnamon bun like braids, red lipstick, and Leia demeanor. Her visage had not changed in the intervening nine years. The video was heavily edited for a PG-13 rating and to speed it up. Bea was to fill in the gaps in dialogue because there was no way to edit out the egregious amount of profanity. It started playing a few minutes into the scene after Leia had been caught playing on her own. Toga half off, Leia stood looking at a mostly naked Darth Vader. Both were appropriately obscured to not show anything naughty.

"The elite, the empire, the traditional parties, the powerful, shared my video to wreck your chance of being heard with Direct Democracy and destroy my chance to see my kid again. If it was so dangerous, why didn't I take it off the internet? I could have easily done that. But I did not because it is art. Let me show you what I see."

Leia moved to the centre of the screen to be obscured by narrating Bea: "Leia is me... but she is also all people who want equality and equity. Leia is a Princess that dared to rebel against the old order. She wants a universe not dominated by an unseen self-serving force, an elite. Every one of us— women in trades, men home-caring children, indigenous people struggling in a colonial world—who strives for a dream that does not fit the norm is a rebel."

"Then there is Darth Vader, the elite of the Empire with all the power. Able to wield a force stronger than any individual. The force of authority, class, chauvinism, colonialism, hierarchy, patriarchy, race, religion, status quo, tradition. The unseen force of the powerful, the system of favouritism and oppression."

In the video Darth Vader raised a hand, to use the force, shooting Bea's words in electric font beams. Leia stood rigid, fighting the force. Bea said, "It is harder to struggle than to submit."

Unable to fight the force, Leia gasped, "Bleep me. Bleep me in my bleep." Removing her clothes, Leia turned away from Darth Vader and got down on all fours.

Owls, Doughnuts, and Democracy, by Jason A. N. Taylor

Bea positioned herself to hide Leia's unmentionables. "Leia is asking for Vader to ride her dirt road." Vader kneeled behind Leia. Leia bit her lip grimacing, rocking forward rhythmically with a slight grunting. "The force trains us to fulfill the role its system has for us regardless of our desire. The force is used to prepare us for the acquired taste. After a while, one gets used to the pain and discomfort. With enough training and preparation, off-roading can be fun." Leia's face softened becoming cherubic as she approached orgasm. "It is the few moments like this that one lives for, when under the thumb of the Empire, the elite. The Empire's hegemony and dominance forces me to live in the norm. Because of it, I cannot live the harmless life I desire. A life where I am heard and respected for who I am. Being forced to live in the norm when you are different is soul-destroying. That short, happy moment is obliterated by the throbbing starfish from getting cornholed by the elite." Leia lay prostrate on the ground with Darth Vader standing above her.

The video split-screened, defeated Leia on one side and Darth Vader's mask face on the other. "The force that the Empire, the elite, the privileged, the establishment uses is wielded by a masked person. There is no individual to blame for the forces, the systemic inequity, injustice and indignities that keep the average, idealist, rebellious, different, person down. Only a pervasive sense that the average citizen is not being heard, resulting in a world not becoming better for the majority."

"Democracy is the opposite of the force." Bea pounded a fist in the air. "It takes the mask off. It takes power away from the elite minority. Direct Democracy is the tool that breaks the system. Direct Democracy will not let me be Princess Leia again!" She took the pins out of her hair and shook her head, unraveled the cinnamon bun braid into flowing tresses.

The screen behind Bea flashed to a bright background, Athena in the centre with an owl perched on her arm. Athena very much resembled Bea. "By describing the meaning of my video, I am defending Direct Democracy from an attack by the elite. A video that explains the system is rigged by the elite to screw us. Isn't it ironic… don't you think?"

"You might not like my art. Or me. But think of the depths, the establishment, the elite have sunk to, victimizing me in this way. Why? Because I am honestly trying to give you more democracy, more say in your affairs. Their machinations to win one more seat may lose me the little custody of my son I have. Think how diabolical it is for them to exploit this video. I may be nasty, yell at cyclists, cycle badly, not let a jerk disabled person get away with bullshit, bend the rules to make rent, and unknowingly break the law to get my child a birthday gift. But my sins are nothing compared to wealthy, powerful, parties and the party forming government attacking me so vilely. Where are the videos of J.T. and Sophie, they must be out there? How come there's no picture of Little Pee Pee's wee, wee wee? There must be a Sikh Separatist movement training video of Jagmeet shooting an assault rifle. Justin and Sophie got a divorce, yet the opposition only attacked him above the belt. This is indicative of the elite protecting the elite. One standard for the establishment and one for us. It is anything goes if the average person is trying to take power from the elite."

"The stupidest part is that for me to do my job as a Direct Democracy Member of Parliament I only need to be honest. They only proved how honest I am. I could have lied and deleted the video. I could have said the video was a deepfake. I am also honest when I say I love the video. I love my son and want this job so I can see him. I truly love democracy. I know Direct Democracy will give us more equality and allow for more diversity of opinion. It will help rebalance the scales of power, taking power from the elite. It may make them give us proportional representation as a consolation prize."

"We must say no to the elite taking more power by keeping us separated with wedge issues. Direct Democracy can unite us and take the power from wedge issues."

"If you think there is no issue with equity in our country, ask yourself why no one has ever asked, 'who is behind the Darth Vader mask' in my video. No one cares because he is a man. It is not shameful for a man. Equity is a problem in Canada. Direct Democracy will create more equality. Vote to be heard. Vote Direct

Democracy." The bright light from the TV. went off, dimming the room enough that Bea could make a ninja's exit out the back. She had to get to her day job.

The shift at the coffee shop kept Bea from dwelling on the fact she had just made a PG-13 summary of her Princess Leia and the Force amateur porno video and released it to the world. She was proud to have stayed away from her phone for the six-hour shift and decided to catch the sunset at the inner harbour before checking in with the owls.

Maneuvering through the throng of cruise ship tourists, Bea heard a fiddler. She turned up Government Street to see that it was the local busker, Darth Fiddler, in a Darth Vader mask. People began to notice as she took a selfie video with him. Soon there were a dozen people lining up to take pictures with Darth Fiddler and her. None of the people were brazen enough to say anything of her Princess Leia and the Force video. Darth Fiddler did not know her but by the end of the meeting she had got his vote.

The interaction with Darth Fiddler had Bea thinking the video must have gone viral. But she was not yet ready to interact with it. She decided to turn her phone off, see the owls and have a good night's sleep. She sent a What's app message to the inner circle to let them know she would be offline.

Shakespeare and Muffin were stretching, getting ready for a night flight. Both owlets were now the size of full-grown barred owls. Bea knew that soon she would not see them together. After a few minutes, Josie called, "WHO COOKS FOR YOU!" The owlets took off to find Josie. Bea could not follow them into the works yard, so she biked home.

28.

Bea avoided her phone first thing in the morning so that she could get a run in but later was unable to ignore the numerous Canadian news clips. All the outlets ran thumbnails with Darth Vader and Princess Leia. CTV had Junior commenting on her video. Unsurprisingly, J.T. did not have much to say but was certain the person who originally shared the video was not a Liberal.

It was time for a happy dance. Bea pounded the floor, proud her strategy had worked. The original Princess Leia and the Force porno was too vulgar, but the PG-13 version changed that. Every news agency could comment on it without referencing Porn Hub or having a reporter awkwardly try to describe Darth Vader technically sodomizing his daughter.

Of all the news clips, Bea was most proud of the *Power and Politics* segment. Evan Solomen argued with Little Pee Pee over who was more morally corrupt: Bea for making the videos or the parties attempting to defame her by sharing them. Evan argued that Bea was not responsible for the depravity she exposed people to because she had no choice but to defend herself from the big parties' attacks. Little Pee Pee tried to argue that Bea was a disgusting trollop who had done irreparable damage to all the children who love Star Wars. When the two agreed to disagree, Evan asked Little Pee Pee what he thought of Direct Democracy. Little Pee Pee responded that he believed in democracy but could not see a deranged person like Bea making decisions for Canadians. Evan corrected Little Pee Pee; Bea was not going to make decisions; rather, Bea would vote for what the people in her riding decided upon. Little Pee Pee still could not get the concept.

With every clip, Direct Democracy had to be discussed to provide context for Bea's Princess Leia and the Force video. Every clip discussing Bea's Princess Leia and the Force video had an ad for Direct Democracy in it.

Notifications were in the thousands; the Direct Democracy social media sphere had burst like a hydrogen bomb. Previous to the Princess Leia press conference, only Reddit and Twitter—with their Not Safe For Work – NSFW settings—had exploded when the original porno was shared. Since releasing the PG-13 version, TikTok, Instagram, and Facebook were melting down. Arguments, opinions, explanations, and questions about the video dominated everyone's feed. Bea found it surreal watching TikToks questioning her sanity, demonstrating how to make the cinnamon braids, outraged that anal was being given a bad name, critiquing the presumption that Princess Leia was for a democratic egalitarian society, taking offence to the wokeness, taking offence at the unwokeness, Americans confused that Canada had elections, speculating if Direct Democracy can work on any of the Star Wars planetary systems, Star Wars cosplayers critical of Bea's costume, angry that Princess Leia's shoes were not accurate to the movie, disturbed that Darth Vader did not have any burns which must have been a slight to burn victims, enquiries regarding Darth Vader's you know what. All these short videos had to at least say, Bea Jensen, Leader of the Direct Democracy party. Direct Democracy's message parroted again and again.

The virality of the message had not translated into a similar rise in the polls. Direct Democracy was at the same percentage as it was the day after the release of the original Princess Leia and the Force video. Bea did her best to tell herself there had only been one poll since she released the PG-13 video. Her faith was renewed when she thought of Ray's rationale for Direct Democracy's success.

Before Bea left for work, she pushed out the best clips from all the social media platforms on WhatsApp for the Direct Democracy Army of Oldsters to share. It almost made her late for work but with some creative interpretation of the rules of the road she arrived on time.

Work was a nightmare.

The regular customer's behaviours were all over the place. Most of them recognized Bea. When they did there were a few variations of response. Avoiding eye contact and verbal communication. Trying to empathize with her, but the proximity to the topic of anal sex resulted in an awkward change to discussing the weather. Wanting to be in her next video. Discussing a favourite conspiracist theory. Leaving when they saw she was going to serve them. Some hung around the counter, lobbing their favourite political theory at her, hoping for the volley to be returned. All of them slowed service down to a crawl. Nothing is worse than government workers not getting coffee in a timely fashion. The vibe was not happy.

Then there were the irregular customers. In a long rant, a religious person told Bea to go to hell. Bea had to respond, "At least you won't be there." Three would-be suiters suggested they get intimate in the washroom, at the beach, or at a nearby hotel. Bea asked them to Google Lorena Bobbitt and snipped in the air with scissors. Many hurled insults from the street. And one guy in a robe had to be kicked out for thinking he was Hugh Hefner.

When the manager had dealt with 'Hugh Hefner', Bea was summoned into the back room. The manager and Bea agreed that it would be best if Bea gave up her shifts until after the election.

Minutes later, Bea was pushing out another video of how she had been victimized. She could not work without being harassed. It was the fault of the Liberals for exploiting her Princess Leia video.

At home, Bea got on Direct Democracy's Discord to rally the troops. The discussion was negative. The inner circle was doing their best to keep the membership's hopes up. It was hard to message 'stay the course' when the course was creating an exponential growth of drama with no rise in the polls. Bea waded into the discussion, trying to buoy Direct Democracy's spirits. Many members voiced anger at Bea's actions, arguing that they distracted from Direct Democracy's message. It was the message of everyone being heard that resonated, not Bea's drama and victimhood.

As the evening darkened to night, Bea alternated between cheerleading on the Discord and making more propaganda. She streamed her reactions to mainstream media, making a video to show the astounding number of dick pictures sent to Direct Democracy in the last twenty-four hours. She posted the graphs Ray made with the caption, 'if a Direct Democracy story goes international, we will win.'

A notification came up from YouTube. A large American progressive internet news network, *The Young Turks* – TYT, were running a story on Direct Democracy. Eyes sparkling, Bea watched

Ana Kasparian provide commentary on the Princess Leia video. "You know, I don't like how this woman, Bea, is making her point. I find it really cringe... but it is effective. What else can she do after the Liberals..?" Ana turned to Cenk Uygur for clarification.

"The Liberals are like the Canadian Democrats," Cenk responded. "Sort of centre left."

"Really? And they attacked a party campaigning for more democracy by sharing a porno video the leader of the party made. A one-candidate party? That's low. I can't believe they did that. Talk about punching down."

Cenk used his catchphrase, "OOFFFFF COURRRSSSE! Ana, Direct Democracy did the one thing no political party can do today. They said they would give more power to the people. They will do anything to keep power. OOFFFFF COURRRSSSE!"

"It is sick. Truly sick. The woman lost custody of her kid over this."

"But Ana, Bea is a fighter. The Democrats could learn from her, but they don't have the guts. Bea threw it right back at them. She said, 'This is me, deal with it...' and 'How dare you shame me and make me a victim? I won't let you.' We need politicians like Bea. Strong and righteous."

"Why didn't we hear about Direct Democracy before now?" Ana questioned. "Bea has a great story with old people using the internet." She laughed at this. "It seems like a great idea. It could easily work here."

Cenk gave a brief explanation of Direct Democracy. Then he said, "We have not heard of Direct Democracy because substance does not matter. It's the 'likes' and controversy that fuels politics, not substance. I watched Bea's early videos when I saw the story. She literally tells her audience she is creating controversy to make Direct Democracy seen. She strives to never inject her political views into Direct Democracy and she's truthful, to her own detriment. Bea Jensen; honest Abe for the 2020s."

This was game-changing. Having Americans comment on Canadian politics is most influential to the Canadian psyche. Having the popular, powerful kid at school take interest in you is what every second stringer wants. All Canadians blush when a T.V. show has a Canadian in it like *How I Met Your Mother's* Robin, or at the success of a Canadian actor like Ryan Reynolds. J.T. benefited from this in the middle 2010s, when American late-night TV crowned him the sexiest politician. Even Canadians who wanted to Fuck Trudeau wanted to fuck Trudeau.

Bea shared the TYT story immediately, then made a stitched video with her added responses to Ana and Cenk's commentary.

The evening got better when Bea checked the polls. Confirming Ray's prediction, Direct Democracy was on the rise again, gaining two points, taking them within three points of the leading Liberal. She smacked the Discord with this new data, guaranteeing they would pull ahead of the Liberals. She left off with: "The best hockey coach ever, Scotty Bowman, said, 'Statistics are for losers,' and 'there is nothing so uncertain as a sure thing.' We must continue to work the system. It has brought us here from nowhere. We have four more days to win. I will be joining corner rallies, taking a shift at the office, knocking on doors, working social media, holding press conferences and prepping for Sunday's last Bea-Con. What will you be doing to help Direct Democracy win?"

The members were reinvigorated by the poll results.

In the evening, the second media tsunami hit: American late night T.V. found Bea's Princess Leia PG-13 video. Steven Colbert's Meanwhile featured the irony of it being used to castigate Bea while describing how the real force is systemic oppression.

Seth Meyers' The Kind of Story We Need Right Now was hijacked by the Jokes Seth Can't Tell crew, Amber Ruffin and Jenny Hagel. They timelined the entire Direct Democracy story with each evil twist and showed Bea as 'the hero we need right now.' They debated whether or not Bea was actually a black lesbian but could not come to a conclusion because Canadians are so foreign.

The Daily Show's Ronny Chieng polled Star Wars fans to see if Bea had accurately explained the Princess Leia-Darth Vader dynamic. Due to lack of personal experience, none of the nerds could comment on riding the dirt road. They did, however, agree that Direct

Owls, Doughnuts, and Democracy, by Jason A. N. Taylor

Democracy seemed like a great political system whose time had come.

Samantha Bee brought out the ice skates to reinterpret the video on ice.

Jimmy Kimmel compared Bea to a good Klan Mom Marg or Handjob Bobert because everything is gooder in Canada.

All these segments included context for what Direct Democracy was, how the host felt it was a positive step, and who Bea was. She dominated American late-night comedy – the media that really matters to Canadians. Each YouTube clip got a million or more views. These did not include all the other social media platforms or traditional TV. Every Canadian social media creator joined the bandwagon, like a Canuck fan after a three-game win streak. Each clip from an American outlet found at least two follow-on shares by Canadian media.

The poll numbers on Thursday night had risen again. Direct Democracy was a point away from tying the Liberals. Fearing that the members might become complacent, Bea printed a sign for the office that read: "Statistics are for losers. There is nothing so uncertain as a sure thing. Direct Democracy does not look at poll numbers." She followed this up with a WhatsApp explaining that they must follow the system and not focus on the score. Poll numbers were banned from discussion.

Friday afternoon, Bea's YouTube feed notified her of something she had been waiting for since she was sixteen. Rick Mercer and the retirees of This Hour Has 22 Minutes responded to her love letter in a video. It started with Rick pretending to open the lost letter and realizing it was from Bea, who' he'd just seen all over the news. He calls a friend, 'Marge Delehunty', aka Mary Walsh, the Xena Warrior Princess of Canadian political comedy. "Marge, I got this letter from Bea Jensen. She's trying something new in politics. I want to help her, but the letter makes me fear for my safety as a gay man. She's a little obsessive. Can you help her?"

"Yes…" Marge answered in a walker, trailing a green-screened Pierre Poilievre and awkwardly trying to brandish her sword. "I'm following up with Little Pee Pee right now. But it's hard to keep up."

Marge took a megaphone from her walker and yelled: "Mr. Pee Pee! Skippy! Pierre! Praise be to God. You've got to change your tact, or you're going to lose your populist image to that upstart, Bea Jensen. I hear she shops at Walmart, lives in a rented apartment, works at a coffee shop and worst of all, she is truthful. What lie can you tell to make people believe you are a true populist? You could start talking about how big your hands are. That could distract a few people from the truth that you're a landlord who's only ever had a government job." Little Pee Pee starts to run. "Try going to a Swiss Chalet or getting mud on your boots; it might help with your image. Oh dammit! He's getting away."

"Thank you, Marg…" Rick's phone was well away from his ear due to the megaphone blare. "I knew I could count on you."

Rick dialled one more number.

"Well, well, well. If it isn't Rick Mercer, the kind of guy I'd want to take clothes shopping." It was Cathy Jones as Babe Bennett, a liberated nineteen-forties gal. "Are you inviting me to Holt Renfrew?"

"No. But I got this letter from a woman you can help. Bea Jensen, leader of Direct Democracy."

"Rick, do I look like some kind of prude? Bea and I are cut from the same cloth. I'm all for women being heard; when I'm not heard, I get a headache, and a man goes to bed unsatisfied, if you know what I mean. Bea's a dish, and she doesn't need my help; she's got spunk… that's not right… she's got cojones… that doesn't fit either. Bea's the kind of woman that has what men have in spades but in a feminine kind of way and that can leave guys feeling a little rubbery, limp, if you will. We need more swell birds like Bea, who can turn it around on all the crumbs out there. I'm just goofing around!"

Bea impulsively commented that she was willing to try and turn Rick if he was into it. But she deleted it and left a more appropriate comment.

Saturday was spent pounding the pavement, going from corner rally to speaking engagement, to buying doughnuts for voters randomly and ending with door knocking. Everyone gave it their all.

Saturday soon turned into a hot Sunday afternoon in Beacon Hill Park. The Direct Democracy crew got to the park two hours before Bea-Con and people were already there dancing. Doughnuts had to be cut into four to give a quarter of the people a chance to have a piece. Bea was most happy when she found the pair of barred owls roosting in the usual spot.

By the time Bea-Con was ten minutes from the official start, there must have been over a thousand people. One in four had some kind of costume, whether it be from Star Wars, politics, or a growing number of owl wannabes. The inner circle of Direct Democracy was on the stage mingling. The DJ put on a funky-sounding sample of a song with cheerleaders singing, "Be aggressive, be aggressive, be aggressive." Bea instantly started to clap to it. It was her new fight song.

Derek identified the song as Faith No More's "*Be Aggressive.*" A song giving instructions on how to give head. Thankfully, the DJ was able to mix the song so that only the *Be Aggressive* lyrics were heard. He was certain Bea would not care, but it would be too much for the rest of them.

Bea MC'd the evening. The first twenty minutes was an interactive pep rally for Direct Democracy with dancing, theatre, and voting like the conspi-racist night. Then she ended it with a barred owl call, "WHO COOKS FOR YOU!"

A Barred Owl responded to the left with, "WHO COOKS FOR YOU, COOKS FOR YOU ALL!"

The crowd went silent.

The owl's mate called back from the other side of the bandshell, caterwauling while the audience stood in awe. The only noise was the owls and some ooo's and ah's. When the owls finished, the music came back on. They all danced. Bea wished Ray and Sam were there to share the perfect moment.

Very quickly, Bea-Con's owl hoots got viral attention from birders, both good and bad. Some of the birders did not like that Bea called to the owls. Others were upset Bea was disturbing them with the rally. Bea knew better; they were urban Barred Owls used to the noise. The video was compared to the Warbler that landed on Bernie Sanders' podium in the 2016 America presidential campaign. The Bea-Con Owl Hoot was one of Bea's favourite videos.

The inner circle of Direct Democracy lingered well after Bea-Con finished. As hopeful as they were, Monday's election meant that on Tuesday, they might not have the same connection. Some of the more rambunctious oldsters sent the more able youngsters to get libations. As rebellious as they were, when the police asked them to leave, they did.

Bea did not let a tiny headache from Bea-Con stop her from a morning run. It was beginning to feel like fall, even though actual autumn was a couple of weeks away. Her lawn sign straw poll showed more Direct Democracy signs than ever before. As she ran past a polling place, some of the people in line recognized her. She waved to them.

Bea went to a corner rally near her house, urging people to vote.

In the late morning, Bea biked to the office to meet Irene, Harold, Wendy, and Rick and go with them to the polling place. The rest of the day was spent waving signs on corners, helping people vote, talking with the media, eating doughnuts, and drinking coffee.

As the polls in Eastern Canada started to close, Bea felt as if she was pregnant again or at least had morning sickness. She took Harold aside. "Did you get nervous before the polls closed?"

"No. But I did get sick once."

"That makes no sense. You got sick, but you weren't nervous?"

"Nope... Never nervous but sick once." Harold poured a discrete splash of liquor into his coffee. "Let me top off your coffee."

Not long after, Derek showed up with the official after-election party supplies, champagne, beer, and charcuterie boards. The DJ from Bea-Con arrived to provide music.

The insider crowd was mulling over the Ontario and Quebec results. All suggested a very close race, with neither the Conservatives nor Liberals having a winning number of seats as the prairie provinces started to count votes.

Bea could not participate in the discussion. Her mind was fixated on whether what she had done would be worth it. It was a lonely place. With nothing to occupy her mind, the consequences of using Sam in the campaign and sharing her Princess Leia and the Force video weighed on her. Would she never see Sam again? She had not talked with him since her second date with Ray. Would the video destroy her chances at a better job if she lost? Could she ask Ray for a job? Was Ray being honest about his admiration for her skills? If she loses, she will get Ray, that is a good consolation prize, right? These questions kept spiralling in her mind with no answer... with each revolution, her worry grew. Alcohol did not seem to make her anxiety less, but she kept testing the hypothesis.

By the time the British Columbia polls closed, the prairies had not provided decisive results either. The prospect of a minority government was becoming more likely. This did nothing to make Bea feel better. She decided to go see her owl family. She told Derek she was going out for air and would be back soon, then turned her phone off.

At the grove, she felt stupid. It was pitch black. Even if the owls were here, she could not see or hear them. Just another foolish decision like the lark Direct Democracy was. As ridiculous as looking for owls in the dark.

Bea sat on the small fence and thought of the owl family. It was a great summer for the owls. She'd seen Muffin branch at this very spot. She was happy Sam was able to share it with her. She laughed to herself, remembering when the owlets dropped a crow leg on Ray. She wanted to see Ray and Sam. She started pondering what she would say when she found out she lost.

When Bea shifted her feet in preparation for getting up, from her left and above, she heard: "Mue", a barred owl contact call. Thirty seconds later, it went "Mue" again. The moon silhouetted a barred owl six metres away.

"Josie? It sounds like you. Thank you for coming. I love that you let me be part of your family. I don't want to be rude since I just noticed you, but I must go." Bea rose from her perch. "People are waiting for me."

Josie made the contact call again, then flew to a tree in a little more moonlight only three metres away. Bea stared at Josie staring at her.

Bea noticed a light coming into the grove. The closer it got, the more certain she was that it was a scooter. It soon passed without seeing her, but she saw Ray. Then it stopped. "Are you here, Bea?"

Josie answered Ray first with a loud "Mue."

Bea had not said anything. Ray's arrival let her know she lost. Direct Democracy lost. Choking on tears, Bea spluttered, "I'm here, Ray. Direct Democracy lost. I lost. We did our best."

"Bea, haven't you looked at your phone? You won. It is a landslide."

"You're joking."

Josie's, "Mue," sounded like it was admonishing Bea.

"Not at all. It's all over. You won."

"Why are you here? Didn't you say you didn't want to be with a public person? Or is it dark enough here for us to have a tryst?"

"When you embraced the Princess Leia video, it made me believe I can do it too. I mean, we'll need some boundaries. I know we can make it work."

"Mue," Josie told them to kiss already.

"I knew you'd come around." Bea jumped up.

"Let's go back to the party." Ray said in mid-embrace. "They're waiting for you to change the world. You made me a believer."

"Direct Democracy has definitely changed me. It gave me that chance to free myself. The shame society heaped on me no longer affects me. I got the chance to be Bea again. It gave me a great family of diverse weirdos. But I'm not so sure it will change the world. Only people can change the world."

"Come on, you are going to parliament with an entirely new, old way of doing democracy. It must change everything."

Bea glanced at her phone and sighed deeply. "People change the world, not systems." The fact that I had to use the rhetoric, oration, and sophistry you warned me of at the poli-sci class tells me our people may not be ready to be engaged in Direct Democracy. I literally got cornholed by Darth Vader to get the vote and message out. Did all the people who watched that video get its democratic message? Or did they insert the conspiracist message that Darth

Vader and the force was a lizard person, Bohemian Grove attendee, or one of the seven Jewish bankers?

"I had to emulate the Trumpsterfire to win. That is what everyone will do from now on. If it was not Stalin, it would be someone exactly like Stalin, the political environment makes the leader. Our social media-based political environment wants salacious, scandalous, and exciting politics because politics has become entertainment... or maybe it always has. Good governance is never salacious, scandalous, or exciting. We need good governance, not entertainment. Maybe the people who elected me will understand this but I'm not sure we have the political information environment to support good, boring governance. I hope so. And I'm grateful they gave me the chance to change my life."

Ray breathed, "You're hot when you're cynical." He gave her a kiss.

The make-out session was stopped by Josie mueing, "Get a room."

"Maybe Direct Democracy won despite me," Bea snorted.

"I can see that." Ray felt that he needed to qualify that statement or get in trouble. "Direct Democracy could not have won without your organizational skills. Your social media and ground game were great. I think the performance could have been dialled back from eleven out of ten to six and you would have won. I think you would have won without sharing the porno."

"I'm happy I put the video out there! I finally got over it. And Rick Mercer responded to me." Bea smiled impishly in the dark. "Maybe all I wanted was for Princess Leia and the Force video to get the views it deserves.

The Imperial March began to play. Bea's handbag backpack lit up. "Oh shit! I better get this." Bea grabbed the phone. "Marcus. A little late for you to call me. How are you going to threaten me today? Oh, you can't. Bye."

"Don't hang up, Bea!" Amy's voice cried. "It's me! Amy! And Sam!"

Bea put the phone on video. "Sam?"

"Yes. In a minute. And congratulations! Amazing! But first I want to talk with you. Marcus has agreed not to change the custody agreement. In fact, he... actually more me and is willing to work on how you can see Sam more. I guess you can say the force is now gone from him. Please only talk with me. I will send you my new number. Let's talk soon because Sam and I want to see you in Ottawa."

"Thank you, Amy... Momma A. Thank you so much."

Amy smiled, then opened a door behind her and said, "Sam. Hey, Sam, wake up. Momma B wants to talk with you. She won."

Sam sat up and rubbed his eyes. "Momma B?"

"Yes, Sam! I won the election. I'm going to be coming to Ottawa soon."

"Mue," Josie said to Sam.

Instantly awake, Sam said, "Was that Josie?"

"Yes, kiddo. I'm in the park. Josie is behind me. Ray is here too. I can try and show you, but the light might scare her." Bea could see Josie looking at the phone with Sam's face on it. "Do you want me to try?"

"Yes!" Bea turned the phone's light on and slowly turned the camera toward Josie. Josie did not move. "Hi, Josie."

"Ok, that's enough. I'm sure Josie does not like the bright light. I must go back to our election party. Love you, Sam!"

"Love you, Momma B!"

Bright-eyed, Bea started to cry. "Amy is letting me see Sam. I won. You're here. Josie recognized Sam. This was the most amazing night of my life. Let's go party with the Party. But I must warn you, Ray, I might get drunk. If I do, you have consent."

Author's Bio:

Jason A. N. Taylor loves ideas and thinking but has struggled with being read because of dyslexia (don't worry, Jason has spent lots of money on editing). Taking inspiration from his parents, both of whom are dyslexic, and with the help of teachers, Jason has persevered and flourished.

Having been the fat and slow kid, Jason strives for equity and compassion. Jason loves nature and sees as much nature in urban owls as in remote, unpeopled places.

Jason lives in Victoria near his favourite places to be, fishing on the Salish Sea or looking for owls on Ləkʷəŋən territory. Jason's day job is as a Safety Professional, where he puts to use his many stories of touching the hot stove, falling off chairs and tripping on stuff. Jason can be found on many social media platforms including:

Facebook: Jason A. N. Taylor
Instagram, Threads, and TikTok: therealjohnowler
Reddit: BigJayTailor
YouTube: cute christa and fishy jay

Cover Artist's Bio:

Angela Stacey is of Cree and Scottish descent. Angela works mostly with upcycled material to make jewelry. Angela paints acrylic on canvas and works with stained glass too. Angela is grateful to have a creative outlet that keeps her grounded and compassionate. Angela hopes her art radiates the peacefulness it gives her. Anglela can be found on Instagram at bugandbuddha.

Manufactured by Amazon.ca
Bolton, ON